THE HIDDEN CITY MURDERS

A JOHN GRANVILLE & EMILY TURNER HISTORICAL MYSTERY

SHARON ROWSE

ThreeCedarsPress

THE HIDDEN CITY MURDERS

A John Granville & Emily Turner Historical Mystery

By Sharon Rowse

Cover design copyright © 2019 Sharon Rowse
Cover photo: A Philip Timms Photo, Vancouver Public Library 6831

Published by Three Cedars Press
www.threecedarspress.com

ISBN: 978-1-988037-28-8

1

Saturday, August 25, 1900

John Lansdowne Granville sat in the Turner's too hot front parlor and listened to the slow, heavy tick-tock of the grandfather clock against the far wall. He wondered idly if Emily's father wound the clock himself every week, or if that duty fell to Bertie Wong, their houseboy.

He could hear the cry of the milkman at the end of the block, and the faint rattle of the streetcar several streets away. It was going to be another hot day, though the early morning breeze off the ocean kept the air cool for now. He'd noted a bit of dew still on the lawn as he walked up the path.

Emily's luggage would be heavy, so the carriage he'd hired was waiting outside. He'd hoped to take his fiancée out for breakfast before driving her to the ferry terminal. But she was running late, which wasn't like her. And the *SS Princess Louise*, bound for Victoria, wouldn't wait.

If she missed it, Emily would have to wait until the afternoon for the next sailing, which would irritate her. And he'd miss seeing her off.

He would have liked to accompany Emily on this trip. In addition to being the provincial capital, Victoria was a pretty harbor town, one that she loved. He'd like to see it through her eyes. And in better circumstances than the last time he'd been there, when Emily had been injured.

But at least he could see her off.

"Granville, I'm so sorry I'm late," came Emily's voice from behind him, and he turned to see her dashing in from the hallway, green eyes glinting with laughter.

"You'll never guess what happened," she said as she flung herself into his arms and raised her face for a kiss.

The kiss was a long one, and he let her go reluctantly. She smiled up at him, then her gaze fell on the clock.

"Is that the time? I'll tell you on the way. Aunt Louisa will never forgive me if I miss this ferry. She has plans for me today."

He smiled at the laughter in her voice. "Then we'd best be going."

Loading Emily's luggage took less time than he'd feared. Unlike his sisters, Emily didn't travel with seven or eight trunks, even for a longer visit. This morning she had one trunk, one large traveling bag and one small one, which the driver quickly stowed away.

Once in the carriage, Granville noted that Emily's expression was a little tense, in contrast to the laughter he'd seen earlier.

"Are you looking forward to staying with your aunt?" he asked.

"Of course," she said. "It's been a busy month, and it will be nice to get away for a few days. I just wish you were coming with me."

"I wish I could. But Scott and I have that meeting with Randall this morning. He said it was urgent. I can't put him off."

"Of course not," Emily said at once. "Though after the injury he received a few days ago, is Mr. Scott really well enough to be working?"

"The doctors say he is. But I'll be keeping an eye on him."

"Good," she said. "Do you know why your lawyer wants to see you?"

"Only that he wants to hire us. Which can't be good."

"And after everything he's done for you on some of your cases, you'll want to help him now. He hasn't told you what the problem is?"

"Not a word. I'll fill you in when he does."

"See that you do," she said with mock ferocity. "I'm still part of your firm, even when I'm out of town."

He winked at her, and she laughed. There were still tiny lines of tension around her mouth, though.

"What has your aunt planned for the next three days?" he asked.

"I don't know all of it, but tomorrow we're invited to a ladies tea."

"That sounds interesting," he said carefully, not sure how to read her tone.

Emily rolled her eyes at him. "Clara thinks so, anyway. She's never met a cream tea that she didn't love, and she's jealous I get to go without her."

Emily's best friend Clara Miles, who often accompanied her on her trips to Victoria, was staying behind because she was part of her sister's wedding party. And the wedding was next week.

Which didn't explain the strain he saw on Emily's face. Was it the talk of a wedding that was the problem? She was still determinedly avoiding any discussion about the details of their own wedding.

Before he could frame the question, she put a hand on his arm and turned towards him.

"I was looking forward to this trip," she said. "But from something Mama let slip, I'm afraid she's put my aunt up to inviting me. With the sole purpose of forcing me to make some final decisions about our wedding."

The glittering social event that Emily's mother was planning for their wedding didn't appeal to Emily. Or to him. But Emily had been avoiding confronting her mother about it.

He could understand why. Despite the rather fluffy persona she presented to the world, that lady could be formidable. And with the best intent in the world, she had a habit of over-riding her youngest daughter's wishes. But any discussion of their marriage had Emily looking cornered. And that worried him.

Was it only the social extravaganza that Mrs. Turner was planning that had Emily running shy? Or was it something more?

"I'm still more than happy to elope with you. Just say the word," he said with a grin. They both knew he meant it, though.

"I'm not quite ready to elope. Even though it means we'd be married a lot sooner," she said with a wry smile. "But ask me again after this trip."

"I'll be sure to do just that," Granville said.

And he would. Emily might not be entirely certain about moving up their wedding date, but he was. They couldn't be married too soon to please him.

Josiah Randall's third floor office was as impressive as the last time he'd seen it. But Granville noted that the waiting room was empty, which was unusual. And there was no clerk working in the outer office. The typewriter was covered, and the desktop empty of everything except a fine film of dust. The telephone sat quiet.

The last time he'd been here, the telephone had been ringing constantly, and several clients had been waiting. Now even the rattle of wagons across the cobblestones outside seemed muted in this deserted room.

The wall clock told him it was a few minutes to ten, and the door to Randall's office was firmly closed. Perhaps the lawyer was meeting with his clerk? But there was no sound coming from behind that door—surely he'd hear at least the rumble of voices.

Sam Scott, Granville's partner in the investigative firm of Granville & Scott, had the same thought. "What's going on here?" he asked, glancing around the room. "You heard any rumors about Randall or his practice?"

"No. You?"

"Not a thing. But this," and Scott waved a hand around the neglected office, "isn't normal. And if he wants to hire us..."

"I know."

The sound of Randall's door opening, loud in the stillness, put an end to their speculations.

"Granville. Scott. I'm glad to see you. Come in," Randall said, opening his door wider. He shook both of their hands, then gestured them to his guest chairs and sat down behind his desk. "Thank you for meeting with me so quickly," he said, steepling his fingers on the desktop.

"Of course," Granville said.

"Least we could do," Scott put in. "You've bailed us out often enough."

An uncomfortable little silence stretched between the three of them. Randall seemed to be studying their faces, and didn't say a word.

In the face of his silence, Granville leaned forward and took the initiative. "What seems to be the problem?"

Randall cleared his throat. "You'll have heard that Archer Peabody was dismissed in June?" he said.

"The prosecutor?" Scott asked.

"Yes," Randall said. "He was unceremoniously dismissed after the fiasco of the Sinclair trial. And the rumor is that Chief of Police Stewart's job is also hanging by a thread, thanks to that same trial."

"The trial at which you so ably represented our client," Granville said. Randall's defense of Sinclair had been brilliant. Also, Peabody was a fool.

"Yes, that trial," Randall said. Then he seemed to be searching for words.

Which was unlike him. Randall had a way with words, which was part of what made him such a good lawyer. The rest was a solid knowledge of the law, coupled with an unerring sense of strategy. And a large dose of creative thinking.

"How does this affect you?" Granville asked.

"Peabody is under investigation for taking bribes on a massive scale. He says he's being framed," Randall said.

There had to be more. "And?"

"And that I'm the one framing him," Randall said.

Scott gave a half laugh. "Who'd believe that idiot?"

"Apparently most of my clients," Randall said. "You might have noticed that there's no clerk out front? I had to let him go. There was nothing for him to do, and I couldn't afford his wages any longer."

"Since Peabody is lying, your name will be cleared soon enough," Granville said.

"Not necessarily. Someone is spreading the rumors," Randall said. "And Peabody is making sure that the right people hear that he's planning to sue me."

"Peabody's planning to sue you? Peabody?" Scott sputtered. "It'd never stand up in court."

"No, it wouldn't. And he must know it," Granville said, watching Randall's expression closely. "I suspect the fellow is talking it up in order to influence people against Randall here."

Who nodded. "Yes. He's likely trying to create confusion about what really happened. To see me tried in the court of public opin- ion, if you will, since he'd lose in a court of law."

"And you want us to look into his shenanigans?" Scott said.

The blunt delivery and fierce look surprised a laugh out of Randall. "That's it. Something is off about this whole business. I can't work out what Peabody hopes to gain by vilifying me and endangering my practice."

"You think someone else might be behind Peabody's actions?" Granville asked.

"I can't imagine who," Randall said. "Or why. But yes, that's what I've begun to suspect."

"When did all of this start?" Granville asked.

"I first began hearing rumors at the end of July. My business started to fall off a few weeks ago."

Granville and Scott exchanged glances.

"When we were in the thick of the mess with the canneries," Scott said. "Two murders and a strike threat..."

"I heard. Congratulations on solving a very messy case," Randall said. "But that case is part of the reason I didn't ask you to look into this for me earlier."

"Which might be part of someone's plan," Granville said. "But only part of the reason? What's the rest of it?"

Their lawyer gave them a wry grin. "I kept thinking Peabody would give up and drop the case. He likes easy wins, and he didn't stand to gain anything by pursuing this. Not that I could see, anyway."

Randall's hands clenched until the knuckles showed white, then slowly he straightened them and laid them flat on the desk in front of him. "I was busy. And it took me far too long to suspect that there must be more behind this than Peabody's sad taste in revenge."

"I don't like it," Scott said, his frown deepening. "Someone knows you too well. They're predicting your reactions."

"Whoever it is certainly seems to be one step ahead of me." Neither the lawyer's countenance nor his melodious voice reflected the frustration his hands had evidenced. "And what worries me the most is that I can't figure out who it is. Or what he's after."

"We'll see what we can uncover," Granville said.

"Thank you. I appreciate it," Randall said. "Please bill me at your standard rates."

"We can discuss it once we have a better sense of what we're dealing with," Granville said.

"I pay my own way," Randall said. "As a lawyer, I prefer to avoid even the suspicion that I accept favors from any of my clients."

That firm sense of principle was one of the things Granville most valued in Randall. Along with his creative approach to solving legal problems.

"Very well," he said. "I'll ask Miss Kent to bill you on a weekly basis, if that is satisfactory?"

"Very," Randall said. "Thank you. When can you start?"

Granville glanced at Scott. Who rolled his eyes. They both needed a break after the near fiasco of the cannery case. And Scott was only just out of hospital.

But they owed Josiah Randall. And the lawyer was clearly worried by whatever was going on. To say nothing of his empty office.

"This afternoon?" Granville said.

When Scott nodded, Granville turned back to Randall. "We'll need any documents you've collected so far. It may take a few days before we have anything to report, though."

"Fine. Thank you," Randall said, and they shook hands.

2

Sunday, August 26, 1900

E mily sat with her aunt at a round tea table dressed with immaculate white linen tablecloths, one of ten tables that had been set up in the shade of the oaks on Caroline Herron's side lawn. From that vantage point, the ladies present could hear the waves crashing against the rocky cliff to the beach twenty feet below, or look out over open ocean as far as the San Juan Islands.

It was a warm summer day, with just the tiniest hint of a breeze off the ocean. Floating on top of the crisp scent of fresh cut grass, Emily could smell the vanilla and sugar of scones baking. She drew in an appreciative breath, wishing Granville could be here to share this with her.

Or perhaps Clara—Granville would be decidedly out of place at a ladies afternoon tea. Not that he'd care. He'd simply charm them all, she thought with a smile.

She drew in another deep breath, frowning a little over the unmistakable scent of fresh, ripe blackberries. Had the Herron's houseboy broken with tradition so far as to serve a *blackberry* cream tea? It was probably too late in the season for the more usual fresh strawberries, served on scones with costly Devonshire cream imported from England. Though strawberry preserves would have been the usual substitute.

Mrs. Herron's cream teas were a summer institution in Victoria society, and Emily had never been to one before. But Aunt Louisa had insisted that Emily come to visit her in time for this one.

"You'll be married before too long, given what your mother tells me, and there's no one better than Caroline Herron to show you what entertaining should look like," her aunt had said. "Though I understand you're avoiding any discussion of your actual wedding day," she'd added with a sideways look that made Emily wonder exactly what Mama had told her.

Emily didn't plan on doing a great deal of entertaining once she and Granville wed. She was far more interested in helping him with his detective business. But there was no point explaining that to her aunt. It would simply result in yet another argument with Mama.

And arguments with Mama were an exercise in frustration, and to be avoided at all costs.

No, it was pure curiosity that brought her here. She'd heard about the Herron teas for so long—and the discussion usually ended up with a quiet comment about the Herron's houseboy, Mr. Ying, and what a treasure he was.

Apparently he could whip up a cream tea to rival anything served in England. Someone else would chime in with the tale of the latest attempt to bribe or steal Mr. Ying away from the Herrons—but Mrs. Herron had apparently won the man's permanent loyalty, though no one was quite sure how she'd managed it.

Here, society's matrons—something Emily planned never to become—relied on their Chinese houseboys for every facet of running a household. And unlike in her own mother's house, that included the cooking as well as all the other myriad details of keeping a household running. Too many of which were still a mystery to Emily.

Supposedly serving an English-style cream tea was the ultimate test of a houseboy's skills.

There were several extremely good tea shops in Vancouver

which served cream teas, as well as those in Victoria. Emily had developed a taste for them after Clara had dragged her to most of them.

She wished again that Clara were here today—she would have loved everything about this lavish entertainment. Today wouldn't be the same without her decided opinions on what made the best scones.

To Emily's mind, Victoria's elegant Empress Hotel served the best cream tea she'd ever tasted. The tea was perfectly steeped, the finger sandwiches delectable, the scones the perfect blend of butter and sugar and vanilla, with sweetened thick cream and strawberry-rich jam—she smiled at the memory. She'd never tasted a cream tea done better, and certainly not at a private home.

Clara, of course, didn't agree. She insisted that the grand Hotel Vancouver did a better cream tea, though she'd never been able to convince Emily of that.

Emily couldn't wait to taste Mrs. Herron's famed offerings and see how they compared to the two hotels. And to tell Clara about it.

Just as the last of the ladies took their seats, several maids began to bring out trays holding steaming china teapots, with matching cream and sugar sets. Emily smiled to see the black gowns, frilled head caps and white aprons they all wore. The old-style costumes gave the event a formal feel, though she noted that the girls wearing the caps and aprons were all quite young. Probably they had been hired just for this occasion.

Once everyone had tea, four of the maids began to bring out baskets of warm scones, then trays covered with little pots of Devonshire cream and small pitchers of fruit sauce. The table Aunt Louisa had chosen was furthest away from the house, so they were among the last to be served, giving Emily time to watch everything and appreciate the coordination it must take to put on an event like this.

Just as a plate of scones was placed on their table, there was a scream from the back of the house, the shrill sound rising and falling.

It was a young woman's voice.

Ignoring her aunt's protest, Emily leapt to her feet and dashed around the corner of the house, following the sound towards the kitchen. As she grew closer, the scent of blackberries and vanilla grew stronger, underlaid now with hint of an odd coppery tang. Could that be blood?

Someone was hurt.

Heart in her throat, Emily ran faster, wishing she wasn't wearing these fancy boots—they were much harder to run in than her ordinary pair. It was a good thing her aunt's maid hadn't laced Emily's stays as tightly as her aunt had suggested, or she'd not have been able to run at all.

The screaming was coming from inside. What on earth was happening here? She hurried into the large airy kitchen that took up most of the back of the house.

All was confusion, with pots and trays everywhere, flour scattered across the floor, and a pot boiling over on the stove, filling the air with the scorched smell of burnt sugar. Three of the maids milled around in a state of panic, their voices rising sharply towards the hysteria of the whoever was still screaming. There was no sign of Mr. Ying.

Ignoring the chaos around her, Emily focused on the source of the sound. She followed her ears across the width of the kitchen, to where a hysterical young maid stood in front of a large standing cupboard.

Emily's heart pounded in her chest as she hurried across the room. She was shocked but not surprised to see the prone form of another young woman—who was also wearing a frilled head cap and full apron.

She didn't see much blood, but the scent of it lingered in the air, and the girl's stillness was worrying. Perhaps she'd simply passed out from the shock of her injury?

Breathing too quickly, she knelt beside the girl and picked up her wrist, feeling for a pulse. For a moment, she thought she had it, then realized she was feeling her own pulse pounding in her fingertips. She drew in a long, slow breath, willing her heart rate to slow. The screaming behind her didn't help any.

"Please be quiet," she said sharply to the hysterical young maid. "I need to see if she's alive."

All the while, her eyes were scanning the victim, looking for signs of blood, and trying to see how badly she might be injured. The poor girl was lying half on her side, as if she'd collapsed while turning away from someone or something.

Emily kept one hand on her pulse, while with the other she pressed down gently on the girl's shoulder, moving her slightly so that she was lying mostly on her back. Then she bit back a cry of horror.

There was a bone-handled knife protruding from the girl's chest, near her heart. It was hard to see the knife against the white of her apron, though a few drops of blood spread crimson against the starched cotton.

She kept feeling for the girl's pulse, though she suspected it was hopeless. Granville had told her that if death is immediate, a wound often bled very little, especially in a stabbing where the knife was left in the wound.

Like this one.

Her heart was heavy with the knowledge as she turned her head towards the other maids. "Did anyone see what happened?"

"No," said the taller of the four on a sob. "She—Betsy—was here. Like this. After we came back from taking the scones out."

"She was alone when you found her?"

The four maids all nodded.

"But she—shouldn't have been. Ying was here," the tallest maid said.

Emily glanced around. There was no sign of the Herron's cook. "But Mr. Ying wasn't here when you found her?"

"No."

"Then one of you needs to call for the police now," Emily said, instinctively using her mother's tone of command. "And the doctor. The other two, take your friend outside and calm her down."

She was instantly obeyed, a fact that surprised her. It was probably a good thing she didn't want servants, or it might go to her head—an idiotic thought to be having under the circumstances, she chided herself.

But then she was sitting in a suddenly empty kitchen holding a dead girl's hand, in the middle of one of Mrs. Herron's famous teas. It was impossible to think of anything that would be appropriate for this.

3

―――――――

A commotion at the doorway had Emily looking up to see several of the other ladies from the tea crowding in like so many colorful butterflies, with Mrs. Herron at the front of them. That lady gasped and put a hand to her throat, but she didn't pale or sway on her feet as several of her guests seemed to be doing.

"What is going on here?" she demanded in a voice that didn't shake. "Has something happened to Betsy?"

"She's been stabbed," Emily said, as calmly as she could. She still couldn't find a pulse. "I'm afraid she might be dead."

At the words, Mrs. Herron paled, and rushed to the other side of the prone girl, kneeling to take the girl's other hand in her own.

"Hush," Mrs. Herron said over her shoulder to her guests, one of whom was in hysterics. "Please, go outside, all of you. I need quiet. And someone call the police."

"I think one of the other maids has done so already," Emily said, relieved to hear her voice didn't shake.

Mrs. Herron nodded, and leaned down towards Betsy. She appeared to be listening for the sounds of breathing. After a moment, she shook her head. "She doesn't seem to be breathing."

Emily had just remembered something Granville had told her about verifying death. "Do you have a hand mirror?" she asked.

"Why yes. It's upstairs on my bureau. Ying can fetch it," Mrs. Herron said. Then looked around her as if expecting him to appear at the mention of his name. "Where is he?"

"I haven't seen him since I entered the kitchen," Emily said absently. She'd stood up and was surveying the kitchen with an impatient eye, looking for something that might serve as a mirror.

"But—where is he?" Mrs. Herron asked, watching Emily with something like confusion on her face.

It was probably shock.

From everything she'd heard, Mrs. Herron was an amazing hostess and a formidable figure in the close-knit society of the province's capital. Not someone who would confuse easily. At that moment Emily spied several brightly polished silver trays, and pounced on the smallest one. That would do.

Holding the tray up the maid's face, she watched for any sign of condensation forming on the shiny surface. Even a hint of moisture would tell them that the poor girl still clung to life.

But there was nothing.

Her hostess watched her actions in silence. Equally silently Emily showed her the pristine surface of the tray. The other woman nodded once.

"She's dead, then." There was sorrow and acceptance in Mrs. Herron's tone.

Emily thought briefly of what her aunt had told her about this woman, who had once braved the harsh world of the goldfields following her husband. She'd likely seen violent death before now.

"Yes."

"Did anyone see what happened?"

"The other maids say not."

"Who found her?"

"I'm not entirely sure, but it sounds as if they all came back inside together from serving the scones, and found her lying here."

"Where was Ying?" It was as if Mrs. Herron had just noticed his absence, and her eyes searched the kitchen instinctively. There was the beginning of fear on her face.

"From the little I could gather, he was here when the other maids took the scones out to the guests, and gone when they returned to the kitchen."

"But Ying—surely he cannot be responsible for this," Mrs. Herron said. "If he is missing, it doesn't look good, does it?"

The two women shared a look as Emily slowly shook her head.

"Did you see anything that might indicate he was the killer?"

Emily was momentarily surprised by the question, then realized she shouldn't have been, given the woman's reputation, and the fact that her husband was now one of the senior magistrates of the province.

"No. But I didn't see anything that would vindicate him, either."

"And he's Chinese," Mrs. Herron said, her voice heavy.

Emily nodded. Both of them knew that the police would look first at the missing Chinaman for their killer, and indeed, were unlikely to look further.

"I know this might sound biased," Mrs. Herron said, her smile a little twisted. "As if I don't want to lose the best cook in the province. But Ying couldn't have done this. I know him. He truly is a kind and gentle man. He would never…" her gaze went to the dead girl and her lips tightened.

"He just couldn't," she finished. "Though it won't matter. No one will care. My husband has influence, but I doubt even that will matter in this case. If they find Ying, they'll hang him for murder."

Emily stared from Mrs. Herron's tight face to the young maid's still features. Betsy looked to be several years younger than Emily was herself. She should have all of her life before her, not behind her.

"Someone must pay for taking this girl's life," she said.

"But not an innocent man," Mrs. Herron said fiercely.

"No, not that," Emily said, suddenly feeling in control again. This was something she could do. "If the police will not do so, we will have to search for the real murderer ourselves."

Mrs. Herron stared at her for a moment. "You're serious," she said.

"Yes," Emily said.

"But how?" Mrs. Herron asked.

It was quiet for a moment, there in the kitchen, with only the two of them and the dead girl, though outside there was panic and the shrill voices of distraught women. And the law would be here soon enough.

"We shall ask questions," Emily said, the plan forming in her head as she spoke.

"We cannot interfere in a police investigation," Mrs. Herron protested.

"We won't. The questions we'll ask are things the police would never consider. And likely wouldn't get answers to if they did ask."

Mrs. Herron gave her an interested look. "Such as?"

"You know your household," Emily said. "And I know how an investigation is run. Between us, we could find out who might want Betsy dead."

"No one could have reason to want her dead," Mrs. Herron said quickly. "She is—was—the youngest daughter of my seamstress, and very sweet."

Emily didn't point out the obvious. This was hard enough for Mrs. Herron. And her impression was that her hostess was not one to flinch from the truth, once the shock had passed.

"Then perhaps Betsy was killed in error for someone else," Emily suggested. "I did notice earlier that in their aprons and mobcaps, with their hair hidden, all the girls looked alike. Or there might have been some kind of accident. Perhaps a fight, and Betsy got in the way."

Mrs. Herron gave her a quick, assessing look, as if only now was she aware of who she was sitting with. "You are Emily Turner, are you not? Louisa's niece?"

"I am."

"I had heard you are engaged to a very capable private detective," Mrs. Herron said slowly. "But I'd never heard that you were involved in his cases."

Emily forced herself not to blush. She was proud of the work she did, no matter what society thought.

"I occasionally ask a few questions here and there," she said lightly. "And Mr. Granville often discusses his cases with me. You learn a surprising amount that way."

Mrs. Herron gave her a shrewd look, then nodded. "I suspect you are underplaying your role. But what you say is true. Given my husband's career, I know quite a bit more about the law than most would expect. Which gives the two of us even more tools to find the murderer, if the police cannot."

"Then you are willing to work together?" Emily asked, not quite believing it. She had never met any one of her parent's age who would even consider that a woman could play a role in solving such a crime. Much less a respected society leader like Mrs. Herron.

"Why don't you come tomorrow, in the late morning?" Mrs. Herron suggested. "By then the police will have interviewed the staff, and we should know how they plan to proceed."

Emily nodded, though she wished she could ask her questions now, while everything was still fresh in people's minds. Especially since she was only here until Tuesday. But the police would not welcome her asking questions now. And her hostess had much to do in dealing with the tragic end to her tea party.

"Yes, tomorrow morning would work well."

"At eleven, then? We could have an early tea," Mrs. Herron said.

"Thank you, I would like that."

Mrs. Herron looked around a kitchen laden with baked goods. "Though I'm afraid I may be serving today's menu. Especially if Ying isn't back. I don't know what I'll do without him."

They exchanged glances. Both women knew the odds against him. Emily was determined that the real killer would be found, whoever that might be, and she could see the same determination on Mrs. Herron's face. Whatever it took.

The noisy entrance of several police officers freed Emily from needing to say anything further. She watched for a moment as they spoke a few deferential words Mrs. Herron.

As one of the officers turned to examine the body, another escorted both her and Mrs. Herron from the room, explaining that it was a crime scene, while a third began to round up the other serving girls.

"Are my guests free to leave?" Mrs. Herron was asking.

"Were any of them in the kitchen?" the officer—Officer Jorgens, Emily noted from his name tag— asked.

"No, none came further than the door. Except for Miss Turner, here."

"Then the others are free to go," Officer Jorgens said, and escorted them both to a deserted table under the shade of a spreading oak.

A plate of scones sat untouched on the table, beside a bowl of clotted cream and a small crystal jug holding a sauce that smelled of fresh, ripe blackberries. Emily noted that the missing houseboy had indeed broken tradition by using a blackberry sauce instead of the traditional strawberry jam.

What a shame she would never taste it. And she was hungry, too. But it would feel like a travesty to eat any of it now.

Emily looked around, taking in the ruins of her hostess's elaborate afternoon tea. Half-full teacups littered the tables, and here and there a brown stain of spilled tea on a gleaming white tablecloth spoke to the trauma of the afternoon.

"Now, would you like to sit down?" Officer Jorgens was saying. "And maybe someone can get both of you a cup of tea?"

Wordlessly, Mrs. Herron shook her head, her eyes fixed on the table in front of her. What was she thinking?

In the silence, Emily watched the four policemen work, looking for anything that might tell her what had happened here this afternoon.

4

Late on Sunday afternoon Granville unlocked the front door of his new house—well, his and Emily's, once they married—and stepped back for Scott to enter. They each carried a suitcase and a bulging leather bag that together held all of Granville's worldly possessions. Which Scott had been ribbing him about the entire way here.

Today was moving day. Yesterday he'd had a few bits and pieces of furniture delivered, and today he'd bid a cheerful farewell to the cramped rooming house he had called home.

"Welcome to my new home," he said, stepping aside so Scott could see the place.

"You've got some big rooms here," Scott said, glancing from the spacious hallway into an equally well-laid out parlor. "But you seem to have forgotten some of the furniture."

He grinned at the understatement. Both rooms were completely empty. "Emily needs to have a say in what kind of furniture we have."

He'd finally worked that out. The first conversation he'd had with her on the subject, he'd told her, "It's my privilege to make a home for my bride," and watched Emily's eyes grow big.

He'd already begun to worry that she was getting cold feet about marrying him. From watching his sisters go through something similar, he recognized the symptoms. But he'd surprised himself with his own statement.

Until that moment, he hadn't realized he was so traditional when it came to their first home. He could almost hear his father's deep tones, talking about the responsibilities of a gentleman towards his bride. It hadn't been Granville he'd been talking to, but one of his older brothers. Still, the words had resonated for him, and his deep love and respect for his late father had carved them on his mind.

But Emily was a modern woman. The traditional approach wouldn't work for her.

At least he'd consulted her in choosing this house. In fact, it had been her choice. Then he'd made her fears worse over furniture, of all things.

"Emily's in Victoria," Scott was saying. "You planning to sleep on the floor until she returns?"

"I've done it before. Besides, I told you I bought a few things."

Scott looked at the bare walls and uninterrupted expanse of hardwood floor. "What, you bought a sleeping bag? Didn't you have enough of sleeping rough in the Klondike?"

"No, though I gained a new appreciation for a well-made bed. Which is why it was the first thing I ordered."

"At least you're showing a little sense," Scott said. "But I need to see this bed of yours. Got to make sure it isn't some battered iron monstrosity that Emily will never forgive you for."

Still carrying his bags, Granville led the way to the formal staircase to the second floor. Glancing into the empty rooms they passed, he pictured the home he'd grown up in, with its spacious rooms, elegant silk-papered walls and lovingly polished antiques. He wanted the same for Emily, but she wasn't someone who appreciated stuffy grandeur. She'd probably find an iron bedstead amusing, but he wouldn't.

"You do know this place echoes," Scott said as they climbed, emphasizing his point by stepping more heavily on several treads.

"Then don't step so hard," he retorted. "In any case, furniture and carpets will fix that. Can't say the same for you."

As his partner grimaced at the jibe, he led the way down the hall towards the bedroom at the far end. Then waved Scott into the room, watching his reaction with amusement.

Scott dropped the bags he was carrying in a corner and looked around. "Fancy," he said. "At least you got a proper bed."

Granville glanced around, pleased with what he saw. He didn't only have a bed, he had a hand-carved bedroom suite of solid oak. The detailing on the bedstead, the washstand, and the bureau with its beveled mirror was excellently done, and he liked the golden finish of the oak. Emily had admired a similar suite she'd seen at a house party they'd attended some months before, so he'd had no hesitation in ordering it.

He'd also ordered a set of quality linens and an electric table lamp with a slate base. There were no carpets here yet, and even this room still felt oddly empty. Not that he'd tell Scott that.

"It's a place to sleep," he said.

"Uh huh. Doesn't look like you'll be doing much else, unless you somehow learned how to cook. Or keep a furnace running."

Neither skill had been part of his upbringing.

"The nights are warm enough. And I'm used to eating at the diner. Besides, it beats a mining camp," he said with a grin. And he and Emily, together, would hire someone eventually.

Before Scott could reply, the telephone rang loudly.

"You've already had a telephone installed? Where'd you put it?"

He now had the luxury of a wall-mounted telephone in the hallway, and a second, desktop one in the room they'd designated as his study.

"Two of them. The hallway and my study. And I'll be right back," Granville said, heading for the stairs.

A direct call meant it could be Emily from Victoria.

"But you've no furniture in the hall." Scott's voice followed him down the stairs.

"Doesn't matter," he called back.

It was Emily.

"Granville. You've already moved into the house?" she said, her voice unexpectedly clear. Usually the line from Victoria was full of hisses and crackles.

"Yes, just this afternoon. Scott helped me move my things," he said. "And you're at your aunt's house?"

"Yes, I am," she said. "I've spent most of the afternoon at the Herron's tea."

Something was off in her voice, a kind of forced cheerfulness laid over a deep tiredness. He thought of the last trip Emily had made to Victoria, when she'd been attacked and injured. His grip tightened on the handset.

"Emily, is something wrong?"

"I can't ever fool you, can I?" she said with a little laugh. "And I'm glad of it. I'm fine, just a little tired. But one of the maids who was serving at the tea this afternoon was murdered. A young woman. A girl, really."

"Murdered? Emily, what happened? Are you in danger?"

"No, no, I'm fine," she said again, sounding more certain this time. "The killer was gone before she was found."

"So this happened during the tea?" He couldn't picture it. How could a ladies tea party end in murder?

"Yes. In the kitchen. We were all out on the side lawn. She was stabbed," Emily said, her breath hitching a little.

Telling him was forcing her to revisit it. Which was the last thing he wanted to put her through. But he needed to know what had happened. That she was safe. "Go on."

"Oh, Granville. She was only sixteen."

"Emily. What an unspeakable tragedy," he said. "You needn't stay in Victoria, you know. Come home early."

"I can't. In fact, I might stay until Thursday," she added in a rush. "I promised Mrs. Herron I'd help her find out what happened."

She planned to investigate the murder of a young woman? He

knew exactly how dangerous that could be. "But aren't the police investigating?"

"Yes, but they're already looking at the Herron's missing houseboy. He's Chinese, and..." her voice trailed off.

"And the Chinese are always the first suspects," he finished for her.

He'd run into a similar situation more than once, and found it infuriating. It was unfounded prejudice, and it often led to the police doing an abysmal job of investigating crimes.

"Yes, exactly," Emily said. "I keep thinking, what if it were Bertie under suspicion? The police don't seem to be asking anything more than the obvious questions."

"It's infuriating to stand by and watch that kind of prejudice," he said.

"I can't. I just can't. Not when I can help," she said. "And Betsy was only sixteen. Sixteen!"

Hearing the sob in her voice, Granville's grip on the earpiece tightened even more. He wanted to urge her to come home immediately, but he couldn't be so unfair to her.

"I'm sorry you're having to deal with that," was all he said.

"Thank you. But at least there's something I can do here. And... I'll need to stay a bit longer."

"I'll be over on the ferry tomorrow morning," he said.

"Granville, no. I'll be coming home on Thursday for Clara's sister's wedding. It would be a waste of your time."

"I don't mind."

"But I do," Emily said. "And you have all those meetings because of our last case. Not to mention Mr. Randall. And I'll be fine. Really."

"I'd feel better if you weren't alone with this situation," he said, meaning every word.

"I know, and I thank you for it," she said. "But I'm not alone. I have Aunt Louisa."

"That doesn't sound comforting, given your earlier fears about your aunt's motives for this visit," he said in his driest tones.

She laughed a little, as he'd intended. "She's not so bad. There's Mrs. Herron, too. And her husband is a magistrate."

Granville had heard of James Herron. He was known to be a very capable magistrate. "Mr. Herron is aware that you and his wife are asking questions?"

"He's helping us," she said, though he thought he heard the slightest of hesitations in her voice. But the line had crackled at that moment, and he couldn't be certain.

"Mrs. Herron really counts on Mr. Ying. He's her houseboy as well as her cook," Emily added. "And she doesn't believe he's capable of this."

She paused to draw breath. "We aren't going to do anything dangerous, I promise. We'll just ask the other maids a few simple questions, then pass the information along to the police."

He didn't bother asking why the police hadn't talked to the other maids themselves. They probably had. And Emily would undoubtedly elicit some key information from the girls that the police would never have known to ask for. He should know—she'd done the same thing in a number of his own cases.

Emily was sounding better as she talked, more like herself, and Granville began to relax a bit.

"Why don't you catch the morning ferry on Tuesday, then," he said. "And I'll meet you at the terminal."

It was as close as he could come to telling her he missed her on an open party line. You never knew who might be listening in, so they were always careful what they said to each other on the telephone.

And caution was particularly important when the call was long distance, as this one was. Or worse, when it involved an active case. Which he supposed this one did, as well.

Except this time it wasn't his case. It was Emily's.

Even putting his own worries for her aside, that was an oddly unsettling thought. He hoped Emily never realized how much he worried about her when she dived into an investigation.

Probably about the same amount she worried when he did the same, he thought with a wry smile as he bade her good night.

"And call me if you need me to come over to Victoria," he said. "I can be on the next sailing, no matter the time."

He could hear the smile in her voice now, as she said, "I truly appreciate the offer, but it won't be needed. I promise, I'm fine."

"I'll hold you to that promise," he said. "And call me tomorrow, let me know how things are going."

"I will," she said, warmth in her voice. "And you can count on my promise. Good night, Granville."

And he was left listening to the buzz of the dead line, wishing that his fiancée was just a little less independent.

Most of the time he wouldn't change a thing about her. Every now and then, however, he could wish her a little more cautious.

She was nearly as bad about ignoring danger as he was.

5

Monday, August 27, 1900

By eleven on Monday morning, Emily was seated in the Herron's downstairs hall, anxiously awaiting Mrs. Herron's appearance.

She'd been thinking of nothing but the death of the poor serving girl and the disappearance of the Chinese cook since yesterday. What had really happened?

It had all been so sudden—one minute it was a festive outing for most of the ladies who made up Victoria society, and the next, they were dealing with a gruesome murder.

Looking out the window, the carefully tended lawn under the oaks looked empty without its decoration of tables and tea things. Emily wondered who had taken care of clearing everything away. She suspected overseeing such tasks normally fell to Mr. Ying. Perhaps he was no longer missing?

Footsteps in the hallway announced the arrival of Mrs. Herron, and Emily spun to face her.

Caroline Herron wore a rich green gown that swept the floor, with traces of lace at collar and sleeves. It was quite similar in style to the pale blue gown Emily herself wore, though more sophisticated, of course. Mrs. Herron was a married woman, while Emily was only engaged.

She spared a moment to worry about the latest of the plans Mama had drawn up for her wedding, and shivered at the thought. Was Granville really serious about eloping? It wasn't quite the thing, but his family background—he was an Honorable, after all, his late father a Baron—would excuse what might be considered fast in those less well connected.

Emily thought eloping could be quite exciting. She didn't feel the same about Mama's plans for a proper wedding. And it was supposed to be her wedding, after all. Hers and Granville's. Under other circumstances, the thought would have made her smile.

Though by now she'd mostly given up arguing with Mama about what constituted a proper wedding for them. There was no point.

"Miss Turner. Thank you for coming," Mrs. Herron said, holding out both her hands.

It wasn't the usual greeting from a lady of Mrs. Herron's stature to a young woman like herself. As she took her hostess's hands, Emily was aware of the bond they had forged in the kitchen the day before, when they'd pledged to identify the real killer, no matter what the police thought.

"I'm glad to be here," Emily said honestly. "And please, call me Emily."

"Thank you. And you must call me Caroline."

It was another unusual gesture, given the disparity in their ages. Mrs. Herron had surprised Emily again. Her hostess had to be in her sixties, while Emily was barely nineteen.

"Thank you, Caroline."

Mrs. Herron nodded. "Now I promised you tea," she said, and led the way into the front parlor.

Spread on the coffee table in front of them was a feast. There were fresh scones, with a small dish of blackberry sauce and another of Devonshire cream. A huge pot of tea with an embroidered cozy keeping it warm sat beside blue and white patterned teacups and small plates and the best silverware.

"Please help yourself," Caroline said. "I know you missed out on your tea yesterday, so I wanted to serve this for you. I do apologize that I couldn't manage the teacakes as well without Ying's assistance, but the scones were baked fresh this morning."

"I am very pleased to try them," Emily said, reaching for a plate while Caroline poured the tea. "I have heard so much about your teas, and with everything happening there was no chance to try even a scone."

Caroline shook her head, her expression somber. "The popularity of my teas was Ying's doing, not mine. And I suspect stories of Saturday's tea will outlive any other tea I have given or will ever give. I wish with all my heart that were not true. And that poor Betsy was still alive."

"Has Mr. Ying been found?" Emily asked.

"The police tracked him down at the home of a friend last night," Caroline was saying. "Somewhere on the outer edges of their Chinatown. He'd attempted to conceal himself under the bed, of all things. Of course he was found out, and he's in jail now. We've hired a lawyer for him, but I'm afraid it will do little good."

"Oh, I'm so sorry. The poor man," Emily said. "So they are sure he's the killer?"

"They certainly aren't looking any further, from what I hear," Caroline said tartly.

"Can he be released while awaiting trial?"

Caroline Herron gave a ladylike but very distinct snort. "Such things are not done in this town. Not for the Chinese workers, at any rate."

They probably weren't done in Vancouver, either. Emily hoped she'd never have cause to find out. Her parent's houseboy—whom she'd nick-named Bertie—while not nearly as skilled as Mr. Ying, was a very capable person. Emily considered him a friend.

Mama would be horrified at the idea, of course, so it wasn't something she ever mentioned. Granville knew, though, and had himself relied on information Bertie had gathered for a couple of his cases. Perhaps Bertie could join their household once they married, and be valued properly for the work he did.

Her hostess seemed to truly value Mr. Ying, from everything she'd said about him.

"You must miss Mr. Ying," Emily said. "Having him work here, I mean." Then she blushed at her own forwardness.

"You're right. I do. He is such a calm presence, and a valued part of everything I do here," her hostess said candidly. "In fact, I can't imagine how I can run this home day to day, let alone do the entertaining that my husband's job calls for, without his very capable assistance."

"Then we must get him back to you as quickly as possible," Emily said.

"I agree," Caroline said. "Now, where should we start?"

"We should probably start with the hardest question," Emily said. "If Mr. Ying didn't kill poor Betsy, then someone else did. Someone who had access to your kitchen. Can you think of who that could have been?"

"We get so many deliveries to the kitchen every week," Caroline said. "I hate to say it, but with so much confusion yesterday, almost anyone might have sneaked into the kitchen. But please, try a scone."

"Thank you," Emily said, and popped a bite of scone spread with thick Devonshire cream and homemade blackberry sauce into her mouth.

She nearly closed her eyes in bliss as the rich flavors of the blackberry scone exploded on her tongue. The stories were right, this was the best scone she had ever tasted, anywhere. Even her friend Clara with her devotion to the Vancouver Hotel's scones would appreciate these.

Then Emily promptly felt guilty.

She knew better, though. Despite the awful circumstances of this case, she had to allow herself to enjoy her own life, or she wouldn't be able to help anyone—including poor Betsy.

It was something she'd been learning from Granville. But this case was the hardest lesson yet.

"The next question, then, is can you think of any reason someone might have wanted Betsy dead?" Emily asked.

She held up a hand as Caroline started to speak. "I know you said Betsy was a sweet girl, and there was no obvious reason for her to be killed. But we can't assume anything. Not if we hope to identify the real killer before Mr. Ying is hanged."

Caroline Herron paled, but nodded. "Yes, I see. I don't know the answer to that question, but the other girls I hired to assist in serving at the tea might."

"Then we need to talk to them," Emily said. "As soon as possible."

"I'll send a message with the stable boy," her hostess said. "And I'll send the carriage as well. We should be able to talk to all of them before tea."

"Good," Emily said. "That will help."

WHILE HER HOSTESS was off arranging for their witnesses, Emily reviewed the notes she'd made in the small notebook she kept in her leather chatelaine, and made a list of the questions they'd need to answer.

On Mrs. Herron's return, she said, "I didn't see any sign of a struggle in the kitchen. Did you?"

Caroline Herron shook her head. "No, I didn't."

"And did the police tell you anything?" Emily asked.

"They told me not to worry," Mrs. Herron said. "That they had the killer, and he'd never do anything like that again. Said they'd make sure of it."

"Oh dear," Emily said. "That doesn't sound good for Mr. Ying. And we have a lot of work to do. When is he scheduled for trial, you know?"

"No," Caroline said. "But I imagine it won't be long. They will want to make an example of him, particularly on this case."

"The Chinese question," Emily said with a sigh. At least once a week there was an editorial in the local newspapers about the

Chinese question, and how it could be addressed. The same news-papers that Emily was not supposed to be reading, at least according to her old-fashioned father.

Too many people believed that Chinese workers were taking their own jobs away, no matter that usually no one wanted the jobs that the Chinese were hired for, like being houseboys and cooks and running laundry services. It wasn't fair.

"Indeed," Caroline Herron said. "Which is why I am so glad to have your help for poor Ying."

"I'm glad to help," Emily said. "And I've been thinking. What if the knife was meant for Mr. Ying, and somehow Betsy got in the way?"

"It sounds more likely than someone trying to kill poor Betsy," Caroline said. "But who would want to stab Ying? And how would we prove it?"

Emily considered the question. "What can you tell me about Mr. Ying?"

"Very little, I'm afraid," Mrs. Herron said. "I have been thinking about it since his disappearance. And I was ashamed to realize how very little I know about him. Ying is an excellent worker, an inspired cook, and unfailingly polite and helpful. He almost runs the house-hold for me. But that is the sum of what I know about him."

"How old is he? Where does he live?" Emily asked. "And what about his family, his friends? Who are they?"

"I know none of the answers to those questions," Mrs. Herron replied. "I would guess he lives in Chinatown, but it is only a guess."

It seemed odd to Emily. She was willing to wager a good sum that Mr. Ying knew a great deal about his employer. But then, Emily tended to meddle in the lives of anyone living under Papa's roof.

And she'd never had to manage a household staff. Perhaps that made a difference. Though it would be harder to clear Mr. Ying's name when there was no one to interview about him.

If this were Vancouver, she'd ask Bertie to find out more about the missing man. But this was Victoria, and she knew no one in the Chinese community here. And she suspected trying to go to Chinatown herself to find answers would cause Papa to lock her in the attic again.

Which would not be helpful in the least. Though she had to admit she was tempted to take the risk and hope he didn't find out.

"It doesn't matter. We'll just have to focus on the murder itself," Emily told her.

"I suppose."

"Did you recognize the knife—the one the killer used, I mean?" Emily asked, stumbling a little as she realized how hard the question might be for her hostess.

Caroline Herron didn't hesitate, though. "I'm afraid so. It was one of a set I've had for years. It was a boning knife that was used on poor Betsy."

Emily was impressed by the calm exactitude of her answer. "And where was the knife kept?"

"In a knife block, on the counter near the wall."

Emily pictured the kitchen as she'd seen it the previous day. "That was right beside where Betsy was found, wasn't it?"

"Yes, it was."

"So, the murderer didn't bring a weapon with them," Emily said. "They simply used something that wasn't already there."

Which meant Betsy must have been killed in the kitchen where she was found. But why?

"So it would seem," Caroline. "I wouldn't have thought to ask that question."

Emily smiled. "I have learned a few things from my fiancé."

"The police didn't ask that question either. At least, not of me."

Emily winced a little. That didn't bode well for Mr. Ying's fate. "Well, at least we're asking it now," she said.

Caroline Herron nodded. "And I am very grateful for your help on this matter."

They exchanged smiles.

"I imagine the coroner will have examined,"—and here Emily paused and swallowed hard, trying not to picture the slight young form she'd found lying so still the day before—"the body by now. But I'm not sure how we would find out what his conclusions were.

In my experience so far, coroners won't discuss their cases with a woman. Which I consider to be most unfair."

"I agree with you," Caroline. "But I don't believe that is a circumstance likely to change in time to help us. However, luckily for us the coroner was willing to talk to my husband."

"And...?" Emily said.

"He said that she was killed by a single stab to the heart." Mrs. Herron said. "The coroner seemed to think it required some degree of expertise with a knife to kill so efficiently."

"Or a great deal of luck," Emily said.

Mrs. Herron nodded. "Expertise would imply someone had killed before. And yet from the little we know at the moment, it seems most likely that Betsy was killed by mistake. Which is hardly the mark of a seasoned killer."

"Unless the killer is truly heartless, and killed Betsy because she was in the way," Emily said.

The two ladies stared at each other. It was a horrendous thought, that a young woman's life could mean so little to someone. But if they were to find Betsy's killer, they couldn't deal in half truths.

6

A commotion in the hall prevented Mrs. Herron from answering.

"I had better go," she said with a sigh. "Until I hire someone to replace Ying, the upstairs maid is the one answering the door, and she is unlikely to hear the bell."

She returned a few moments later with one of the four maids from the day before in tow. "I have set up the other three in the kitchen, until we have talked to Jane, here," she said.

"Hello, Jane," Emily said, recognizing the girl as the one she'd talked to the day before. "I hope the shock of yesterday's events hasn't been too difficult for you?"

Jane, a tall, thin girl who couldn't have been more than seventeen, swallowed hard and blinked furiously, but her voice was clear. "No, Miss. I just want to do what I can to help catch that horrible man what did this."

Mrs. Herron patted her shoulder. "Thank you, Jane. We all want that. Please, have a seat on the sofa," and she indicated the tight backed burgundy sofa opposite where she and Emily were seated.

Jane sat down immediately, and sat on the edge of the sofa, looking somewhat nervously between Emily and Mrs. Herron.

"Jane, I know you answered a lot of questions yesterday, and I'm sorry to have to ask you the same questions all over again. But this is important, so please answer us as if you've never heard the question before. Can you do that?" Emily asked.

"I'll try," Jane said earnestly.

"Did you see who stabbed Betsy?" Emily asked.

Jane's shook her head. "No. She was like that when we got back."

"And where were you coming back from?"

"I was carrying out trays with the scones and dishes of blackberry sauce and clotted cream," she said. "All of us were. Well, all of us except Betsy, who had taken the cucumber and cream cheese sandwiches out of the refrigerator and was cutting off the crusts."

"So who was in the kitchen with Betsy when you found her?" Emily asked.

"Mr. Ying. He was standing at the head of the stairs to the cellar," Jane said and her eyes welled with tears.

Emily nodded, and made another note.

"We will find out who did this to Betsy," Mrs. Herron said.

The unflinching determination in her voice must have affected Jane as strongly as it did Emily, because the girl gulped a little, but wiped them away her tears, and nodded firmly.

"And… I thought I saw someone else behind the cellar door—just a glimpse through the hinges on the door," Jane continued. "But I'm not sure."

So someone else had been there. The killer? "Did you mention that to the police?" Emily asked.

Jane looked slightly offended. "Of course."

And they had still arrested Mr. Ying? Why were they not looking into the fact that someone else had been there yesterday?

"But I didn't tell them…" Jane began.

"Go on," Mrs. Herron said when the girl hesitated. "Even the smallest detail might help us find Betsy's killer."

"I didn't tell them that I thought Mr. Ying was talking to him."

"Him?" Emily said, holding her breath. How much had the girl seen?

"Well, whoever was behind the door," Jane said. "I mostly just caught a glimpse of something dark."

"Dark?" Emily said.

Jane nodded. "Black, maybe. Like a shirt. Or a jacket. And he must have been standing several steps down on the stairs to the cellar."

"Could it have been a dark blue?" Mrs. Herron asked.

"Like navy? Maybe," Jane said slowly. "But I couldn't tell if the cellar light was on, so the real color might have been lighter, and just in shadow."

Emily made a note. "What about his voice? The man on the stairs. Did you hear it at all?"

Jane shook her head.

"Not even enough to tell if it was a man or a woman's voice?" Emily persisted.

"No," Jane said. "I just heard Mr. Ying's voice, talking so softly I almost couldn't hear him. That's why I didn't tell the police," she said in a rush.

"Go on," Emily said.

"He—Mr. Ying—seemed angry, though," Jane said. "And scared."

Scared made sense, Emily thought, given who and where he was. But anger?

"Angry?" she said. "Why do you say that?"

Jane blinked, and looked scared. "I can't tell you—I didn't really hear the words. It was just a feeling I had."

"Was he speaking English?" Mrs. Herron asked.

"I think so," Jane said. "But I couldn't be sure."

"And you never saw who he was talking to? Then or later?" Emily asked. "Anything that might help us identify him?"

"No—it was only a glimpse, and I wasn't really paying attention. I was thinking about getting the trays out to the guests before everything got cold."

Which was understandable, but most unfortunate.

"It's all right, Jane," Mrs. Herron said, reaching across and patting the girl's hand. "We know you're doing your best."

"My best isn't good enough," Jane said, her jaw set. "Not when they killed Betsy like that. I wish I had heard more. Or seen something useful."

Her voice broke on the words.

"Anything you can tell us will help," Caroline Herron said. "Do you know how long they were talking?"

"I don't know," Jane said. "I just noticed them as I was taking the trays out. We were so busy. It was all ready at once."

"It must have been very hard," Emily said. "With everything that was going on yesterday, and so much to do, and then Betsy being killed. I imagine it's very hard to remember what happened when."

"Yes. That's how it was, exactly."

"Anything you can remember will help us," Emily said. "Can you try to take us through everything that happened from the time you arrived here yesterday?"

Jane nodded, her face intent. "I'll try," she said.

"I appreciate that," Caroline Herron said.

Jane nodded and gave her a faint smile. "We spent the first hour or so making scones and blackberry sauce like Mr. Ying told us. Once the scones were nearly done, we filled all the teapots. All four of us took them outside on trays—the teapots with tea cozies to keep them warm, and the milk and sugar."

She rubbed a hand across her face, and blinked hard. "It seems impossible that was just yesterday, and Betsy was still alive."

Mrs. Herron patted her hand again. "I know, dear. I'm not finding it any easier," she said as Jane blinked away tears.

"The only thing you can do for your friend now is to help us find her killer," Emily said softly.

Jane nodded. "I'll try." She looked from one to the other. "But won't the police do that?"

Emily exchanged glances with her hostess. Apparently the girl hadn't heard the stories about their local police force's attitudes toward Chinese suspects.

"We may ask questions they haven't thought of," Mrs. Herron said tactfully.

"And we'll make sure to keep them informed," Emily added quickly. "Go on. You had just finished taking the teapots outside."

"Oh, I see," Jane said with a tiny nod. Their explanation had made sense to her. Or maybe she had heard the rumors.

"After we came back to the kitchen, Betsy finished taking trays of scones out of the oven—they were all a beautiful golden brown. Then Mr. Ying sent her downstairs to fetch the silver platters. Jane was putting the scones on cooling racks, while Annie and I were moving the coolest scones onto trays. Meg was putting the garnish on the trays. In between stirring the sauce, so it wouldn't burn."

"Where was Mr. Ying in all of this?" Emily asked.

"He was putting out the bowls—the good china, the one with the garland pattern," Jane said with a glance at her employer.

Caroline Herron nodded.

"And then Meg and I each took a tray of scones outside, and when I got back Mr. Ying had disappeared."

"But Betsy was there?" Emily asked.

"Yes. She had taken the blackberry sauce off the heat and was stirring it as it cooled. It couldn't be lumpy, you see."

Emily could imagine that a lumpy sauce would count as a disaster at one of Mrs. Herron's teas, and made a mental note to herself never to throw a formal tea.

Though by contrast to a murder, a lumpy sauce was a paltry thing.

And Mrs. Herron was handling this investigation extremely well. Emily wondered how she'd learned this kind of fortitude under difficult circumstances.

It would be interesting to know what her life had been like as the wife of one of the early Gold Commissioners, long before Emily herself was even born. British Columbia had been a British colony then, not even a province of Canada. Perhaps Mrs. Herron—Caroline, she reminded herself—could be persuaded to talk about those days? After they'd solved this murder and Ying's name was cleared, of course.

"When we came back inside for the rest of the scones," Jane said. "Ying had just finished ladling the sauce into pitchers, and Betsy had filled the dishes of clotted cream. Which is specially imported from Devonshire, you know," she added earnestly.

Jane seemed to take as much pride in the tea as her employer did, Emily noted. No wonder Mrs. Herron's teas were always so good.

For a moment Emily wondered how Caroline Herron had created such loyalty in the people who worked for her. It would be a useful thing to know, for her investigating as much as for her and Granville's eventual home.

"And there was no sign of anyone else in the kitchen?" Emily said.

"No, not then," Jane said. "The four of us started taking the trays with the clotted cream and the blackberry sauce out to put on all the tables. That was when Betsy was cutting the crusts off the sandwiches and Mr. Ying was standing by the stairs."

"Then what happened?" Emily asked.

Jane paused for a moment. "Well, I was the first one back inside. And I looked for Betsy to ask how the sandwiches were going, but she wasn't at the counter where she'd been cutting them. Instead I saw her lying on the floor against the far wall, all crumpled like."

Jane drew in a breath on a sob and dabbed at her eyes with the handkerchief she held balled in her hand. "I called her name and rushed over and fell to my knees beside her. I took her hand and it was still warm. At first I thought she passed out, but then I saw the knife. And she… she wouldn't wake up."

Emily's eyes threatened to tear up at that image and she had to force herself to focus on the questions she needed to ask. Betsy deserved for her killer to be found, and quickly. "Did you see Mr. Ying?"

"No, I didn't," Jane said, her voice still hitching a bit. "The cellar door was half open, too, which it never is, and from where I sat I could see down the stairs. But there was no sign of anyone. By then the other three were inside, and Annie was having hysterics. So I called for help, and that's when you came."

"Where do the cellar stairs lead?" Emily asked. "Is there a way through the cellar to the outside?"

"Yes, if you know the way, there's a door on this side of the house, nearest the drive. It's a bit of a maze, though," Caroline Herron said

"Who knows about it?"

"We all did," Jane said.

"So likely everyone who has ever worked at this house knows about that exit," Emily said.

Mrs. Herron nodded without comment.

"So that is likely how Mr. Ying left," Emily said. "And possibly how the killer got in."

"But why kill Betsy?" Jane said. "Everyone loved her. And she was only working here that one day. Just like the rest of us."

Emily wondered if Mr. Ying had been the intended victim, and Betsy had simply been in the way? Or was there something Betsy had seen or done that made her a target for a killer? Unfortunately Jane's story had given them more questions than answers.

"Is there anything else you think we should know?" she asked her.

"No," Jane said. "But I'll tell Mrs. Herron if I think of anything."

THE INTERVIEWS with the other three serving girls provided much the same information as the conversation with Jane. Though none of them had been quite as observant as Jane, they hadn't contradicted anything she'd said, either.

At the end of nearly three hours of interviews, both Emily and her hostess were exhausted. They looked at each other in frustration.

"So there might have been someone else in the kitchen that day. Must have been, since Ying couldn't have done it. Which the police know, and don't care about," Mrs. Herron said. "And we have too little information to act on. Was that even worth doing?"

"Interviews are always worth doing," Emily said. "You never know when something will prove helpful. At least we now know for sure that there was likely someone else there that day. And we have a good guess how he and Mr. Ying left without anyone seeing them."

Mr. Ying's actions in fleeing the scene struck Emily as ill considered, though. If he truly was as innocent as Mrs. Herron—Caroline—believed him to be. Unless he had been taken hostage by the killer? Was that even possible?

Or perhaps, given the prejudice against the Chinese, he expected to be arrested anyway.

"I suppose this was time well spent then," Mrs. Herron was saying. "What do we do next?"

"I'd like a tour of your cellar, if I may?" Emily said.

"Of course. Would you like a cup of tea first?" Mrs. Herron asked automatically.

Emily made a face and shook her head. At which both she and Caroline began to laugh. Which helped to release the tension.

Murder investigations were much harder than Emily had realized, especially when she kept seeing the image of poor young Betsy lying sprawled on the floor. No one should die like that, but at sixteen the girl had barely begun to live.

Emily set her jaw. Whoever had killed Betsy like that had to be found and made to pay for his crime. Whatever it took.

THE HERRON'S cellar ran the full width of the house, but only half the length. Dug out of hard-packed ground, with a well-trodden earthen floor and rough timbered walls, it was filled with six-foot high shelves built of untreated wood. One-third of the cellar seemed to serve as a pantry and cold storage, one-third was general storage, while the rest held maintenance and garden implements.

Emily was impressed that the lighting was electric, though it seemed to her an unnecessary extravagance for a cellar. A series of light bulbs hung nearly eight feet above the hard-packed dirt floor. Unlike most cellars she'd seen, this one was actually bright enough to identify the labels on various cans and jars in the pantry area, at least if you held them up towards the light.

The lights were strung along pathways made by the placement of the shelving on either side, and seemed to twist and turn at random. Mrs. Herron was acting as Emily's guide, and she gave a wry smile as she led the way through the maze.

"The arrangement makes sense when you use the various areas," she said. "But it confuses everyone who sees it for the first time."

"Perhaps if they are looking for something," Emily said, looking at the pathway of wires running along the ceiling. "But you could use the wiring as a map to find your way from one side of the cellar to the other."

Mrs. Herron looked up.

"Yes, you're right," she said. "I had never thought of it that way. So whoever was in our cellar that night might not have been someone who has been to the house before."

"I'm afraid that's probably true," Emily said, looking carefully around her. "So that's one less piece of information we have to go on."

Emily studied the lighting. Her eyes traced the wiring until it came to an end and looped back on itself. "I noticed the cellar only seems to take up half the space of the house," she said. "Was there a reason it wasn't built under all of the house?"

"Yes, that side of the house sits on solid rock," Mrs. Herron said. "It would have required extensive blasting to continue the cellar. Quite frankly, it wasn't worth it. Aside from the expense, we simply didn't need that much storage space. So we only dug out the part that was easy to do."

"So you had this house built?" Emily asked.

"Yes, we did. Does it matter?"

Emily shrugged. "Probably not. Although in an investigation, one never knows. But really, I'm mostly curious. It's a besetting fault of mine, I'm afraid."

Mrs. Herron smiled at that. "I admire your honesty."

Emily was still looking at the lights. "I would like to see if I can find the exit without any prompting," she said. "Do you mind?"

"Not at all. I'm very curious to see what you have in mind."

"I'm not entirely sure yet," Emily said, as she moved forward. She was following her instincts, as she perhaps too often did.

If whoever had stabbed Betsy had been an intruder, how would they have found their way into the house?

If they had been following the lights along the ceiling, they must have done as Emily was doing, slowly winding her way through stacks of shelves. The further she went, the more it seemed this was a foolish idea. She wasn't getting anywhere.

And knowing that Mrs. Herron was walking silently behind her, expecting answers, wasn't helping any.

Just as she was about to admit defeat, Emily turned yet another corner into yet another aisle of garden related items. And suddenly she could see light from a small window set into a door at the far end of the rows of shelves.

"Is this it?" she asked Mrs. Herron, pointing towards the door. "The exit, I mean?"

"That door that opens out onto the carriageway," Mrs. Herron said.

"And it's the only other exit from the cellar?"

"It is."

"If Jane is right about what she saw," Emily said, her eyes were searching every inch of the path towards the door. "The killer must have exited this way. And he may have left some trace. Does anything seem out of place to you?"

Mrs. Herron didn't reply, but Emily glanced over her shoulder to see her hostess was carefully looking at the items on the shelves they passed. Emily didn't say anything more until they had exited from the cellar.

"Do you see anything out of place?" she asked.

"No," Mrs. Herron said. "But then I spend little time in this part of the cellar. We really need Ying for this. He always seemed to know exactly where everything was down here, as well as which things would be needed each season."

"It's possible you could talk to him in jail," Emily said. "Though I'm sure that would cause quite a stir. Do you think it would be worth it?"

"I don't care about that," Mrs. Herron said. "A small bit of gossip is nothing compared to a man's life. However, I think Ying would need to walk through this part of the cellar in order to tell us anything. And I don't think even my husband has enough influence to make that happen."

"That's probably true," Emily said. "But there may be a way to make it happen."

"How?"

"If the police think you have an idea to help solve their case, they might be willing to bring Mr. Ying here, don't you think?"

"What a devious idea," Mrs. Herron said. "I'm impressed. Yes, I think that might work."

"It sounds like a suggestion that needs to come from you, though," Emily said. "Something along the lines that you're concerned something seems out of order. Would you agree?"

"I definitely agree," Mrs. Herron said. "And I'm sure I can come up with the right words to get them to act. And to allow me to be present when they bring Ying through here. If only to quiet my very reasonable fears, you understand."

From the look on Mrs. Herron's face, Emily had no doubt that she would be able to do so. They smiled at each other.

"I look forward to hearing what Mr. Ying has to say," Emily said. "In the meantime, I'd like to have a look at the area just outside the door. It might tell us something."

"Very well."

Once outside the door, Emily looked carefully for any signs that anyone had come this way recently. She suspected the killer had entered the house through this door, as well as left by it. And that Ying had exited the house the same way—though perhaps not at the same time. She was hoping to find some evidence that might prove exactly that.

Though they still had nothing to prove that Mr. Ying himself was not the killer. Only Mrs. Herron's belief in him.

The fine gravel of the carriageway continued right to the doorway they were standing in, so there were no footprints. There were no unusual marks on the door itself or around the cast iron handle.

"Is this door ever locked?" Emily asked, bending closer to examine the elaborate handle.

"No, I'm afraid it isn't," Mrs. Herron said. "We use it so often, you see."

So that didn't help. Emily looked carefully around her. There were no helpful bits of paper the killer might have dropped. No torn bits from his clothing. Nothing at all that would help them trace him.

Emily turned back to Mrs. Herron.

"This hasn't been as helpful as I had hoped," she said. "Do you know if Mr. Ying has told the police anything useful at all?"

"I believe he has simply refused to talk," Mrs. Herron said.

"Then we'll have to hope he sees something in the cellar that we didn't," Emily said. "In the meantime, I'll talk to my fiancé. He might be able to suggest something I've missed."

She was looking forward to talking with Granville that evening. She missed him.

7

Despite an early start, it wasn't until mid-afternoon that Granville finally found the time to review the thick file of documents Randall had given him on Saturday. It had turned into another scorching day, and the mercury was projected to rise even higher by evening. The preparations for moving to a new office space were proving far more disruptive than he'd anticipated. Between the heat and the lack of decent fans, everyone's patience grew short.

Emily's absence added more tension, since she was the one who had worked directly with the architect on the design of their new space. No one else had her depth of knowledge. And the move itself was still a week away.

Thinking about Emily brought back sound of her voice when he'd called her the previous evening. Despite the crackling of the telephone line, he could hear her grief over the murdered girl. And she'd been the one to find the body.

He could imagine all too well how hard that had hit her. Yet she'd forbidden him to drop everything and take the next ferry across to her. She'd assured him she'd be fine.

And he couldn't ignore her wishes.

Resolutely, he turned his attention to the waiting stack of Randall's documents. Bolstering himself with another cup of coffee, he opened the thick file. He began to skim through the pages, stopping in some places to read more intently. When he was done, he closed the folder, placing it carefully on the desk in front of him.

And looked across the partner desk to see Scott watching him with the beginnings of a grin on his face.

Once they moved to their new offices, it was going to seem odd to have his own office, and not look up to see Scott sitting there.

"Have you read this thing?" Granville asked, tapping a forefinger on the file.

"I took a look."

"And what did you think of it?"

"That it's exactly the kind of mess we'd usually hand off to Randall to review for us," Scott said promptly.

Unfortunately, Scott was right—that was what he'd been thinking too. "Since we can't exactly hand it back to Randall to explain to us…"

"Why not?" Scott said.

Granville frowned at him, then realized Scott was serious. And it wasn't a bad question.

Randall was the best person to see through the convoluted legal language and thinking that lay inside this folder. But this time, it was Randall's own reputation and career on the line.

"Because Randall asked us to take this on for a reason," Granville said. "We have to respect that. So who else could help us with it?"

"You mean another lawyer?"

"Can you think of one you'd trust to do the kind of job Randall would?"

"Nope."

"Nor can I," Granville said.

"Then what about asking Mac and Miss Kent to take a look?" Scott said. "They won't be much help on the legal stuff, but they might see something we're missing."

On several previous cases, their receptionist and the fellow who was now their accountant had teamed together to unravel some fairly complex financial shenanigans. But this was different.

"This doesn't seem to be a financial case," Granville said.

"No, but they're pretty good at seeing how things tie together. And isn't that what we need here?"

He had a point. "It's worth a try, I suppose. Very well, we'll leave it with Miss Kent. She can explain it to Mac."

"I'm glad you see it my way," Scott said.

"At least it's better than sitting here reading through this file again. It's far too hot in here for that." Granville said, glaring at the barely turning fan overhead.

"Our new offices will have no shortage of fans." Scott said. "And I expect you've got something else in mind for us to do today?"

"I do indeed," Granville said with a grin. "We need to have a chat with Mr. Peabody."

"That should thrill him," Scott said. "As I recall, he wasn't too fond of us by the time the Sinclair trial ended."

"At least he didn't try to sue us."

"I'm sure we can change his mind if we try," Scott said.

AFTER HE'D BEEN FIRED from the prosecutor's office, Archer Peabody had hung out his shingle as a defense attorney. Granville and Scott found him on the second floor of a dingy building at the far end of Water Street, in the low rent part of town. The office was small, the furniture cheap, and the clientele absent.

And Peabody was not pleased to see them.

"What do you two want?" he asked with a scowl.

"We have a few questions," Granville said. "If you have the time?" And he indicated the empty waiting room.

"I gather you're working for that fraud Randall. I suppose I can spare a few moments," the lawyer said grudgingly. "Since I suspect it will get rid of you faster than arguing about it."

"Interestin' reasoning. It just might at that," Scott said with a broad grin.

"So what did you want to know?" Peabody said.

"Let's start with why you call Randall a fraud?" Granville said.

"He won his case by twisting the truth about everything from what really happened to who the real killers were. And that kind of behavior can't be allowed in this town," Peabody said, pursing his lips.

The expression on his chubby face made him look like a petulant child.

"So you sued him as an act of public charity?" Scott said.

"I sued him because his actions ruined my good name. Now let's see how he likes it." Peabody's tone was laced with venom, his face had gone purple and he was leaning forward with his fists clenched.

Everything in the file Granville had read suggested Peabody had a vendetta against Randall, so he'd expected a diatribe of this sort. It surprised him that the fellow was being so honest about getting even, though.

The odd thing was, Peabody seemed to believe every word he said. Granville had expected to uncover a total fraud, not to find that the other lawyer believed his own nonsense.

Could someone else be behind all this, and feeding Peabody's delusions? If so, who else had it in for Randall? And why?

"Who is funding this endeavor?" Granville asked.

"What do you mean?" Peabody said. "I'm a lawyer. My costs are my own."

"Hmmm," Granville said. "But in the meantime, your own clients must suffer."

"I have no clients. Thanks to Randall," Peabody muttered.

"Eh. What's that?" Scott asked, picking up on where Granville was going with this. "How are you paying your bills, if you have no clients?"

"That's none of your business," Peabody said. "Now, I think we're done here."

They probably were, since they were unlikely to get anything more out of the fellow.

"Thank you for your time," Granville said, standing and donning his hat.

Peabody scowled, but said nothing more as Granville and Scott took their leave.

"That's it?" Scott said once they were in the hallway outside Peabody's office and heading for the stairs. "With a little encouragement, I'm sure he had more to say."

And Scott grinned and cracked his knuckles theatrically.

Granville smiled and shook his head. "It's a good thing I don't believe everything you say," he said. "But our friend back there told us more than he knew."

"He did?"

"He did. Someone is definitely funding his bills. And probably encouraging the fellow in his crusade against Randall."

"Yeah, I got that," Scott said. "But we still don't know who. Or why."

"We know more than we did from reading that file of Randall's," Granville said. "The attack on Randall didn't start with Peabody."

"Didn't we know that already?"

"I can only speak for myself," Granville said. "But I thought Peabody was getting his revenge by making Randall look bad."

"So did I," Scott said. "And he isn't, is he? He thinks he has a legitimate grievance."

Scott paused while he navigated a turn in the narrow staircase. For a ludicrous moment, Granville pictured Scott's broad shoulders getting stuck there.

"Is Peabody really that bad a lawyer?" Scott asked. "Or has ego twisted up his thinking?"

"Probably both," Granville said. "It doesn't really matter. If someone else is behind this, he recognized in Peabody an opportunity to take Randall down. And took it."

"And all we have to do is figure out who that is?" Scott said sarcastically.

"Exactly," Granville said with a grin.

Scott just shook his head. "So what's next?"

"Next we talk to someone who knows all the scams being run in this town," Granville said.

"Why do I get the feeling we're about to confront Vancouver's biggest gangster?" Scott said.

"Probably because we are."

"You'd think you'd have had enough of bein' shot at," Scott said.

"It's been a week since our last confrontation," Granville said. "And you've been out of hospital for most of that. It's getting a little boring, don't you think?"

Scott groaned. "When is Emily coming back from Victoria, again?"

"Not until Thursday. Why?"

"You aren't so eager to get shot at when she's around," Scot said.

He just grinned.

8

Robert Benton's office was in a space carved out of the back of one of his warehouses. After climbing a narrow staircase to reach it, the spacious outer office filled with mahogany furniture and leather chairs was always a visual surprise to Granville, no matter how often he'd been here before. After a brief wait, one of Benton's thugs opened the heavy doors into the even more elaborate inner office and thunked it shut behind them. Benton sat in a typical pose, his hands steepled on the polished marble expanse of his desktop, with a Cuban cigar smoldering in the heavy ashtray beside him.

"I don't recall scheduling an appointment with either of you," he said, looking from one to the other.

"We have no appointment, I'm afraid," Granville said.

"Ah. And here I thought I was in for a dull morning," Benton said, picking up the cigar and drawing deeply.

He didn't offer them one, as he sometimes did. Which told Granville something about Benton's mood. "We aim to please," he said, ignoring the groan from his partner.

Scott's sister was Benton's paramour, and everything about that situation made his partner uneasy. But there was nothing to be done about it. Benton was still their best source of information about the shady side of the city—and the most dangerous one.

"What trouble have you embroiled yourself in this time?" Benton asked, breathing out rich, slightly spicy smoke that hung in the air between them.

"Nothing serious," Granville said. "We're looking into some rumors we picked up about a local lawyer, and we're wondering if you'd heard anything about what's behind them."

"A local lawyer," Benton repeated. "Let me see. Would that be Josiah Randall, by any chance?"

It figured Benton would have heard about it. "That's the one," Granville said, watching Benton closely.

He hoped Benton would remember—and value—the role Randall had played in saving Scott from a murder charge—which had saved Benton himself from his lady's severe displeasure. Frances Scott would likely never have forgiven him if he'd allowed her brother to hang for a murder Scott hadn't committed.

Judging by the look on Benton's face, however, they might have played that card once too often already. Best not to mention it now.

"And what might that information, if it exists, be worth to you?" the gangster asked, exhaling more smoke.

"What did you have in mind?" Granville asked.

"A favor. To be named later."

"Don't do it, Granville," Scott said in a harsh whisper. "Not an open-ended favor like that."

"What kind of favor?"

Benton gave him a hard smile. "Whatever kind I happen to need."

Granville suspected the fellow knew exactly what kind of favor he intended to ask. He was testing them. Well, let him. Josiah Randall had helped him and Scott more than Granville cared to think about.

"I agree. But with caveats," Granville said.

"Go on," Benton said, sharp eyes assessing both of them through the veil of smoke he'd created.

"The favor you ask me can't be anything illegal," Granville said.

"Or anything that would endanger our friends or family. And it's only me you're asking the favor of."

"Both of us," Scott said, frowning at Granville, then scowling at Benton.

Who burst out laughing. "That's all?"

The man sounded disappointed. Dammit. He could have asked for more, then. "It's enough," Granville said.

"Good, then. You both owe me a favor, to be collected later," Benton said on another puff of smoke. "As for your lawyer, I hear he's being set up. And rather creatively, too. As I imagine you've already figured out."

"Who's behind it?"

"That I don't know. And the local rumor mongers are depressingly silent on the subject." He winked. "Probably too boring for them."

Interesting. "Why Randall?" Granville asked.

Benton looked amused. "I'm tempted to say why not, just to see your expressions," he said. "But I plan to use that favor, so I won't."

He had the feeling he was going to regret whatever favor he'd granted Benton. But he'd given his word, so he'd accept whatever the fellow intended to ask. "Then why?"

"Have a look at Randall's more recent cases," Benton said. "Rumor has it that he's treading too near someone's patch. And Randall is both persistent and very good at what he does. He can't be bought off, and he can't be cowed."

That wasn't good. Granville knew all about staking and protecting one's own patch of ground—literally as well as figuratively. And eighteen months on the gold creeks of the Klondike had taught him first hand just how vicious someone defending their claim could be.

"So Randall presents a threat to someone," Scott said. "Which means he has to be brought down? Just like that?"

"That's about the size of it," Benton said.

"And you've heard no rumors on who that someone is?" Granville asked.

"I've heard a bit of noise," Benton said with a gleam in his eye.

"But nothing as concrete as a rumor. Which is most unusual. If you do find out, I'd appreciate you passing it along."

"In return for the favor?" Granville asked.

Benton laughed again. "I do find you amusing," he said. "Which is just as well for you. But no, not in return for the favor. That will be another matter entirely."

It had been worth a try.

"Can you tell us more about whatever patch Randall is encroaching upon?" Granville asked. "The noise you mention must contain some detail."

"Only that there's money involved. And it's probably illegal," Benton said.

"And you aren't involved?" Scott said. "How's that possible?"

"Careful, Sam," Benton said, drawing deeply on his cigar. "I like your sister. It doesn't extend to you."

"But Frances likes me," Scott said.

"And she only knows as much of my business as I let her know," Benton said.

"Well, if you think that, you don't know Frances very well," Scott said. "She's always known more than she should. And more than those around her think she knows, too."

Granville put a hand on Scott's arm. He wasn't sure what was going on between his partner and Benton, but baiting the gangster was a bad idea. No matter how fond Benton might be of Scott's sister.

"We'll follow that line of questioning, then," Granville said. "And since that favor of yours sounds a large one, we'll be back if we run out of rumors."

Benton breathed out smoke, watching them through it with hooded eyes. "The more you two talk, the bigger that favor is growing," he said.

Which, from Benton, was close to a lethal threat. "Let's go, Scott," Granville said.

Benton probably didn't fully mean it, but he was suddenly in a worse temper than Granville had seen before.

And deadly as he knew Benton to be, Granville had rarely seen that side of him as clearly as he'd seen it today. What was going on there?

Was it having to admit how little he seemed to know about Randall's case? Benton wasn't a man who liked being in the dark about anything illegal happening in what he—and most everyone else on the wrong side of the law—considered his town.

Or was the problem whatever was brewing between Scott and Benton?

Granville hoped it wasn't the latter.

———

Not until they were exiting the building, and safely out of earshot of Benton's henchmen did Granville turn to his partner.

"All right, give," he said. "What's going on between you and Benton?"

"Nothing," Scott said, his jaw set stubbornly.

"Don't give me that. You were baiting the man. And given who and what Benton is, that's madness."

"What if I was? What business is it of yours?"

"You're my partner, Scott. If Benton decides to take you down, who do you think is going to be standing right beside you?"

"You needn't be," Scott muttered.

"You're trying to tell me that after everything we've been through, you expect me to stand aside if Benton decides to go after you?"

"Yes," Scott said. "Anything else would be foolhardy."

"Well, call me foolhardy, then," Granville said. "Just don't try and tell me that you wouldn't do the same for me."

Scott grumbled, but didn't argue.

"No comeback?" Granville said. "Scott, what is going on?"

"I don't like how he's treating my sister," Scott said.

"What, Frances? He treats her like spun glass. And you know as well as I do that she's more than capable of holding her own. Even with Benton."

"Especially with Benton," Scott said with a wry grin. "No, not that sister. The other one. Lizzie."

"Lizzie?" Granville said. That, he hadn't expected.

Scott's youngest sister, Elizabeth Scott, had had a hard life. Scott and Frances were both trying to help her overcome the scars, both mental and physical, those years had left her with.

Which included an addiction to the opium pipe.

"What dealings with Benton have with Lizzie?" Granville asked.

"She and her daughter, little Sarah, are still living with Frances," Scott said. "Lizzie is much better, but she still relies too much on laudanum. And Benton's been taking it upon himself to call her on it."

Granville frowned. "Benton has? Why would he think he has the right to do so? You're her brother."

"Benton pays all of Frances' bills," Scott said wryly. "Which means he's paying Lizzie's bills. And in Benton's mind, paying the bills gives him all kinds of rights."

"And does Frances agree with him?" Granville asked.

"Well,…" Scott looked away.

"She does?" That surprised Granville. "That doesn't sound like Frances. What aren't you telling me?"

"Nothing you need to know," Scott said, still not meeting Granville's eyes.

"Now it's me that doesn't need to know? Are you forgetting who helped you find Sarah and bring her back from Denver?"

"No. But it's not that kind of problem."

Granville rolled his eyes. "It never is. And I'm not going to get a straight answer, am I?"

Scott ignored the question.

Granville glanced at his friend, then grinned. "Fine then. Let's go talk to Frances. She never met a question she wouldn't answer."

"No," Scott said. "Not this time."

"This is a perfect time," Granville said. "It's time for tea, and Frances will be home for guests."

"Not now, Granville," Scott said. "Things are—tense—with

Lizzie right now. I don't want anything to upset her. And it will upset her if she suspects we're talking about her with Frances."

"We'll be circumspect," Granville said, with a wink. Scott's youngest sister need never know that they were concerned about her.

But the discomfort combined with worry on Scott's face changed his mind. If his pragmatic friend was that unsettled by whatever was going on, then Scott was right. This wasn't the time.

If the situation hadn't improved in a few weeks, though, he'd have a chat with Frances himself. She'd tell him what was really going on between her siblings and her lover.

And what needed to be done to fix it.

9

Tuesday, August 28, 1900

The next morning Granville took his new route to the office. His house was only five blocks away, and it was a pleasant walk despite the building heat. But he'd barely noticed the manicured gardens he passed, the slight hint of a breeze.

Most of his thoughts were focused on his conversation with Emily the night before. He had a bad feeling about the murder investigation she was involved in. But so far, it wasn't enough to act on.

It was a relief to walk into the normality of his office, to exchange greetings with Trent, and get an update on his schedule for the day from Miss Kent. Even the pending disruption of their upcoming move was a welcome distraction.

Then came the telephone call from Randall.

"I need help," he said, in a broken, pain filled voice.

"Where are you?" Granville demanded.

"My office…"

"You're alone?"

"Yes," Randall said on a harshly indrawn breath.

"Don't move. I'll be right there," Granville said, and hung up.

As he did so, he thought he heard a breathy laugh, which worried him even more.

"Is Scott in yet?" he hollered through the open door as he grabbed his coat, hat and the revolver he normally locked away.

Miss Kent appeared in the doorway. "No, he said he had an appointment and would be in by ten."

"Thanks," he said as he stepped past her. "I'll be out for the rest of the day. Trent, you're with me."

Luckily all of them knew not to ask questions when he got that tone in his voice. Trent Davis, their young apprentice, just nodded and grabbed his own coat and cap.

"Where are we off to?" Trent asked as he trotted behind Granville and down the carpeted stairs.

"Randall's office. Something is very wrong. I think he's been attacked," Granville said as he crossed the lobby at a fast clip and exited onto the street.

"Want me to hail a hack?" Trent asked from behind him, looking up and down the street in search of one.

"It's only a few blocks. It's faster to walk," Granville said, stretching his stride until Trent was half-running to keep up with him.

It took them less than ten minutes. When they reached the solid granite office block where Randall had his offices, Granville took the stairs up three flights, rather than wait for the elevator operator. Flinging open the door of Randall's office, Granville strode into the outer office.

The room was empty, but otherwise everything looked normal. All the furniture was intact, and the file cabinets closed. There was no sign anyone had broken in, no sign of a search. Then he heard a groan from the inner office.

"Randall?" he said as he hurried to the doorway, Trent hard on his heels.

"Here," came that weak voice. "Not... going anywhere."

And again that breathy laugh.

Granville soon saw why. Randall was curled up on the floor,

covered in blood. He'd been beaten, and badly. It was hard to tell how extensive the damage was—there was too much blood. But it looked like at least one of his legs might be broken.

He was aware of Trent standing in the doorway behind him, heard the lad suck in a shocked breath.

Granville quickly knelt beside Randall and felt for his pulse. It was thready, and too fast. But at least it was regular.

"Still alive," Randall said, almost too softly to hear.

There was a whistling in his breathing that Granville didn't like, either. If his ribs were broken, and one had pierced his lung, it would sound like that.

"Call the hospital to send an ambulance," Granville said to Trent. "Then go down and wait for them, and bring them up here. Tell them it's urgent."

"Will Mr. Randall be all right?" Trent asked.

"Go. Now," Granville said instead of answering.

There was nothing he could say that would help. He didn't have the answers any of them needed. And Randall needed help fast.

"I'm gone," Trent said, and Granville could hear him on the telephone in the outer office, talking to the operator.

He glanced around the spartan office, grabbed Randall's suit jacket from the coat rack and draped it over the injured man. It would help with the shock. Then took off his own suit jacket and rolled it up, tucking it under the injured man's head.

Randall was probably losing too much blood, but Granville couldn't see any wounds that were bleeding too fast. He'd have to move him to see more, or even to bind any of his wounds. And that ran the risk of causing more damage.

The best thing he could do was to keep Randall warm, and get him to the hospital as fast as possible. Luckily it wasn't far away.

He heard Trent hang up the telephone, then clatter down the stairs. Then there was nothing but the sound of Randall's ragged breathing, far too loud in the stillness.

"Who did this?" he asked softly.

For a moment he thought Randall was already unconscious. Then the words came, more labored than before.

"Don't... know."

"Never mind, just rest. The ambulance will be here soon," Granville said, and put a hand on the other man's shoulder in reassurance.

It was probably less than five minutes before he heard the wail of the ambulance siren, but it seemed forever until he was watching two stocky men carefully loading the lawyer onto a stretcher, and carrying him to the elevator.

"I'm coming with you," he said to the ambulance attendants, grabbing Randall's keys from his desk and locking up before he followed them out.

"Trent, see if you can track Scott down, then meet me at the hospital."

Trent's worried face was the last thing Granville saw as he climbed into the back of the horse-drawn ambulance.

THREE EXHAUSTING HOURS LATER, Granville was pacing from one end of his office to the other, waiting for a call from St. Paul's Hospital. The doctor who'd met them at the ambulance at City Hospital had stabilized Randall, then immediately transferred him to St. Paul's for the complicated surgery. There was still no word on the extent of his injuries, though the first doctor had confirmed they were every bit as bad as Granville had suspected.

He wasn't sure Randall would make it.

Nor were the doctors at St. Paul's. They'd refused to tell him anything further—not surprising, since he wasn't family—and they'd sent him away, after telling him that there would be no news for several hours.

He'd hoped the operation wouldn't be that long. The doctors here were good, but even using chloroform as an anesthetic, few survived an operation that lasted longer than two hours. And despite the now common use of carbolic acid to bathe wounds and fight infections, the risk of a serious infection from extensive surgery was still huge.

It had already been more than two hours. With no news. The lack of action was grating on him.

He would have gone back to the hospital, if he thought that would make any difference. But it wouldn't. Randall's life was in the doctor's hands. And God's.

All he could do was find out who had done this to his friend. And make sure they paid for it.

He'd sent Scott and Trent out to see what rumors they could pick up. The beating had been thorough, and professionally done. Probably by at least two men, from what he'd seen. Maybe three.

This was no impulsive attack. Someone had ordered it. Either to take Randall down temporarily, or to take him out of the game entirely.

Whatever the game was.

Benton had told them Randall was challenging someone's patch. It was an odd choice of words—something that might normally describe a rivalry over something profitable. A rancher, looking to expand the grazing land for his cattle. One gang taking on another.

Randall was a lawyer, and an exceptionally good one. Whose patch could he be challenging?

On the surface, Peabody seemed to fit—Randall's able defense of Walter Sinclair had publicly exposed Peabody's incompetence.

But a beating like the one Randall had taken? That wasn't Peabody's style. And it didn't fit with the legal action the disgraced lawyer had already taken.

It didn't make sense.

Unless someone had wanted to make sure Randall couldn't appear in court?

If it weren't for Benton's words, Granville's first suspicion would be that the attack on Randall was revenge. He'd have been looking through Randall's past cases for someone angry enough that they wouldn't be satisfied with forcing Randall out of business. Someone who was determined to make the lawyer suffer physically as well. Maybe even kill him.

And he'd still pursue that angle.

But he wouldn't ignore Benton's words, either. Benton was

rarely wrong when it came to what was going on in what he considered his town. He wasn't exactly careful with the truth, though. Or not all of it.

And yesterday there had been something odd about Benton's approach to the whole matter of Randall's troubles. It wasn't anything Granville could identify. But it was enough to make him wary of relying too heavily on what Benton had told him.

He'd start by looking into whether Randall's business dealings extended beyond his legal practice. And if so, was there anyone he dealt with who had motive to do something like this?

When he'd skimmed the file Randall had given him, he hadn't noticed anything that suggested the lawyer had other business interests. But he hadn't read it that closely. And there might be other files in the lawyer's office.

Until Randall had recovered enough for a conversation—if he ever did—Granville would make the decisions on his behalf. Randall had hired him to find out who was set on destroying him, after all.

Now he was going to find out. And he'd use whatever means he had to. Starting with Randall's financial records, and whatever else he could find in Randall's office.

Since there was nothing else he could do to help his friend. And he hated waiting.

Especially when the news was likely to be bad.

10

Promptly at ten on Tuesday morning, Emily again joined Caroline in the front parlor of the Herron mansion.

"Now, would you care for tea?" her hostess asked.

Emily gave her a sideways look, and Caroline Herron gave a slightly strained laugh.

"I can see you have something else in mind. Your aunt did warn me that you were hard to divert when you were engaged in a subject."

Emily blushed a little. "I appreciate the offer of tea, but we only have a few hours before luncheon and there are so many questions that need to be answered."

"Oh, don't apologize, Emily," Caroline was quick to say. "I share your impatience with unnecessary formality, especially when there is something of importance to be done. And solving this murder—and bringing Ying home again—is of the utmost importance. Justice must be done here. And I am very afraid it might not be if we don't intervene."

"I feel the same way," Emily said. "And we have no time to waste. Were you able to arrange for Mr. Ying to tour your cellar with the police yesterday afternoon?"

"I was."

"And what did he have to say about the cellar?"

"He said that nothing looked different to him," Caroline was saying. "But I think he was lying. And more, I think he was frightened."

"Why do you say that?"

"For two reasons. I do know Ying fairly well, even though I don't know much about his life away from here," Caroline said, waving her hand to encompass her home. "And he was speaking in broken, almost pidgin English this morning. Yet his English has always been remarkably good."

She took a sip of her tea. "Apparently Ying's command of English has deteriorated badly while he's been in jail," she added dryly.

"Which sounds like a good way to stall the police inquiries," Emily said.

"Yes. But they brought the police interpreter along, and he claimed to be unable to understand Ying. So either Ying speaks an obscure dialect, or he was being deliberately impossible to understand."

Emily wondered if the interpreter was Ah Quan. She and Granville had encountered the court interpreter on a case of Granville's, several months earlier. Might that matter on this case?

"I wonder if the translator shares Mr. Ying's fear?" Emily said. "Which might impact what either of them was willing to tell the police."

"That's possible, I suppose," Caroline said, then sat in silence sipping her tea.

"You said there were two things…" Emily prompted her.

Her hostess looked up at that. "Hmmm… oh, I am sorry. I was just wondering what both men might be afraid of. If you were right."

"How did Mr. Ying show his fear?" Emily asked.

"When we were in the cellar, I saw his eyes dart to several shelves, then quickly back to the police, as if to see if they'd noticed. They hadn't, of course. Then he looked back at the first shelf, as if unable to help himself. As if he had to check. And there was such a frozen look on his face..."

Caroline poured herself another cup of tea with a hand that shook. "I've seen fear before. But I've never seen it so starkly. And never on Ying's face."

"The police didn't notice?"

"No. The expression was only on his face for a moment, and they weren't paying him much attention. They are sure they have their killer, after all. Most of their attention was on the cellar itself. And to be fair, our cellar is rather like a museum of sorts."

It was certainly the biggest cellar—and the most crowded one— that Emily had ever seen. "Have you any idea what Mr. Ying might be so worried about?"

"I'm afraid not. I think only he has that answer, and he seems unlikely to tell us. No, we are at a standstill, I fear."

Emily considered that. If the Ah Quan was the interpreter, perhaps he could be persuaded to tell them what he knew? "I think we need to look at the cellar again," she said, and stood up, shaking out her skirts.

Caroline looked rather amused at this breach of protocol, but she followed Emily towards the kitchen without a protest.

THE CROWDED CELLAR looked exactly the same to Emily as it had the day before. She turned to meet Caroline Herron's eyes.

"Which shelves did Mr. Ying look at?"

"Follow me." Caroline led the way, her footfalls in her dainty laced boots silent against the hard-packed floor. She paused in front of a set of shelves about half-way between the kitchen door and the outer door.

"This one first," and she indicated a shelf at her own shoulder height, almost five feet off the ground. "It was eye-level for Ying, and his eyes stayed there, as if he couldn't believe what he was seeing."

She moved along to the next shelf, touched a shelf a foot lower. "Then this one."

And the shelf beside it. "This one. And this one." Pointing at the next shelf down.

Caroline stepped back until she was standing beside the shelf she'd originally stopped in front of. "Then he looked back over his shoulder at this one again. His face is never easy to read, but it seemed to me that he couldn't quite believe what he'd seen, that somehow he'd look again and it would be different, if you know what I mean?"

Held speechless by the emotion in Caroline's voice, Emily just nodded.

"And then—the fear in his eyes. I'll never forget it. I don't know what he was seeing, but I hope I never know that kind of fear. It was only for a second, then his expression went blank again, as if he wasn't even there anymore." She blinked rapidly. "I'm afraid for him."

Emily nodded, her eyes busily scanning the shelves Caroline had pointed out. They seemed to be a random collection of unwanted or worn out items of all descriptions. How anyone could tell if something was missing—or added—she couldn't imagine. So what had the man seen?

"Don't worry, we'll clear his name," she told Caroline. "But we have to figure out what he was looking for, first. What is all this stuff?"

"I don't know," Caroline said. "Some of it came from our old house, and has been down here since we moved in."

"On these shelves? Specifically?"

Caroline looked from Emily's urgent face to the crowded shelves. "Oh," she said. "I was so shaken by Ying's expression... It hadn't occurred to me that I might know. I've become too used to relying on him to know what's here."

She stepped closer to the first shelf she'd pointed out, and frowned. "I see old lamps, and a collection of vases, and ... oh, this was my daughter's when she was five or so."

And she reached in and pulled out a bedraggled looking stuffed bear with one button eye hanging loose. "She loved this bear."

"So these are things that belonged to your household in your previous house, then?" Emily said.

"Yes, that's right."

"And on the other three shelves?"

Caroline walked back and looked more closely. "Yes, those ones too. Oh, there's one of the thistle candlesticks. Ugly thing. That was part of a set of dishes that James's great aunt gave us, with those spiky thistles all over it. How he hated that set."

"These are all things you no longer use, then?"

"That's right," Caroline said, looking a little guilty. "We probably should never have moved them, just sorted them and given away or thrown out most of it. But we had the space, and it was just easier to move everything."

"But if these were moved here from your previous house," Emily said, "Then why are they not packed away in boxes?"

Caroline looked at the shelves as if seeking for an answer. "Maybe it was easier to find things, in case they were needed?"

"But everything on the shelves below this one is packed in boxes," Emily said.

Caroline bent over enough to see the contents of the shelf below. "So they are. But when were they packed?"

She wiped the thick dust from the top of one box, and peered at it. "I can't quite make this out…"

Emily leaned a little closer. "I think it says April 1891."

"Thank you," Caroline Herron said with a quick smile. "I really should get spectacles, at least for some things. But they are such awkward things, I tell myself I can see just fine. And I can, most of the time. But in all this clutter…" She shook her head, laughing a little at herself.

"It's a good thing I trust Ying," she added. "He could be stealing from us and I probably wouldn't notice."

Emily felt a chill trace down her spine at the words. Was that what this was about?

"Was 1891 the year you moved into this house?" Emily asked.

"Yes, nearly ten years ago now—I can hardly believe it's been so long. These boxes would have been packed and moved at the same time as the things on the other shelves. I don't know why those items were unpacked when these were not. We'd have to ask Ying."

Emily's eyes were carefully searching the shelves, looking for any sign that something that might be missing. It wasn't easy. There were so many items packed higgledy-piggledy onto those three shelves that it was hard to focus on just one thing.

She stepped back to look at the whole shelf, instead of each individual item. Seen that way…

"Mrs. Ha—I mean, Caroline, does it look to you as if the items on this shelf," and Emily pointed to the one that Mr. Ying had looked at longest. "Are they more jumbled about than the other two shelves that have been unpacked?"

"I don't know what you…" her hostess began, as she copied Emily's posture, and stared at the same shelf.

"Oh. Oh, yes, I see. And I think you're right. It's as if someone was going through things in a hurry, and tossing them aside."

"Yes, exactly. Whereas these other shelves look as if they've been unpacked quickly, but the placement of items has a kind of order to it."

"As if someone wanted to make things easy to find, as well as making sure nothing got broken," Caroline agreed. "But who would do such a thing? And why? It makes no sense."

"I think we'd best focus on the why first," Emily said diplomatically.

It was obvious to her that Mr. Ying must have played some part in whatever this was. But she didn't want to make finding Betsy's killer any harder for Caroline than it had to be. They didn't have many facts yet.

Just a murder. And the look of fear on Mr. Ying's face.

11

Emily stared again from one shelf to the next, trying to make sense of the jumble.

"One or more of the items on those four shelves had to be valuable to someone. Maybe the killer?" she said, half to herself.

"Something the killer could steal and sell, then?" Caroline said. "That makes sense."

"Or perhaps something was hidden here, and when the killer came to retrieve it, he couldn't find it," Emily said. "Which might explain the argument between him and Ying that Jane told us about."

"But Ying wouldn't..." Caroline began, then hesitated, looking from shelf to shelf.

Clearly there was a something different here. And Mr. Ying must have known about it, if Caroline hadn't been exaggerating about how well he knew the cellar and its contents. Which would be a hard truth for Caroline Herron to face.

"Mr. Ying may have done no more than to allow a friend to store an item here for safekeeping," Emily said.

"Or he may have done much worse," Caroline said. "I have to

face the facts as they are. Please don't try to sugar coat anything for me. In the long run, it will only make things worse."

Emily nodded, and her admiration of Caroline grew. "At least this gives us something to follow up."

"I don't understand how a few shelves of junk could end up with poor Betsy dead."

"Whatever is behind this must be very important to the killer. Or else he is someone with a very short temper and little regard for human life. In which case, it is hard to imagine why Mr. Ying would allow such a man into your home. Not if he is as loyal as you believe him to be."

"He is loyal," Caroline said. "After so many years, I simply cannot believe that I am wrong about him."

She paused for moment, staring at the shelves in front of her. "But the fear I saw on Ying's face was very real. Whoever the killer is, he must have threatened Ying with something serious enough that he felt he had no choice but to betray us in this way."

"Or he felt his actions were a lesser betrayal than whatever he was threatened with," Emily said.

"What do you mean?" Caroline asked.

"The threat could have been to Mr. Ying himself. But what if someone threatened you or your family? What would he do?"

"He would tell me," Caroline Herron said decisively.

"Are you sure?" Emily persisted.

Caroline gave her a sharp look. "Well, no. I can imagine that there might be circumstances where he would not do so. Especially when I think of the fear I saw."

Emily nodded, unsurprised.

"But if you're thinking that Ying may have allowed a killer access to this house in order to protect us?" Caroline said. "That makes no sense."

"I think we are only seeing the edges of what happened here," Emily said. "But I am wondering if he would have been so unwilling to say anything to the police, if he were just protecting himself."

Caroline's brow furrowed. "You really do think Ying's actions were about protecting us?"

"I think it's a possibility worth following up on," Emily said. "Don't you?"

Caroline smiled. "I do, indeed. But how?"

How indeed? For a moment, Emily felt like a fraud. She had no ready answers.

"The only real clue we have is what might be missing from the shelf," Emily said slowly. "May I ask you a few more questions about them?"

"Please, go ahead," Caroline said.

"This candlestick that was given to you by your husband's great-aunt," Emily said, reaching for it. She lifted it out and examined it.

The piece was about six inches high, and heavy, made of pottery rather than china. The sprig of thistles that ran up one side of it was naturally colored and three dimensional, carefully shaped and painted to show off each separate petal and sharp barb. "This seems the oldest item here. And this sprig of thistles must have been individually made and applied. Has it any value?"

Caroline laughed. "That? I doubt it."

"How old is it?" Emily asked.

"I have no idea. My husband inherited it from his great-aunt's estate. It has been in her family for some time, that's all I know."

It was certainly not of any style Emily had ever seen. And it truly was ugly. But you never knew. "And you said something about a collection of items that he inherited at the same time?" Emily asked her eyes scanning the shelves for other pieces.

"Yes, there were quite a number of pieces, all in a similarly deplorable style. Including a full set of dishes, I think. My husband truly hated them, but I thought them so ugly as to be amusing," Caroline admitted with a smile. "Nothing I'd ever put on a dinner table, or even a tea table, though. They should be here."

"I don't see anything like this one," Emily said.

"They must be here, somewhere," Caroline said, taking the time to look hard at the shelves. "But you're right, I don't see them either.

Probably they were never unpacked. They should be in some of these boxes nearby."

"Perhaps," Emily said. "But maybe we should look."

"Do you really think some ugly old dishes are what our killer stole?"

"I think sometimes very old items can become collectible. Sometimes because they are unusual. Unless you have a better idea for finding the killer and saving Mr. Ying?"

"You take that box. I'll take this one," Caroline Herron said.

OVER AN HOUR LATER, they were both dusty from head to toe and surrounded by open boxes and discarded packing paper.

Caroline looked up from unpacking the last box in front of her.

"You were right," she said. "I can't find any of the other pieces that came from that set. They must have been stolen. Unless they were all packed together and that box got lost in the move. It can happen more easily than you'd imagine."

It seemed unlikely to Emily that a complete set of dishes would fit in one box. "But then I wouldn't expect to find this candlestick," she said diplomatically.

She lifted it off the shelf, and examined it more closely. "It has a chip on the back, which would diminish its value to a collector. And usually candlesticks come in pairs. Where is the other one?"

"Not here, obviously," Caroline said with a sigh. "And I do remember a pair of them, because I couldn't imagine anyone ever using them. The pair would likely have been packed together, too. So you think the second candlestick and all the other items were stolen."

"Yes. I do."

"And do you really believe these old things were valuable enough that someone would kill for them?"

"I suspect the killer thought them so. But would you mind if I borrow this candlestick for a few days?"

"Be my guest. Keep it if you like. What do you have in mind?"

"No, I'll be sure to return it. I think it ugly, too," Emily said with a smile. "But if these items do have value, it would be useful to know how much they might be worth. And how big the market is for them."

"That's well thought of. You will check with the museum?"

"Yes, though since it has only existed for twenty years, I doubt their collection will contain similar items."

"I'm surprised you know that," Caroline said.

"I've been to the museum several times," Emily said. "Recently I've developed something of an interest in the early history of British Columbia."

She felt a little embarrassed to admit it to Mrs. Herron, who was such a leader in Victoria society. Supporting music, literature, or the arts was considered appropriate for women. An interest in history was for men, and was considered even less ladylike than an interest in detecting was.

Caroline simply nodded as if it was quite a usual response, which she knew it was not.

"My aunt tells me there are one or two decent antique dealers in town, though," Emily said. "As well as a dealer in imported china. Collecting is rather a passion of hers, so I thought I would ask her to accompany me, and start there."

"That is very good thinking, and could prove quite useful."

"Especially if we talk to Mr. Ying again," Emily said. "And I think it is time to do so. There are questions only he can answer, and with what we've learned today, he may be willing to talk to you. Can your lawyer arrange it?"

"I'm sure of it. You wish to be there?"

"Yes, I'd appreciate it."

"Good. I'll set it up for tomorrow afternoon?" Caroline said. "Unless you were planning to visit the antique stores tomorrow?"

"No, I'm hoping to do that this afternoon."

"Then I will arrange the meeting for tomorrow, and call for you at one, if that suits?"

"I look forward to seeing you then," Emily said.

Several hours later Mac followed Miss Kent into Granville and Scott's shared office, both of them carrying stacks of files. Since Scott's half of the partner desk was empty, Miss Kent sat there. She began to spread out stacks of papers, while Mac pulled up a chair to the side of the big desk.

Granville stared at the piles of paper. Had all of those documents come out of Randall's files? No wonder he hadn't taken in much when he'd skimmed through them.

"What have you found so far?" he asked.

Miss Kent and Mac shared a look. "You go first," she said.

"Randall's financials are pretty straightforward," Mac said. "At least on the financial side. The ledgers are clear, everything seems to be accounted for, and I saw nothing that raised questions for me."

"Seems?" Granville said. "Did you find something that wasn't entirely accounted for?"

Mac nodded, and leaned forward to pick up a stack of papers that Miss Kent was pushing towards him. He shuffled through them, then pulled out a written list from half-way down the stack.

"For a lawyer, Randall does a fair bit of business outside of his legal work. And he has a good head for investments, from what I can see here," Mac said, and handed the page to Granville.

Who skimmed through it, then looked up.

"Two houses and a small apartment building on the east side as well as two small businesses. This is a nice mix of assets," Granville said, impressed and a little surprised. "Randall has an interest in all of them?"

"Randall owns all of them," Mac said dryly. "Though he has mortgages on all but one of them. They seem to be ably managed by the individuals running them. And he's instituted some form of profit sharing for most of them."

"Profit sharing?" Granville said.

"The managers—in the case of the shoe repair place, for instance, it's the cobbler—receives a regular wage plus a share in the profits based on how quickly those profits are growing. Same for the fellow who manages his rental properties. Which is smart in a real estate market where the prices are rising as quickly as ours."

"Incentives," Granville said. "Quite similar to how a few of the more progressive landlords work with their tenant farmers in England."

Granville's father, the 5th Baron Granville, had been one of the first to implement something similar on his own estates, and Granville had seen first-hand how effective that could be. Was a variation of that something he could put into practice in his own businesses? It was something to consider. And to discuss with Emily, who always brought her own unique perspective.

"I haven't seen the farming model," Mac said. "But Randall's been smart about how he implemented this here."

"Meaning you didn't find anyone on this list with a grudge against Randall?"

"Right again," Mac said. "Not a financial grudge, anyway."

"And non-financial?"

"I put out a few feelers on all of these," Mac tapped a finger on the list. "Seems Randall has shown some interest in the daughter of the fellow who manages his rental properties."

"And that's a problem?"

"I hear his manager isn't too happy about it," Mac said dryly. "But I couldn't find out why. Or how serious it is, for either of them"

"That's worth looking into," Granville said. "Miss Kent, what did you uncover?"

"I've been looking into Mr. Randall's legal cases for the last eight months," she said, waving a hand at the two dozen stacks of paper laid cross-wise in front of her.

"And?" Granville asked.

"Most of his clients have reason to be happy with him. And a few of his opponents probably hate him."

"Most of his clients?" Granville repeated. "Can you be more specific about the ones who might not be so pleased with him?"

"Of course. But you need to understand that this is a first look through these files."

"Fair enough," Granville said. "What have you found so far?"

"That Mr. Randall won a lot of his cases. But he did lose some," she said. "And of those losses, two resulted in the loss of substantial funds for those clients. And in three other cases, the loss resulted in jail time for the client."

"Is there any indication of those client's reactions? Did any of them turn against Randall?"

"All of them paid his bills, but the money came from the retainer they paid up front, so that doesn't really tell us anything," she said, running a finger down a list written in what Granville recognized as her neat script.

"Go on," he said, curbing his impatience and reminding himself that her thoroughness was what made her analyses so effective.

And Randall was in no hurry at the moment.

She glanced up at him and nodded. Probably taking in his impatience at a glance. She looked a little nervous, and he suddenly wished Emily was here.

"There are two files where the client sent a note to Mr. Randall vowing revenge," Miss Kent said quickly.

She passed him two stacks of paper. "In the first one, the client was convicted for accidental death and thrown in jail. Mr. Randall represented him in his appeal. When that too failed, he threatened to make Mr. Randall pay."

"I see," Granville said. He flipped through the file, noting the client's name and the details of the two notes. "And the second one?"

"Lost a great deal of money. He went directly to sending notes threatening to make Mr. Randall pay."

She'd summed it up nicely, Granville thought, flipping through the second stack of papers. "What about the opponents?"

Miss Kent passed him another six stacks of paper, and he skimmed through each stack, then looked up at her.

"Why do you think each of these might wish to harm Randall?" he asked. "I don't see threatening notes, except on the last file."

She gave him a small smile. "In half of the cases, the lawyer was fired by the client immediately following the trial."

"Randall embarrassed them, made them look incompetent," Granville said. "Same thing he did with Peabody."

"He ran rings around them," Mac put in.

Miss Kent smiled at Mac.

"Yes," she said. "He seems to have a very creative approach to the law."

That was one way of putting it. "It's a very effective one," Granville said. "Luckily for this firm."

"Not so luckily for the other lawyers," she said. "From my reading of these cases, they all three cut too close to the law in pursuit of profit, and paid off a few officials to ensure they'd get away with it."

"And Randall exposed their shenanigans in front of the jury, I see," Granville said, flipping between the three cases. "But why would any of these three want to injure or kill Randall?"

"Because in each case, there are new laws being passed to prevent the shortcuts these crooks have been profiting from," she said. "One has already gone bankrupt."

"And the other two have had to go legitimate," Mac added with glee. "Well, semi-legitimate. I asked around about them, too. They're not happy about it, not happy at all."

He'd just bet they weren't. "Would you make up files for each client so that these don't get mixed up? Then return the files to me?" Granville asked Miss Kent.

She nodded.

"And can you both include any notes you made about those particular cases. Oh, and Mac? I need more on any problems with his tenants. And also if Randall is scheduled to appear in court in the near future. And if so, on which cases."

"Sure thing," he said.

As the two stood up to leave, the telephone rang. It was the hospital.

GRANVILLE PAUSED in a corridor outside Randall's ward. The big windows that ran along the west side of the corridor gave him a lofty view of the ocean and the endless sky above it. A small window high up was open a crack to let in the air. Despite the dust and stink of manure from the street, the hint of breeze carried the smell of the sea, free from the odor of illness and the harsh bite of disinfectant.

He drew in a deep breath, then went in search of Randall's doctor. And was just in time to catch the fellow before he went on to his rounds.

The news for Randall was good, but guardedly so. The surgery had gone well. They'd repaired most of the internal damage caused by the broken rib and set his leg. This afternoon Randall had regained consciousness, if only briefly. He wasn't ready for visitors, and might not be for days yet.

They question of whether Randall would survive at all hovered unspoken between them.

"If I'm going to find out who did this to Randall, I need to speak to him as soon as possible," Granville said.

"I understand, but I can't allow it until he's much stronger. I'm not sure he'd be able to respond to questions in his current condition in any case," Dr. Serson said.

It was sounding worse by the moment.

"How serious are his injuries?" Granville asked.

The doctor frowned. "Normally I wouldn't even be discussing my patient's condition with anyone but family. But since this patient doesn't seem to have family here, and since you brought him in— I'll answer your questions."

Granville hadn't known that Randall had no family here, but it didn't surprise him. People moved here from all over to build a new life for themselves. Often they left behind family and friends, and the distance alone did a good job of severing, or at least weakening, most ties.

"And? Will he recover?"

"He took a severe beating," Dr. Serson said. "There may be internal damage that we didn't find. And I don't like the fact he was unconscious for as long as he was."

"Which means what?"

"Which means that only time will tell."

Granville wasn't settling for that. "How does he look?"

The doctor frowned. "He looks bad," he said bluntly. "But he's young and fit, which is in his favor. So he may make a full recovery. Or he may succumb to his injuries."

He hesitated, put a hand to his stethoscope. "His recovery could be long. And expensive. If he doesn't have sufficient funds, some of the treatments he needs may be unavailable."

Granville waved that off. "I'll cover them. Whatever it takes," he said. "What happens next?"

"Good enough," the doctor said, and made a note on the chart. "For now, there's little we can do except keep a close eye on him and wait for his body to heal itself."

Not what Granville had been hoping to hear. "Randall was alone in his office when I found him," he said. "But it looks to me that whoever did this to him intended to kill him. Would you agree?"

"It is certainly one of the severest beatings I've seen where the patient was still alive when he was brought in," Dr. Serson said, watching Granville carefully.

"I'd hate for his attackers to hear that Randall is still alive, and try again. Can you keep it quiet that he survived?"

"I'm glad you're taking precautions. None of the nuns will talk about him, but it would be easy enough for someone to check with the morgue to find out if he's dead."

"Fair enough," Granville said. "Then perhaps it would be enough to let out that he's hovering at death's door."

"Which, unfortunately, has the advantage of being true. But we'll do our utmost to keep him alive. Any way we can."

Thanking the doctor, Granville made his way out of the hospital, and drew in a breath. Again he could taste the salty freshness of the sea.

At least Randall was alive. And he was a fighter. He'd make it.

In the meantime, he was going to find the cowards who'd done this to one of the finest men he knew. And make them regret that they'd ever laid a finger on him.

***

His face grim, Granville turned his steps towards the police station. Which was not somewhere he'd gone willingly in the past.

Vancouver's police force had a reputation for corruption. Though several attempts had been made to clean up the force, bribery was still too entrenched—and too lucrative.

But Benton's talk of someone defending their patch—which is what his hints amounted to—was still the best lead he had. And a campaign like that wasn't something that could easily be kept quiet. He knew at least one source that might have heard something about such a feud.

Under pressure from the city council to clean up his force, the Chief of Police had hired several new patrolmen earlier in the year. And one of those new hires had proved both painfully honest, and willing to work with Granville to see that justice was done. If it weren't for Officer Clay Daniels, Sinclair might well have been hanged for a murder he was innocent of.

When he reached the station, an impassive officer told him

Daniels wasn't in, so he left a brief note with the desk sergeant. In the interests of discretion, he said only that he'd like to meet when his shift ended, but didn't leave a location—Daniels would know where, since they'd used Mary's Diner as a meeting place during the Stewart case.

1 3

A fter a late lunch with her aunt, the two ladies stood on the sidewalk in front of Messrs. Allen and Cox Fine China. Emily noted that the shop was well positioned in the heart of downtown, and presented an immaculate front with a neatly swept sidewalk and gleaming front windows.

"Is this the place, Aunt Louisa?"

"Yes, this is the best place in town for china. I'm not too sure what they'll make of your candlestick though," her aunt said, giving the item in question a disparaging glance.

Emily hid a grin. Not that she didn't agree with her aunt, it was the importance that lady placed on decorative items that amused her. Emily liked to have nice things around her, too, but if they pleased her eye, she didn't much care about the "marque" or who made them or any such nonsense.

She suddenly wondered how Granville felt about such things. It had never occurred to her before, but he'd likely been raised amongst priceless antiques, and took them for granted. What if he wanted their own home decorated in moldy furniture and stuffy styles? Could she bear it?

On the other hand, he always dressed with such understated

elegance, she couldn't imagine him expecting anything less in his home. Which simply gave her something else to worry about. How was she going to meet that standard?

As Aunt Louisa pushed through the glass doors into the shop, she thrust her worrisome thoughts back into the shadows, grateful to focus on the case. Inside, they were met with the cheery jingle of a shop bell and welcomed by a portly gentleman who clearly recognized Aunt Louisa.

"Welcome, my dear lady," he said moving forward surprisingly quickly on small, neat feet. "And what can we do for you and your lovely companion this fine morning?"

Emily glanced around her. Fine china of all shapes and colors was lovingly arranged in finely crafted glass cabinets that covered three walls of the room. Whoever had done the display had studied museum displays, and taken advantage of every trick. Every item showed to its best advantage—and any price tags were carefully tucked out of sight. Shopping here would be a pleasure for anyone, and likely irresistible to a collector.

"It is nice to see you again, too, Mr. Allen," Louisa was saying. "Though it is actually my niece who needs your expertise today."

Taking that as her cue, Emily smiled and moved forward. Pulling the candlestick out of her handbag and unwrapping the protective tissue she'd wrapped around it, she placed the thing on the glass counter top. Where it sat looking dated and out of place in this gleaming shop.

"Oh my," Mr. Allen said, moving forward to examine it. He glanced at Emily as he reached for it. "May I?"

At her nod, he picked up the piece and turned it over carefully in his hands. "Earthenware, and a good example of the naturalist style. I see it has several chips missing from the thistle decoration as well as a larger one from the lip," he said. "That is unfortunate."

Judging by the disappointment in his voice, the piece must indeed have some value. She'd been right!

"Yes, it is a shame." Emily said. "However, I'm hoping to get some idea of its value in its current condition. And to learn a little more about the piece, as well."

Mr. Allen shook his head. "I'm afraid in its current condition, I can only offer you thirty dollars. Perhaps forty, if the collector I'm thinking of will go that high."

It was much more than Emily had been expecting. And the expression on Aunt Louisa's face nearly made her laugh out loud.

"And if it were not chipped?" she asked.

"Then you would be looking at least double that amount," he said. "Four times if it were part of a pair. And possibly much more."

Beside her, Aunt Louisa gasped. "For that ugly thing?"

It was Mr. Allen turn to laugh. "Yes, indeed. Although I'm inclined to share your view of this over-ornate style. But it has become popular again amongst certain collectors. And there's no accounting for taste."

"Popular again?" Emily repeated. "How old would this be?"

"This style was popular in the middle of the last century. If I'm not mistaken, this particular design debuted at the Crystal Palace exhibition in London in 1851 and was wildly popular for a short time. It fell out of fashion, but has been rediscovered in the last ten years or so."

"By whom?" Aunt Louisa said in an undertone.

Mr. Allen apparently had sharp ears, because he glanced at her and his lips twitched.

"Unfortunately very few pieces have survived from fifty years ago," he said. "Especially in the currently popular patterns, like this one. Which makes these items much more valuable as a result."

"What if this were part of a set, including both candlesticks, a tea set and a complete dinner set. How valuable would something like that be?"

Mr. Allen's eyes lit up. "With the whole set complete?"

She nodded.

"If it were all in this same thistle pattern? Hmmm," he said, tilting his head a little to one side as he seemed to be consulting some inner resource. "Then a set like that would easily be worth four or five thousand dollars."

Behind Emily, Aunt Louisa gasped. Emily felt much the same,

but she didn't want to do anything to interrupt the flow of information.

"Perhaps even more," Mr. Allan was saying. "And if you knew someone who owned such a set and was interested in selling it, we would be more than happy to represent them, and we'd make sure to get them the best possible price."

Emily debated her options for a moment. How much to tell Mr. Allen? On the one hand, she didn't want to do anything to endanger Mr. Ying, or to make his situation worse. On the other hand, there could not be that many serious collectors of this kind of pottery, especially in a town the size of Victoria.

If Mr. Allen would release the names of any collectors he knew, there might be a way to solve this case without going near Chinatown. The information could save Mr. Ying's life.

But how to persuade Mr. Allen to tell her what she needed to know?

"I do know of such a collection," she said. "But there are some difficulties to be addressed before any sale can be thought of."

"Perhaps my firm might be of some use in addressing those difficulties?" Mr. Allen offered.

She pretended to hesitate. "Oh, I am not sure. It is such a delicate matter."

"Absolute discretion is guaranteed," Mr. Allen said. "We value our relationship with our customers above all. I believe your aunt can speak to that?"

Aunt Louisa nodded.

"They are indeed very discreet," she said. "It is why I bring most of my business here. I would not hesitate to trust him with the most delicate matters."

Emily nodded decisively. "Very well then. I am undertaking this on behalf of a friend, whose name you would know if I mentioned it. These dishes were inherited from her husband's great-aunt. They did not value them, so the dishes were stored away."

Mr. Allen made a *tsk*-ing sound. Likely he'd prefer that owners of unwanted china consult him about the value, she thought with an inward grin.

"My friend has recently discovered that the rest of the set, with the exclusion of this chipped candlestick, has been stolen."

Mr. Allen's eyes, which had lit up at the beginning of her narrative, flashed disappointment. "I see," he said.

"My friend suspected that the collection must have value, and hopes to address the theft," Emily added. "If the pieces can be recovered, then she would be looking to sell all of them through a reputable dealer. On very favorable terms."

"Recovering stolen items such as these would not be an easy task," Mr. Allen said. "Indeed, some might call it impossible."

"Yes, so I feared. However, the information you have shared gives me hope. Since this is a specialized market, with few items available and only a limited number of collectors..." Emily paused, and gave him a significant look.

"Surely you aren't suggesting I tell you the names of the collectors," Mr. Allen said, looking first taken aback, and then horrified. "It would be a betrayal of their confidences."

"I would not dream of asking anything about your dealings with these collectors," she said. "Only the names of those who collect this kind of pottery, which must be at least somewhat public information. And these collectors would then have an opportunity to buy an amazing collection of"—what had he called it?—"naturalist earthenware."

There was a gleam in Mr. Allan's eyes again, which told Emily he was at least considering her argument.

"After all, it isn't as if the collectors have anything to hide," she said, hoping she could carry it off. "But they would likely be the first to have been approached by the thieves."

After further discussion, and with a bit of assistance from Aunt Louisa, who had been briefed on the situation and was not above a bit of gentle blackmail, Mr. Allen gave in. He quickly wrote several names on a slip of paper, folded it carefully twice over, and held it out to Emily. "I am trusting to your discretion, as you have trusted to mine," he said.

"Thank you. You can rely on it," she said as she reached out a gloved hand to take it from him.

As soon as she and Aunt Louisa were back in the carriage, Emily unfolded the slip of paper and glanced at the list. Two names. She was disappointed that she didn't recognize either of them. "Could there really be only two local collectors of this pottery?" Emily asked.

"I'm surprised there are any," Aunt Louisa said tartly. "Ugly stuff."

Emily had to laugh. "I agree. But obviously it has value for at least a few people."

"So what happens now?" Aunt Louisa asked. "Do we take this list to the police?"

"No, that wouldn't get us anywhere," Emily said. "They believe that Mr. Ying is guilty, and they won't look further. Which is why Mrs. Herron and I are digging into this."

"Well, maybe you and I should keep looking into what happened to the earthenware, then," Aunt Louisa said, holding out a hand. "May I see the list? I might recognize some of the names."

As Emily hesitated, her aunt laughed. "Don't worry, I'll keep it confidential," she said. "Now give me the dratted list."

With a smile, Emily handed the paper over, and waited to see her aunt's reaction. The names meant nothing to her, but then she knew little of Victoria's society, other than the people her aunt had introduced her to.

She watched in fascination as Aunt Louisa's eyes widened. "But... I know both of these men," she said. "Does this mean that one of them is a thief?"

"Not at all," Emily said. "It could mean that. But it could mean also mean that one of them bought the Herron's earthenware without knowing it was stolen. Or the collection might have been sold elsewhere, and these men know nothing about the stolen collection."

"Oh." Aunt Louisa sounded deflated and Emily hid a grin. Unfortunately, detective work was nowhere as exciting as people tended to think it was. Though it did have its moments.

She remembered the time-stopping feeling of having a gun pointed at her, and suddenly missed her fiancé very much. Detecting was much more interesting when she shared it with Granville.

"It's also possible that the collector we are looking for is someone Mr. Allen doesn't know," Emily added.

"So what do we do next?" Louisa demanded.

"Tell me what you know about the two men on the list," Emily said.

"Why?"

"I think we should pay them a visit."

Aunt Louisa gave her a skeptical look. "Surely you don't expect them to simply tell you they have the stolen goods?"

Emily smiled. "Not unless they don't know the items are stolen. Which is possible." Though probably not very likely, if the collecting community was as small as Aunt Louisa had told her.

"At least you still have some sense, for all your detecting," her aunt said.

Emily ignored that. "But if they do know something, they might let something slip. Or possibly one of them could tell us more about other collectors of this naturalist earthenware. So, would you feel comfortable paying a visit to each of them?"

"I can do better than that," Aunt Louisa said. "Victoria has a Collectibles Society that meets once a month. And that meeting is being held tonight at the Empress Hotel. Would you care to join us?"

"Of course I would," Emily said. "How could you doubt it?"

Emily looked at her aunt's solemn face, then started to laugh. "Oh, you're teasing me."

She hadn't known Aunt Louisa had it in her.

As soon as Emily could get a private moment to do so, she called Granville's office telephone. She got no answer, so she called the general line.

"Granville and Scott investigations. Miss Kent speaking," was the pleasant reply.

"Laura, it's Emily," she said.

"Emily, how is Victoria?" Laura asked.

Obviously Granville hadn't told her about the murder.

Emily wondered if he'd shared it with Scott. Probably. And she was glad of it. The two partners worked well together, and they'd counted on the other one having their back ever since they met on the Chilkoot Trail at the start of their arduous journey to find Klondike gold.

"Victoria is…interesting. I'll tell you about it when I'm back," she said. Now was not the time. "At the moment, I need to talk to Granville. Rather urgently, I'm afraid. Do you know when he'll be in?"

"No, but I know where he is," Laura said. "I can send Trent with a message for him to call you as soon as he can, if that would help?"

"Is he planning to come back to the office today do you know?"

"Yes, I think so. He and Mr. Scott are meeting here at six."

Then the message could wait for his return. There was nothing more she could do today, anyway. And luckily Aunt Louisa had nothing planned this evening. She'd be glad to have a quiet evening.

"It can wait until then, but thank you for offering. Please pass on my message, and tell him I'll wait for his call. I'm at my aunt's home," Emily said, and gave her the number.

14

____

When Granville got back to the office, Scott and Trent still hadn't returned. But there was an urgent message from Emily.

"You spoke with her?" he asked Miss Kent.

"I did."

"And how did she sound?"

"She sounded very much herself," Miss Kent said with a smile, clearly aware of his concern. "I offered to have Trent bring you the message immediately, but she asked me to wait until your return."

Which probably meant that her investigation was gaining momentum and she wanted to discuss it with him, but that Emily herself was fine.

"Thank you," he said, meaning it. "I'll be in my office. Please see that I'm not disturbed."

"Would you like a cup of tea?" Miss Kent offered.

"Thank you, but I'll wait until the other two return," he said.

She nodded, and he retreated to his office, firmly closing the door behind him. Then she put his call through.

"Atkin residence," came Emily's voice as soon as the operator had made the connection.

"Emily, it's Granville. How are you?"

"I'm well," she said. "Very well, in fact. And looking forward to seeing you on Thursday. And you?"

She did indeed sound fine. "I'm well," he said. "And looking forward to seeing you also. You needed to talk to me?"

"It's this case," she said, all in a rush. "If I were home, I'd talk to Bertie, because my friend's Chinese cook is now the main suspect. And I need to ask a few questions about him. I don't know whom to talk to here, though."

Now he was worried again. He'd quickly learned that China-town existed on the fringes of Vancouver's society—an unknown land to most non-Chinese. In theory, the same laws applied there. In practice, he wasn't so sure.

And the same would likely apply in Victoria, where the China-town was even older and more established than the one here.

"You know Chinatown isn't safe for non-Chinese," he said. "And that holds especially true for women."

"I think some of the rules might be a little different here," Emily said. "But I don't really know, so it's frustrating. I have questions that need answering, and I can't follow where those questions lead."

"I've found that's true in every case," Granville said ruefully. "Investigations seem to be a series of dead ends, with tiny bits of information gathered along the way, until finally we know enough to put the pieces together."

"Is that meant to be reassuring?" she asked tartly.

He gave a crack of laughter. "Not very helpful, is it? I'm afraid it's the truth. Which is often not reassuring."

Now she was laughing too. "It's my own fault. I've seen enough of your investigations to know that. But it's hard when it matters so."

She must be thinking of the girl who'd been killed.

Murder was always hard, but the victim was so young. Only a few years younger than Emily herself—making it very personal for her.

"You are helping her in the only way anyone can now," he said.

"And you will uncover the truth. Despite our best intentions, there are no quick answers in a murder case."

"Thank you for that," Emily said. "I needed to hear it."

"I'm at your service," Granville said wishing he could see the blush that phrase always brought to her cheeks. And that he could be there with her, instead of here. A telephone call was not a satisfactory substitute.

"There was one other thing," Emily said. "There may be a theft involved in this case. And the stolen items would be very identifiable."

That sounded like something expensive but unique had been stolen. Possibly a collectible item? But Emily was being very careful in her wording. She must be worried about the possibility of the switchboard operator overhearing something damaging.

"Interesting," he said.

"Isn't it?" she said. "I hope to learn more tomorrow, and I can update you when I see you on Thursday."

"I'll be at the ferry terminal," he said. "You're still planning on taking the morning sailing?"

"I am," she said. "And thank you."

After he'd hung up the telephone, Granville glanced at the half page of cryptic notes he'd taken while they talked.

There was nothing he could do for Emily at the moment, so he filed the note in the folder he'd started after she told him about the murder.

But he'd find an opportunity to talk to Bertie about the three of them visiting Chinatown while Emily was in Vancouver.

GRANVILLE WAS REVIEWING his notes and updating the case file when Scott and Trent finally returned from their quest for rumors in the attack on Randall. "Well?" he asked as the two tromped into his office, looking tired and hot. "What did you find?"

"Nobody seems to know anything about the attack," Scott said. "Or if they do, they're not talking."

"That's odd."

"Isn't it?"

"It was a waste of your time, then?"

"Didn't say that, did I?" Scott said with a grin.

"What do you mean?"

"There should at least be a few rumors floating around," his partner said.

"Even a couple beers didn't pry anything loose," Trent put in. "And no one even tried to blame it on thugs hired from out of town."

"Which means it's probably someone local," Granville said slowly. "And not a single person had anything to say?"

"Nope. None of 'em," Scott said.

"Which is either fear, or they really don't know anything," Granville said.

"I'd guess fear," Scott said.

"Making Benton the obvious suspect," he said. "Think he was lying to us?"

"In my experience, lying is Benton's favorite thing," Scott said. "Though I can't see what he'd gain from moving Randall out of the way."

"Nor can I," Granville said. Though he was sure the gangster hadn't told them everything, Benton as the mastermind behind the attack on Randall simply didn't make sense. He needed to have another chat with him. A cordial one.

Because Benton wasn't a man you offended. Not if you were smart.

"What about your favorite weasel?" Scott said. "Gipson is fond of hiring thugs to beat people up."

It was indeed Gipson's style, as Granville could personally attest after an unpleasant encounter in the Klondike while Gipson was trying to steal their claim. He'd ended up staked out on a frozen lake that time. Luckily Scott had found him in time.

"True. Though I don't know that anyone actually fears Gipson," he said.

"Not to this extent, anyway," Scott agreed.

"But Dagan's thugs, now. They might be worth looking at," Granville said, thinking about the east side gang he'd tangled with on the Sinclair case. "The beating fits their style, and Dagan used fear as a weapon."

"I thought Dagan was in jail after the Sinclair case?" Trent said. "Is he out?"

"Nope, he's still behind bars," Scott said. "But the gang's still active. I heard his second-in-command took over. Guy named Lew Gurak."

"Except why would either of them go after Randall? Even if they were hired to do so, I still can't work out what anyone gains from killing our lawyer," Granville said.

"Wait a minute," Trent broke in. "You said something about what they gain by killing our lawyer. Is Randall dead then? I know he looked bad, but I thought he'd make it."

"He's hovering on death's doorway, as far as whoever worked him over is concerned," Granville said. "And I'd like to keep it that way. His doctor said Randall came through the surgery well. But infection is always the biggest risk."

"Then he'll make it?" Trent asked.

"If there's no internal damage they didn't find," Granville said. "And if he's very lucky."

Scott nodded soberly. "You're thinking you don't want anyone going after Randall again. So you'll put it about that he didn't make it."

"That's it. It's safer for him if everyone thinks he's already nearly dead."

"Good," Scott said. "Makes our job easier, too."

"Except it means we have to figure out who attacked him—and who's behind it—before Randall is well enough to leave the hospital," Granville said. "And right now we don't have the slightest notion what's really going on."

Which was ironic considering that he'd just reminded Emily that confusion was the normal state of affairs at the beginning of an investigation. It didn't make it any less frustrating, though.

"So we've got about a week," Scott said. "Where do we start?"

Granville had to smile at his partner's confidence. "We're having dinner with Officer Daniels."

"Now him I like," Scott said. "But why dinner?"

"Daniels gets off shift at seven, which means he's not free until half past the hour. And he's fond of Mary's Diner."

"That's a good reason," Trent said. "I'm hungry."

Scott rolled his eyes, but refrained from pointing out that their apprentice was always hungry.

15

Granville and Scott met Trent at Mary's Diner just after seven, taking a booth in the back corner. There was no sign yet of Daniels—it was still too early.

"Trent, what did you find out?" Granville asked as he signaled the waitress for a pitcher of beer and four mugs.

He'd sent Trent to talk to Scott's sister, Frances. The boy thought the lady walked on water, and she was by turns amused by and tolerant of him. If there was any way of finding out what Benton had been up to that morning—without anyone getting killed—this might be it.

"Miss Frances was her usual lovely self," Trent said loftily.

It wasn't the lad's usual style, seeming more like a mix of Trent's idea of how a gentleman talked about a lady, and Granville's own style. Which amused Granville immensely.

He waited for Scott's reaction. Which wasn't long in coming.

"Lovely self?" Scott said. "This is my sister you're talking about? Lad, you've lost what little sense you had, if you think that's a good description of my sister."

"But she is lovely," Trent said hotly.

"She's stunning, all right," Scott said. "But she's a firebrand. Lovely is a poor word to describe Frances."

When Trent just stared, Granville decided it was time to intervene. Hiding his smile, he said, "Never mind all that. Had she heard about Randall?"

After another furious scowl at Scott, Trent looked at Granville and nodded. "She had. She was real sorry to hear about it, too."

"How did she hear?" he asked.

"Mr. Benton told her. They had lunch together."

Which is what Granville had been hoping. Benton often joined his lady for lunch on Tuesdays. Scott gave Granville a look that said he'd just figured out what his partner was up to, and wasn't best pleased by it.

"Did she tell you what Benton said?" Granville asked.

Frances Scott was as sharp as they came, and Granville wouldn't be surprised if she'd guessed why Trent had stopped by for a visit even before the lad opened his mouth. What Frances didn't choose to share might be as telling as what she'd said. And he'd suspected more than once that Benton counted on exactly that.

Trent, who was still smitten with the incomparable Frances, wouldn't have picked up on the nuances.

The lad was nodding, and beaming. "I didn't even have to ask. She seemed to be feeling chatty today, and she told me that Mr. Benton was even more upset about the attack on Mr. Randall than she was."

"In my town, too," Trent added, in a half decent imitation of Benton's growl. "That's what Miss Francis said he said. And that it was no way to solve a business problem, and something about someone needing a lesson."

"I don't suppose Frances mentioned a name for that someone?" Granville asked.

Trent frowned. "No. I guess she didn't. I didn't really notice, because..."

"Because you were busy watching her lovely eyes?" Scott put in with a grin.

Trent shot him a scathing look. "Because she told me enough else about him I didn't miss the name," he said with dignity.

"What exactly did she say?" Granville asked.

"She said someone has these grand plans and that Randall was in the way of a key part of them," Trent said.

Presumably this someone was their suspect. Did that mean he was a lawyer too? Or simply a crooked businessman who was ruthless about removing any obstacles in his path?

Unless Benton was manipulating them for some reason of his own.

"She also said that he's a sort of investor, too, has a bigger stake in things. Kind of like Benton, only not..." Trent said in a rush.

"An investor like Gipson?" Scott said.

Trent frowned. "No, I don't think she meant him. But that's all she said about the guy."

"Anything else about Randall?" Scott asked.

"No. But it's a start, isn't it?" Trent asked.

A name for this someone would have been even more helpful. Did Benton truly not know who had ordered the attack on Randall? Or had the gangster chosen not to share it for some reason of his own? He needed to find out.

"It is a start, and more than we've been able to come up with. Well done," Granville said, and Trent looked pleased with himself.

By the time Officer Daniels arrived, looking hot and weary after what had obviously been a long day, the three of them had nearly exhausted the possibilities that Trent's new information had given them.

"The frustrating part is no one seems to know the villain of this piece," Scott was saying.

"Benton knows something, though," Granville said. "And yet he's not sharing it. Why not?"

Scott groaned. "Because he's Benton. You're not going to confront him again, aren't you?"

"If I have to. We need to find whoever's been trying to kill Randall."

"You do know Benton is going to kill you one of these days, right? You'll push him too far, and that'll be it for you."

Granville just laughed, while Trent looked anxiously between the two of them.

"You don't mean it," Trent said to Scott. "Tell me he won't kill you," he said to Granville.

"Have I walked into the middle of something?" Daniels asked as he reached their table.

"Not at all. Have a seat," Granville said, and moved along the bench seat of the booth to make room for him.

"What seems to be the problem this time?" Daniels said once he was seated, looking from face to face. "There is a problem, I take it?"

"You've heard about the attack on Josiah Randall?" Granville asked, pouring him a mug of beer.

"What attack?"

As they filled him in, Daniels pulled a notebook and a pencil stub from his pocket. Started to scribble something. Then he looked up at Granville. "Before you tell me too much, is this official?"

Official police business, he meant. Which he'd have to report to Chief Stewart. And rumor was that the chief of police, despite being put on notice by the Police Commissioners, was still taking bribes.

"It isn't official yet," Granville said.

"That only held while Randall was still alive," Daniels said quietly.

"Between the four of us, then," Granville said, lowering his voice. "Randall is still alive. But he won't stay that way if whoever delivered that beating finds out they failed to kill him. So I've put it about that the attack looks like it will be fatal."

"You don't think the police can protect Randall?" Daniels asked him.

"I'm not sure enough to risk his life. Are you?"

With a sigh, Daniels put his notebook away. "No, I'm not. Unfortunately. This is off the record then—for now, at least. Go on."

They filled him in on everything they'd learned to date.

"The only real information we have is that this is likely about profit," Granville said. "Randall probably got in someone's way, and caused him enough trouble that they decided to stop him. I don't know if the beating was meant to kill him, but most men wouldn't survive it. And that's all we know. Nothing about who that someone is."

"The usual rumor mills haven't a word to say on this," Scott added. "It's odd."

"We were hoping you'd run across something on your rounds, or talking to your fellow officers, that might tie into this case," Granville said. "Does any of it sound familiar? Even the smallest thing could give us a direction."

Daniels took a deep draught of his beer. "Nothing comes to mind," he said. "But you haven't given me much to work with."

"We don't have much," Trent burst out. "That's the problem."

Granville silenced him with a look. "You'll let us know if you do hear anything?" he said to Daniels.

"I can do that," the officer said. "Though, now I think on it, I have noticed the rumor mills have been quiet lately. Even though I'm still new on the force, and don't have many connections yet, I should still be hearing something."

"You're not?" Scott asked.

"No."

Granville drained his mug, and signaled for another round. "I have the decided feeling that this is much more complicated than it seemed initially."

"What did Randall get himself into?" Scott said. "He seems such a level-headed fellow."

"It's up to us to figure that out," Granville said.

"Let me know what you find out," Daniels said. "And I'll help where I can."

Coming from Daniels, that wasn't an empty promise. It made a welcome change, having at least one member of the police force on their side.

The Collectibles Society met at eight o'clock that evening in a sectioned off part of the ballroom at the Empress Hotel. A folding wall had been set up to block off the empty two-thirds of the larger room, which Emily found ingenious.

She hadn't seen the ballroom before, and she was awed by the height of the ceiling, the gilt touches everywhere, and the acanthus-patterned William Morris carpet that covered the entire floor. She could almost see how it would be—full of lights and music and dancers, with the scent of flowers hanging heavily on the air. It must be totally overwhelming.

Perhaps she could persuade Granville to bring her to attend a ball here one day. He professed to hate all the fuss, but he was a wonderful dancer—and very elegant in his black evening attire.

The members of the Collectibles Society while stiffly polite, were hardly elegant, and the meeting was as dry as the ball she was picturing was gay. Though they made her welcome, it was quickly evident that the men and women gathered here were far more interested in what her aunt had to say than they were in Emily.

Even the men whose names had been on Mr. Allen's list were barely polite when Emily mentioned mid-century naturalist earthenware. Mr. Martin gave her a stiff smile, while Mr. Andrews half-listened to her questions for a few moments before turning away to answer some comment of Aunt Louisa's. It was clear both of them were both much more interested in discussing the latest collectibles gossip with her aunt. Emily found the subject drier than dust, but being ignored by most of this company suited her very nicely.

Keeping her eyes down, and making sure not to meet anyone's gaze, Emily moved towards the back of the room, and began the process of melting into the wallpaper. Sometimes she could learn more by being invisible than she could by asking difficult questions. And her instincts told her this was one of those times.

Besides, Aunt Louisa was in her element here, and she had quite taken Emily's quest to heart. If her aunt didn't end the evening with another collector or two added to their list, Emily would eat her bonnet. And she was rather fond of that bonnet—a fancy twist of lace and feathers on a wisp of satin.

From the seat she'd chosen, Emily could hear bits of conversation from half the room. The two women in front of her were discussing teacup patterns, while several others a few feet further into the room were discussing silver patterns. Two gentlemen over in the corner seem to be discussing changes to the process of silver-smithing.

From somewhere to the right of where she sat, she could hear a man's voice saying something about the Crystal Palace. A mumbling voice she couldn't quite hear answered him, and then a woman's voice said the words "naturalist style." Was that her aunt's voice?

No, Emily thought not. She moved a little trying to see who was talking, or at least to be able to hear them better. But she didn't want to move too quickly, and give away her interest. Not yet.

She was too late though. Whoever had been talking had stopped now, and the only conversation she could hear from that direction seem to be about German beer steins.

She sat back with a sigh. It was going to be a long evening. She just hoped it proved worthwhile.

After what her pocket watch told her was half an hour, which had seemed interminable to Emily, her aunt reappeared from somewhere.

"Come with me, Emily," she said, seizing hold of her arm. "There's someone you must meet."

BEING half dragged along beside her aunt wasn't an experience Emily wanted to repeat. But she was curious who her aunt had found, and why she was in such a hurry for Emily to meet him.

"Mr. Carstairs, I wanted you to meet my niece Emily," Aunt Louisa said as they drew closer to impeccably dressed man a few years older than her aunt. "Emily, Mr. Carstairs."

He had a heavy, sensual face and a charming smile. But there was something about his high color and full lips that she found off-putting. And a cynical look in his eyes that she definitely didn't like.

The man greeted her with a slight bow. "Louisa, she's a credit to you," he said.

Emily was irritated by his condescending tone, though she was careful not to let it show.

"How do you do," she said, with a curtsey that was exactly the depth society required—and not one whit deeper. She'd have like to give him one exactly as shallow as his bow had been, but reminded herself she was here for a reason.

"Mr. Carstairs is an expert in various types of pottery, dear," Aunt Louisa said.

Emily wished she could caution her aunt against overdoing it. Her aunt had never called her dear in her life.

"I was just telling him how interested you were in mid-century earthenware," Aunt Louisa was saying. "When it struck me that you would enjoy talking to him."

"Why thank you, Aunt Louisa," Emily said, only just managing to suppress a smile at her aunt's performance. She hadn't seen her this animated since her uncle had died. Was it because of the case, or was she interested in this man?

Emily turned towards Mr. Carstairs, to find he was watching her skeptically. "If you really wouldn't mind, there was one thing that I was curious about."

"I'd be pleased to answer your questions," he said in a tone that belied his words.

"Thank you," Emily said. She considered simpering up at him, simply because he annoyed her, but decided she couldn't pull it off.

"I've been reading a catalog from the Crystal Palace Exhibit in London fifty years ago," she said. "And I was intrigued by the illustrations of something called the naturalist style."

She clasped her hands together and wished that Granville could see her. It would amuse him.

"They were so delightful," Emily continued, "with the buttercups, and the leaves, and all manner of growing things—as if the garden itself had been turned into clay. Aunt Louisa tells me the style is long out of fashion, but I see such similarities between it and some of the work that William Morris did over the next twenty years or so."

Which was true enough, as Granville would say. Except that Morris had taste, unlike most of those working in the naturalist style, judging by the Herron's candlesticks. She left out that part, though.

"So did the naturalist style evolve into the Arts and Craft movement?" she finished breathlessly.

"Not at all. The naturalist movement fell out of favor fairly quickly," he said, quick to correct her. "In fact, Morris's work, and the Arts and Craft movement itself, was in reaction to much of the work done for that exhibition. They found it artificial, much too ornate and ignorant of the connection between the work and its materials. Ironically, it is the work of Morris and his fellow artists that makes the naturalist style collectible now."

His gaze moved back to her aunt, and his voice warmed. He dropped the cynical act that Emily had seen earlier. If it was an act.

"These earlier pieces are so exaggerated, in fact," he said, "so much a mockery of what they were trying to be, that they are now seen as a different kind of perfect."

Her head spinning a little at the inversion, Emily could see why her Aunt Louisa had introduced him as an expert. He knew quite a bit about this fairly obscure form of china. And he was clearly passionate about it.

Though she wasn't quite sure if that passion was because he thought the work impressive, or because he found it so bad. Whatever the reason, given this level of interest, she wondered if he might be a collector. And one who hadn't been on Mr. Allen's list.

Her aunt's beaming expression suggested she was thinking the same thing. Or was she simply returning Mr. Carstairs's interest in her?

It was an unsettling thought, to think of her staid aunt with a suitor. And one as self-satisfied as this one?

Surely Aunt Louisa had better prospects, assuming she even wished to wed again. That she could be interested in this man as possible husband was beyond Emily's understanding.

Why should her aunt even consider marrying again, after all? She had her own money, her own house, the freedom to do as she chose. If she wanted suitors, she could find them, and there was no one to place restrictions on her. It seemed an ideal setup to her.

Emily turned her attention back to Mr. Carstairs, trying to see him without any bias. *Could* he be the collector they were looking for? There was only one way to find out.

Drawing in a silent breath, Emily said as politely as she could manage, "I hope one day to own one of these pieces myself, though my aunt cautions me that they are hard to come by now, and priced accordingly?"

From the corner of her eye, Emily could see Aunt Louisa give her a sharp look, but luckily, she said nothing.

Mr. Carstairs nodded, and gave a little bow towards Aunt Louisa. "Your aunt is a very intelligent lady, and she is quite right."

"So it is a dream I must give up then? Owning a piece of this pottery, I mean," Emily said.

"Not necessarily. Pieces do come up for sale occasionally. They are not inexpensive, however."

"Oh, how marvelous," Emily said. "Is there a particular store where I might find them for sale?"

He smiled. Probably at her naiveté as well as her supposed eagerness, Emily thought wryly.

"No, these items are rather too specialized, as well as too rare, for most shops to carry."

"But then…?" Emily said

He gave her an indulgent smile, but was that a warning look in his eyes? "Societies such as this one have been formed to allow aficionados to find their collectible of choice. Your aunt here can probably keep you apprised of any news related to the pieces you seek."

"Oh but…" Emily began.

Aunt Louisa chose that moment to step in. "Yes, indeed I can. But now I think it's time to introduce you to Mrs. Smith, who is collects a more affordable style of china. Otherwise I can tell that you and Mr. Carstairs would be discussing the naturalist style all evening. And that would never do."

The two of them exchanged a look that Emily couldn't quite interpret. Or perhaps she simply didn't want to interpret it. That glance looked suspiciously flirtatious to her.

"Of course, of course," Mr. Carstairs said. "It was a great pleasure to discuss one of my own favorites with a new collector," he said with a little bow to them both and a sideways look at her aunt.

"But Aunt…" Emily protested as Aunt Louisa dragged her off.

It was partly for show, but she was also feeling annoyed at being interrupted just when she was on the brink of getting some very valuable information.

"You need to learn the art of subtlety, Emily," Aunt Louisa said quietly once they were out of his earshot. "Detective business or not. He was beginning to suspect your motives."

"You mean you weren't flirting with him?" Emily said before she could stop herself.

"Well, of course I was," her aunt said. "Flirtation is often a lady's best weapon. We need information, after all. And he has it."

"But…" Emily said began, not even sure what she could say without mortally offending her unexpectedly helpful aunt.

"You were too eager," Aunt Louisa said with a sharp look at

Emily. "Now it is up to him to follow up. And I judge him too much of a collector to resist. I would expect a call from him tomorrow."

Emily was impressed with her aunt's take on the man. And surprised that her aunt had read her so well. She nearly told her so, then realized it would probably sound condescending. And inappropriate, given their relative ages and life experience.

"Yes, I see," she said instead. "So what do we do now?"

"Now we chat with Mrs. Smith," Aunt Louisa said. "And then we can make our departure."

"Already?" Emily said.

"There are no other collectors here with an interest in pottery, much less in naturalist earthenware. Staying would be a waste of time. And quite frankly, I enjoy spending an hour or so with this group, but any longer than that and I am heartily bored."

They exchanged a smile and went looking for Mrs. Smith.

WHILE HER AUNT was engaged in saying her goodbyes to several groups of people, Emily was hiding behind a large fichus tree in a corner near the doors of the huge room. She was busily thinking about her recent encounter with Mr. Carstairs.

In retrospect, perhaps she had over-reacted to that cynicism she thought she had seen. He was probably innocuous enough, if a little full of himself, and a little too interested in her aunt. And quite obsessed with his pottery.

But did that obsession truly extend to mid-century naturalist pottery? And run deep enough that he wouldn't flinch at buying stolen pottery? Pottery a girl had been killed for?

In this very civilized setting, it seemed impossible.

Emily was trying to decide if the idea truly was impossible when yet another middle-aged gentleman in a tweed suit sidled up beside her. She gave him a sideways glance, but didn't recognize him. This one was no taller than she was, and too thin and too pale—at least for a gentleman.

"Couldn't help noticing you were talking to that Carstairs

fellow," he said, in a plummy English accent that struck her as not quite authentic. "Sorry we haven't been introduced, and all that, but I wanted to warn you. My name's Wilkes, Bartholomew Wilkes. And you shouldn't trust Carstairs, y'know."

Now Emily was intrigued. "Oh? And why is that?" she asked, copying her mother's most disapproving tone to perfection.

It was a gamble, but she judged that attitude the one most likely to keep Mr. Wilkes talking. Luckily, she seemed to have guessed right.

"He's a collector," Mr. Wilkes said.

Emily glanced at the crush around her. "Isn't everyone here a collector? Including you?"

He gave her a lopsided smile. "You have me there. And you're right, we're a bit odd, the lot of us."

"And your point is?" Emily said rudely, feeling very daring.

"Well, there's odd, and there's… well, I hate to say it, but twisted is the word that comes to mind."

"Twisted? What in the world do you mean?"

"It takes some of us that way," Mr. Wilkes said earnestly. "Collectors I mean. It goes from a hobby to an obsession. And from an obsession…"

"It becomes a mania?" Emily said.

"That's exactly right. A mania." Mr. Wilkes considered her admiringly. "You have a way with words, you know."

"Thank you," Emily said. "But about Mr. Carstairs? You were saying?"

"He hides it better than most. But he definitely has the collection mania. And don't be deceived by the polished charm he displays so easily at an event such as this one. Carstairs is an obsessive man, and dangerous with it."

According to Aunt Louisa, anything one collector said about another had to be taken with a sifter full of salt. No doubt her aunt would tell her to ignore this.

But what if Mr. Wilkes—and she had to smile at the name—was right? What if Mr. Carstairs was not only the collector she was looking for, but the man who had killed Betsy?

Emily glanced at the slight man with the moon face and protruding eyes staring at her, and doubted it could be quite that simple. Nothing else about this case was.

She fidgeted with her fan, suddenly wishing she could simply go for a bicycle ride to clear her head. Bicycling along one of the paths that led to the ocean would be a welcome relief after the stress of the murder and trying to find the killer.

But Aunt Louisa seemed almost as bad as Papa when it came to any type of exercise for women. And she couldn't go alone. So that was out.

Besides, she didn't know anyone who had a bicycle she could borrow. Unless Mrs. Herron—Caroline, she chided herself—owned a bicycle? And would like to ride with her? It seemed unlikely, but it didn't hurt to ask.

"I see you doubt me, Miss," Mr. Wilkes's earnest voice brought Emily's attention back to her surroundings. "But I beg you to believe me. The fellow is not to be trusted. And certainly not by a young woman such as yourself."

"Oh, I'm sure I'm safe enough in company," Emily said lightly. "Though I appreciate your concern for my safety."

She worked to keep the ironic note out of her voice, and hoped her expression didn't betray her.

Apparently not. "I'm glad to hear you say it," Mr. Wilkes said. "A man like Carstairs takes people in, until it is too late. He should be locked up, really he should."

His voice trailed off as Aunt Louisa bustled up to them. "We really must be going," she said to Emily.

Mr. Wilkes tipped his hat to both of them and faded back into the crowd.

"I was surprised to see you so deep in conversation with Mr. Wilkes, of all people," Aunt Louisa said as they waited for the attendant to fetch their wraps. "Whatever was that about?"

Emily gave her a laughing look. "You'll never believe it, Aunt..." she began as they handed a coin to the attendant and exited the ballroom.

1 7

Wednesday, August 29, 1900

Wednesday morning brought clear skies and the promise of another hot day. Arriving at the office in the early coolness, Granville pulled the blinds against the morning sun, then reviewed his notes from the previous day. With a wry grimace, he concluded that he now had more questions than ever.

Who was behind the attack on Randall? And why?

And if Benton knew more than he'd told them, why was he being so cagey about this one?

The only thing that was clear was that Randall had become a threat to someone, and it had nearly cost him his life. That was the piece he needed to focus on. He reached for the folders Mac and Miss Kent had left for him, and began to read.

It was over an hour later when Scott arrived. Granville looked up from his reading, and met his partner's grin with one of his own. Scott looked from the small stack of folders under Granville's hand, the ones that he had yet to read, to the much larger stack on his right.

"You look like you're having fun," Scott said.

"Hardly," Granville said. "I'm going through Randall's files again. I'm very glad I never became a lawyer, let me tell you."

Scott laughed. "Dry stuff, huh?"

"Dry indeed. But somewhere in all this paper is the motive for murder. Which isn't dry at all."

"Good point," Scott said. "Grudges always spice things up nicely."

"You'd think so," Granville said. "But this language is so tedious that even the nastiest of cases nearly has me nodding off."

"Need some help wading through it all?" Scott offered.

"Thanks, but I'm nearly done." And he thought he might have found something interesting. But he wanted to review the rest of the cases before he said anything.

"I'll see about getting you some coffee, then. Keep you awake through the rest of that stack," Scott said.

"I'd appreciate it," Granville said fervently.

Two cups of coffee and another hour later, Granville slapped shut the last file. "Done," he said.

Scott looked up from what looked like a stack of invoices. "You made it through all of those?"

"I did. But I had a few moments of nostalgia for wading through freezing cold rivers in the Klondike, let me tell you."

Scott laughed. "That bad, hey? At least you weren't longing for that hellish climb up from Dyea. The day either of us long for that is the day I know it's time to pack this business in and head north."

For a moment Granville was there again, on the mountainside between Dyea and the top of the Chilkoot Pass, in the driving snow and howling wind. Halfway up that horrendous climb, bent forward against the slope and the weight on his back. Half the climb behind him, half ahead.

Climbing up and up. Single file on that icy slope, sixty pounds on his back. Breath harsh in his lungs, one painful step at a time. Each man following on the heels of the man in front of him.

Then reaching the top, stashing his load, and heading down to do it all over again. Climb after climb.

It had taken them two days to carry all their gear up.

No, he couldn't imagine wanting to repeat that experience. Ever. Even lawyering would be less awful.

"Most of the gold sites have been worked out, from what I hear," he said. "There isn't much gold left in the Klondike."

"There's always work," Scott said with a shrug. "And other mines. They're still taking gold out of the Fraser River, even."

"Not a lot of it," Granville retorted.

"Doesn't take much to keep a man alive."

That was true. But it took quite a bit to keep a wife alive. And eventual children.

Picturing Emily's smile, Granville figured his gold mining days were pretty much done. But for the first time he wondered if Scott felt the same.

"Well, I'm not nostalgic about that climb yet," Granville said. "And I think I found something."

"You did?" Scott got up and came around the partner desk to Granville's side, looming over his shoulder to peer at the file in front of him. "What did you find?"

Granville had to laugh at his expression. Scott was as eager to be free of the office as he was.

Neither of them were cut out for poring over paper for days at a time. Or even hours. They were much better at the doing—out talking to people, digging into the truth, wherever it lay. Even confronting the villains.

Maybe especially that last.

"Miss Kent sorted these six folders out for me," Granville said. "These are the lawyers who might have had a grudge against Randall because they lost a case to him. I read through all the files, but I focused on these six."

"Why?"

"Well, if Benton isn't just misdirecting us for some reason of his own," Granville said, ignoring the snort Scott gave at that. "Then Randall is a threat to someone. My best guess? Whatever big fish is behind this, Randall got in his way."

Scott chortled. "A big fish? You must've spent too long in the salmon canneries on our last case. The stink of the cannery line got to you."

Granville had to laugh. "At least I can enjoy eating fresh salmon again, now that I'm not smelling that stink every day."

Scott winced. "Not me. It's steak all the way for me."

He grinned at that. "So I've been looking for a case where Randall's actions might block a big fish's activities."

"Makes sense. And?"

"And these three cases would create problems for someone. Two of them don't seem to lead to anything big enough to get Randall killed over. But this last case," and he tapped the file in front of him. "This is our most likely candidate."

"Okay," Scott said. "Who and why?"

Granville turned to the last page, pointed to a paragraph he'd underlined in pencil.

"This is one of the judgements Randall won," he said. "It was between an importing firm and their customer. The fellow that lost, a Mr. Sikes, ran a small firm that imported a variety of goods from the Far East, especially from Japan and China. He'd promised Randall's client an order of Chinese dinnerware in a particular blue and white pattern, and the client had paid up front."

"So?"

"So Sikes delivered porcelain with a poorly rendered copy of the desired pattern, and blamed the quality on the manufacturers in China. The client refused delivery, and Sikes wouldn't reimburse him. Randall called in a porcelain expert to explain the difference to the court. Sikes's lawyer, a fellow named Bragg, tried to argue that the expert was wrong, but he failed. The judge called it theft, made Sikes repay the entire invoice, and barred him from charging people up front in future."

"I don't see how that could get Randall killed," Scott objected. "This Sikes sounds like a small player to me."

"He does indeed," Granville said. "But importing is big business. And this kind of fraud—promising one thing and delivering another, especially when the order is paid up front? It could be very lucrative, if it were done on a large enough scale. What if Sikes himself is only part of something much bigger?"

"Like a big importing firm with a lot of small, seemingly independent branches, you mean?" Scott asked.

"Exactly like that," Granville said. "And because these are relatively small orders, some clients might not even notice the difference in quality, and most wouldn't bother to sue. Lawyers are expensive, and most lawyers won't take on a case this small. Even if they will, the client usually wins too little to cover their legal fees."

"But not in this case?"

Granville smiled. "Randall's defense of his client was inspired. He made this small case important enough for the judge to rule hard against Sikes's business practices, which is very unusual."

"So other merchants who have been similarly defrauded might take notice," Scott said slowly. "And might want to hire Randall as well."

"If this one case was connected to something bigger, it wouldn't be long before Randall started to figure that out," Granville said. "This is the only such case in his completed files. I need to get my hands on his list of recent clients, the ones who haven't gone to court yet, to see if my theory holds up. And we'll need to talk to them, too."

"It sounds like you need to talk with Mac and Miss Kent about that," Scott said. "But since this Bragg case is about shipping, why don't I take Trent and go hunt up rumors on the docks?"

"That sounds like a plan," Granville said. "I want to check in on Randall again, too. After I talk to Mac and Miss Kent."

With a nod, Scott left. Matching action to words, Granville sought out Mac and Miss Kent, and briefed them on what he'd found and what he needed from them.

"Try not to get into trouble," he finished with a wink. As he left, Granville could hear Miss Kent's laughter and a guffaw from Mac.

18

It was mid-morning by the time Granville reached the hospital, but Randall was either still unconscious or deeply asleep. He was very pale, and the bruising was much worse than yesterday, blooming purple and blue on every visible piece of skin. Granville went looking for Dr. Serson, hoping for some positive news. But the fellow was in surgery, and would unavailable for some hours yet.

Leaving the hospital, he walked across to the streetcar line. He got off on Pender and walked towards the office. It was hot, and all he could think of was a mug of cool ale. And perhaps something to eat.

Which put him in mind of another information source that had served him well on the Sinclair case. He consulted his pocket watch. The timing was perfect.

Turning down Richards, he directed his feet towards the Terminal City Club, and the lawyers and businessmen who would be planning strategy and exchanging news in the bar there over a light luncheon. One of the members would be sure to have heard something about the attack on Randall. Even if it was only a rumor to augment—or contradict—Benton's terse remarks.

And the India Pale Ale the club served had become a favorite of his. Especially when paired with their roast beef dip sandwich.

LOCATED in an unremarkable office building just a block from the harbor, the Terminal City Club was modeled after a traditional English club, complete with dark paneled walls and a smoking room. Granville was greeted in the lobby by the club secretary, who gave him a nod and a brisk "Afternoon, Sir."

"Good afternoon," Granville said. "Is O'Hearn around? Or Draper?"

"I haven't seen Mr. O'Hearn this afternoon, but I believe Mr. Draper is upstairs in the bar."

That didn't surprise him. Andrew Draper was the business reporter for the *News Advertiser*, and he made it his business to know what was happening on his beat. Given the amount of time the fellow spent in the bar of this club, it amazed Granville how accurate and thorough Draper's business stories were.

Though perhaps it shouldn't have. The club bar was a gathering place for ambitious young businessmen. And the dapper reporter with the jovial manner and the unforgettable mustache had a very hard head for alcohol. He'd also proved to have a good ear for lies, as well as a sharp nose for a story. Those particular characteristics had made him a good source on the Sinclair case.

They also made him just the fellow he needed to talk to now.

Making his way up an impressive staircase, complete with stuffed moose heads—which were definitely not a feature of a typical English club—he turned down the hall and into the crowded bar. There he was greeted with handshakes and slaps on the back from the gentlemen he knew, and smiles from those he didn't.

Draper was easy to spot—he was standing with several others at his usual table, beer in hand. Granville ordered a pint of ale and a round for the table, and made his way over to them.

"Granville, good to see you," Draper said immediately. "You haven't been around much lately."

"We just completed a case in Steveston," he said. "Which isn't a convenient distance from here."

Since Steveston could only be reached by boat or by a jolting, hour-long carriage ride over poor roads, his comment was received with laughter. The bartender brought the round he had ordered, placing a full glass in front of each man. Which lightened the mood still further.

"What brings you by today?" Draper asked, his eyes narrowing a little.

Granville could tell that the reporter's instincts for a story had been aroused.

"I've just come from the hospital. I'd planned to visit my lawyer —I don't know if you know him? Josiah Randall?—but he's been attacked. And it looks to be fatal, I fear," he said.

"Randall is dying? But that's dreadful news," Draper said. "He's a good man. And he's one of the best lawyers in town. Despite that idiotic lawsuit Peabody has launched against him."

"I've certainly found him so," Granville said. "I can't imagine who might have beaten him so badly. Or why."

"Nor can I," real estate agent Grant Marshall said, joining the conversation. "From my dealings with him when he was acting on your behalf, he was impressively capable. Though far too thorough for my liking," he added with a wink.

It was probably true, too. Marshall had recently assisted him and Emily in finding what would be their new home, as well as in the purchase and renovation of new premises for their offices. Since Randall had handled the legal documents for them, he and Marshall had met several times. And Randall never missed a detail when it came to legal documents.

"Could Peabody's lawsuit have something to do with it?" he asked.

A dark suited businessman he didn't know snorted. "Peabody? The fellow doesn't have an aggressive bone in his body. It's what made him such a loss as a prosecutor. Chief Stewart just liked him because Peabody let the chief run the show."

"And didn't question anything the police themselves did," added another.

"So who put him up to the lawsuit?" said Draper thoughtfully. "It's out of character, isn't it?"

There was a brief discussion about whether Peabody had been outraged enough to sue, or if someone had put him up to it. Most agreed with Draper—left to himself, Peabody didn't have the gall to sue another lawyer for his own incompetence.

"Still, why would someone put Peabody up to it?" Granville asked.

"Randall has been making a bit of a name for himself," a dark-haired fellow by the name of Konrad said. "That can be dangerous."

Granville gave him an interested look. One of the lawyers Randall had defeated so soundly had been named Konrad. Was this the same fellow? "Oh?"

Konrad nodded. He drained his whiskey and reached for the fresh round Granville had ordered. "There's those that appreciate him. And those that don't."

There was a murmur of agreement.

"Pistols at dawn?" Granville said with a grin.

That was met with another round of laughter.

"Nothing so straightforward," Konrad said, tipping his glass to Granville in a silent toast. "Business rivals are fair game. When the stakes rise, the weak ones can find themselves cut out."

That certainly fit in with what Benton had said. And it also suggested a knowledge of exactly what was going on with Randall. Though he wouldn't call Randall weak—unless Konrad meant that one man alone was weaker than those who had more money and muscle behind them?

Granville made a mental note to find out more about Konrad.

"Is that what was happening with Randall?" he asked. "He was being cut out?"

"I think it's a good guess," said Konrad, drinking deeply. "The fool was getting above himself."

And wasn't that an interesting statement. "So who would cut him out?"

"Well, I don't rightly know," Konrad said. "All I hear are rumors."

"Rumors?" Draper said, leaning forward now. "About Randall? I hadn't heard."

Granville could almost see the ends of the reporter's luxuriant mustache quivering as he caught wind of a story. He sat back to watch the show.

"It's just a rumor, you understand," said Konrad, looking alarmed now. "You can't quote me."

"Of course not," said Draper, but there was a gleam in his eye that Granville was glad wasn't focused on him. "But that's the man I need to talk to."

"Which man?" asked an unwary Konrad.

"The one I *can* quote," Draper said with a straight face.

There were grins around the table at how well Konrad had been set up. Konrad was looking panicked.

"I don't know anything," he protested. "And I certainly don't have a name."

"What do you have?" Marshall asked.

"And how did you come across information that even I hadn't heard?" Draper added with a hard look.

"It's only rumors," Konrad said. "I heard some other lawyers were upset with Randall. Including Peabody. Who seems pretty bitter about the whole thing, and increasingly angry."

"Why?" Draper asked.

"Randall's too honest," Konrad blurted out. Then he turned pale and swallowed down half his whiskey.

"And you know this how, exactly?" Draper asked.

"Just things I heard. Here and there," Konrad said.

"Here and there," Draper said. "But you're a lawyer, aren't you?"

"That's irrelevant," Konrad said. "I'm not part of this."

Oh yes he was, Granville decided. He didn't know exactly how yet, but he'd be finding that out.

"But you know who is involved," Draper said shrewdly. "And what's behind it, I'll bet."

Konrad drained his glass, and signaled the bartender for another. Glanced around the table. Then he leaned in, and lowered his voice.

"You didn't hear this from me," he said. "But there are some lawyers who are willing to bend the law further than others. They're rather unhappy with Randall."

Granville thought of the files Miss Kent had identified, and suspected he could name at least three of those other lawyers. It was a start.

Then he pictured Randall's battered face as he'd last seen him, his harsh attempts to breathe. He wasn't buying Konrad's story. There was more to this case than a few unhappy lawyers.

There had to be a bigger fish behind this somewhere. And he was going to find out exactly where. Then he and Scott were going fishing.

19

By half past one on Wednesday afternoon, Emily found herself seated beside Caroline Herron in a well-lit but windowless room inside the Victoria courthouse, an imposing edifice of brick and granite that had been built some ten years earlier to serve the needs of the young province. Both women wore plainly trimmed but elegantly cut day dresses of fine lawn. Emily's dress was a pale peach, as befit her unmarried status, while Mrs. Herron wore a deep goldenrod tone. Emily thought they added a much-needed touch of color to the drab room they sat in.

Neither woman said much as they waited for Mr. Ying to be brought in, though they exchanged glances when the clerk on duty firmly closed the door behind himself as he exited. It had been made quietly clear to them that this was no place for ladies, despite the courteous treatment they'd received. Mrs. Herron was married to a magistrate, after all.

Emily glanced at Caroline and rolled her eyes. The magistrate's wife smiled back at her.

The police officer brought in Mr. Ying, chained hand and foot, and handcuffed him to the chair. He wore rough gray prison garments that looked too large on him, though his long queue was still coiled neatly around his head.

"Are all those chains really necessary?" Caroline asked.

One of the guards who'd brought the prisoner in gave her a blank look. "The man's a murderer, ma'am. He shouldn't even be talking to ladies like yourself. It isn't safe, even with the chains."

The other guard gave him a look that silenced him, then nodded to Mrs. Herron. "We'll make sure you're safe," he said.

"Thank you. We'll be fine," Emily said, and Caroline Herron nodded a dismissal at them.

"We'll be right outside if you need us," the second officer said.

"And we'll be watching every move through the door," the first officer warned the prisoner. "So don't try anything foolish."

Emily was surveying the healing cuts and yellowing bruises on Mr. Ying's face with horror. She nearly asked him if they'd happened before or after he was arrested, but at the last moment remembered to hold her tongue. She and Caroline had decided earlier that it was best if Caroline spoke first. Mr. Ying was more likely to trust her.

"Ying, I am so sorry to see you here," Caroline was saying. "How are you?"

The Chinese man gave a small shrug and glanced towards the window in the door, where the guard's eyes were visible.

"It's all right. My husband assures me they can't hear us," Caroline said. "We can talk freely."

"Why do you come here?" Mr. Ying said. "There is nothing for you to do. Nothing anyone can do."

"I know you didn't kill poor Betsy. And I am determined to see you set free," Caroline told him. "Miss Turner and I have been asking questions about what really happened the day of the tea party."

For a moment Emily saw the fear Caroline had mentioned in Mr. Ying's eyes. What was he so afraid of?

"You must not," he said rapidly. "It is a danger for you."

Who did Mr. Ying think would be threatened by two ladies

asking questions? Emily wondered. Even the police didn't take them seriously.

"Nonsense," Caroline was saying. "We are only asking a few questions. We will be careful, and we shall be quite safe."

Mr. Ying looked away. "You do not understand," he said softly.

What if the murder was somehow be connected to Chinatown? Was that what Mr. Ying feared?

"We have not yet talked to anyone in Chinatown, if that is your concern, Mr. Ying," Emily said, watching him closely as she tested her theory.

She thought he looked a little calmer at the words.

Still his voice was fierce as he said, "I go to trial. Let your husband's justice find answers."

"Fine," Caroline said. "But only if you answer a few questions for me."

Ying closed his mouth tightly and stared into the distance, refusing to look at her.

"You know how determined I can be," she told him. "And if you won't talk to me, I'll go to Chinatown and find someone who will."

So Caroline hadn't missed her cook's reaction to Emily's words. Good. And she was watching Mr. Ying's reaction as carefully as Emily was doing.

Both of them let out a soft breath of relief when he stopped staring at the far wall and looked at his employer instead.

"What do you ask?" he said.

"I know about the missing pottery from the cellar, Ying," Caroline said. "That hideous stuff that Mr. Herron inherited. I don't even mind that it's gone. I just want to know why. And who?"

Mr. Ying's lips tightened, and for a moment Emily was afraid he wouldn't answer. But it seemed his loyalty was as strong as that Caroline Herron felt towards him. He nodded.

"Who was it, Ying?"

"Not...that," he said, his voice a hoarse croak. "But I can say the pottery was stolen."

Caroline's own lips tightened, and for a moment Emily was

afraid she'd try to order him to tell her, and spoil everything. She should have had more faith.

"Is that why Betsy died, Ying?"

He looked away, as if ashamed. "Yes," he croaked out. "That knife. To threaten me."

Emily felt a little rise of excitement. She'd been right. Then she looked from Mr. Ying's bruised face to their dismal surroundings and felt ashamed. This was no time for pride.

"Why?" Caroline asked. "Just tell me why?"

Ying looked at her for a moment. "You say ugly things, and hide them away in cellar. Those things for one who collects, much prized."

"How did they know we had such things?" she asked.

He looked away. "My fault. I feel proud, and talk too much of your home. Then they make threat to your little ones if I not help them steal."

Caroline Herron paled and drew in a harsh breath at his words. But to her credit, she didn't look away.

"You should have told me," she said. "We'd have found a way to stop them. And keep my grandchildren safe."

Emily was watching both of them closely. Something was missing here. If Mr. Ying was helping the thieves, then why would they attempt to stab him? She decided getting a reaction from him was worth the risk that he would stop telling them anything at all.

"If you were helping them, why would they attack you?" Emily asked.

Mr. Ying drew in a sharp breath, then closed his eyes as if the movement pained him. Emily wondered what other bruises he bore underneath the rough prison garb.

"They didn't attack him," Mrs. Herron said softly, her eyes trained on Ying's face. "And he wasn't helping them. The theft must have happened while we were setting up for the tea, when it was so busy."

She paused, raised a handkerchief to her mouth for a moment, as if to hold back the words. Or perhaps what they meant.

"Betsy wanted to talk to me," she said after a moment. "She

must have seen something in the cellar, but I was too busy with the tea and didn't have time to listen. And so she died—the thieves killed her before she could betray them. I'm right, am I not, Ying?"

He nodded once, a jerky motion of his head. "I tell him she is not a danger to them. I tell him I take care of it—talk to girl, tell her items are sold, and that you know about sale. But—no time. He too angry. He kill her anyway."

Mrs. Herron nodded back.

"I thought so," she said to Emily.

Then to Ying she said, "You tried to stop him, didn't you, Ying? It's why you're so bruised now."

The Chinese man was staring at the floor. He didn't answer her question. But then, it wasn't really a question.

And looking from Mrs. Herron to Mr. Wong, Emily began get a glimmer of how it might all fit together, though she still had too many questions. "But how does Chinatown fit in?" she asked impulsively.

He didn't seem to hear her. And he refused to answer anything else, no matter what Mrs. Herron said. She even offered to send her grandchildren away, somewhere safe, until it was all over, but he shook his head.

"No place safe enough," he muttered, just loud enough that Emily heard him.

<hr>

EMILY AND CAROLINE left the jailhouse in preoccupied silence.

"At least we now know most of what happened when poor Betsy was killed. And something about why it happened," Emily said as they stepped into the Herron carriage. "But we still know nothing of who was involved. And how are we ever going to get Mr. Ying to tell the police that he wasn't responsible for her death? That he tried to stop it?"

"We cannot," Caroline Herron said as she settled her wide skirts on the plush seat. "If Ying won't testify on his own behalf—and I can tell from how he was speaking that he will never do so—then there is no way to force him."

Emily stared at the woman she'd come to admire. "Surely you aren't giving up?"

Caroline glanced over, her face set in determined lines. "Of course not. Ying might not be willing to help himself, but I will do whatever needs doing to see him clear of this. Especially since it is my grandchildren he seems to be trying to protect with his silence."

"Good," Emily said. She thought a minute. "Given Mr. Ying's reaction to any mention of Chinatown, he definitely doesn't want us asking questions there. It might be a place for us to start, don't you think?"

"I don't know about that. Certainly, Ying would know who to talk to, but I'm not sure it would be so easy for the two of us."

Emily wondered at her hesitation. She would have expected more from a woman so determined to clear her cook's name.

Caroline must have seen something of what she was thinking in her face. "Have you ever been to our Chinatown, Emily?" she asked.

"No, I haven't. But I've spent some time in Vancouver's China-town. I expect they are similar?"

"Actually, not at all. Our Chinatown is much older than yours. It was established by men who came north from San Francisco during the gold rush in the 1850s, and nearly three thousand Chinese people are living there now."

Emily stared at her. "That many? It must be huge."

Caroline smiled, though her eyes were still sad.

"Our Chinatown covers four blocks of the downtown, and is really quite impressive. And since it seems it might be important to this case, I think you need a tour. Do you have the next hour free?"

"I am free until dinner," Emily said.

"Good," Caroline said, and gave the order to her driver.

As the carriage drove down Cormorant Street, Emily could see the change in the buildings that told her they'd entered Chinatown. There were the same solid three-story brick buildings she'd seen in the center of town, built in the Italianate style with elaborate plaster cornices and window arches. But here the buildings had carved wooden balconies that overhung the wooden sidewalks. Large red lanterns hung beside lacquered doors, and signs written in flowing Chinese characters in gold, yellow, and red were everywhere.

"It looks new," Emily said, mentally contrasting it with some of the much smaller and often battered-looking wooden structures along the edges of Chinatown in Vancouver.

"Most of the buildings in this section were built in the last five years or so," Caroline said. "The earlier buildings were much rougher. You can still see some of them, if you look."

Emily soon saw what she meant. Mixed in with the brick buildings were rough-built wooden structures and two-story buildings that looked familiar. And temporary beside their more elegant brick cousins.

As their driver wound his way from Douglas to Store Street and back again along the connecting streets, Emily looked from one side of the street to the other, trying not to miss anything. Caroline Herron pointed out the Chinese hospital, church, school, an opera house, two temples, several association houses, and two opium factories as the carriage rolled past them.

"It seems much more permanent, and more settled than Vancouver's Chinatown," Emily said, trying to take it all in. "Perhaps because this Chinatown was established so long ago?"

"That would make sense," Caroline said. "Since Vancouver is a much younger city than Victoria. The Hudson's Bay Company trading fort was established here nearly a hundred years ago."

Emily had heard the story before, and at the moment she was more interested in Chinatown's present than its history. "What are the narrow openings I see between some of the buildings? Where do they lead?"

"You have a good eye for detail. It's one of the mysteries of Chinatown, from what I've heard. In behind these buildings we can see, there is a maze of dwellings and businesses, all connected by narrow alleys, stairways and passageways."

It sounded very like parts of Vancouver's Chinatown. Emily sat a little straighter, and tried to see into the narrow openings, but to no avail. "I can't see a thing," she said. "Can we stop the carriage and explore?"

"I'm afraid we wouldn't be welcome," Caroline said. "Except in a few of the shops. Not without an invitation and a guide. And even then, we'd likely not be permitted entrance without a male escort."

Emily grimaced, but nodded. Exactly like Vancouver's Chinatown. "So what is back there? In the alleys, I mean?"

"I have only heard the rumors, you understand," Caroline said. "I'm not sure anyone who isn't Chinese truly knows much of it. But in those hidden alleyways I hear you might find gambling parlors and opium dens, brothels and joss houses. And also crowded tenements with hidden courtyards where children can play and old men raise pigeons in the sun."

Emily's eyes widened. "Opium dens? In addition to the opium factories?"

Caroline nodded. "Opium smoking has always been accepted in Chinatown, and since it's quite legal, the factories purchase business licenses from the city, and openly process the raw opium. The smoking opium which results is then sold in grocery stores in Chinatown. When the factories are working, you can smell the cooking opium throughout the city."

"What does it smell like?" Emily asked, fascinated.

"Some say it smells like potatoes boiling. Myself, I've found the smell has an undertone of roasting peanuts as well."

"And the opium dens? Are they less legal than the factories? Is that why they're hidden in the courtyards, while you can see the factories from the street?" Emily asked.

Caroline smiled at the question. "Opium manufacture and use are both legal. But we saw two opium factories as we drove by. I have it on good authority that there are at least nine in Chinatown."

"Oh," Emily said, looking more closely at the buildings they were rolling past. She saw another alleyway, and a door that looked as if it might lead into a hidden passage rather than a building. "So the other factories are in the inner alleys and courtyards, just like the opium dens. Are they worried about them being discovered?"

"More cautious than worried, I believe. Unlike the gambling parlors, which are illegal and tend to be raided frequently by city police, opium dens are fully legal. If not exactly acceptable to most outside of Chinatown."

Emily thought about that for a moment. "So in effect, Chinatown is a hidden city within the city of Victoria," she said. "Some facets of the Chinese culture are accessible to anyone, but many are hidden, accessible only to those who know about them."

"Yes, that is it exactly," Caroline said.

"No wonder you hesitated when I asked you where we might start asking questions about Mr. Ying and the murder. The answers probably lie in these hidden alleyways," Emily said. "What are joss houses?"

"Places of worship, I believe, and integral to the Chinese culture. But they can also be meeting houses."

"For the associations you mentioned?" Emily asked. "What are those? Are any of them criminal associations?"

"I suspect some of them might be criminal, or at least have those elements," Caroline Herron said. "But that comes more from what I've seen of human nature over the years than it does from what little I know of Chinatown."

They shared a smile.

"Some of the associations are also known as *tongs*, though I am unclear whether that name has a particular meaning," Caroline said.

"I've heard a little about the *tongs*, much of it confusing," Emily said. "People most often seem to equate the *tongs* to the criminal element."

"I doubt that's strictly true," Caroline said. "Or even partly true. But the associations I'm know most about are the benevolent associations, who run the hospitals, the Chinese legal funds and the like. And the benevolent associations also seem to keep the peace within Chinatown, though I'm not sure what their structure is. There are also associations for everyone from the same area of China, as well as ones for people with the same last name."

Emily was trying to take it all in, and feeling a little lost. It seemed an even more complex society than she'd realized, perhaps because it was older than Vancouver's Chinatown, and had longer to develop all these various associations.

"It sounds almost impossibly complex for someone who isn't Chinese to understand," she said.

"I think it is," Caroline said. "My husband has told me a little, here and there. I know he dealt with one of their benevolent associations when there were disputes on the goldfields, things like that."

"But in this case, someone was hired to steal your pottery, which was to be sold to someone else. And Betsy was killed over it. Where would you go to ask questions about that?" Emily asked.

"And that is exactly the problem," Caroline said. "Now that it is clear Ying won't tell us anything helpful, I wouldn't even know where to begin."

Emily nodded slowly. "Thank you for showing me your Chinatown. I hadn't truly understood the problem before."

"I know. You almost have to drive along these streets to even begin to understand the complexity of it," Caroline said. "Which is going to make it even harder to free Ying. I am beginning to wonder if there is even any way to save him."

As the Herron carriage drove homewards, Emily was so busy trying to think of a way to find answers in Chinatown she barely noticed how smoothly the carriage rode on what Papa would have excitedly called "the newest invention in springs." There must be some way of finding out what Mr. Ying was holding back.

As the carriage drew to a stop in front of her aunt's home, Emily turned to face Caroline, and noted with alarm that she looked drawn and tired, and seemed to have lost the spirit she'd been showing all day.

"Would you care to come in for tea and discuss what we've learned?" Emily asked "Aunt Louisa might have something to suggest we haven't considered, since she knows so many of Victoria's collectors."

"I thank you, but I don't have the heart for it now," Caroline said.

Emily started to protest, but Caroline Herron was no longer listening. Head bowed, she spoke as if she'd forgotten she wasn't alone.

"I wish now I had never held that wretched tea party," she said in such a soft voice Emily had to strain to hear her. "Then my ugly pottery might still be gone—as if I cared—but Betsy would still be alive. And Ying would not be stuck in that jail, facing a death sentence."

Before Emily could think of a word to say, the driver came around to open the door for her, and the moment was lost.

20

Granville strode back towards his office, feeling the anger simmering in him at Konrad's dismissive attitude towards Randall's supposedly fatal injuries. He wanted to punch someone, but this case called for subtler methods.

When he swung open the office door, Miss Kent looked up, startled. He closed it carefully behind him and she gave him a tentative smile.

"Is Scott back yet?"

"No, he and Trent are still out. As is Mr. McAndrews."

He nodded. "I'll be in my office. When Scott comes back, send him in. And when Mac gets back, why don't you and he join us."

Once seated behind his desk, Granville jotted down the revelations from the discussion at the club, along with his conclusions. His thoughts in order, he stared out the window, watching the light breeze stirring the ivy on the brick building across from them. He was getting the first glimmering of what this case might be about, and how he'd avenge Randall.

Just then, Miss Kent knocked lightly and stuck her head around the door. "Mr. Scott isn't back yet, but Mr. McAndrews is. Did you want us to join you now, or wait until Mr. Scott is back?"

"Now would be fine," Granville said. "Why don't you both come in." As they did so, he noted that both of them carried sheaves of files as well as their notebooks. That was a good sign.

"We have a lead," he said as soon as they sat down opposite his desk. "Or at least the beginnings of one. I'll brief you in a moment. But first, if either of you has found anything new, I'd appreciate hearing it."

"I looked into the fellow who manages Randall's rental properties," Mac said. "He's still none too happy about the interest Randall was showing his daughter. But it seems he hasn't liked anyone else who showed interest in his daughter either. Though he's never gone past yelling with any of them. And since he apparently likes working for Randall, I doubt he'd even go that far in his case."

"So we can discount him, then. Good. Did you have any luck with Bragg's client list?" Granville asked. "Or were you able to discover anything else in Randall's files, Miss Kent?"

They exchanged glances.

"I didn't get very far," Miss Kent said. "I think between us we've already pulled out everything of value. But Mac—I mean Mr. McAndrews might have something for you."

Was that a blush? Granville had thought Emily was being romantic—even though it wasn't like her—when she'd mentioned a possible interest growing between these two. But it appeared she might have been right.

A fact he hastily decided to ignore.

"Mac?" he said.

"I found that list of Randall's scheduled court appearances you wanted," Mac said. "And I'm not sure, but I think the two cases I marked are similar to the one you were most interested in."

Granville glanced quickly down the list, taking careful note of the names of the opposing lawyers. Jasper Konrad and Oliver Lessing.

So that was where Konrad fit in. No wonder he was glad to see Randall out of the picture. And reluctant to be quoted about it. "Interesting. Have you got...?" he began.

Mac handed him two thick files. "These are Randall's client files for the cases involved," he said,

"Thank you," Granville said. "I'll take a look."

"And your lead?" Mac asked.

He grinned. "My potential lead has just solidified nicely. I was told that there's a group of lawyers who are rather unhappy with Randall, and are plotting against him. And I rather suspect that, based on the files, that we can name at least five of those lawyers."

Miss Kent smiled. "Let me guess. Cheever, Griggs and Bragg. And possibly Konrad and Lessing?"

"Those are the names I was thinking of."

"And this information is solid?" Miss Kent asked.

"It came from Konrad himself. Who, by the way, swears he isn't directly involved in this group."

"Of course he isn't," Mac said.

"Naturally not." Granville said. "And to prove that, he'll be giving up the names of all those who are involved. Because if Randall dies, it makes every one of those involved murderers."

"He isn't going to die, though, is he?" Miss Kent asked. "I thought he was recovering."

"The doctor thinks he'll make it. But these lawyers don't know that."

Miss Kent's smile widened. "How can we help?"

"It's possible that one of these five is responsible for the attack on Randall. It's also possible that there is someone else behind this group. Perhaps someone who has a great deal to lose from the changed laws resulting from Randall's cases," Granville said. "Can you look into these lawyer's clients and see if anyone fits?"

"Including Mr. Konrad's clients?" Miss Kent asked.

"Definitely including Konrad's clients."

Miss Kent and Mac exchanged glances. "Court proceedings are published," she said. "Let me see what I can learn. But this may take some time."

"I'll help her," Mac said. "And if there's a money trail, I'll find it."

When Scott and Trent finally returned, the three met in his office.

"We didn't find much," Scott said. "No rumors at all about Randall. Still. And not much happening on the docks, either."

"So there's nothing to suggest crooked dealings in the importing business?" Granville asked.

"Well, nothing that's causin' rumors, anyway," Scott said with a grin.

"It's real quiet," Trent said. "Bar fights, and stuff. But nothing big. Could be the heat, though."

He might have a point. The heat had been oppressive the last few days, with almost no breeze to move the humid air. It was the kind of weather to provoke meaningless fights, but serious schemes would wait for cooler weather.

"We might finally have a lead in another direction," Granville said. And he filled them in on his meeting at the Terminal City Club, and what Mac and Miss Kent had uncovered.

"This thing with the lawyers is the first motive I've heard that fits the facts we have," he added. "And if the biggest threat Randall poses is to other lawyers, that explains the lack of rumors."

"Lawyers getting together to take down other lawyers, huh?" Scott said.

"You can't trust 'em," Trent put in heatedly. He caught Granville's eye, and added hastily, "Except Mr. Randall, of course."

Granville wasn't at all surprised the lad felt that way, given his father's frequent run-ins with the law. "There are other good lawyers in town, too. But most lawyers know the law well, which means they know exactly how to bend it. And some of them don't hesitate to do so."

Scott was frowning. "You don't think it's just a group of rogue lawyers behind this thing, do you?"

"No, I don't," Granville said. "The attack on Randall was too vicious, for one thing. He was very lucky it didn't kill him outright.

Then there's the information Benton gave us, which doesn't fit that scenario—there are too many disconnected pieces. I still think it's more than we're seeing. Maybe our big fish."

Scott grinned at him. "Our big fish? You mean your big fish?"

Granville rolled his eyes. "Have it your way. My big fish, then. But whatever we call him, if there's someone behind the attacks on Randall, we can't underestimate him," he added, all amusement gone. "Which is why I've arranged to meet with Robert Carver in half an hour."

"Carver? The sleazy lawyer who helped Putnam cook the books on the Sinclair case?" Trent said. "Why would we want to meet with him?"

"I thought he'd been disbarred," Scott said.

"Apparently not," Granville said. "He's been reprimanded, and is on his best behavior, or so I hear. But Carver is a smart man. And he helped us out before.

If Randall is being attacked because of his legal work, Carver is likely to have heard about it. And if Gipson's involved in some way, he might have heard that, too."

"Seeing as how Carver got involved with Gipson before," Scott said.

"Exactly. I'm hoping Carver will be willing to share what he knows with us."

"It's a start, I guess," his partner said.

Granville laughed. "We're at the stage of an investigation where we're turning over rocks to see what crawls out."

"Like more lawyers," Trent muttered under his breath.

———

GRANVILLE REMEMBERED Carver's third floor office well, though the last time he'd seen it, it had been night and he and McAndrews were busy searching the place. The front office was empty now, as it had been that night.

He wondered if Carver had hired a new clerk. Or whether the fellow could afford to do so. Given his history, it might be difficult to re-establish his practice.

He should have known better.

Carver's large oak desk was stacked with files, and his calendar, in the glimpse Granville had of it before Carver closed the book, was full. He wondered how much of that business was legal.

The lawyer looked pleased to see them, though. Standing, he came around the desk with his hand outstretched. "Granville. Scott. And Trent, isn't it? It's good to see you."

"And you," Granville said.

"Please, have a seat," Carver said, waving them to the deep leather wing chairs opposite the desk. "And excuse the mess. I'm still restructuring my practice after my—absence—in June."

He winked, and Granville remembered why he liked the fellow.

"Now, what can I do for you?" Carver asked as they made themselves comfortable.

"You've heard about Josiah Randall?" he asked.

"I have," Carver said. "And I was very sorry to hear it. He's one of the good ones, and as sharp as they come. You'll be investigating, then?"

"He's our lawyer," Scott said. "Got me out of jail, for starters."

Carver nodded. "Sad news for you, then. And for the legal profession here, too."

He seemed to mean it. Which made it more likely he'd help them.

"We're looking into what happened, and who might be behind it," Granville said.

"And running into dead ends at every turn," Scott added.

"And you were hoping I could help?" Carver said ironically. "I'm honored. I'll be happy to help. And not only because I owe you, either. I liked Randall, even when we were on opposing sides. Unfortunately, I'm not sure how much help I can be."

"We know about Peabody suing Randall," Granville said. "But Peabody is definitely being funded by somebody. There's also talk of other lawyers conspiring against Randall for being too honest."

"And you think there's something else behind that?" Carver said shrewdly. "Such as whoever is funding Peabody's lawsuit?"

"I think Randall was in someone's way," Granville said.

"Someone or some group. And yes, most likely it's whoever is funding Peabody."

He'd learned the hard way never to ignore the money trail, and so far, this case seemed to be all about someone's profit. "Those thugs that beat Randall so thoroughly knew what they were doing," he added.

"Professionals, you think?" the lawyer asked.

"That would be my guess."

"Which means there should be rumors floating about," Scott said. "Especially after word got out about Randall. But so far, no one's talking."

"And we asked everywhere," Trent put in. Then sat back, looking pleased with himself. Despite Granville's warning that in this meeting, he was to listen and learn. And not talk.

Given the lad's opinion of Carver, it had seemed safest. He should have known Trent wouldn't be able to stay quiet for long.

"And isn't that interesting," Carver said, making a few quick notes on the legal pad in front of him. "I haven't heard anything either. Which, as you say, is unusual. Let me make a few calls and get back to you."

"You might want to speak with a lawyer named Konrad. He certainly wanted to get even with Randall," Granville said, and filled the lawyer in on that conversation. "Be careful, though. This appears to be a dangerous time to be a lawyer."

"Thanks for the warning. I'll manage," Carver said. And his eyes were gleaming as he showed them out.

21

All through the meal that her aunt's cook served, Emily kept picturing the defeated look on Caroline Herron's face as she'd last seen it. She had no appetite for dessert, and excused herself from the table as soon as the meal was finished.

"Are you well, Emily?" Aunt Louisa asked. "It isn't like you to turn down dessert."

"I am feeling badly for Mrs. Herron, and worried about the case," Emily said. "It seems we were right about the link between the stolen pottery and poor Betsy's murder. But for every piece of information we uncover, we seem to run into another dead end."

"Was the information we uncovered yesterday about the collectors of earthenware not helpful then?"

"It was very helpful, Aunt Louisa. Thank you again," Emily said. "But after talking with Mr. Ying in prison today, it's clear he is determined to make no effort to clear his own name. And whatever he fears, it seems to be connected to Chinatown."

She decided not to mention the threat against Caroline's grandchildren, except to Granville. It wasn't likely to help matters if more people knew about the threat. And talking about it seemed disrespectful to Caroline, somehow.

"Whatever did the man say?"

"It wasn't so much what he said. His reactions to our questions suggest a link of some kind between the theft of the earthenware and Chinatown."

"What kind of link?" Aunt Louisa asked.

"I don't know. And I can't see how any of the naturalist earthenware collectors connect to Chinatown. But it may be that the thieves were hired there."

"That sounds possible," Aunt Louisa said. "Have you learned anything about them? The thieves, I mean."

"No, nothing. But *someone* has frightened Mr. Ying into staying silent, so we're left trying to uncover who that might have been. Then we need to connect that person to whoever bought the stolen pottery."

"It's like a giant puzzle," Aunt Louisa said. "And it seems logical, when you explain it."

"Yes, but it's frustrating too," Emily said. "We're making such slow progress, when all I can think of is seeing poor Betsy avenged."

"You need to think of something less tragic for a bit," Aunt Louisa said. "Are you sure you won't have at least a little dessert? My cook, Lau, made a Charlotte Fool, and it's one dish he's rather good at."

Emily shook her head. "No, thank you. I think I will call Mr. Granville. I want to talk to him about the case. If I may use your telephone?"

"By all means," Aunt Louisa said with the wave of her hand in the general direction of the telephone stand in the hall. "You must miss him. Your fiancé, I mean. Young love. It is so nice to see."

Emily rolled her eyes as she left the room. With her concerns about Mr. Ying's stubborn silence and what it would mean for all of them, it wasn't until much later she realized her aunt was teasing her.

EMILY SAT at the telephone table in her aunt's hallway, thinking. What did she need to tell Granville? Aside from arranging which ferry she was taking, since he was collecting her at the terminal.

She really missed him, and talking on the telephone was a poor substitute. She was suddenly fiercely glad she'd be seeing him tomorrow.

She also desperately wanted to discuss this case with him. Talking over the details of various investigations had been helpful to both of them in the past. Sometimes she wondered what regular couples talked about. And she could use his perspective now, when she seemed to have come to yet another dead end.

But she was wary of saying too much over an open telephone line. You never knew who might be listening in. Some of the switchboard operators had a habit of doing so, and they were inveterate gossips.

Still, Granville had a way of hearing what wasn't said. Maybe she could refer to previous cases of his as a kind of shorthand? She made a face at the memory of all those hours of actual shorthand she'd taken. Such a waste of time—she'd never need it now.

Although it could be very handy in keeping track of the details of this case. And most people couldn't read shorthand, so her notes would be more private. She'd have to see if she could find a stationer that carried shorthand notebooks this afternoon, so she could spend time sorting out her thoughts on the ferry ride tomorrow.

It took several moments for the call to connect through to their office in Vancouver. She had called Granville's private number, so it didn't surprise her when his voice came on the line. She could picture him, sitting there at the old partner's desk, looking down on the busy street.

"Emily?" his so-familiar voice said. "Are you all right?"

His voice sounded odd. Tense, and a little hoarse. But it could be the telephone line.

"Granville," she said. "It's good to hear your voice. And yes, I'm just fine."

"I'm glad to hear it," he said.

He sounded like he *really* meant it. And was that relief in his voice? What was happening in Vancouver, anyway?

"And how is it going in Victoria?" he asked.

"Very well," she said, and paused. "But..."

"But you're having problems with the case you told me about the other day," he finished for her.

"Yes, exactly." He seldom missed the nuances in any conversation. She loved that about him.

"You're safe, though? Not in any danger?" he asked. "You haven't been hurt again?"

Emily nearly laughed. So that was what was wrong. He was worried about her because she'd been attacked on her last visit to Victoria. Which was due to an unrelated case. And all of those men were in jail now, thanks to Granville.

She bit back a smile. Well, maybe she'd helped a bit.

"No, I'm fine, really," she said, emphasizing the last word. It was harder than she'd expected, having such a conversation over the telephone. "This isn't like the last time I was here, when I was injured. There's no one after me this time."

There was a pause, and Emily heard the hissing of the line, and wondered if their connection had been dropped. Then his voice again, deep and calm.

"I'm glad. So tell me about your case."

"I feel like there's a missing piece," she said. "And I'm not sure how to find it. If I were in Vancouver, I would ask Bertie."

"You need a name, then?" he asked, catching the reference immediately.

"Yes. But I don't know who to talk to here."

"Have you considered talking to Ah Quan?" Granville said. "He's the man who helped us..."

"In the missing heir case," Emily said. "Yes, I know. I'd thought about asking him for information. Though I was advised on the last case that he wouldn't talk to a woman, remember?"

"It might be worth trying," Granville said. "All he can do is say no."

He was right.

"You know, I think I might take my partner in crime with me," Emily said. "She's the wife of a magistrate, which might help."

She tapped a finger against her chin as she thought about it. "I'll call her, ask if she can set up a meeting. And if that doesn't work, perhaps her husband would be able to ask Ah Quan what we want to know."

"And since you'll be here in Vancouver for a few days, perhaps the two of us can also talk to Bertie," Granville added. "Or his uncle."

Emily smiled at that. Bertie's uncle was a power in Chinatown, if a dangerous one. If he chose to, he could probably give her the information she needed. And Granville was using the references to previous cases in exactly the way she'd thought of doing.

"That would be most helpful," was all she said. She was confident he would know exactly what she meant.

"You are still planning on taking the afternoon ferry tomorrow?" Granville asked.

"Yes. Which might mean I have time to meet with Ah Quan before I sail."

"Then I wish you luck with your meeting," he said. "And I look forward to seeing you at the ferry dock tomorrow afternoon."

"And I you," she said, her tone equally formal. Then she couldn't help herself, and her voice softened. "Good night, Granville."

As she made her way back to the dining room, Emily felt much happier than she had earlier. She always felt better after she talked with Granville. Except when they were disagreeing about something, which thankfully happened rarely.

Except on the matter of their wedding date. He really wanted to move it closer, but she still needed more time before she was ready to discuss that notion with Mama. The idea of a formal church wedding with hundreds of attendees terrified her. But anything less grand wouldn't be acceptable to her indomitable parent.

Who was pushing harder for Emily to begin making decisions about the details of her wedding. And there were so many of them.

Guests. Invitations. Flowers. Attendants. A dress... She felt over-whelmed at the very idea of all the planning that was ahead of her.

And possibly the notion of all she'd be responsible for as a married lady was increasingly daunting, she admitted to herself.

Though she'd get to live with Granville, see him all the time. Wouldn't that be worth everything?

She had no answer for herself.

Still, at least she had a next step in this frustrating case. And tomorrow she and Granville could discuss all the details, in person. She felt a little jolt of energy run up her spine at the thought of seeing him again.

Maybe she should just work on her mother to set an earlier wedding date. How long could planning a wedding really take, after all?

AUNT LOUISA WAS STILL SIPPING her coffee, staring thoughtfully into space. The empty dessert plate in front of her suggested that the Charlotte Fool had lived up to its billing.

Which gave Emily another idea. "Aunt, does Mr. Lau live in? Or in Chinatown like Mr. Ying?"

"He lives in Chinatown, though I regret to say that is the only similarity. Lau's cooking is still not up to the standard Ying sets. That man needs to be released from jail if only to ensure he can continue to bake those sublime pastries of his."

Emily gave her aunt a sharp look. Was she serious? The twinkle in Aunt Louisa's eye told its own story, and Emily relaxed.

"Aunt, could I talk to him? Mr. Lau, I mean? He must know Chinatown as well as Mr. Ying does. And perhaps he knows Mr. Ying as well, since you and the Herrons are practically neighbors."

Aunt Louisa gave Emily a thoughtful look. "After talking to Mr. Granville, you haven't given up on finding out if the theft and murder at the Herron's originated in Chinatown, have you?"

"No," Emily said. "And I won't, either. Not if that is what it takes to solve this murder case. Even though I have a better sense of how complex that society is, after Mrs. Herron drove me around a little today. None of us wants to see an innocent man hang."

"Indeed we don't. Come along then. Let us go and talk to Lau."

AUNT LOUISA's kitchen was a cozy room, with windows looking out on the back garden and a huge fireplace made of local river rocks. A young, traditionally dressed Chinese man was wiping down the marble counters.

"Lau," Aunt Louisa said. "You know my niece Emily, I think. We have a few questions for you. Could you leave that and come and talk to us, please?"

The three of them pulled up chairs at the battered wooden table on the far side of the kitchen, near the windows which would let in morning sun. Aunt Louisa and Emily sat on one side of the table, Lau chose the other.

"If I may," Emily said, with a glance at her aunt. "Mr. Lau, as you may know, Mrs. Herron and I are looking into the death of one of the girls who was serving at Mrs. Herron's tea."

He nodded.

"And we need your help," Emily said. "Do you know Mr. Ying, Mrs. Herron's cook?"

Another nod.

Emily was a little disconcerted by his silent regard, but persevered. It was too important to give up. "He has been accused of the murder. We don't believe he is a killer. But we need your help."

No response.

Emily and her aunt exchanged glances.

"Lau, can you help us?" Aunt Louisa asked.

"Yes, Missus," Mr. Lau said.

"Did you and Mr. Ying ever talk?" Emily said.

"A little," Lau said.

"Mr. Ying was being threatened," Emily said. "Do you know anything about that?"

"A little," Lau said.

Well, at least that was progress, Emily told herself. "Do you know who threatened him?"

Mr. Lau shook his head.

"Did he tell you why he was being threatened?" Aunt Louisa asked.

Lau hesitated.

"We know about the theft," Emily added. "And we aren't worried about that. It's the murder that Mrs. Herron cares about."

"He say they want something belong to Herrons," Mr. Lau said. "He say they threaten family."

"You mean Mr. Ying said that?" Emily asked.

"Yes."

Emily nodded. It was the same story Mr. Ying had told them. "Mr. Ying also said there was someone wanting to buy the stolen items," she said. "Did you know about that?"

"I know."

"Do you know who was wanting to buy the stolen pottery?"

Mr. Lau started to say something then stopped.

Emily and her aunt exchanged glances.

"If we are to save Ying from being hanged, we need to know who really killed that girl," Aunt Louisa said. "Even the slightest bit of information might help. And Ying needs your help now."

"Someone from *tong* talk to Ying," Mr. Lau said after a long pause.

"*Tong*?" Aunt Louisa said with a frown.

"A Chinese association," Emily told her aunt. She turned to Mr. Lau. "And that someone is the reason Mr. Ying is so afraid?"

Mr. Lau nodded.

"Who threatened him? Can you give us a name?" Aunt Louisa asked.

Now it was Mr. Lau's turn to look afraid.

"What about which *tong* this someone was from?" Aunt Louisa persisted.

Mr. Lau looked frozen in place, his eyes locked on his employer.

"Do you know who stole the missing items?" Emily asked quickly, before Mr. Lau's obvious fear paralyzed him entirely.

"No," he said.

"Is there anything you can tell us that might help save Mr. Ying's life?" Emily asked.

"No," he said again.

"Thank you, then, Lau," Aunt Louisa said, rising. "We appreciate your help. We'll go back to the parlor now. Could you bring us a fresh pot of tea when you get a moment, please?"

"Thank you," Emily said, then followed her aunt through the green baize door and out of the kitchen.

Comfortably settled back in the parlor, Aunt Louise turned to Emily. "What was that about the *tongs* being Chinese associations? They must have a great deal of power, then. From what you've told me, they have Ying terrified. And given what I just saw, I'd say Lau is as well."

"My understanding about *tongs* doesn't go deep, Aunt," Emily said. "And the rumors are confusing. But depending on who you talk to, the *tongs* seem to be some combination of a community organization and a secret society. Each *tong* is different."

"Really?" Aunt Louisa said. "And can the police do nothing?"

"Despite the rumors, most of the *tongs* are not criminal organizations. And I understand that they largely regulate themselves," Emily said. "Besides, the police seem able to do very little about non-Chinese criminal gangs. How effective do you expect them to be investigating the Chinese associations, when they don't even speak the language?"

"I suppose that's true," Aunt Louisa said. "So you think it is these *tongs* that Ying is so afraid of?"

"I just don't know," Emily said. "But perhaps if I can find someone in Chinatown willing to answer my questions, we might have some hope of finding the killer. Or at least helping Mr. Ying save himself."

"So what do we do next?" Aunt Louisa asked

"We keep looking for collectors of naturalist earthenware. And hope they can lead us to the killer," Emily said. "Though we'll have to be very careful about how we ask questions. It isn't the kind of conversation that will be overlooked by whoever the guilty party is."

"No, indeed not," Aunt Louisa said. "But perhaps if I drop a word or two in the right ear, it might start a rumor that would flush out the man we're looking for."

"That needs to wait until we have a bit more information from Chinatown, Aunt," Emily said, wishing her aunt didn't look quite so cheerful about the prospect. "Until we know what we're dealing with, asking questions could be dangerous."

"I'll be careful," Aunt Louisa said.

"There's already been one death over this ugly pottery," Emily said. "I couldn't live with myself if you were murdered too."

Aunt Louisa looked shocked. "They wouldn't murder me," she said.

"Someone killed that poor girl," Emily said. "Who probably just saw something that the killer felt threatened him. She might not even have known that whatever she saw was important. Who knows if one of your questions could prove threatening to such a killer? Even if it seems innocuous to you."

Aunt Louisa looked shocked. "You don't live in a safe world, do you?" she said.

"Not really," Emily said after a little thought. "But it's real. And it isn't boring."

"No, I can see that," Aunt Louisa said. "I think perhaps I've been underestimating you."

Emily smiled. "Don't worry about it. My parents do so all the time."

Aunt Louisa laughed. "I suppose they do at that. Though they'd be surprised to hear it. And I suspect your mother less so that your father."

It was Emily's turn to be surprised. Her aunt saw more than she'd given her credit for. "While I'm in Vancouver, Mr. Granville and I will be visiting that Chinatown. We have contacts there who could be helpful in this case. At least in telling me who we might to talk to in Chinatown here."

"Or what we need to ask about," Aunt Louisa said. "Yes, very well. I'll wait on asking my questions. As long as you promise to tell me what you've learned."

They exchanged a smile.

"I promise," Emily said.

2 2

Emily and Caroline Herron arrived at the courthouse at half past eight for their appointment with the court interpreter. It hadn't been difficult to convince Caroline that they needed to speak with him. Nor had the magistrate's wife had any difficulties in arranging the meeting. The meeting itself proved less than helpful.

Ah Quan was polite, and respectfully answered each of their questions. Unfortunately, he either didn't know much, or he wasn't prepared to tell them much. And neither Emily's careful questions nor Caroline's plea on behalf of Mr. Ying seemed to make any difference.

After a frustrating quarter of an hour, Caroline thanked him, and the two ladies left. As they sat in the carriage heading home, Emily turned to Caroline.

"Well, that was a waste of time," she said. "Do you suppose your husband would have any better luck?"

"I doubt it," Caroline said. "I suspect that as the official court translator, Ah Quan is very circumspect when it comes to questions about murders involving his countrymen."

"And also about questions concerning Chinatown, apparently," Emily said.

Caroline nodded. "Which makes sense, if you think about it," she said. "I did speak with my husband, by the way. He confirmed my understanding that the *tongs* wield a great deal of influence there."

"That's good to know," Emily said. "I'm hoping to learn more while I am in Vancouver for my friend's wedding. We—my fiancé and I—have some contacts in Vancouver's Chinatown who may be willing to share information. As long as they don't deem our questions dangerous to their own interests."

Caroline Herron lifted her brows. "You do lead an interesting life. I confess, I hadn't believed life for a woman today could be as interesting, or as dangerous, as when I was a young bride, traveling the rough roads to the goldfields of the Fraser with my husband. It was an experience I've always valued. But you seem to have your own version of the frontier."

Emily smiled. "Vancouver is still a very young town, by anyone's standards. And I confess that exploring that 'frontier', as you name it, is one of the main attractions of my work with Granville and his firm."

Caroline gave her a shrewd look. "But not one of the main attractions of your fiancé himself, I gather?" she asked.

Emily pictured Granville as she'd last seen him, and blushed deeply.

Caroline smiled.

"No, I thought not," she said. "And I'm glad to hear it. Marriage is hard work, but with the right partner, there is no more rewarding journey."

She glanced out the carriage window. "Now, enough nosy questions. We are nearly home. Have you time to come in for tea, or did you want to collect your luggage and have the carriage take you straight to the ferry?"

"I think I'd best collect my luggage now, though I thank you for the offer of tea," Emily said, still feeling a little warm and wishing she could tug at the suddenly too tight neck of her soft green dress.

The one that she'd been told matched her eyes. She'd chosen it knowing she'd be seeing Granville later today.

"I really do appreciate the offer," she added quickly. "But are you sure you can spare the carriage to drive me?"

Caroline waved it off. "Think nothing of it. It's the least I can do, given everything you've been doing to help me. Have a wonderful trip, and stay safe in Chinatown."

"Thank you. I will," Emily said.

"And I will see you when you return," Caroline said with a smile.

EVEN ON RAINY DAYS, Emily loved the ferry journey, the bracing salty smell of the sea, and the heavy thud of the engines reverberating through the deck as they chugged across open ocean, then wound their way through several small, heavily forested islands.

And today was sunny, with blue cloudless skies reflecting back on seemingly endless seas. A breeze that tasted of salt cut the heat that continued to build.

Still, Emily found the ride long and tiring. She was too worried to appreciate much of it. With nothing else to do, her mind kept turning over every fact she'd learned since poor Betsy's murder. And it wasn't enough.

It was so frustrating. The more she learned, the less sense it all made. As Aunt Louisa had pointed out, it was as if she was assembling a complex jigsaw puzzle. Except this one had been turned over, so that all she could see was the plain back of it. She couldn't see the picture the puzzle pieces made at all.

Letting out a little huff at the nonsense she was thinking, she took another turn around the deck. And in the distance she could see a familiar coastline. She was nearly home. Finally.

She suddenly felt better.

Both Granville and Scott were in the office early the next morning. When the telephone on his desk rang just before eight, Granville looked up from the files Mac had handed him the night before. He grabbed a pencil and made put an asterisk against the paragraph he'd been reading, then picked up the handset.

"It's Carver," the lawyer said. "And I think I might have something for you. But I'll need to brief you in person."

Granville glanced at the file in front of him. He'd only skimmed half of it. "I can be there in twenty minutes, if that suits you?"

"Yes, that's fine. And I think you should bring Scott along."

And wasn't that interesting. What had Carver learned to make him suggest that?

He immediately decided that he and Scott would go armed to the meeting. Guns were technically illegal in Vancouver, but that law was ignored often enough that sometimes carrying one was worth the risk of arrest.

Glancing across the desk at his partner, who had looked up when the telephone rang, he mouthed "Carver," and raised an eyebrow. Scott nodded.

"We'll see you then," he told Carver.

"What was that about?" Scott asked as he hung up the earpiece.

"Carver wants to meet with both of us for an update."

Scott watched as Granville took his revolver from the top drawer of his desk, and checked that it was loaded. "You expectin' trouble?"

"There was something in Carver's voice," Granville said. "It never hurts to be prepared."

"Right," Scott said, retrieving his own gun. "We leaving right away?"

"I need to finish this file first. Mac was right about these upcoming court dates Randall had scheduled."

"Right how?"

"They're quite similar to Bragg's case. And if Randall had won these two, it might have been enough to change a few laws. Not to mention leaving Konrad and Lessing losing their own cases rather badly."

"Which wouldn't go over well," Scott said. "Though the law-changing stuff sounds like a question for Carver."

"Exactly. Especially since it also sounds like a reason for someone to want Randall out of the way."

"Someone like Konrad or Lessing?"

"Them as well."

"You thinking of your big fish?"

"Yes."

"Any word on how he's doing?" Scott asked. "Randall, I mean."

"Nothing new since yesterday. The doctors are still optimistic."

"And they're keeping quiet about him being alive?"

"So far," Granville said.

"Let's hope they keep it that way."

"Indeed."

WHEN THE TWO of them arrived just over half an hour later, Carver's outer office was again deserted. Scott looked pointedly at the empty chairs, the dust that was thickening on the reception desk. Then he looked over at Granville.

"You sure he's still in business?"

He ignored the comment, leading the way to Carver's closed office door. He rapped once, entering when Carver's voice gave him leave.

"Granville. Scott. Good to see you both," Carver said, rising and coming around his desk to shake hands. "Have a seat."

When they were settled, Granville leaned forward. "What do you have for us?"

"Not as much as I'd hoped," Carver said. "Mostly rumors."

"What have you found out about our conspiring lawyers?"

"You're right about there being a group of them. I've found four, so far. And a fairly conscienceless bunch they are, too," Carver said. "In fact, Peabody is the best of the lot. Which isn't saying much."

Carver named four lawyers; Peabody, Cheever, Griggs and Bragg—all of whom had lost key cases to Randall.

"You know all of them?" Granville asked.

"I do," Carver said. "And the odd thing is, there isn't a leader in the bunch."

He didn't miss the implication. "So you think someone else put them up to it?"

"Like our big fish?" Scott asked with a grin.

Carver smiled back. "Very like your big fish, I'd say. And whoever he is, he keeps a low profile. If he exists, no one is talking about him."

The lawyer paused, glanced from him to Scott. "All of them are talking about you two, though. And tying your names to Randall's. I didn't hear much, but I didn't like what little I heard."

"That's why you suggested Scott come along today?" Granville asked.

"That's why."

"We can take care of ourselves," Scott said.

"That's your reputation," Carver said. "But keep an eye out, anyway."

"I don't suppose you'd share the name of your informants?" Granville asked him.

"You suppose right."

"Would you be willing to ask them if they'll talk to me?" Granville asked. "I'll protect their privacy. And we can keep any meetings quiet."

Carver gave him an assessing look. "I could do that. But I wouldn't expect too much."

"They might rather answer our questions through you," Scott said. "Keep us at arm's length."

Carver gave him a thoughtful look, his eyes going from Scott's gun hand to the protective posture he'd taken beside Granville. "They might, at that."

"You'd be willing to ask them?" Granville asked.

Carver nodded. "I like you two. Don't ask me why."

"We seem to have that effect on people. The ones who aren't trying to kill us, anyway," Granville said with a grin. He glanced at Scott, who nodded. "And I think we'd better hire you for this case. For all our sakes."

"That's good thinking," Carver said. "Very well. A dollar should suffice to ensure our discussions are protected under confidentiality."

"I'm serious about hiring you. At your going rate," Granville said. "The attack on Randall needs to be avenged. I want to see that whoever is behind it—our big fish—pays for what he's done. In full."

"Are you sure you want to hire me?" Carver said. "There's really no need. And my legal reputation isn't the best at the moment."

"It will be after you expose our big fish in open court," he said with a confidence he didn't entirely feel. "We'll find the evidence to take him down, but I'm relying on you to make sure it holds."

Carver swallowed hard. "I'll do my best to make you proud."

"Never mind that," Scott said. "Just help us avenge Randall."

Granville nodded. "As Scott says. What about Konrad and Lessing?"

"They aren't part of this group as far as I know," Carver said. "But they're cut from the same cloth."

"Figures," Scott said.

"Why do you ask?" Carver said.

"We need to hire you officially first," Granville said. "Then we'll fill you in on why you're going to be following up with these two for us."

Carver grinned, and reached into a drawer. "Client forms coming up," he said.

BACK IN THE OFFICE, Granville called everyone together.

"Scott and I just met with Robert Carver," he told them. "He's already started looking into the group that are conspiring against Randall, as well as any rumors that may be circulating amongst their peers. I've briefed him on what Konrad said yesterday, and given him the rest of the names you Mac and Miss Kent came up with as a place to start."

"Carver? Isn't he the one who was almost disbarred?" Mac said.

"That's the one," Granville said. "He's reformed."

At Mac's skeptical look, he grinned. "There's no one better to understand the mindset of this misfit group of lawyers who have it in for Randall. Not to mention, he knows his way around financial fraud. We've retained Carver to work with us for this case."

"And a good thing, too, if you're sure of him," Mac said. "I'm no lawyer, and we really need someone with legal training to have a look at everything we'd been putting together."

"Why don't you and Miss Kent set up a meeting with Carver to discuss your respective findings? It might prove productive," Granville said.

He handed Mac the lawyer's card. "I won't have time to follow up with him once Emily arrives today, so consider him your legal resource for the duration of this case."

Mac nodded, and Miss Kent made quick squiggles in her ever-present stenographer's notebook.

Neither of them looked particularly happy at the notion of working with the renegade lawyer. Granville hid his grin and took pity on them.

"It looks like you were right about the similarity between Bragg's case and the ones Konrad and Lessing are opposing counsel for. And Carver's already confirmed four members of the group, all of whom appeared on your lists; Peabody, Cheever, Griggs and Bragg."

"That was quick work," Miss Kent said.

"So far, I've been impressed," Scott put in.

"What's our budget for this?" Mac asked in a brisk, all-business tone.

"On this case, spend what you need to," Granville said. "We need the big fish caught before he orders anyone else killed."

"Just don't anyone tell Carver we said that," Scott added with a wink, easing the tension in the room.

By six o'clock that afternoon, Granville, and Scott were at the ferry dock on Vancouver Harbor waiting for Emily's ferry to arrive. A light breeze off the water cooled what was becoming an unseasonably warm day. On a little hill above them, the ornamental trees surrounding the palatial homes glowed gold with the first hint of autumn hues.

As Granville checked his pocket watch for the third time, Scott raised his brows and grinned at him.

"They're late," Granville said.

"Yes, but isn't that the ferry on the horizon there?" Scott said, pointing. "And a good thing, too. Or you'd be pacing this dock, and interrogating the harbor master on where exactly that ferry is."

Scott was probably right, Granville thought ruefully. He didn't like being separated from Emily in any case, and knowing that she was involved in a situation where a young woman had been murdered made it worse. Carver telling him and Scott them to watch their backs meant Emily could be in danger here, too. Which didn't help.

It was an unsettling thing to know about oneself.

2 4

Emily watched as the dock came closer and closer, and her worry was replaced by a sudden wash of gladness at being home. All of the passengers were pressed along the railing, some waving gaily at those who were waiting for them. On this perfect summer day, it almost felt like an outing, just being here. Even though it wasn't, not exactly.

She could see Granville standing there, feel his eyes fixed on her, though they were still too far out for her to confirm that. Scott was beside him—there was no mistaking his burly height—with Trent beside him. It was so good to be home.

She still had mixed feelings about Cecily's wedding—normally she hated formal events—but she couldn't miss this one. Clara would never forgive her if she did.

It would be so good to spend time with Granville. And to catch up on his case, and to discuss hers...

Her murder case. The solution to which continued to elude her. And she felt so responsible for finding justice for young Betsy.

Though now none of it seemed quite real. Victoria and the death of young Betsy had felt more and more unreal, the further away she travelled.

As she disembarked, Emily walked faster and faster, leaving behind the porter who was maneuvering her luggage.

"Mr. Granville," she said, as soon as she got near enough for him to hear. And held out her hand for him to shake.

He took her proffered hand and lifted it to his lips in courtly fashion. She shivered at the kiss he'd pressed to her gloved palm, covering the moment with a warm smile for Trent and Scott.

"I'm very glad to be home," she said, tucking her hand into the crook of Granville's arm. "I've missed all of you. And I have so much to tell you."

But she slanted a very private look at Granville. Who gave her a smile that nearly melted her knees.

"And we have much to tell you," was all he said. "But I think it best to wait until we are out of this crowd."

She nodded, still trying to get her breath back.

———

IN THE CARRIAGE on the way home, Granville shared the details of Randall's case, with a few asides from Scott.

"But he will recover?" Emily asked. She liked Josiah Randall, and greatly admired his courtroom skills.

"The doctors are nearly certain of it, though he's recovering very slowly."

"We're putting the word out that he's at death's door, though," Trent said. "It's safer for him, that way."

"How is that possible?" Emily said. "Surely the doctors…"

"Once I explained the danger Randall was in, the doctor went along with it," Granville said, "They have him in isolation, which limits even further the people who know anything about his condition."

"I'm impressed that you managed all that," Emily said. "I've never heard of such a thing."

"The doctor seems a good chap," Granville said.

"And it helps that Granville here has offered to cover all the extra costs," Scott said.

Of course he had. Emily gave him a warm smile, and squeezed his arm a little.

"And the case itself?" she asked.

"Is proving challenging," Granville said. And explained about the lawyers, and Benton's hints, and the big fish.

"This big fish, if he exists, would have to be efficient as well as elusive," Emily said. She paused, and looked from one to the other of them assessingly. "I assume that explains why all three of you are armed. And well-armed too, if I'm any judge?"

Trent nodded and grinned at her. "Nice catch," he said.

Emily met Granville's eyes. "Are you in danger?"

He didn't prevaricate, or pretend to misunderstand her, as most men would have done. "No one has tried to kill us yet. But this investigation is risky. And we're not risking our lives—or yours—if that changes."

"Thank you for not hiding that from me," she said.

"You need to know," he said bluntly. "And I'll make sure you're safe."

She could hear the promise in his words, see it in his eyes.

"We all will," Scott said, and Trent nodded vigorously.

"Thank you," she said, meeting Granville's eyes, then looking at the other two. "All of you. But not at the expense of your own lives. I won't have it."

2 5

───────

Friday, August 31, 1900

The following morning, Granville collected Emily from her parent's home a little after nine and handed her into the hired carriage that was waiting at the curb.

Emily admired the sleek lines of the carriage, which wasn't one she'd seen before. "Is regularly hiring carriages something new you're doing since I went to Victoria?" she asked ask she settled herself into the plush velvet upholstery.

"No. I hired it this morning, along with the driver," he said.

"Very nice. But why? It isn't as if we have far to travel. I thought you preferred to walk or take the streetcar. Or even a hack."

"Normally, I do," he said. "But it will be useful during the wedding festivities. And traveling this way is faster and more convenient."

"And this has nothing to do with a possible killer?"

"Which killer? Your case or mine?" he said with a wink. "Besides, mine is only a would-be killer."

"Are you sure you want to go into the office today?" he asked while she was still shaking her head over his attempt at distraction. "Can you afford the time, with the wedding tomorrow?"

Not for the first time, she appreciated the fact that Granville had grown up with sisters, and ones who were far more involved in the social whirl than she would ever be.

"Since I'm not part of the wedding party, all I need to do is show up at the church tomorrow," she said. "My dress has been ready for weeks. I'd thought that Clara might need my help today with errands for her sister Cecily, or similar things. But I talked to Clara briefly last night, and she says she's fine."

Fine might be stretching it, Emily thought with an inward grin. But Clara had also said she wasn't going to draw Emily into what she termed "this madness".

"Clara and I have arranged to go for lunch after church on Sunday and catch up, instead," Emily added.

"On Sunday? You can't go alone," he said.

"Granville, it's lunch. On a Sunday. We'll be perfectly safe."

"With this case being so uncertain, you could be in danger too," he said. "It isn't worth the risk. I promise not to sit at the same table as the two of you, but you can't go alone."

Emily rolled her eyes at him, but the vision of him sitting by himself having lunch at Stroh's, surrounded by a sea of women gossiping about him was too funny. Especially while she sat at a different table having tea with Clara. She had to laugh.

Then she had to tell him about it, gasping it out between gusts of laughter.

He grinned, knowing exactly what she meant. "Mrs. Smythe would dine out on gossip like that for weeks," he said, mentioning an inveterate gossip who was also a friend of Emily's mother. "Who are we to deny her?"

Which set her off again, even while she savored the moment created by the private joke between them.

It didn't take them long to reach the office, or very much longer to greet Laura and Mac. Laura was looking her best, Emily thought as she watched her friend. She didn't look as strained as she had before taking this job, and her eyes were lively. Mac had noticed, too. He couldn't take his eyes off of the other girl.

Emily hadn't had a chance to talk to Laura recently, other than briefly about the plans for the move from this office to the new one several floors down—which was happening on Monday!—and which Laura had well in hand.

But once Betsy's murder was solved and she was back home for good, Emily looked forward to a catching up on everything, from how the office was running to exactly what was going on between her friend and the young accountant. Meanwhile, she had a murder to discuss with Granville.

Who was standing waiting by his office door. If he was impatient, it didn't show, but Emily suspected he was as anxious to hear more about her case as she was to tell him about it.

There hadn't been time yesterday—and it hadn't seemed right to discuss Betsy's murder and her own frustration with the case in front of Scott and Trent, at least not yet. But both of them were off this morning searching for information on Randall's attacker, and she and Granville had his office to themselves.

Closing the office door behind her, Emily melted into Granville's embrace. After a particularly satisfying kiss—interrupted by Laura with the tea tray —they sat down on either side of the partners desk. Granville smiled at her.

"Now this looks right," he said. "I picture you sitting across from me at the breakfast table every morning as we discuss our day."

Emily took a sip of tea, not sure whether to be pleased or annoyed. She was still feeling a little lightheaded from that kiss, but this was no time to let it distract her.

"You see that happening at the breakfast table, but not in the office?" she said. "Don't you take me seriously here, too?"

"Of course I do. But we are so seldom alone. In our own home, we would be."

"Oh," she said. And blushed hotly, suddenly at a loss for words.

She hadn't been picturing actually living with him—not really. Her mind hadn't got much past the drama of arranging their wedding.

Now she was imagining the two of them together all day. And all night. Suddenly she couldn't quite meet his eyes.

"Now tell me about your case," Granville said. "All the details you had to leave out of your telephone calls."

That she could do. Emily put down her tea cup, leaned forward and began to fill him in.

When she was finished, Granville looked at her for a moment, a strange look in his eye. "You've put yourself in the middle of a complex, and potentially very dangerous case. And you're doing all the right things."

Emily blushed again. "Did you think I wouldn't?" she asked, half teasing and half defensive. "You keep saying I'm good at investigating."

"You are," he said. "And I knew you'd grow better. I didn't expect it to be this quickly, though. Or on a case this difficult."

Now she blushed in earnest, but she smiled at him too.

"I keep feeling like I'm missing things that should be obvious," Emily said, hesitating a little. "And making all kinds of mistakes. That can't be normal."

"I'm afraid it is," he said. "You just have to keep investigating until it starts to make sense. Sometimes talking about it helps. What makes you feel as if you're missing something?"

She thought about it for a moment. "I can't see the connection between stolen mid-century collectible pottery, the two Chinese cooks, and young Betsy's murder."

He nodded. "Tell me what you know about each one separately."

"The pottery was stolen from the Herron's cellar, and is very valuable, particularly to a small number of avid collectors," she said slowly, numbering it off on her fingers.

"Betsy was last seen alive in the kitchen. At nearly the same time, the Chinese cook was seen talking to someone who was hidden on the stairs leading to the Herron cellar," she said, turning down two more fingers. "Which suggests that the theft might have happened that day.

It also suggests that Mrs. Herron's cook may be involved in the theft. And that Betsy was killed because of something she saw or overheard."

And she turned down another finger and her thumb, making a fist that she gripped tightly enough that her knuckles whitened, until she realized what she was doing and released it quickly.

Granville watched her without comment. "Go on," he said.

"It's almost straightforward, up to that point," Emily said. "If Mrs. Herron's cook played a part in the theft, and if he had a partner, then that partner is likely the killer. Possibly the partner feared betrayal and killed Betsy to ensure her silence."

"But?" Granville said when she paused.

Emily smiled at him. "I gather there is always a but?"

Not waiting for an answer, she continued. "But who is that partner? The Herron's cook—Mr. Ying—has been arrested, and refuses to talk. Though he told Mrs. Herron and myself in confidence that he's keeping silent because the killer threatened to harm Mrs. Herron's grandchildren if he speaks. But he won't name the killer, even to us.

He seems very nervous at any mention of us asking questions in Chinatown, though. And my aunt's Chinese cook does too. But Ah Quan didn't even mention Chinatown."

Granville had listened thoughtfully and without interrupting her until this point, which she very much appreciated.

"You don't think this Ying is the killer, then?" he asked now.

He didn't miss much, either.

"No, I don't," Emily said. "And neither does Mrs. Herron, who knows him rather well. But I still can't sort out how he's involved here. Or what Betsy could have seen or heard that made someone decide to kill her."

She let out a little huff of frustration. "None of it makes any sense. And I don't understand how whoever stole the pottery collection would know about the value of it, much less find a collector willing to pay that amount. The Herrons themselves thought it ugly and worthless."

Emily gave a strained laugh. "In fact, if he'd asked her, I suspect Mrs. Herron would have given the whole collection to her cook. She values him far more than she does that pottery."

Granville sat back and thought for a moment. "If I asked you which one question worries you the most, what would you say?" he asked.

"That's easy," Emily said. She didn't even have to think about it. "It's the Chinatown connection."

She impatiently brushed back a stubborn wisp of auburn hair that kept breaking loose from her French braid and getting in her eyes.

"I still can't see how it fits," she said. "But Mr. Ying is afraid of something to do with Chinatown. And I know too little to guess what that might be. Or even if it's important."

He grinned. "Then what a good thing I've arranged through Bertie for a meeting with his uncle this morning."

"You did?" Emily felt her smile growing wider and wider. Bertie's uncle was a power in Chinatown. And ever since she'd argued with him to save Granville's life, he'd seemed to have an odd respect for her. If he chose to, he could probably give her the information she needed.

"Oh, Granville, thank you," she said, beaming at him.

<hr>

As the hired carriage rolled toward Chinatown, Emily was surprised to find how much she enjoyed the comfort of the carriage, and the convenience of being able to talk freely, even here in Vancouver. Not that she'd really want to own one—just that it was an interesting thing for an investigator to know.

"I'm very grateful that Bertie's uncle agreed to meet with us," she said. Her words were directed at Granville, but she glanced under her lashes at Bertie, seated impassively opposite them, trying to gauge his reaction to her words. He was pretending not to be interested in a word they said.

She had come to know her parent's houseboy better than that. She'd noticed that since his arrival nearly a year ago in Gold Mountain—as many of the Chinese called the West Coast of North America—Bertie was interested in everything happening around him.

She'd also learned he paid attention to everything, and thought about it all long and carefully while engaged in the more mundane of his duties. One day she'd have to get him to tell her what he really thought of everyone he'd met here.

"Have you thought about what you want to ask Wong Sun?" Granville asked.

"All I need is a little information about Victoria's Chinatown," she said. "And perhaps an introduction to someone there who might be willing to answer some of my questions about the death of poor Betsy."

Bertie's eyes widened a little. She'd probably horrified him with the last request, Emily thought, fighting back a nervous giggle. He usually didn't show any emotion at all, so for Bertie that was a strong reaction.

She carefully didn't look at Granville, though from the tension in the arm touching hers, he wasn't any better pleased with her plan than Bertie was.

Well, she hadn't expected either of them to like it. And she really needed to talk to someone in Victoria's Chinatown. It was such a complex society, she knew she'd never understand how it worked without a lot of help.

She'd listen to reason on how to accomplish what she needed to while still staying safe. She wasn't being foolish about any of this. She simply had a murderer to expose.

And an increasingly uneasy feeling that she didn't have much time left in which to do so.

Emily's latest declaration made him uneasy, but Granville had seen her thrive in difficult situations before. She had a way with people, and Wong Sun seemed to like her. He had every confidence that she would handle this situation well, too.

No matter how worried her daring might make him.

As the carriage-driver made his way through the congestion of wagons, carriages and streetcars on Pender Street, Granville kept picturing Emily's expression when he told her Bertie would be escorting them to Vancouver's Chinatown. She couldn't have been more pleased if he'd bought her a pair of emerald ear bobs. He pictured his sisters' various reactions to a similar situation, and hid a grin. His fiancée was unique.

"What is amusing you, Granville?" Emily asked from her seat beside him in the carriage.

She really didn't miss much. "I was remembering our last visit here," he said, with partial truth. "You and Bertie saved my life then. I'm hoping you won't need to do so this time."

She grinned at him. "I hope so too."

She'd looked so tired when she arrived. He could see that this murder investigation was weighing on her. He hoped they could find some answers for her here, or at very least a lead.

Bertie directed the carriage to stop in front of a nondescript two-story building, then led them through a faded side door—a different one than they'd used in the past, Granville noted. Just how many entrances were there into the hidden areas of Chinatown?—and down a winding maze of corridors and stairways until they reached an ornately carved red door that Granville did recognize.

This was the home of Wong Sun, Bertie's mysterious uncle. That he was a power in Chinatown was not in doubt. What else he was, Granville was certain it would be a mistake to ask.

It didn't stop him from speculating, though.

The room Bertie led them into was large, and dimly lit. Shadows cast by the oil lanterns at intervals along the walls flickered and danced, and some kind of incense hung heavily in the still air. This was the room Granville had been in twice before, the room where he'd been beaten into insensibility for asking the wrong questions on his first visit.

The visit Emily had rescued him from, with Bertie's help.

The room felt no different from his last visit—quiet, cavernous, more than a little threatening. The dry rustle of silk robes alerted Granville that Wong Sun was now in the room with them. Granville turned to face the older gentleman and bowed, aware that beside him Emily and Trent were doing the same. Out of the corner of his eye, he could see Bertie, bowing more deeply than any of them. And showing proper honor to his uncle.

"Thank you for agreeing to see us," Granville said as Wong Sun inclined his head. "We have a most puzzling situation and would appreciate your wisdom."

"My nephew tells me the young lady has a question for me," Wong Sun said.

Emily stepped forward a little. Granville braced himself, ready for any sign of trouble as he waited for her to speak.

"I was at a tea party where a girl was murdered," she said. "In Victoria."

Wong Sun's face showed no expression. "I am sorry," he said, in a voice like dry sand.

"Thank you," she said. "It is a tragedy. And I am hoping you can help me in solving the crime."

"Oh?"

At the single word, Granville's eyes fixed on their host's face, watching for the slightest sign of anger or offense. Emily needed to tread very carefully.

Here in his own world, Wong Sun was dangerous. And they knew too little of the politics of Chinatown itself.

He glanced over at Emily's face. She knew it too, he realized. Good. She often had a talent for saying exactly the right thing. He hoped it didn't fail her here.

And his eyes locked on Wong Sun again.

"The man who is accused of the crime, Mr. Ying, is one of your countrymen," Emily was saying to Wong Sun. "I believe him to be innocent, but he refuses to defend himself. And there is some connection to Victoria's Chinatown I don't understand. Any suggestion of my asking questions there seems to worry Mr. Ying."

"Go on."

There was nothing encouraging in words or tone, but Wong Sun had not yet refused to answer Emily's questions. Which from this man was an enormous concession. Granville looked at his fiancée to make sure she realized that.

Of course she did.

Emily inclined her head in respectful acknowledgement of the latitude Wong was giving her and smiled at him.

"I was hoping you could suggest a name," she said. "Someone in Victoria's Chinatown who might speak for Mr. Ying. Or at least help me better understand what is keeping him silent in the face of a murder charge, and what he fears."

"No one in Chinatown—here or in Victoria—will speak with a woman about such matters," Wong Sun said, the dry tone at odds with his crisp British accent.

"Oh," Emily said. "I see."

There was no smile now. But she was quick to swallow her

disappointment. "Is there anything you can tell me, then, that might allow me to help Mr. Ying?"

She impressed Granville again with her quick thinking, especially in difficult circumstances. And this elegant and very Chinese room with its subtle overtones of menace certainly qualified.

"There is some small information that has come my way, which may assist you somewhat," Wong Sun said in a voice like the wind over dried leaves.

"I would very much appreciate anything you might be able to tell me," she said, dipping her head in acknowledgement.

"I hear the girl was killed by a hasty man, one with a bad temper and no judgement," he said.

"Then killing Betsy was not part of the plan?" Emily asked.

"From the little I hear, only a fool would have decided to kill her."

"And would you have heard this 'hasty man's' name?" she asked.

Her tone was carefully neutral, despite the anxiety she must be feeling. Granville could tell from the tension in her stance that she was worried about offending Wong Sun. Not surprising, since he clearly knew the information that she so desperately needed.

"I would not."

Emily's gaze flicked to Wong Sun. "Might you have heard who hired this incompetent man?" she demanded

"I did not hear that anyone hired him," was the inscrutable answer. "Though he worked with a Chinaman, one another man hired to steal the pottery."

Granville stared from him to Emily and back again, his mind racing. How much money could there possibly be in naturalist earthenware, that anyone other than an avid collector would be interested in it?

Emily was frowning over Wong Sun's words. "Then did Mr. Ying kill Betsy?"

"No. He did not."

No hesitation there, Granville noted. Though perhaps the real question should be—who had hired this Chinaman, and how was he connected to the fellow who'd killed the young woman?

And how much danger did either of them pose to Emily? His hand automatically slid towards the knife concealed at his belt at the thought, and it took an effort of will to move it back.

As Wong Sun's words died away, the silence stretched in the cavernous room. Despite the tension she felt, Emily noted how cool the room was, even with all the candles burning. Cool enough that the fire was welcome. It was hard to believe that outside they'd been practically melting in the August heat.

She drew in a slow breath, trying to will herself to stay as cool as the room as she scanned the faces around her. Of them all, only Bertie looked uncomfortable.

She wondered what Bertie knew that had him looking like that. And if it was something she should know as well. Probably.

From the moment of Betsy's murder, she had been chasing after answers. And finding only more questions.

Granville's search for whoever had nearly killed Mr. Randall seemed to have fared no better.

No matter. Granville had taught her to work with what she had. Which in this case, meant trusting her instincts.

Wong Sun held the power here, and for some reason he'd decided to help her. Within limits. He had balked at naming Betsy's killer. Or naming the thief, or the man who'd hired the thief. Why?

She couldn't ask again. That much was already clear.

So who had hired the thief who "worked with" Betsy's killer? Was it the collector who coveted the Herron's pottery? Or someone who wasn't really relevant to her case? Even Wong Sun himself?

The odd phrasing of his answer hadn't escaped Emily either, though she wasn't sure quite what the connection implied.

She felt her knees shake under her at the realization of how much she didn't know here, and how dangerous each question she chose to ask could be. Only determination kept her upright. She would not give in to such a weakness. This conversation was too important.

Now it was up to her. She had to figure out which questions he was willing to answer. And which answers would give them the leads she needed to find Betsy's killer.

She just had to stay focused on the reason she was here in the first place. "The thief who was hired in Chinatown, you heard that he 'worked with' the killer. Is the killer also Chinese, then?"

"No, he is not." There was a trace of contempt in Wong Sun's voice, although nothing showed on his face.

"And the man who hired the thief? Might you have heard whether that man is connected to Victoria's Chinatown?" she asked carefully.

"I hear he sometimes works with the *tongs* there," was the careful answer.

Could she ask more? It felt risky. "And have you heard that this man worked with the *tongs* to hire the thief who stole the naturalist earthenware collection?" she asked, choosing every word with care.

"That is what I hear."

"Does this man live in Victoria, then?"

"I hear he does not."

He didn't? Emily wished she knew what it all meant. She was aware of Granville standing tall and silent at her back and was very glad of his presence.

"But he is Chinese?" she asked. She was pretty sure she knew the answer to this one.

"I hear he is not."

Oh dear. That wasn't the answer she'd been expecting. From the little she'd found out about them, the Chinese *tongs* served only the Chinese community...

Though it also meant Wong Sun himself was not directly involved. Which was something of a relief.

"Might you have heard why the *tongs* would be willing to work with this man, then?" she asked then, pleased to note her voice didn't quiver, not matter how unstable her knees felt at the moment.

"I hear that perhaps this man is a good customer."

He was? A good customer of the *tongs*? How interesting.

Emily nearly asked what the fellow purchased from the *tongs*, but thought better of it. She wasn't sure how far Wong Sun's tolerance would stretch.

She tilted her head a little. "Might being a good customer entitle such a man to ask the *tongs* for special treatment?"

"Such a thing might be possible."

"And might there be a particular kind of special treatment?"

"I hear that information has great value," Wong Sun said. Then as Emily shifted her weight slightly from one foot to the other, not quite sure what to ask next, he gave a nod that wasn't quite a bow to each of them and vanished through the velvet curtains as quietly as he'd entered.

Apparently their conversation was over.

Leaving Emily unsure what to make of the information she'd been given. Which seemed to have raised more questions than it answered.

AFTER THEY RETURNED Bertie to her parent's home, the carriage ride to the office was a silent one, with both of them caught up in their own thoughts. When they reached the office, Emily was pleased to see Laura and Mac chatting in front of the reception desk.

"Laura, it's tomorrow that the movers will be packing up our offices, isn't it?" Emily said in a voice loud enough to be heard clearly by all of them. "Though I suspect very little will get done on Monday either."

"I suspect you're right," Granville said with a grimace, as Laura nodded.

Emily smiled at him. "It will be worth it."

"More than worth it," he agreed. "But it will be good to have the disruption behind us."

Behind Granville's back, Laura rolled her eyes, and Emily grinned at her. The other woman had been the one efficiently handling most of the details of the upcoming move. And there were a lot of details.

"But I've arranged for Laura and myself to meet at Carver's offices on Monday," Mac said.

As Emily wondered what they would be talking to the lawyer about, she watched Laura's face fall.

"You'll have to go alone," Laura told him. "I need to be here to oversee the movers."

"If you arrange that meeting for mid-morning on Monday, I can be here and oversee everything, and both of you can go," Emily said. "I'm not returning to Victoria until Tuesday."

Laura smiled. "Thank you."

"Why don't we all plan to be here on Monday," Granville said. "Just in case. Moves can get complicated. Mac, can you set that meeting for Tuesday, instead?"

Mac nodded, and Emily shot both of them a grateful look.

This move was going to be complicated enough without Laura's detailed knowledge of all the arrangements.

WHEN HE AND Emily were finally back in his office, and once again seated on each side of the partner's desk, Granville looked across at his fiancée. How was she feeling about the meeting with Wong Sun? He couldn't read her expression, and she wasn't meeting his eyes.

What was she thinking?

"You were hoping for a contact inside Victoria's Chinatown," he said. "Which is not quite what Wong Sun gave you. Are you disappointed?"

"No. Or not exactly, anyway," Emily said, tracing some kind of pattern with her finger on the desktop. "I did get more information than I'd expected. As well as more questions."

Something was worrying her.

"What is it, Emily?"

"I'm not sure what to make of that information." She was so focused, her words nearly tripped over each other. "I can't exactly doubt Wong Sun..."

"But you can't trust him, either."

"Wong Sun said he'd heard that someone hired a Chinese man, who stole the Herron's pottery. And that man—I'll call him the thief —somehow worked with another man. The "hasty man," as he called him. And it's the hasty man who killed poor Betsy."

"Yes," Granville said. "Assuming that what Wong Sun 'heard' was the truth."

"Which it might not be," Emily said. "I know. But what he did say suggests that he knows the truth about who killed poor Betsy. Or at least part of it."

"It does."

"I'm inclined to believe what he said, at least for now. It gives me information I didn't have before. And he didn't have to tell me anything, after all. I wonder why he did?"

"I don't know. And I don't imagine Wong Sun would tell us," he added wryly.

Emily laughed at that. "I can't see why there is so much interest in the theft of some old pottery collection in Victoria, though. Why would Wong Sun even know about it?"

"How valuable is this pottery collection?" he asked.

"Very," she said. "Though only to a collector. Granville, it is the ugliest pottery imaginable. All spiky bits everywhere. It's as if someone stuck a fistful of thistles onto teacups and plates and saucers, then turned them into clay. Hard clay. Just think about using them—food would stick to every single spike."

He bit back a laugh at the face she was making. "I'm sure there is great artistry involved if they are that realistic."

"Thistles, Granville," she said. "Expensive thistles."

At which he did laugh. "I've learned that any time I seek answers from Wong Sun on a case, there are likely to be unanswered questions."

Emily smiled back, green eyes dancing. "Yes, you're right. But at least I have information I didn't have this morning. I suppose I'll have to be content with that."

2 8

Saturday, September 1, 1900

Bright and early on Saturday morning, Granville dropped by Scott's rooming house and dragged his friend out of bed, with Trent trailing along behind him. Over Scott's loud complaints, Granville promised to buy all of them breakfast if Scott would just hurry up.

"At Mary's Diner?" Trent asked, so eagerly that Granville grinned and gave him a nod.

"What's so urgent it can't wait for a reasonable hour?" Scott demanded, as he rummaged through a pile of clothing on the floor, apparently looking for a clean shirt.

"I have a wedding to attend this afternoon. And a would-be killer to catch. There's no time to waste," Granville said, leading the way down the stairs with the other two thundering after him.

"He has to go to a wedding, so I get too little sleep. Hardly seems fair, does it?" Scott said to Trent, who couldn't seem to decide whether to laugh or keep yawning.

After a hearty breakfast, they were in the office just after seven. By the time the rest of the team arrived—which included Emily, to

Granville's surprise—they had compared notes and discussed the facts they had on Randall's case until all three of them were heartily sick of it.

"Finally," Trent said when he heard the outer door creak open and the three voices chatting. "We need some new minds on this stuff. I can't even think straight anymore."

He wasn't the only one. "Perhaps Mac or Miss Kent have uncovered some additional facts that might help," Granville said.

"Well, they met with Carver yesterday afternoon. Maybe that'll give us something," Trent said.

"They did?" Granville said. "I'd thought that was scheduled for Tuesday?"

"It was, but they moved it up. Something one of them learned that had them all excited. Not sure which one. Because I was stuck behind the reception desk," he added in a disgruntled tone.

"And you're only mentioning this now?" Granville said, exchanging exasperated glances with Scott.

"Why did it matter? You couldn't ask them before now anyway," Trent said.

"We could have invited Carver to join us for breakfast," Granville said. "Or at very least, to this meeting we're about to have with Mac and Miss Kent."

And with Emily, apparently. He was pleased she'd come in today, though he couldn't imagine how she'd found the time.

"Oh." While Trent was thinking about that, Miss Kent popped her head in the door.

"Would you three like tea?"

"If you're making a pot, that would be appreciated," Granville said. "Then why don't all of you join us here?"

"Yes, we'll do that," Miss Kent said, and disappeared again.

Fifteen minutes later, they had all squeezed around the oversized partner's desk that dominated the room.

"Aren't you glad we'll be moving to our new offices soon?" Emily said, glancing around the crowded office. "I think my favorite is the new meeting room."

Miss Kent nodded. "I agree."

"And your new office is the same size as this one," Emily told Granville. "As is Mr. Scott's office. Just wait 'til you see it all set up with your new desks."

"I'm looking forward to it. Though in an odd way I'll miss this old desk."

"I won't miss staring across at you all day," Scott said. "Now I might even get some work done."

He grinned, then turned to Mac and Miss Kent, who'd taken seats side by side. "How did the meeting with Carver go?" he asked.

"We compared information, and he's going to get back to us on what he might need in court, depending on which direction his investigations take. Also, we confirmed that Cheever, Griggs, Peabody, Bragg, Konrad, and Lessing are all members of this group of lawyers. Based on our information, he's going to take a closer look at a couple of other lawyers and see if they are as well."

"Which accounts for six of the eight of the lawyers on your original lists. That's an excellent start," Granville said. "Is Carver planning on talking to any of this group of six?"

"Not yet, I don't think," Miss Kent said. "I had the impression he wants to discuss things with you first."

Granville exchanged glances with Scott. "I'd like to talk to Konrad again before Carver does," he said. "We'll have to see when we can fit it in."

Emily was watching him closely. "You have a feeling about Mr. Konrad and Mr. Randall, don't you?"

"I wouldn't call it a feeling," he said. "But there was something almost gleeful in his voice when he talked about this group of lawyers getting even with Randall. Which makes no sense, when he and Randall haven't even faced off in court yet."

"Actually, they have," Miss Kent said. "Konrad was the junior lawyer on a case Bragg lost to Randall. Though from the transcripts, it seems Bragg treated his junior rather badly, while Randall was kind to him."

Granville smiled. "Thank you, Miss Kent. That may just be the piece I was looking for. I'd appreciate a typed copy of your notes on that case, if you can?"

"Of course," Miss Kent said. "I'll have it for you by the end of today."

He glanced at Emily and laughed. "I'll be rather busy with the wedding festivities today. Just leave the typescript on my desk when you're done."

No point telling either of them he intended to confront Benton again first.

ONCE AGAIN SEATED UNEASILY in Benton's outer office, Granville contemplated the blank expressions of the two thugs who guarded the closed door to the gangster's inner office. He wondered idly if the two men spent the entire day standing there. Both were armed, but judging by their over-developed muscles, they hardly needed the weapons.

"How long d'you think he'll make us wait this time?" Scott asked in a voice that was meant to be heard, nodding towards that closed door.

"Depends how badly he wants to see us."

Another five minutes ticked slowly by on the large gold framed clock on the far wall. Then Scott had his answer as the three of them were ushered into the even more ostentatious inner office. The expanse of blue marble that was Benton's desktop caught and held Granville's eye every time. The unexpected beauty of it in these surroundings suggested the gangster was far more than he seemed.

And why was he was spending so much time thinking about furnishings?

Benton didn't look surprised to see them. Nor did he look offended, which surprised Granville. There was no cigar burning in the ashtray beside him, either.

But then, he'd kept them waiting for more than ten minutes. Perhaps he considered that enough of a win in their ongoing battle of wits.

"And what can I do for you three today?" he asked.

"As you've probably heard, we're looking into a number of lawyers and their clients who have reason to be dissatisfied with—or even threatened by—Randall's recent courtroom wins," Granville said.

"So?"

There was no expression on Benton's solid features as he spoke. Trent bristled, while Granville and Scott exchanged glances.

"You told us you'd be interested in hearing whatever rumors we might uncover about this case," Granville said.

"I did say that, I suppose. Foolish of me."

Two could play that game. "I'm sorry we've wasted your time," he said, and stood up.

"No need to be hasty, now," Benton said, unperturbed. "Since you're here, you might as well say what you came to say."

"If you're willing to share information, I'd be happy to," he said, ignoring Scott's alarmed look.

"Fair enough. As long as your information has sufficient value to me."

"And who decides that?"

"I do, of course. Are you going to argue with me?"

"No. I'll simply take it into consideration for future situations. Which, as our firm continues to grow and take on more challenging cases, might become an issue for you."

"And would that be a threat?"

He grinned. "Of course not. Call it an operational goal."

Benton laughed. "You continue to be entertaining. And you still won't work for me?"

"I have a firm. One with lofty operational goals," Granville said, deadpan.

Benton shook his head. "So tell me what you've heard about this lawyer of yours. And what you want from me."

"Randall's success in several lawsuits against several firms that import goods from the Far East has won him a number of enemies," he said. "Some of whom want to discredit him. One of whom apparently sought to eliminate him."

"And that one?"

"Granville calls him the big fish," Scott put in. Throwing a sly grin at Granville as he did so.

"The big fish," Benton said slowly, as if testing the words. "Something of an exaggeration, but I like it. So you have no idea who this big fish is?"

"Not yet," Granville said. "Do you?"

"If I did, would I be asking you?"

"Possibly. If it served your needs."

Benton chuckled. "True enough. Very well then. I've become aware that someone's keeping a close eye on the goods that flow through our port."

"Someone?" Granville said.

"Possibly your big fish."

"And?"

"And I'd be very interested in a name for that big fish."

"You don't know who he is?"

"No. He's very small potatoes. His name hasn't mattered to me before."

"But you know he has it in for Randall."

"That was a guess until now. I knew Randall's success was starting to change the import laws. And that would probably annoy whoever this is."

"You mean the big fish," Granville said. "Annoy him enough to hire Randall killed?"

"Again, possibly. Whoever this is, he's subtle, even invisible."

"Hardly your style," Scott said.

"No," Benton said. "It isn't. And he hasn't got in my way. Yet."

"Smart man," Granville said, noting Benton's lack of response to Scott's dig with relief. Were things better between the two of them, then?

"For now," Benton said.

"You think he'll challenge you at some point?"

"I think every thief, no matter how smart, grows greedy."

"You should know," Scott muttered, and again Benton ignored him.

"Why didn't you tell us this before?" Granville asked quickly, before Scott said something the gangster couldn't ignore.

"I'm telling you now."

"I need specifics."

"There are none. Only the faintest of rumors."

"Rumors about what?"

"Slight increases in imported goods. Nothing that would help you find him. Randall's cases are your best bet," Benton said in a tone that made it clear the subject was closed.

Granville wondered what exactly the gangster was smuggling that he'd pay such close attention to the flow of goods through the port. "And you'd like our big fish's name when we uncover it."

"Of course. Since you're searching for him in any case."

"And does that fulfill the favor we owe you?" Granville said, knowing it was a long shot.

"Of course not," Benton said with a broad smile. "That favor is far more valuable."

Which was hardly reassuring. But at least he had a few more answers. With Benton, that counted as a win.

Once they were halfway down the street—and well out of earshot of Benton or any of his men—Granville turned to face Scott.

"It seemed a little less tense in there than I'd expected. I gather things have been resolved between you and Benton on the Lizzie issue?" Granville said.

"Yup," Scott said. "I took care of it."

Trent stopped and frowned at both of them. "You did not. Miss Frances took care of it." He turned to Granville.

"You should have seen it." There was a trace of awe in Trent's voice. "Miss Frances took Benton on like someone lit a fire under her. 'You leave my sister alone. Lizzie is fine," she says. "For her, laudanum is a blessing. Unlike when she smokes opium, she's eating. Not wasting away to nothing.' It was great."

"Sure was. And it shut Benton up right fast," Scott said.

"Good," Granville said, and resumed his quick pace.

Trent tugged at his arm.

"Hey, slow down. Where are you off to, anyway?"

"I have a wedding to attend, remember?" Granville said, length-ening his stride.

Trent made a face. "But it's hours yet."

He grinned, but didn't slow down. "These things take more time that you'd expect. You'll find out, one day."

"So what am I supposed to do?"

Granville and Scott exchanged a look over Trent's head.

"We're going back to the office," Scott said. "And you're supposed to help Miss Kent with whatever she needs to get things ready for our move on Monday."

"But what about what Benton said?" Trent wailed.

"Benton said some things about his dealings with whoever has it in for Randall that require thinking about," Granville told him. "So while you're packing boxes, you can think about them. Next time we meet, we'll sort out what's next."

"But what *is* next?" Trent asked, half running to keep up with them. "Haven't we run out of leads on this case?"

"No, we haven't," Granville said. "We have six lawyers, and their clients, to dig into."

"You think one of them is the big fish?" Trent asked.

"He may be. Or not," he said. "But I think one of them will lead us to the big fish."

It was Saturday, Cecily's wedding day. Emily was determined to put all thought of murders and assassins out of her head, just for today. They had no place at a wedding.

The church was lovely, decorated all in white, with hints of pink. Clusters of late roses bloomed against delicate orchids and dainty ferns around the altar and along the center aisle, and wide white satin bows adorned the end of each pew. And Cecily made a beautiful bride.

As the notes of the Wedding March swelled through the church, Emily turned to watch her glide up the aisle. Her gown was corded white silk, embroidered in intricate patterns and trimmed with exquisite lace, and her long train swept elegantly behind her. Her veil was a cloud of delicate lace around a face glowing with joy, and her bridegroom in formal black looked at her with something close to awe.

Mama kept telling Emily that her own wedding day would be the happiest of her life, and looking at Cecily, she could almost believe it. And she made a decision.

She'd talk to Mama tomorrow about finding a new wedding

date, one that would make both herself and Granville happy. How bad could a wedding really be, after all?

Then her eyes swept the crowded church, ending on Clara's face, where her friend stood at the front of the church with seven—*seven!*—other bridesmaids. One of the bridesmaids looked furious with another standing beside her. And Clara looked exhausted.

It was all too much. Too elaborate, too much display of wealth and social standing, too public. The idea of the formal church wedding like this one—with so many details and everything just so—was daunting. And all of it in front of hundreds of people, who would gossip over everything that happened? That terrified her.

No wonder Mama wanted two years to plan such an event.

She could feel Granville's warm presence on the ha wooden bench beside her, sense him watching her as much as he did the bride. It was a relief to know he didn't want a large formal wedding either.

But then there was the matter of their wedding date. He really wanted to move it closer. And she did too, didn't she?

Then why hadn't she already talked to Mama?

And why did the notion of all she'd be responsible for as a married lady seem increasingly daunting?

She'd get to live with Granville, after all. See him all the time. Wouldn't that be worth everything?

What was this unsettled feeling, when everything she thought seemed wrong and she felt jangled and out of sorts with herself? Was this what was known as cold feet?

The bride reached the altar, and stood like a statue beside her groom. The bridesmaids fanned out in a river of pale pink one side of her, while the groomsmen marched stiffly to their place by the groom's side. It made a lovely tableau.

Seated on the bride's side of the church, all Emily could see was the backs of carefully styled heads and those elegant dresses as the minister droned on. Wishing he was a little less wordy, Emily tried picturing herself standing there, with Granville tall and straight at her side. And swallowed hard.

Maybe she simply wasn't cut out for marriage?

Just then Granville picked up her hand and held it in his much larger one. A current of heat ran through her. Emily met his eyes and smiled.

Or maybe it was formal weddings she wasn't cut out for. It was time for her to stop waffling and talk to Mama about her wedding.

But not until this case was finished.

3 0

Tuesday, September 4, 1900

Early Tuesday morning, Granville drove Emily to the ferry terminal for her return to Victoria. She almost wished she didn't have to leave again—her life was here. But she couldn't leave poor Betsy's case unsolved, and her killer free. She just couldn't.

"I could still come with you, you know," Granville said as they neared the ferry docks.

He'd offered before, and once again Emily was tempted. It would be easier with two of them. And she missed him when she was away.

But this was her case. Hers. And she was close to finding Betsy's killer, she could feel it.

How could she tell Granville that she didn't want his involvement?

"I know, and I wish you could," she said, smiling at him. And that was true, too. "But you have your own case here. And until you solve it, Mr. Randall is still in danger, isn't he?"

"With the two of us, we could solve your case faster, then come home and solve mine," he said persuasively, and dropped a kiss in her palm. "It's likely to be more efficient in any case. We work well together."

Emily tightened her hand on his. He turned his hand over, holding it in his warm grip.

"We do," she said. "But I just can't."

He gave her a searching look. "Betsy matters to you," he said.

"Yes. She does."

"And this is your first case."

She swallowed hard. Nodded.

He smiled at her, and began to talk about the people they'd met after church yesterday.

He understood. Emily's heart swelled and she held his hand tight, loving him more than ever.

Then with an effort she concentrated on what he was saying.

As the ferry chugged its way around a thickly forested island, Emily let her eyes rest on the stretch of nearly flat ocean ahead of her. Standing on the top deck, along the railing near the bow, she had a nearly unobstructed view of where they were going. It was a good place to think.

Which made it her favorite place to spend a ferry journey, and today was perfect for it. The air was fresh and invigorating, but the only breeze came from the momentum of the ferry itself, the sea an endless blue stretching ahead of her.

If only she had so clear a view of her case.

The conversation with Granville had helped, but there were still so many questions. Everything depended on her asking the right ones, in the right way, of the right person. And she wasn't sure she could do so.

Granville didn't seem to doubt her, though.

She smiled at the thought, and drew in a deep lungful of the sea air. On a day like this, with the sun glinting off the ripples in the ferry's wake, how could she doubt? And no matter what, she wasn't going to let poor Betsy down.

At least the chaos of the move was behind her. That was one thing finished. Granville and Scott Investigations now occupied their new offices, and they were open for business today. Which hadn't been easy.

Knowing they couldn't afford to close the office for more than two days, she and Laura had planned everything, right down to where every piece of furniture would go. Even to the coat tree in the lobby and the placement of the telephones.

Laura had done a stellar job of making all the arrangements, double checking every last detail. The movers they'd hired had been efficient and willing to work with their plans.

But even all that planning hadn't prevented the chaos of the move itself.

So many things had gone wrong it hurt Emily's head to think about it. It had taken all of them working together to pull it off. The whole thing had been exhausting. But oddly satisfying.

She let her mind drift forward, to the case that awaited her. It felt like she'd abandoned it, unfinished, when she'd had to go back to Vancouver. Even though she'd been working with Granville on it part of the time. And despite the new leads she had.

Leads she could never have found in Victoria.

Suddenly she felt very alone, and worried that her investigation would have gone cold, and stalled beyond recovery while she was away. Now, too late, she was second guessing her decision not to accept Granville's offer to come with her.

How was she ever going to solve a case this complicated on her own?

On the short carriage ride back to his office, Granville worried about Emily. She had promised to be careful, and he knew how capable she was—but she was tracking a murderer.

When the carriage pulled up in front, he paid the driver and dismissed him, then firmly put away his concerns. Emily would be fine, and if she needed his help, she'd ask for it. He had to believe that.

And he needed all his focus here today. He had his own would-be killer to catch.

Walking into their elegant new lobby on the second floor, he heard the familiar efficient rattling of a typewriting machine, which stopped the minute he opened the door. He glanced around.

After the hectic mayhem of the previous day's move, he hadn't expected everything to be in place today. The overwhelming impression was of a prosperous, well established business.

The typewriter wasn't Miss Kent, however. An unfamiliar young woman was seated behind the polished maple reception desk. She had dark hair pulled neatly back, snapping dark eyes, and an eager look.

"Good morning," she said in a professional tone, with just the right note of welcome. "How may we help you?"

He stared at her for a moment.

Had Emily told him the firm had hired someone new?

They had discussed the possible need for a new hire, someone dedicated to reception duties. Such a hire would free up Miss Kent and Trent to fully focus on investigative work. Which would make sense at some point, especially now they had the space.

He hadn't expected it to happen so quickly.

And without his input.

"Good morning," he said. Before he could decide how to ask what she was doing there without sounding insufferably rude, Miss Kent appeared through the meeting room door. She looked from his expression to the new receptionist and back. Her eyes widened, and she looked flustered.

He'd never seen the unflappable Miss Kent lose her calm before. What was going on here?

"Mr. Granville," she said. "I hadn't expected to see you so soon."

"The ferry sailed on time, which is unusual," he said politely. And waited.

"I'm so sorry, Mr. Granville," said the young woman behind the reception desk, flushing a little. "I should have recognized you."

How was she supposed to have recognized him? He'd never seen her before.

Granville wished Emily was there. He was feeling more than a little irritated that she'd set this up without telling him, but she'd have had things running smoothly if she'd been here.

Now Miss Kent, whom he'd never seen this nervous, was blushing deeply. "This is my fault," she said hurriedly. "Mr. Granville, this is Miss Rizzo. She's here to help us out this week."

"I'm very pleased to meet you, Miss Rizzo."

"And I you, Mr. Granville."

The exchange of pleasantries seemed to ruffle Miss Kent even further. "Umm... could I speak with you in your office for a moment?" she asked. "If you have the time, of course."

"Of course," he said. "Is everyone else here now?"

Miss Kent nodded.

"Good," Granville said, then looked past her at the younger woman.

"Miss Rizzo, would you let everyone know that I'd like to see them in the meeting room for a quick meeting in…shall we say fifteen minutes?"

He glanced back at Miss Kent, who flinched, but nodded.

"Of course," said their new—apparently temporary—receptionist. "Would you like me to make some tea for your meeting? And I believe we have biscuits, too."

"Excellent idea," he said, gesturing Miss Kent towards his office. He wasn't convinced they needed a full-time receptionist, but Miss Rizzo certainly seemed capable enough.

"I'm so sorry, Mr. Granville," Miss Kent said the moment they were in his office. She was practically vibrating with tension. "We… I meant to tell you."

He considered her for a moment. "You mean my fiancée meant to tell me, don't you?" he asked, suddenly struck by the humor in the situation.

She obviously heard something in his voice, because she visibly relaxed, and a hint of a smile appeared. "I'm afraid so," she said. "But the move yesterday was such chaos, and we weren't even sure this would work out. Then Emily was so focused on the journey back to Victoria, and solving her case…"

Granville smiled at that. "Yes, I know. So why don't you fill me in on what she had meant to tell me."

"Well, when Emily realized how much work there was still to do here after the move… And that Mac, I mean Mr. McAndrews, and I still had work to do on the legal files, to say nothing of meeting again with Mr. Carver. Well, Trent would have been sitting at reception half the day. And just when you might need him…"

"The two of you realized we needed extra help for a bit," he finished for her.

"Yes, that's it."

"I gather it's only for a week." For now, at least. And he held back his grin at Emily's latest plot. "But where did you find Miss Rizzo on such short notice?"

"Well, she trained with us, Emily and I, at the typewriting school," Miss Kent said. "And she's a few years younger, but very good. She hasn't found a position yet, so she's going back for the fall semester to work on additional skills. And the school doesn't start for another two weeks, and she and I are neighbors, so I said I'd see if she was available. And she was."

Granville felt a little overwhelmed by the flood of words, but at least now he understood what Miss Rizzo was doing in his office.

He wondered what Scott thought about it, and whether his partner had been consulted, either.

Probably not.

He nearly laughed at the thought of Scott's likely expression when he ran into Miss Rizzo. Despite having been raised with two sisters, Scott wasn't all that comfortable around women.

"Thank you for breaking the news to me, Miss Kent," he said with a straight face. "And now I think it's time for a strategy meeting on our current case, don't you?"

"I do indeed," Miss Kent said with such an obvious look of relief that he nearly spoiled it all by letting the laughter he'd been squelching spill out.

***

TEN MINUTES later they were all seated around the carved walnut table in the meeting room. Granville looked around him. Scott sat at the far end, with Trent beside him and Mac and Miss Kent across the table. Only Emily was missing. And temporarily, anyway, Miss Rizzo.

There was ample seating for all of them. Even with a dozen people, the meeting room still wouldn't feel crowded, he noted with a quick surge of pride. And the blinds and overhead fans kept the room cool, while still letting in enough sun to wash the room in the bright morning light. The subtle touches of color in the wallpaper and the carpets kept the room professional while still retaining a welcoming aspect.

He thought he recognized Emily's friend Clara's influence, and for a moment wondered what their home would look like. Emily would surely ask for Clara's help when it came to decorating there. When she was home again he'd ask her.

But for now he tucked the thought away—it was too close to his fears for her safety. His focus needed to be on finding their big fish.

Trent's head was swiveling from one end of the large room to the other and back. "This is better," he announced. "There's room for everyone, now. We should have done this a long time ago."

Scott looked at Granville across the length of polished wood and rolled his eyes.

"It looks much better in here than when we left yesterday," Granville said in surprise.

"Miss Rizzo and I came in early to straighten everything up," Miss Kent said.

They'd done a great deal more than straighten, Granville realized, remembering the boxes of paper and files that had been everywhere yesterday. "Thank you," he said. "We really appreciate all the work you've done."

"It was nothing," she said.

"Hardly," he said. "And if you find you need Miss Rizzo's assistance for a little longer than a week, that can be arranged. Please feel free to come and discuss it with Scott and I."

"Thank you, I will," she said with such pleasure that Granville found himself wondering exactly what he'd just committed himself to.

Scott looked amused.

Great.

"Now that the move is over, and Emily has returned to Victoria for the time being, our entire focus needs to be on the catching Randall's would-be killer," he said. "Preferably before someone finds out Randall is still alive."

"How is Mr. Randall doing?" Trent asked. "I gather he's still in hospital?"

"He is," Granville said, "On the whole, he's been recovering far faster than anyone expected he would. Yesterday his doctor said that if it weren't for issues of his own safety, he might be considering a date for sending him home."

"That's good news," Scott said.

"It is. However, I spoke with his doctor this morning, and it appears Randall had a small setback and is unconscious again. The doctor isn't recommending visitors today."

"That's too bad," Scott said.

"I'm hoping for better news tomorrow," Granville said.

He'd been warned these could be the first symptoms that Randall was bleeding internally, but until he knew more, there was no point in upsetting the others.

"And we're still pretending he's dead?" Trent said.

"Hovering near death," he said.

"Same thing," Trent muttered.

Granville hid his grin as he continued. "Randall's doctor has agreed to continue the charade until whoever wanted him dead has been dealt with."

"Good," Scott said. "Then we'd best get on with it."

"My plan exactly. This morning, Scott and I will track down Konrad. We have a few questions for him," Granville said with a nod to his partner. "Trent, is there anything you need to follow up today?"

"Not unless some more rumors cropped up. Which I doubt. There's still nobody talking."

"Then you're with us."

"Good," Trent said with a huge sigh of relief. "I hate it when nothing's happening and no one will tell you anything."

He wasn't alone in that feeling.

Granville turned to Mac. "How are you and Miss Kent getting along with those legal records? Any progress?"

"Nothing substantial, I'm afraid," Mac said. "To be honest, I suspect we won't find much more in the records we currently have until we have someone to focus our search on."

"Which is what Scott, Trent and I will focus on today—finding that name," Granville said. "We'll be out for most of the day. If you have information or if we need to meet again, we should be back around four."

G ranville, Scott and Trent ran their quarry to earth in a back corner of a decrepit bar on the docks. The place was badly lit and nearly deserted. Konrad was working his way through a plate of fried salmon, eggs and potatoes, served with thick slices of toasted sourdough. He looked like he hadn't slept, with dark circles under his eyes and a grey complexion. As they entered, he raised his cup to call for more coffee, and his hand shook.

"Kinda late for breakfast, isn't it?" Trent said in a carrying voice.

"Rough night, Konrad?" Granville asked as the three of them slid into the booth the lawyer occupied.

Konrad's appearance wasn't the only thing that seemed to have lost its polish since he'd seen the fellow last. He jumped at the unexpected voice, then glared at Granville, completely ignoring Scott and Trent. "I don't see that's any of your business," he said. "And what are you doing here, anyway?"

"Looking for you."

"Well, you found me. Now you can leave."

The owner came by and filled Konrad's cup. When he raised the pot towards Granville in mute invitation, the latter nodded as Konrad glared at him. Soon they all had cups of rich-smelling coffee in front of them. Granville fully expected the coffee in a place like this to taste like tar, but he was pleasantly surprised to find the flavor almost matched the aroma.

"I get it. You're not leaving," Konrad said. "So what do you want?"

"I want to hear more about that group of lawyers who hate Randall's ethics so much."

"It isn't enough that you set Draper on me?" Konrad asked.

"Draper followed up with you?"

"Of course he did. He thinks there's a story in it."

"And is there a story?"

"No, there is not," Konrad said. "And I've told him that I'm not even part of the group. But that doesn't stop Draper. He calls every day, sometimes twice a day."

Konrad paused to stir sugar and cream into his coffee, the motions jerky with anger. "You want to know what I told him about the group? What I think about Randall? Go ask him."

"If there's no story, then why are you still so angry with Randall?"

"You'd hate him too if you were me," Konrad muttered into his coffee.

"Possibly," Granville said. "However, he's my lawyer, and I was always as grateful for his ethics as I was for that sharp legal mind of his."

Konrad gave Granville an angry look, then stared at the unappetizing mess of egg, ketchup and potato that still covered a third of his plate. Pushing it away, he swallowed more coffee. "If you won't leave, then I will," he said.

"Not until you've answered my questions," Granville said, and let the fellow see the butt of the gun he was wearing at his waist, hidden under his jacket.

Konrad's pallor took on a greenish hue. "There's no need to be hasty," he said. "What did you want to know about the group?"

"How did it come to be?"

Konrad shrugged "I guess there's no harm in telling you. It started with the usual grousing lawyers do after they've lost a case.

Then they started comparing notes, and worked out that the judgements Randall had been getting could spell trouble for all of us. And they couldn't have that."

Granville noted the telling 'us', but he held back the pithy words he wanted to say. First, he needed information. Then he could give the fellow the tongue lashing he deserved.

"And?" he prompted Konrad.

"And they kept talking about what we could do to stop it. To stop him."

Exactly as he'd suspected. And exactly as Benton had suggested the big fish might act—nearly invisible behind the scenes. Interesting.

"Which judgements were you all so worried about?" he asked.

Konrad reached for his coffee. "How do you mean?"

Granville said nothing.

Konrad put down his cup. "It's all boring legal details you wouldn't care about," he said. Then as the silence stretched again, he added, "Mostly to do with importing and exporting."

"Like the case you have pending with Randall?"

Konrad reached for his cup again. "I suppose you could make that argument."

And Granville was looking forward to seeing Randall do just that, once they'd found whoever had attacked him. "Could?" was all he said.

Konrad's face flushed, and a small tic beside his eye quivered and jumped. "It's similar," he said.

That was the best he could do? "So you—and your case—will benefit from Randall's death?"

"Well, I suppose you could say that. Though I had every expectation of defeating him soundly in court."

"As the others of your little group have done?"

Konrad flushed, and his tic sped up. Granville wondered how he survived in court with a tell like that. "It doesn't mean I wanted Randall dead."

Doesn't mean he didn't, either. Granville chose a different line of attack. "And who is the leader of your little group?"

Konrad looked offended. "I told you I'm not part of that group. And there is no leader. Everyone is equal."

Right. Granville didn't believe him on either point. "I see. So what can you tell us about them all?"

For the first time Konrad glanced at Scott and Trent. Granville wasn't sure if it was the intent look on Trent's face or the glimpse of the gun that Scott was casually displaying, but the lawyer's eyes widened. He suddenly looked like a rabbit that had spotted a fox, and Granville fought back a grin at the image.

"They have some good ideas, and they're going to get back at Randall," Konrad said.

"Randall is dying from a vicious beating," Granville said. "Did one or more of your group attack him? Did you?"

"Of course not. We're lawyers," Konrad said as if that explained anything. "None of us would *kill* him."

"Someone has. A slow, painful death," Granville said, leaning towards Konrad and lashing at him with his voice. "Did one of your group hire that someone?"

"No! Of course not!"

Granville just looked at him.

"At least I…I don't think so."

"If someone did, who might it have been? Who hated Randall the most?"

"All of us. Maybe even me. But I didn't kill him. Or hire someone to attack him. I just complained."

"I thought you hated him," Trent said suddenly.

For a moment Granville was afraid it would break the hold he had on Konrad, but it seemed to be the right thing to say.

"I do!" Konrad nearly shouted. "And I'd stop at nothing to humiliate him. Or hurt him financially. But to beat him to death? To hire someone to kill him?" He shuddered. "Not that. And I can't imagine someone I know could do that."

And yet someone had.

Granville eyed the broken man across the table. It was too bad. He'd liked Konrad for the murder, simply because of the animosity the lawyer clearly bore for Randall.

Plus the fact that he didn't care for Konrad.

Sometimes the most spineless creatures were the most danger-ous. They'd attack suddenly, without warning, and hold nothing back.

He suspected the attack on Randall had been like that. Randall had known someone was working to discredit him, but he obvi-ously hadn't expected a physical attack. Granville knew Randall owned a gun, a sleekly lethal black revolver. But he hadn't been wearing it that day.

"Vancouver is a pretty small town," Granville said. "The odds are good that you know whoever is behind this attack. Probably quite well. I'm asking for a name. Now!"

Konrad startled, and attempted to glare at Granville to cover it up. He failed miserably. "No. I can't…"

"I need a name."

"I don't know! But, if I had to say someone…"

"You do."

"Then, I'd say Oliver Lessing."

Another name he recognized. Granville nodded. "Good. Why him?"

"He's had issues with Randall before. He holds a grudge even worse than I do. And the man has a mean streak that he hides most of the time. But I've seen it the odd time in court. He waits his time, sets people up. Then he strikes. And he has no mercy. None."

Interesting. Konrad had insisted he himself would never trans-late his hate into a physical attack. But he thought Lessing would do so. Why? "Would he attack Randall directly, himself?"

"How should I know?" Konrad retorted, then sat back and closed his eyes for a moment. "No," he said, slowly. "No, I don't believe he would. I think he'd hire someone to do it for him. He doesn't like people to know what he's up to. Hiring someone would keep his own role anonymous."

"Who would he hire?" Granville asked. And held up a hand to stop Konrad's automatic protest. "If you had to guess."

"He mentioned Gurak's thugs to me once. It was to do with a case where he was going to lose until a key witness vanished.

Which he did, shortly thereafter. If he did so once… Talk to Gurak," Konrad finished abruptly.

"Thank you. I will," Granville said. "And we'll leave you to finish your breakfast." He stood up, and Trent and Scott followed his lead.

Konrad looked at the congealing grease on his plate, then gave Granville a weak smile as he turned to go.

Leaving Konrad to his cold food, Granville, Scott and Trent took the shortcut up Gore Street and headed back towards Draper's office at the *News Advertiser*. Granville had cancelled the carriage and driver after Emily had returned to Victoria, but as the streets narrowed and grew dustier, he wished for a moment he'd kept them. Or at least hired a hack.

His boots were going to be disgraceful after this little jaunt, and he'd be brushing them himself tomorrow. Life had been easier in London, with a valet to take care of the mundane details of presenting oneself as a gentleman.

Easier, but less satisfying.

He grinned at the thought. He was really feeling out of his depth if he was missing his long-gone valet.

"So what did you think?" Scott asked Granville as they strode along, walking three abreast. "D'you still like Konrad for the attack on Randall?"

"No, I don't, dammit," Granville said. "The fellow doesn't have enough spine."

"Yeah, that sums him up."

"But he hates Randall," Trent said. "Really hates him, I mean.

He wasn't even trying to hide it. And you said yourself you thought it might be hired thugs that done this. Konrad could've hired them."

"Yes, he could have. But I don't think he did."

"Well, why not?"

"Konrad's the kind would get all het up and knife you in the back," Scott said. "If he thought he could get away with it. Then he'd blame the circumstances. He "couldn't help himself." I don't see him as the kind to beat someone to death, or even hire that done."

Granville nodded. "Spineless," he repeated.

"Oh," Trent said. "Yeah, I guess I've seen guys like that. Snakes, I call 'em."

"Exactly," Granville said.

"What about Lessing?" Scott said. "You think Konrad could be right about him?"

"I don't know him at all. But I found Konrad's sudden accusation more than a little suspicious."

"Konrad sure had a lot of detail about how nasty the guy is," Trent said. "He sounded like someone who hoards grudges."

Granville laughed. "You could be right, at that."

"Doesn't mean he's wrong about Lessing," Scott said.

"Doesn't mean he's right, either," Granville said.

At that moment Scott nudged him with an elbow. "We're being followed."

"What?" How had he missed that?

Using the windows of the tailor shop they were passing as a guide, Granville could barely make out a bulky figure in an ill-fitting black suit following on the sidewalk behind them, some thirty feet back.

"The one in black? No hat?" Granville said in a voice pitched for Scott and Trent's ears only.

"There are three of them," Scott said as quietly. "The other two are across the street."

A quick glance verified his partner's words.

"I see them too," Trent said, just above a whisper.

"Good thing you both decided to come with me," Granville said. "Though I could have handled it."

"Same way you handled Gipson's thugs in the Klondike?" Scott said, grinning at him.

"That was years ago. I was still green then," Granville said, keeping a close eye on the three following them.

"Uh huh."

They walked in silence for another block. The three followers kept pace. "Recognize any of them?" Granville said.

"Nope. They're too far away to be certain of anything."

"Me neither," Trent said.

"How long have they been following us?"

"Since we left Konrad, I think," Scott said. "I caught a glimpse of them a couple of times, but I wasn't sure until now."

"So they could have been following us since we left the office. Or they were keeping an eye on Konrad. But why now?"

"Somebody must've got stirred up," Scott said. "Maybe it's the questions we're asking?"

"Or because we talked to Konrad?" Trent said.

"Could be either. Otherwise it's a pretty big coincidence." Granville considered their surroundings. This wasn't one of the safer parts of town. "Think we should ask them? Now, before we get into really unfamiliar territory?"

"Seems only polite," Scot said.

"My thoughts exactly. See that alley just past the brick warehouse?"

"Across the street?"

"That's the one. You two ready?"

At their nods, Granville wove his way between the carts and wagons lining Water Street, Scott and on his heels. All three turned down into the dank, narrow alley that ran between two brick buildings.

Down at the end the alley widened out into a small courtyard. The place was filthy, smelling of garbage and worse. There was no hope for his boots now, he realized with a reluctant grin.

The light was dim back here, with three- and four-story buildings all around, but it was the perfect place for an ambush. They waited in silence, listening for the slightest sound. Would their followers take the bait?

They did.

Granville heard cautious footprints coming down the narrow alley. Then came a moment of heavy silence.

Three dark figures erupted out in a concerted rush, straight for them. They were decent fighters, heavily muscled and strong, and well matched in size to him and Scott. Though he was concerned about Trent, who seemed to grow taller by the month, but hadn't yet filled out.

Granville ducked a well-aimed punch, then leaned away from the kick that followed. If the thug had connected, that blow would have done some damage.

It was just as well they were in a courtyard. In these tight quarters, the three thugs with all their bulky muscle were at a disadvantage.

Granville came back with a left, right combination, and his opponent shook his head slightly as he stepped back. Behind him, he could hear Scott and the thug he was fighting were exchanging blows, thick meaty sounds that meant they were well matched. Trent too seemed to be holding his own, using his lighter frame and agility to run rings around his heftier opponent.

His own opponent tried for another kick, and he stepped into it, using their momentum to lay the fellow on his ass. Where he lay for a moment, half stunned, then surged up. Straight into Granville's fist.

With the fellow dispatched, Granville turned to see if Trent or Scott needed help. Just in time to see Scott's opponent fly across the small courtyard and smack into the brick wall of the warehouse with a thud. The thug slid down the wall and lay groaning in the dirt.

Trent was getting in a few good blows, but his opponent, though clearly winded, was hitting back harder. Granville stepped forward and stuck out a foot, sending the third thug sprawling. Trent immediately grabbed a loose piece of board and hit the downed man over the head, knocking him cold.

Then the lad met his questioning look and grinned through a bruise spreading over the left side of his face. "Piece of cake," Trent said. "Now what?"

"We tie these three up, call Officer Daniels and let him know where he can find them. Then we carry on with our mission." He considered the three vanquished thugs. "You recognize any of them?"

Trent shook his head, though Granville noticed he winced as he did so.

"Nope, 'fraid not," Scott said. "You?"

"I think your former opponent looks familiar," Granville said. "But the light is bad. Let's see if he'll tell us anything."

Scott found some frayed lengths of rope coiled on top of a barrel and began tying the three men up. Granville walked over and nudged the groaning man with his boot.

"Hey. You. Who do you work for?" Another groan was his only answer. Which wasn't a surprise.

"You're one of Gurak's men," he said.

Scott stopped wrestling with the rope and looked at the fallen man in surprise. Then he nodded slowly. "I think you might be right."

Granville nudged the fellow again. "Well? I'm waiting."

"Never heard of him," came the sullen words.

"No? Well, you have a choice. You can tell me who you work for, and I'll let you go. Or you can wait for Officer Daniels—who can't be bought off, by the way—and answer his questions. Which will it be?"

The fellow gave vent to a fervent curse, then spat out a few words.

"You'll have to say it louder," Granville said. Earning himself a glare from close set dark eyes he'd definitely seen before.

"Yeah, we work for Gurak. Now tell him to let me go."

"Who hired you?"

Silence.

Granville nudged him again.

Another curse, followed by a glare. "Dunno. You'd have to ask Gurak that. I'm sure he'd be real happy to tell you."

"Fine. Tell Gurak I'll meet him tonight at his usual dive. Eight p.m. Agreed?"

"Sure. It's your funeral," Gurak's man said darkly.

Granville nodded to Scott. "Just his hands," he said. With a grin, his partner bent to untie the rope he'd used on the fellow's legs.

"It'll take him a bit to get himself free," Scott said, as the three of them strode up Carrall Street.

Trent was quiet, which was unlike him, and Granville kept an eye on him. If they hadn't just been attacked, he'd have sent the lad back to the office, but for now, he was safer with him and Scott.

"Even longer if he frees his fellow thugs too," he said. "They won't be following us again. Not today, anyway."

"Good," Scott said. "And after we talk to Gurak, not any other day, either."

Granville, Scott and Trent found Draper at his desk at *The News Advertiser*, his eyes narrowed and his fingers hammering madly on a large Remington typewriting machine. "Just a minute," he said without looking up. "Last paragraph."

Granville and Scott exchanged grins. "I've heard Miss Kent say exactly that," Scott said as they watched, his voice nearly swallowed by the roar of sound that was the newsroom. "But she doesn't look at her keys. Ever."

Draper did. He seemed to be using only three fingers on each hand, but the keyboard kept up a steady rattling. Suddenly it stopped, and the reporter rapidly read through what he'd typewritten, and nodded once. Then he glanced up, and sprang to his feet.

"Granville. Scott. And Trent, isn't it? What can I do for you three?" He gave Trent's quickly darkening cheek a concerned look, but didn't mention it.

"I'd like to buy you a drink," Granville said. "We have some questions about the Randall story, if you have the time?"

"Sure thing. Let me just get this to my editor." And Draper hurried off.

Ten minutes later the four of them were walking into the

Scrivener's Ink, where Draper led them straight to a table at the back. The place was half-full, and judging by the number of nods he got, Draper was known here.

"Journalist's hangout?" Granville asked, taking in the smoke-stained walls and long walnut bar with a nearly a dozen imported beers on tap.

"You mean the name of the place didn't give it away?" Draper said with a smile. "Beer?" he asked, looking from Granville to Scott to Trent.

At their nods, he signaled the bartender, holding up four fingers. Then he lit a cigarette, waved out the match and stared soberly at Granville. "So. Randall. How's he doing?"

"Not well, I'm afraid," Granville said. "I spoke with the hospital earlier, and he's still unconscious."

Which was an exaggeration, though unfortunately not much of one. At best, Randall's setback meant he wasn't improving as quickly as the doctor had hoped. Though they still said he was holding his own, whatever that might mean.

"Sad news. Sorry to hear it," Draper said. "So let's see if we can do something about the scum that got him, shall we?"

"Indeed. I gather you followed up with Konrad about the other lawyers," Granville said. "Are you getting anywhere with the story?"

"I have a few other names," Draper said guardedly. "But before we get into that, is this the same deal as last time? We share information, I don't publish until there's been an arrest, but I get the exclusive?"

"That's the one," Granville said. "You good with that?"

"I am indeed," Draper said as a foamy jug of beer and three glasses were set in front of them.

"This round's on me," Granville said, waving away Draper's protests and handing several coins to the bartender. "Have one yourself," he told the fellow, adding another coin.

"Thank ye' kindly," the bartender said. "We have fresh sandwiches available if you're hungry. Roast beef, a nice thick cut."

"The food's good here," Draper said. "And lots of it."

Granville glanced at Scott and Trent, who both nodded. Trent was still unnaturally silent, which was a concern. The food would do him good.

And it was nearly two. No wonder he was hungry. "Two apiece, and with chips. Thanks."

Scott looked up filling their glasses, leaving a thick rim of foam atop the amber liquid. "He means French fries," he said with a grin, which the bartender returned.

"O' course," said that individual over his shoulder as he hurried back to the bar.

"IPA?" Granville asked Draper as he accepted a brimming glass from Scott.

"Naturally. I won't drink anything else," Draper said. He raised his glass. "To Randall."

They drank, and Granville leaned forward. "So, about these lawyers," he said. "What do you know?"

"Not enough," Draper said. "I can't get anyone to admit to a thing. Not on record, anyway. But just between us? I can't see any of them doing it."

"Not enough anger?"

"No, the anger's there. Though I couldn't get a read on where it's coming from. But what I couldn't find is a reason for the attack on Randall. Not even a suggestion that it was a "heat of the moment" reaction."

"But why would they admit something like that to a reporter?" Scott asked. "They know the law better'n anyone."

"I didn't expect a confession," Draper said. "But in this business, you learn to hear the truth—and the lies—in what isn't said."

"So what did you hear?" Granville asked.

"Trumped up anger, and not much more. Not enough for a decent story, not even a photo cutline," Draper said. "What have you found?"

"I'm leaning towards one of them hiring thugs to administer the actual beating," Granville said.

"But which one?"

"And that would be the question," Granville said. "I spoke with Konrad this morning, and he suggested Lessing."

"Did he now? That's interesting," Draper said.

"I thought so. Why do you?"

"Because they're rivals. They specialize in the same areas of the law. And from what I've noted over the years, they don't like each other much. I've even heard rumors that there was a girl involved."

"So Konrad might be trying to take down a rival, then? That could explain it," and Granville filled Draper in on what Konrad had said.

The reporter laughed heartily. "You've never seen Konrad in court, have you?"

"No, why?"

"Because he just described himself."

Granville and Scott exchanged glances. Scott rolled his eyes, which summed up Granville's own feelings nicely.

"I'm done with these idiots," he said. "Scott and I are meeting with Gurak later. We'll see if he can at least tell us something useful."

"Gurak, is it? That should prove interesting. If I didn't have a deadline, I'd insist on coming along, just for the entertainment value."

"I take it you know Gurak?"

"Of him, at least," the reporter said. "He's a bully, but not nearly as lethal as he thinks he is. Or as Dagan was. I wish you luck."

Draper shook his head, his luxuriant mustache quivering, as if in sorrow at Granville's fate. "The least I can do is buy another round before you go. Sustenance for your journey, as it were."

"How could I say no?"

When the ferry finally docked in Victoria, Emily found a porter to help her with her bags. Then her eyes searched the dock for the carriage her aunt usually hired. There it was. That was a relief.

Then she looked a little closer. Aunt Louisa hadn't just sent the carriage to meet Emily, she'd come herself.

Spotting her aunt sitting so straight-backed on the leather upholstered seat, Emily's heart sank. Aunt Louisa would want to hear about the wedding, and who was there, and what the bride wore. Every tiny detail of it.

She'd probably want to know even more details about the planning of Emily's own wedding.

Emily's step slowed. She dreaded the thought of the next half hour, filled with society gossip and uncomfortable questions, when all she could think of was getting back to finding Betsy's killer.

But Aunt Louisa surprised her. Oh, she wanted to hear all the details of Emily's trip. And she was full of questions. But not a single one of them was about weddings.

Instead, she wanted to hear about what Emily had found out in her search for the man who'd killed Betsy.

And she wanted to tell Emily everything she herself had managed to uncover.

And that she'd invited Mrs. Herron for tea the next day, so that all of them could compare notes.

Emily nearly laughed aloud. She'd been wrong—she wasn't solving this case on her own. She had a team here, too. They might have no experience in finding a killer, but they brought other strengths.

Far from being stalled, her case was moving forward almost too quickly. Suddenly she was scrambling to catch up.

DINNER THAT EVENING was a quiet affair, with just Emily and her aunt present.

"I know you've had a long day, so I had Lau prepare simple dishes that we could serve ourselves," Aunt Louisa said as they seated themselves at one end of the long mahogany table.

Emily gave her a sharp look. "You want to talk more about the case," she said.

Aunt Louisa smiled. "My ridiculous curiosity demands all the details of your investigation," she said. "And perhaps I can help. We're private now. It was harder in the carriage."

Which was true enough, since the carriage driver could hear every word.

Emily began to describe her visit to Vancouver's Chinatown in colorful detail, including the meeting with Wong Sung. When she was done, Aunt Louisa sat back with a look of satisfaction on her face.

While Emily sat back with a small frown on hers.

Aunt Louisa noticed immediately. "What's wrong?" she asked.

"I hear things differently when I'm telling you about them," Emily said. Her frown deepened.

Aunt Louisa nodded as if this made sense to her. "And?" she said.

Emily laced her fingers together and contemplated them, not

sure any of it was making sense to her. "I was told a thief was hired to steal the Herron's pottery," she said slowly, thinking out loud.

"Go on," Aunt Louisa said.

"And that thief 'worked with' a hasty man. It was this hasty man who killed poor Betsy."

Aunt Louisa just nodded. Bless her for not asking the obvious questions. Not yet.

"I was also told that the man who hired the thief deals with the *tongs* in Chinatown here," Emily said slowly.

Her aunt frowned at this, but kept her silence.

"And that man hired the thief, but he didn't hire the hasty man —Betsy's killer," Emily finished.

"I think I'm following you," Aunt Louisa said. "And this is worrying you because…?"

"Because based on Ying's obvious fear when Chinatown was mentioned, I thought the man who killed Betsy had to be Chinese," Emily said. "And since the man who hired the thief also does business with the *tongs*…"

"That seemed to confirm it," her aunt said.

"Yes."

"We're assuming that the Collector didn't hire the thief himself, I take it."

"No, I was told so. Or rather, I was told that the man who hired the thief doesn't live in Victoria. And I think our collector must do so."

"I would agree. So it isn't the Collector," Aunt Louisa said. "But…" she began.

Emily held up a hand to forestall the question. "And the hasty man who killed Betsy is not Chinese either."

"Not Chinese?"

"No," Emily said slowly, still thinking it through. "Though apparently the thief is from Chinatown."

"How trustworthy is this information?" Aunt Louisa asked.

"Not at all," Emily said promptly. "But I can't see how anyone has anything to gain by lying about this."

"So where does the Chinatown connection fit? And the *tongs*?"

"I don't know. Yet," Emily said. "And Mr. Ying isn't talking, so we're just guessing about what he is afraid of. Maybe he's afraid of the thief who was hired to steal the pottery? If that man was some kind of enforcer for the *tongs*. And Mr. Ying knows what he is capable of...?"

"That sounds possible," Aunt Louisa said.

"Or perhaps Mr. Ying is afraid of the hasty man, who is the actual killer."

"The killer who isn't Chinese," Aunt Louisa said. Now she was frowning, too.

"Yes. That killer," Emily said, intent on her own line of thought. "The other maids said that Mr. Ying and the killer had an argument on the stairs, right before Betsy was killed."

"So Ying definitely knows who the killer is."

"Yes. But he isn't talking," Emily said. "It's definitely possible the killer threatened Mr. Ying then. But if the killer is not Chinese, then why does any mention of Chinatown make Mr. Ying nervous?"

"What if the killer is someone who is known and valued in Chinatown?" Aunt Louisa suggested. "Even though he isn't Chinese."

"Yes, that might make sense," Emily said. "But why would the killer—the 'hasty man'—be involved in the theft of the Herron's pottery in the first place?"

"Well, if the killer really isn't Chinese, then perhaps he is someone who works for the Collector," Aunt Louisa said.

"So the Collector might have sent the hasty man in order to protect his own interests?" Emily said. "That could be possible, I suppose. Though why would the Collector need to hire a Chinese thief, if he already had the hasty man working for him?"

"Misdirection?" Aunt Louisa said. "The actual theft was done by a hired thief, someone with no connection to the Collector at all."

Emily frowned. "That sounds awfully complicated, especially if the Collector had sent his own man along too."

Aunt Louisa leaned forward a little, clearly caught up in the case. "Or what if the thief had to be Chinese? Perhaps Ying refused to work with a thief who wasn't Chinese."

"There were a lot of fresh fruit and vegetable deliveries to the house on the day of the tea," Emily said thoughtfully. "A Chinese thief would blend in."

"That could be it," Aunt Louisa agreed. "Or perhaps the Collector arranged to hire the thief through one of the *tongs*, and then decided he couldn't trust such a man with his precious new acquisition."

She smiled at Emily. "We collectors can be a suspicious, paranoid lot."

"I've noticed," Emily said, almost smiling at the thought. Then she focused on the mystery in front of them. "So the Collector sent his own man along to make sure the pottery was safe? I can see that happening."

"Whoever the Collector is, he's a very poor judge of people," Aunt Louisa said tartly. "Stealing the pottery was bad enough. But sending a fellow who would end up killing an innocent young woman over it? Criminal stupidity."

"I know," Emily said, and they sat in silence for moment, mourning a young life lost.

Then Emily looked up sharply. "Wait a minute. Maybe we're still making this too complicated. We have only your cook's word that someone from a *tong* is involved at all. And you said yourself that he is young."

"He has proven less experienced than I'd thought when I hired him," Aunt Louisa said. "But he is a good worker. And with the present shortage of experienced cooks..." She let the words trail off, and gave a resigned shrug.

Emily was still focused on remembering exactly what Wong Sun had said about the killer.

"Wong Sun named the killer a hasty man, one with a bad temper. And no judgement." She paused, her mind making connections that she hadn't considered before. "That sounds to me like someone with an obsession. And if he isn't Chinese..."

"He sounds to me like a collector," her aunt said on a sigh.

"What if whoever wanted the Herron's pottery grew obsessed with the idea of owning what is apparently a unique collection?"

Emily said. "And decided to participate in the robbery itself? Is that even possible?"

"I wish I could say it wasn't," Aunt Louisa said. "But I have seen collectors caught up in the frenzy of need to possess a particular object."

"You have?" Emily tried to imagine it.

Her aunt nodded. "Yes. Oh, not in a situation as serious as this one, of course. In one case, the collector simply paid far more than they could afford to obtain a prized item. And in another, the collector was utterly relentless in persuading the original owner to sell."

"But could anyone, even in that kind of frenzy, actually kill a young woman? Just over pottery?" Emily was appalled all over again as she said the words.

"I've heard the argument made that we all have the ability to kill," Aunt Louise said. "In order to protect that which we hold most dear."

"But... pottery?"

Her aunt patted her arm. "It might not be a collector."

"But we can't ignore the possibility."

"No. We can't."

They looked at each other.

"So where do we go from here?" Aunt Louisa asked her.

"We work the case from two ends," Emily said decisively. "Chinatown for the connection with the thief, and the Collector for the connection to the hasty man."

"Both of which sound potentially dangerous," Aunt Louisa said. "We'll have to be careful."

Emily nodded.

"Where will you start?"

"Since we're meeting with Caroline Herron for tea tomorrow," Emily said. "I think I'll ask her to accompany me to Chinatown beforehand, since she seems to know it fairly well. Do you want to come with us?"

"No, I want to ask a few questions about my fellow collectors. But we can compare notes over tea."

Emily smiled. "Be careful, then."

"Of course," her aunt said. "But what do you hope to learn in Chinatown? If the thief was hired there, they are certainly not going to tell you."

"Maybe not," Emily said. "However, I intend to ask about rumors of someone who collects pottery and also has ties to Chinatown."

The plan sounded weak to her own ears, so it didn't surprise her that Aunt Louisa gave her a skeptical look.

"If that's what you want to ask, why not talk to my cook again?" Aunt Louisa said. "It's possible Lau knows something that might be helpful. And he's unlikely to try to kill you. Unlike whoever you might try to question in Chinatown."

"You don't mind?"

"Not as long as I can join you," Aunt Louisa said with a smile that looked suspiciously like a grin.

Aunt Louisa's kitchen was warm and welcoming with the scent of tonight's chicken casserole and the bread for tomorrow, though Mr. Lau looked surprised to see them. And none too pleased, either, in Emily's estimation. She wondered why.

Was it because they had invaded his domain unexpectedly? Or was he reluctant to talk further about the theft of the Herron's pottery, and the death of the young woman that had followed?

Her guess was the latter. It seemed obvious. And neither he nor Mr. Ying had wanted to talk about the *tongs* at all. Emily's presence in his kitchen probably warned him, quite accurately, what the subject of their conversation was likely to be.

For a moment she wondered what it must be like to be in his position—he was young, his English still shaky, and, judging by tonight's meal, he lacked the polish an older cook like Mr. Ying had acquired. He probably feared risking his job by displeasing his employer, despite the local shortage of good cooks. He hadn't proven himself yet.

But clearly he feared something or someone else even more.

She gave him a smile, hoping to set him at ease, and waved

towards the table. "Why don't we all sit down. I have a few small questions for you."

Rather than reassured, he looked even more spooked. Which wasn't the reaction she'd been hoping for.

"We talked before I left town about Mr. Ying, and the Herron's stolen pottery," Emily said in her calmest voice.

Mr. Lau glanced over at his employer, then nodded once.

"I'm not asking you about the thief who took the Herron's pottery," Emily said. "I'm more interested in the man who bought it. And I have heard a rumor that he is a white man."

Mr. Lau's eyes widened a little, but he said nothing.

Emily let that thought hang for a moment. Then she continued. "This white man supposedly does business with the *tongs*. Have you ever heard of such a person?"

"*Tongs* do business with some white men," Mr. Lau said.

"Have you ever heard a rumor that one of these white men also collects pottery?" Emily asked him.

"Maybe."

"And do you know this man's name?" Emily said.

Mr. Lau shook his head.

"Or anything about him?"

"People say he like the fragrant smoke," Mr. Lau said.

The man who had bought Mrs. Herron's stolen earthenware was an opium addict? That shocked Emily.

But could she trust what Mr. Lau was telling them?

"Is this man the reason Mr. Ying was so afraid?" Emily asked.

Mr. Lau gave a quick nod.

Too quick? Emily wondered. What did Mr. Lau stand to lose if anyone learned of this conversation? Could she trust what he was telling them?

Still, at least he was answering her questions.

"Who threatened Ying?" Aunt Louisa asked.

Now Mr. Lau looked even more wary.

"Did someone from one of the *tongs* threaten Mr. Ying?" Emily asked, testing him.

He dipped one shoulder. "Maybe. I not know."

"Is there anything you can tell us that might help save Mr. Ying's life?" Emily asked.

"No." The single syllable was flat and harsh.

Emily exchanged glances with her aunt, who shook her head slightly. Clearly she thought he was done answering questions, and Emily agreed with her. Pushing Mr. Lau harder now would only make things worse, though she suspected he knew more than he was saying.

It was so frustrating.

But once she learned more, she might be able to ask better questions. Ones that would convince this man to tell them what he knew.

"So what do we do next?" Aunt Louisa asked when they were back in the dining room.

"We look for someone who collects naturalist earthenware, and is addicted to the opium pipe," Emily said. Flatly.

Aunt Louisa drew in a harsh breath. "Is that what fragrant smoke means?"

"Yes, I'm afraid so," Emily said. "Though I'm not sure I trust your cook's information. If it's true, though, we will have to be extremely careful about how we ask questions. It isn't the kind of conversation that will be overlooked by whoever the guilty party is."

"No, indeed not," Aunt Louisa said. "And if it isn't true?"

"If your cook is frightened enough of someone to lie about everything? Then I suspect we need to be even more careful."

Aunt Louisa nodded. "Yes. But if I drop a word or two in the right ear, it might start a rumor that would flush out the man we're looking for."

"Be careful, Aunt Louisa," Emily said. "Someone out there is dangerous. And more than willing to kill to protect himself."

Aunt Louisa just smiled. "Don't worry, dear. I'm not a fool."

"I never thought you were," Emily said. "But I do think our killer is likely both charming and devious. As well as lethal."

"Oh, my."

"And I have an idea as to how we can expose him. Aunt Louisa, when does the Collector's Society meet again?"

"Not until next month. Why?"

"I think we should host a dinner party for them," Emily said. "But next month is too far away. I'd like to have everyone come this Thursday night."

Aunt Louisa looked intrigued, but a touch worried. "I think that a wonderful idea, but we can't hold it here. Lau is nowhere near a capable enough cook to pull off something like that."

"I thought of asking Mrs. Herron. I suspect she'd be willing to undertake it, even without Mr. Ying. Because of Betsy."

"I suspect you're right, dear. But this is short notice."

"I know," Emily said. "I'll call her tonight, and ask. Which reminds me. I need to telephone Granville first, before he thinks I've confronted the killer in Chinatown or something equally awful," Emily said, rising and shaking the creases out of her long skirts. "He worries too much."

"He might have reason," Aunt Louisa said under her breath as Emily turned towards the hall.

"I heard that."

A soft laugh, and her aunt's softly spoken words followed her. "You're very lucky, you know."

As Emily waited for the call to connect through to Granville's office in Vancouver, she considered her aunt's words. She was very lucky, and she knew it. Though she had the odd feeling that on this topic, she and her aunt were referring to very different things. And that she really didn't want to know what her aunt was thinking.

Then the call connected and Granville's voice drove the annoying speculation out of her head.

"Emily?"

"Granville. You're working late. Is it very busy?"

"No, I'm just catching up on a few things after our move. Obviously you made it safely to Victoria."

"I did indeed," Emily said. "With no incidents at all. And how are things there?"

"We've been focusing on our search for the big fish today."

"Is that going well?"

"Not in the slightest," he said pleasantly, and she laughed.

"Wasn't it you that reminded me that cases take time and patience?" she teased him.

"I take it your case is going well, then?"

"Not in the slightest," she said, and he chuckled.

"You'll have to marry me. No one else would be able to tolerate either of us," he said.

Emily had to rub her throat before she could get the words out.

"Oh, I intend to marry you," she said. "I'm not letting you get away." She waited a beat. "My aunt would never forgive me."

He laughed at that, the deep sound reverberating down the crackling line. "So how is it really going?" he asked. "Are you seeing any progress at all?"

"It feels like all I've done is gather more facts that don't fit together," she said on a sigh. "There is one thing, that struck me as unusual. And might suggest the link between the Chinatowns in Vancouver and Victoria."

"Oh?"

"By the way, how is Lizzie, these days?" she asked, hoping he'd make the connection she needed him to. "I recently learned that she and my collector share a relaxing pastime."

Lizzie was recovering from an addiction to the opium pipe, an addiction that Mr. Lau had just told her the Collector shared.

"Hmmm," he said. Then the line crackled so loudly it was a moment before he could say anything else. "And you think that pastime might be the connection we were looking for last Friday?"

"That's certainly what I wondered," she said. "It seems to fit, doesn't it?"

"It does."

"Unfortunately it just opens up more questions for me," she said. "It doesn't solve any of them. You?"

He was silent for a long moment. Thinking? Or was someone else there? Why was he working so late?

It didn't sound like his case was going any better than hers. And he hadn't mentioned what the big fish was up to. Her arms prickled up in pins and needles at the thought.

The silence stretched too long, but before she could decide whether to ask what was going on there, he deflected the question.

"Why do I get the feeling I won't be seeing you until you've solved this case—and finished visiting your aunt," he asked lightly.

"Probably because it's true," Emily said.

"If I can be of any assistance in helping you solve the case faster, I'm more than ready to do it," he said.

Emily had to laugh. "Flatterer," she said.

"But you will be careful, won't you?" he said, his voice turning serious.

"Of course," she said, making the decision in that instant not to tell him about the dinner she was contemplating. Not until Mrs. Herron had agreed, and she knew for sure it was happening. "I'm not actually going to arrest anyone, you know. Now tell me about your case."

"I have six possible suspects," he said. "Two of whom might be guilty."

He still sounded tense. "If you only knew which two," she said mournfully, and he laughed.

"You're coming to know me too well," he said.

She smiled at that, glad he couldn't see her face, and the worried look she was sure it still carried. "Everything is all right there, though?"

"Of course it is," he said. Too quickly? "And with you?"

"Yes," she said. "I'm just impatient."

"I know. But both our cases will come clear in time."

"How much time?" she asked, getting the laugh she was looking for.

But it was too hard, this non-discussion that anyone could be listening to, when what she needed was to really talk to him. It would have to wait.

"Look, my aunt is waiting," she said. "I'll call you tomorrow night, all right?"

"See that you do," he said lightly.

And she hung up, feeling more frustrated than ever that she couldn't discuss things with him properly over an open telephone line. She wished she could just ask him to catch the next ferry over. And he'd do it, too. She knew it.

Regardless of the damage it would cause to his case, or even to his professional reputation.

Which was why she'd never ask.

By the time Granville and Scott arrived at the Black Bull just after eight, they had to fight their way through a boisterous crowd. The pub occupied the whole of a large and decrepit warehouse, and it was already packed to its corrugated tin walls. It took ten minutes to get near the long wooden bar, rough-cut from some enormous tree, and they had to yell to place an order.

Still, the ale was good, and cold enough to almost make up for the heat that had built up under the old tin roof. Granville headed for a spot along the back wall where they could watch the noisy crowd without being too obvious about it. At the far end, two musicians were setting up, both fiddlers tonight. He wished them well, trying to be heard over this crowd.

Several tired looking parties came in, and the noise level approached a roar.

"I forgot third shift at Hastings Mill lets out around now," Scott hollered in Granville's ear. "We should have come earlier."

Granville was watching the door. It was close to nine. He'd expected Gurak to be late, copying his former boss. A ripple of movement just inside the door told him the fellow had arrived.

Five men walked into the space created by the ripple—all

wearing the same cheap black suits as the three they'd fought off earlier. Gurak was tall and heavily muscled, but despite a deep scowl, he lacked Dagan's sense of menace.

Granville fought back a grin. No point alienating the man before he had to. "Looks like he's trying to convince people he reigns supreme here," he said to Scott. "Not sure it's working."

"That's why you suggested meeting him here? Give him a false sense of security? Sneaky," Scott said, making no effort to hide his own grin.

Granville shrugged. "Flies. Honey," he said, at which Scott laughed, the deep sound quickly lost in the din surrounding them.

"If Lessing is involved, Gurak can give him to us. We need his help," Granville said, just loud enough for Scott to hear him. He left his ale on a nearby table and began to make his way towards the door, knowing Scott would have his back.

"And we have nothing to trade in return? Oh, this'll be good," his partner said from behind him.

As he approached Gurak, Granville was careful to keep his hands open and slightly away from his sides, away from his knife and his gun. Gurak's thugs watched him cautiously, but didn't stop him. And when he reached out a hand, Gurak met it in a brief shake.

"We need to talk," he said.

"The first round's on you," Gurak said.

"Fine. Let's take this outside."

Gurak nodded, and motioned for Granville to take the lead. Granville felt the hairs on the back of his neck rise as he turned his back on the five men, but he hadn't come here with the intention of challenging the fellow.

He moved far enough away from the door that the noise was reduced to a buzz. The sun was nearly down, and the first streaks of red tinted the sky, silhouetting the familiar outlines of downtown buildings to the west. He could clearly see Gurak's face, still scowling, as the man came nearer.

Gurak stopped half a foot from him. "Well?" he said, challenging him.

"The fellow who hired your three men today," Granville said, as Gurak's men ranged silently behind him, and Scott took up his stance at Granville's shoulder. "What do you know about him?"

"Why?" Gurak asked.

"You trust him, then?" Granville asked, deliberately not responding to the brusque question.

"The pay's good. What's it to you?"

"Did you know he sent your men after my partner and I?"

Gurak's scowl deepened.

So he had known.

"I don't have a problem with you," Granville said. Not yet, anyway. "Which is why I let the three who attacked us go. It's the man who hired you I want."

"That didn't work so good for Dagan."

"He shot and killed two men. You haven't."

Gurak's stance relaxed the slightest bit. The fellow had believed him? Interesting.

"You have problems with the man that hired me?"

"I do," Granville said, wondering how Lessing would have connected with a thug like Gurak. Perhaps he'd defended him in court at some point?

If it was Lessing.

His mind went to Randall, who had barely survived the beating he'd received. Had Gurak's men been the ones who attacked his friend?

He shelved the thought for now. He'd deal with it later. And someone would pay.

"Why?" Gurak asked.

Granville just looked at him, his face set.

Gurak shrugged heavy shoulders. "What you need to know?"

"Everything."

Gurak said nothing. His scowl returned.

"Did he give you a name?" Granville clarified.

"No.

"How did he set up your assignment?"

"He send someone to meet with me."

"Here?"

"No, a bar down on Dupont Street. This morning."

"Describe him."

Gurak rocked back on his heels, as if trying to gain a little distance from him.

Granville wondered if he'd let the fury he was feeling show a little too much. Then decided he didn't care. "Well?" he demanded.

"Brown suit, broad brimmed hat. Not tall." And he measured a height of about five foot six with his hand against his own chest. "Brown hair, pale blue eyes. Easy to forget."

Except he'd matched the description of Lessing that Granville had been given earlier quite nicely. "How old?"

"More than thirty. He look down, look away. Scrawny little man." Gurak's disdain for the fellow who'd paid him leaked through his words.

So if Gurak was telling the truth, Lessing didn't want to be noticed. Or remembered.

"Anything else that struck you about him?"

Gurak started to shake his head, then stopped. "He is cheap. Tries to underpay me."

Something else to ask about Lessing. He thanked Gurak for the information, politely, but with an edge in his voice that had the gangster looking nervous. As they strode away from the Black Bull, Granville noted that Scott was giving him a sideways look.

"What?"

"I should've never doubted you," his partner said with a broad grin.

"Enjoyed that, did you?"

"Yup. Somehow I doubt he'll try to kill you again."

"Too bad. I'm not done with Gurak yet."

Granville's tone had Scott looking hard at him. "What? Did I miss something?"

"I think his boys were the thugs who nearly killed Randall."

Scott stopped in his tracks, stared at him. "Them? On Lessing's orders? You think Lessing is the big fish?"

"It seems possible. Or someone is working very hard to make us think so."

Scott's lips tightened. "We need to take care of him, whoever he is. And soon."

"I can assure you, we will make him pay," Granville said, and it was a vow. "And Gurak and his boys, as well."

3 8

Wednesday, September 5, 1900

The following morning Granville woke early, and glanced around his unfamiliar bedroom, feeling disoriented for a moment. Without a carpet, and the room tended to echo. In fact, the whole place echoed. And it smelt far too new.

But time and more furnishings would take care of those. At least he now had a bed, with a mattress that was just firm enough.

Ironically, he'd just spent the night in the best bed he'd slept in since leaving England more than two years before. Yet between thinking about the previous evening's confrontation with Gurak, and about Emily's call, he'd been awake half the night.

It worried him, knowing she was alone in another town, on an island as large as Britain. Separated from him by miles of ocean. And she was hunting a killer.

It wasn't much past six when he got to the office. He spent some time updating his case notes, and even more time staring out the window at the as the sky gradually lightened, listening to the clatter and clang as the city gradually wakened. He was relieved when the clock struck the quarter hour, and he could leave to meet Scott for breakfast.

He strolled into Mary's Diner just before seven and scanned the room. It was busy with the usual morning crowd, the air thick with the heavy smell of frying bacon and strong coffee. He was hungry, and everything smelled good. Scott was already there, and had snagged a corner booth. Good.

Granville tipped his hat to Mary as he passed the counter, and she winked, patted her hair under the hairnet and grabbed the coffee pot. "The usual?" she said to both of them as she poured his cup and refilled Scott's.

"Please," Scott said, and Granville nodded.

"Coming up," she said, hollering the order to the kitchen as she made her way around the tables, filling coffee cups as she went.

Granville watched her go, amused despite himself at what he thought of as diner ballet. He kept expecting her to run into someone, or pour coffee on them, but she lightly twisted and turned her bulky body from one end of the restaurant to the other without a single mishap.

He looked back to see Scott watching him. "What?"

"What's eating you now?" Scott countered.

There was no point arguing. Scott knew him too well. "I talked to Emily last night," Granville said.

Then neither of them said anything as another waitress deftly slid heavy plates of eggs, sausage and toast in front of them.

"Emily's all right?" Scott asked in swift concern as soon as she'd left.

"I think she's fine. It's hard to tell over an open telephone line. Except that she sounds as nearly as frustrated with her case as we are with ours."

"Speak for yourself," Scott said, deadpan.

"Eat your sausages," Granville said. "She did have one new piece of information to share though."

"Well? Don't keep me waiting," Scott said, and forked up a mouthful of sausage.

"It seems the collector who bought the stolen pottery is an opium eater," Granville said, and dug into his own meal.

"What? This is the pottery the girl was killed over? And the guy who bought it has a link to Chinatown?"

"It is and he does," Granville said. He reached for his coffee mug, drained it and signaled for a refill.

"And?"

"If we believe what Wong Sun told us, then someone hired a thief to steal that pottery collection for the collector. And that thief was Chinese," Granville said, slowly spreading butter on a thick slice of toasted sourdough.

"Go on," Scott said.

"If the collector smokes opium, it means he's at least somewhat familiar with Victoria's Chinatown. Emily suspects that the thief was hired there," Granville said. "And I think she's right."

"But I thought Wong Sun said that someone other than this collector hired the thief," Scott said.

"He implied it. But all the Chinese men who are even peripherally connected to this theft live in Victoria. And apparently all of them are nervous every time Chinatown is mentioned. Including the fellow who is currently in jail under suspicion of committing that murder."

"And if the thief was brought over from Vancouver, you wouldn't think he'd still be hanging around making people nervous," Scott said. And took a swig of coffee. "I take it they're still scared?"

"They are. Which again suggests the hiring was local," Granville finished for him.

"That makes sense," Scott said. "So?"

"So I've been asking myself why this collector didn't hire the muscle he needed himself? If he's an opium eater, it means he has connections in Chinatown. Where the thief was hired."

Scott stared at him for a moment. "Maybe he feels safer if he's not linked so closely to the theft?"

"Perhaps. It also suggests some connection here, and most probably a criminal one. Someone who would hire the thief for him," Granville said.

"But isn't Emily's collector only interested in fifty-year old earthenware? Why would he have those kinds of connections?"

"A number of my father's friends were collectors," Granville said. "In my experience, a collector who collects only one thing is rare indeed."

"So you're thinking Emily's collector might collect something else? Something a criminal might be interested in?"

"That's it," Granville said.

"Which could be a good thing," Scott said. "More connections for us to follow."

Granville wasn't so sure of that. He didn't like to think of Emily drawing another criminal's attention in this case. It was bad enough that young Betsy's killer might be aware of her investigation.

"If we can find those connections quickly, it might help solve her case before the killer can harm anyone else," he said. Like Emily.

"So we find them quickly," Scott said. He was frowning, though. "But we have a lot of theories. Not much proof. Now what?"

Granville checked his pocket watch. "We have enough time to pay a quick call on Randall before we meet with the team."

THEY NEVER MADE it past the nurses on duty.

"I'm afraid you can't go in," the young nurse in the nun's habit said, holding up a slim hand as if to prevent them from going around her.

"Is Randall worse?"

"He needs quiet and rest until we determine the cause of his fever," she said.

"He's running a fever?" Granville said.

"I'm afraid so."

Any infection could be serious. "Will I be able to see him today?"

"I'm afraid you'll need to ask the doctor directly," she said firmly.

"Do you know when Dr. Serson will be available?"

"I'm afraid not."

He'd have to call later. There was no point asking anything now. He already knew he wouldn't get an answer.

WHEN HE AND Scott got back to the office, the meeting with the team was a brief one. Especially since Granville didn't want to share his worries about Randall. Or the ones about Emily, either.

Mac and Miss Kent looked tired, but he was relieved to see that Trent was looking more alert this morning, despite a spectacular black and purple bruise that covered half his face.

"I'll keep this short," Granville said. "We have information on Emily's case as well as about our big fish to share."

He briefed them on what Emily had told him, and the conclusions he and Scott had come to earlier. And on the meeting with Gurak the previous evening. When he finished, there was a little silence.

"It sounds to me as if you're leaning towards Lessing as the one behind all this," Mac said after a moment. "So would it make sense for Miss Kent and I to focus on Lessing, and on any interactions between him and Randall?"

"At this point, both Konrad and Gurak are pointing the finger at Lessing. And we know too little about the fellow," Granville said. "So yes, by all means dig into Lessing as deeply as you can.

Meanwhile, Scott, Trent and I will meet with Carver again, to get his take on the various lawyers involved. Miss Kent, could you have Miss Rizzo set that up for us around ten?"

"Of course," she said, making a note. "But if I may…?"

"By all means. Go ahead," he said.

"You aren't sure that Lessing is the one behind all this, are you?"

"No, I'm not," he said, smiling at her. "But how did you know?"

"You don't seem relieved to put a name to the big fish," she said. "Which suggests you have doubts."

"We'll make a detective of you yet," he said, and her cheeks turned crimson.

"Thank you," she said softly.

"Scott? Trent? What's your read on Lessing?"

"We don't know much about him, for all that everyone's telling us he's the bad guy," Scott said.

"Yeah. It feels like we're being railroaded," Trent said. "I don't like it."

Granville didn't either. Though he was relieved to see the lad was able to talk easily, despite his bruise.

"Which is why we keep digging," he said. "Why don't we all meet again at five this afternoon. There are answers out there somewhere, and it's our job to find them."

Carver's outer office was once again deserted. Glancing at an un-watered aspidistra growing forlornly in a corner, Granville wondered if the fellow could reinvent himself as a lawyer here. Or whether he'd end up having to leave town in order to establish himself somewhere new.

This time Carver must have been listening for them, though, because he came out to greet them immediately. If he was surprised to see the three of them, he covered it well, and his outstretched hand and welcoming smile didn't waver. Not even the sight of Trent's bruise elicited so much as a twitch.

Perhaps he might make it here after all.

"Granville," he said. "And Scott and Trent as well. I was pleased when your girl said you'd be by this morning. I gather things are pretty hectic for you, between this case and your office move."

"It's Randall's case I'm most concerned about," Granville said. "And I gather you have information for us?"

The lawyer nodded and ushered them into his office. "I don't like what I'm hearing," he said as he sat down, the well-worn leather of his oversized chair creaking slightly beneath him.

"About Randall?" Granville said.

"Yes. There's an animosity there, an anger against him that's disproportionate to the facts that your people have found, and anything I've been able to uncover," Carver said. "It isn't normal."

"As though someone is feeding that anger for their own purposes, perhaps?" Granville said.

"Yes. Just like that." Carver leaned back, frowning. "And I can't put my finger on where it's coming from."

"I heard a paler version of that from Konrad last week," Granville said. "I wondered if he was the source. But we've just had breakfast with the fellow…"

"Interrupted his breakfast, you mean," Trent said gleefully. Then subsided under Scott's glare.

"As I said," Granville said, forcing back a grin at the lad's cheek. "And much as I'd like to declare him the villain, I don't think he has enough spine. Not to beat someone that badly."

"Ah," Carver said thoughtfully. "He certainly seems to hate Randall, though."

"He sure does," Trent said.

"But I think I'd agree with your assessment," Carver finished.

"Konrad pointed us towards Lessing, another lawyer," Granville added. "Said he could see Lessing hiring someone to kill Randall. I don't know the fellow. Do you?"

"Yes," Carver said. "He's slimy. And ruthless in court. And someone who might not hesitate to deal with a threat, by whatever means."

"Which is what Konrad said, too. He also suggested Lessing had someone to attack Randall."

"Who?"

"A local thug, name of Lew Gurak," Granville said. "He used to be one of Dagan's men."

"Dagan? The one Randall made mincemeat of in court right before everyone learned I wasn't really dead?" Carver said. "I heard about that. It was hilarious. And more than a little frightening. Randall is beyond good."

"That's the one. It seems one of his henchmen assembled what remained of his old gang, and is back in business. Apparently

Lessing once hinted to Konrad that he'd hired Dagan's gang to deal with a recalcitrant witness in an earlier case."

"And you think this Gurak might be happy to kill Randall in revenge for Dagan?" Carver said.

"Dagan's men are stupidly loyal," Scott said.

Trent opened his mouth, but at a glance from Granville closed it again and sat back.

"I suppose Lessing could be have hired him," Carver agreed. He was frowning.

"Scott and I talked to Gurak last night," Granville said.

"He talked to you?" Carver sounded shocked.

"He did," Granville said, remembering his last run-ins with Dagan's boys with an inward smile. "And he also described the fellow who'd brought him the contract. Fellow matched Konrad's description of Lessing pretty closely."

Granville watched the lawyer's reaction closely. "You still don't think Lessing is our big fish, do you?"

"No, I don't. It just doesn't fit what I know of the fellow. Or this case."

"Sounds like you've given this a lot of thought," Scott said.

"I have. And whoever is after Randall likely won't be obvious," Carver said. "This whole thing feels as if someone slipped poison into a pool, where it's spread unnoticed, until all of it is poisonous. Only this time it's a pool of people."

It was an apt analogy, and hit into the heart of what had been niggling at Granville since Randall was attacked. "Nothing I know about Randall explains this level of aggression against him, either," he said. "And even from my small knowledge of lawyers, their reactions make no sense."

"Agreed," Carver said. "Every case has a winner and a loser. None of us win every case. Nor should we expect to. Though we'd never tell the client that, of course," he added with a wink.

Sobering immediately, he added, "I consider Peabody's attempt to sue Randall a ridiculous over-reaction. It makes him look like a fool. But planning to kill another lawyer over something like that? That is insane."

"It is certainly beyond reason," Granville said. "And it didn't stop with Peabody. Now there's a whole group of them. Someone is really good at this."

He felt the small hairs stand up on his arms at the thought. And what it might mean for Randall.

"We have to stop him," Scott said.

"We do," Granville agreed. "Unfortunately, it doesn't leave us with any suspects. From what I've been told, Lessing isn't a fellow who could spread poison without anyone noticing. Not subtle enough."

"No, subtle is not a word that describes Lessing," Carver said. "I can't see him as the one behind this. Not if we're right about the poison. Lessing doesn't know how to influence people."

"It's far too early in this case to dismiss him entirely, though," Granville said. "Even if you're right about what we're looking for."

"And we still don't have any idea why this is all happening?" Scott said. "Why Randall?"

Carver shrugged helplessly. "The genius of our poisoner is he's successfully blurred our ability to guess why he's after Randall."

"*And* who he is," Trent put in.

"Yes, but the one follows the other," Carver told Trent, who looked confused.

"No matter how carefully we dig into Randall's files, we're unlikely to spot the poisoner in the confusion he's created," Carver said.

"Then where do we go from here?" Trent asked, undaunted.

Granville and Carver looked at each other.

"Scott and I also paid a visit to a reporter," Granville said. "Draper has apparently been hounding Konrad for a story, and I wanted to follow up on it. He doesn't have much yet, but he's still digging. And the fellow has good instincts."

"So he might uncover some hint of whoever's behind all this," Carver said. "Makes sense. You'll follow up there?"

"Of course."

"And what are you planning now?" Scott asked Carver.

"Since we're dealing with someone who spreads their own kind of poison, I'll do some further digging into the six lawyers that make up that little conspiracy," Carver said. "Criminals who think they're invisible often get cocky. And careless."

"Have a look at their clients, too, if you will. It could still be one of them," Granville said.

Although he'd be very surprised if their big fish gave himself away so easily.

Then he wondered with a touch of wry amusement if someone this subtle—and this deadly—still qualified as a fish? If it was a deadly poisonous one, a pufferfish for instance, then perhaps he did.

"I'll be in touch with your office if I find anything," Carver was saying. "And you'll do the same?"

Granville agreed, refraining from mentioning that Carver still had no one answering his telephone. He sensed that the lawyer wasn't yet fully committed to resuming his practice. Though he couldn't fault the fellow's work on this case. Which was all he cared about right now.

Once Randall was safe, though, he just might have a chat with the fellow about his plans.

Despite his poor judgement when it came to getting involved with Gipson, Carver was a capable and creative lawyer. He'd bent the law, badly, but he'd more than made up for it by helping them bring the real culprits to justice.

And for some reason he liked the fellow. It would be a shame to lose him due to a few poor choices.

4 0

At ten on Wednesday morning, Caroline Herron's carriage stopped in front of her aunt's stately Tudor-style mansion, and Emily hurried out to meet it. The coachman was quick to hand her inside, and Caroline met her with a welcoming smile.

"Thank you again for agreeing to host the dinner for the Collector's Society," Emily said. "I'm hopeful it will get us closer to exposing Betsy's killer."

"Not at all," Caroline Herron said. "I am pleased to do so. I want to catch him just as badly as you do. And your aunt's offer of Lau's assistance helped immensely."

"As long as you're not expecting him to cook," Emily said with a sigh. "I am afraid it would not go well."

Caroline laughed. "No, I assure you. I have borrowed a very good cook from a friend of mine. But it is so good to have you back, my dear. I've missed you."

And she reached forward and gripped Emily's gloved hands in her own. "Without your help, I've made no progress at all in freeing Ying from his current imprisonment."

"I'm sorry to hear that. Though I do think we may be starting to make progress," Emily said. "And I also wanted to thank you again for agreeing to take me to Chinatown today."

"I'm looking forward to it," Caroline said with a smile. "But you feel we are making progress?"

"Yes, I do. I couldn't stop thinking about the case while I was away, and I have some new information. I think some of the pieces of this case are beginning to align."

"Oh?" Caroline said, straightening her back even further and giving Emily an alert look. "What has been happening? What have you found out?"

As they drove towards Chinatown, Emily filled her in on what she'd learned in Vancouver, as well as the discussion she'd had with Aunt Louisa the previous evening. Caroline listened attentively, but she didn't interrupt once until Emily had finished.

"But this is marvelous," Caroline said then. "What do you hope we can accomplish in Chinatown today?"

"I would really like to identify the thief who actually stole your pottery. He, of all people, is sure to have the answers we need."

"The thief being the man your informant said was Chinese?"

"Yes, exactly," Emily said. "But I am afraid that by asking about the thief in Chinatown, we'll lose our chance of getting any answers at all. Would you agree? Or do you happen know someone who might be able to get answers about who the thief is?"

"From everything you've just told me, I cannot think of anyone who could ask that question in Chinatown and actually get an answer," Caroline said frankly. "So, with that in mind, what do you intend to ask?"

"I'm hoping to hear rumors about our Collector. And since he seems to have stronger connections to Chinatown than we'd expected, I've been wondering if he might specialize in chinoiserie as well as early Victorian pottery."

"You don't think the connection is his opium smoking?" Caroline asked in surprise.

"What if it's more than that?" Emily said. She had been thinking about it since Granville's joking comment about chinoiserie. "It seems collectors often specialize in more than one type of collectible."

Caroline glanced over, and seemed to be studying Emily's face. "I can see where that might be a possibility. But do you really think this collector might be the one who killed Betsy?"

"I'd rather not think it," she said bluntly. "Collectors are as much a part of our social circles as you and I are. They seem no different from us—other than having a rather odd hobby."

"Agreed. And?"

"Someone who could kill an innocent girl for no real reason is a monster," Emily said. "I'd prefer to think Betsy's killer will be easily identifiable as a monster, once we find him. Not someone who appears in every way to be just like me. Or you."

She swallowed hard as she finished speaking. Everything about what she'd said made her feel ill. But that wasn't going to stop her. Not until she'd caught him.

Caroline nodded, and patted her hand. "But?" that lady said.

"But I have learned enough about collectors, from what my aunt tells me and from my own observation, to know we'd be remiss in ignoring the possibility that our hasty man is the Collector himself," Emily said. "Collectors have a passion for their own particular art form, and some have fewer moral restraints in their pursuit of that passion than others. I can believe—though not easily—that there might be one who would kill for their passion."

"I hate to agree with you," Caroline said. "But I've seen greed drive men to unspeakable deeds. From what you describe, collecting can become a form of greed. And one that might become as addicting—and destructive—as certain forms of gambling."

"Yes," she said. "That's an excellent comparison. And something we need to keep in mind today. In asking about the Collector, we might be looking for a killer driven by a compulsive form of greed. One who has poor judgement and worse impulse control."

"A 'hasty man', indeed," Caroline said. "So how do we do look for information on such a person here?"

"I thought we might visit several of the grocery stores you

mentioned that sell everything," Emily said. "With an eye to purchasing several choice pieces of Chinese porcelain."

And she smiled at her new friend. "Perhaps you could advise me on a few items for my dower chest. What do you think?"

"That," said Caroline decisively, "Is a devious but brilliant strategy. And I love shopping for chinoiserie."

"I saw that you had several lovely pieces in your home, and particularly admired the blue and white pieces. That's why I asked for your help," Emily said.

She just hoped Granville would forgive her for shopping for these things without him. After their most recent excursion to Chinatown, she suspected he'd have strong opinions on everything she bought today. She could only hope their tastes matched.

If not, she'd simply give the stuff away. They had too much else in common to let a little thing like a difference in their taste for exotic china come between them. Especially now.

THE FIRST STORE they stopped at stood right on Fisgard Street just past the intersection with Government. It was one of the more modern buildings, in the Italianate style, but decorated in bold reds and golds.

As she descended from the carriage, Emily looked around her with fascination. It felt very different standing on the broad planked sideway with people jostling by on either side of her, and she was glad it wasn't raining. Trying to avoid umbrellas here would be challenging.

Through the shop's doorway, she could smell herbs and spices, as well as the sharp scent of salted and dried fish. One odor was particularly overpowering, and she reached into her reticule for her handkerchief and held it against her nose for a moment.

Observing the motion, Caroline smiled. "Dried shark fin," she said. "Ying tells me it is a Chinese delicacy, but the smell is a bit overwhelming for the rest of us."

"I suspect the Chinese dislike the smell of Limburger cheese," Emily said, returning the smile.

"Probably. Shall we go in?"

At Emily's nod, Caroline led the way through the open doors. Inside the shop was crowded with goods packed on rows of wooden shelves, which created narrow aisles leading off every which way. Emily's eyes widened, and she stared from one row to the next.

The smell of dried fish was even stronger here, and the sheer variety of scents and colors and textures surrounding them felt overwhelming.

"I think I saw some interesting porcelain near one of the windows," Caroline said, and wound her way around a display of open baskets filled with unidentifiable dried foods towards the far side of the shop.

As they came to a halt in front of a set of shelves filled from floor to ceiling with porcelain patterned in all colors, the shopkeeper, a somewhat rotund Chinese man shorter than either of them, came forward and greeted Caroline by name.

"It is my honor to see you again," he said. "How may I help you today?"

Emily noted that he wore a dark, English style suit, but his long queue was wound around his head in the Chinese style. The blend of cultures here was fascinating.

"It is my young friend here who might need your assistance," Caroline said, indicating Emily with a sweep of her hand. "She is particularly interested in Chinese porcelain."

"Ah. Many different styles available here, if you not see something pleasing to you."

"I'm looking for pieces for my new home, since I'll be marrying soon," Emily said, then blushed furiously at talking about her wedding to anyone, much less a stranger.

"I wish you good fortune. Your husband is a lucky man."

"Thank you," Emily said, trying to beat back her blushes.

"I like these blue and white pieces," and she gestured towards a shelf in front of her. "But while lovely, they seem to be intended for everyday use. I am looking for more decorative pieces."

The fellow nodded. "Ah, yes. Perhaps large vases interest you? Or containers? Also blue and white?"

"Yes, I think so," Emily said. "And I'd be interested in older pieces, too, if you have them? Antiques."

"Come, then," and he turned to make his way deeper into the store, past shelves filled with a jumble of items, from bowls and dishes to cooking pots, decorative fans, lengths of silk, woven baskets and bamboo furniture.

Emily couldn't stop staring from one shelf to the next, wishing she had time to stop and examine everything. She had to remind herself that she was there for a reason. She could visit here again, and take her time. After she'd found young Betsy's killer.

They stopped in front of a display of large porcelain vases and containers in various patterns of blue and white. "This is very favored," the shopkeeper said.

"They are beautiful," Emily said, leaning closer to examine the intricately painted detail of a willow tree by a bridge on one vase. Perhaps a pair of these, one either side of the hearth in the parlor... "Caroline, what do you think of this style?"

"You have excellent taste, my dear," that lady said. "A pair of these would be a good start, particularly if you were looking to build a collection over time."

Recalled to her purpose, Emily looked about for the shopkeeper, who had stepped a discreet distance back from them. He was still close enough to be in earshot though, she realized with amusement.

"Well, I do like these," she said. "And I may indeed buy both. But... I had hoped to start with several much older pieces."

"I can find antique vases for you if you wish?"

"Yes," Emily said slowly, making sure her voice held a hesitation. Then she turned impulsively towards Caroline. "Oh, I don't know. I don't know enough about buying this kind of china, and I'd hate to make a mistake."

Caroline smiled at her a little condescendingly and looked

towards the shopkeeper. "Do you know someone in town who is an expert and collects these porcelains?"

Emily held her breath, hoping he wouldn't simply refer her back to Mr. Allen at Allen and Cox.

The shopkeeper bowed slightly. "Yes, I can give you names if you like? Both are Englishmen."

"That would be wonderful," Emily said, clasping her hands together in assumed joy.

"And these vases?" the shopkeeper asked.

Emily glanced back at the shelf. They were lovely. She was sure Granville would appreciate them. Her gaze flicked to Caroline, who gave a half-nod.

She needed those names. And why not buy the vases? They were much more interesting that the household linens her mother wanted her to take in interest in.

"Yes, I'll take them," Emily said. "Can you ship them?"

"Of course."

She left with a receipt for the two vases, and a carefully lettered list of two names.

That pattern was repeated in the next three establishments they visited, though Emily managed to make smaller purchases in all but one of them. In each case though, she left with a short list of names of collectors of chinoiserie, which she and Caroline compared when they were back in the carriage.

After the fifth shop, Caroline called a halt. "We'll be late for tea with your aunt if we don't stop now. And I'm exhausted."

Emily was too, but she hated to stop now. "Just one more," she said. "I'd like to be sure."

Caroline smiled, but shook her head. "You have one collector who is named on three of the five lists. Another who is named on all five lists. And both of them are hinted to be opium smokers. One of them strongly so."

"Mr. Carstairs," Emily said.

Something in her tone must have given away her dislike of the man, because Caroline gave her an enquiring look. As Emily explained how she'd met the fellow at the Collectors Society, and her impression of him, Caroline nodded.

"That fits with the man we're looking for. What of the other?"

"Mr. Gainer? I've not heard his name before. And so far no one has mentioned him having any interest in naturalist earthenware."

"So Mr. Carstairs may be the stronger suspect," Caroline said thoughtfully. "Good. Let us go and have tea, and see what your aunt has to say."

"But I'd still like to find something a little stronger than rumors about opium use…" Emily said as Caroline called for her carriage.

ONCE EMILY, her aunt and Mrs. Herron were ensconced in Aunt Louisa's cozy parlor, with a pot of tea and a plate of small pastries in front of them, Emily turned to her aunt and raised a questioning brow.

"You must have news," she said. "You are practically beaming."

"Indeed I have," Aunt Louisa said. "I spoke with several of the ladies of the Collector's Society earlier this morning. And I just happened to drop the rumor I had heard about a collector of naturalist earthenware who spends a great deal of time in Chinatown. And you'll never guess what they told me."

"They named Mr. Carstairs," Emily said with a tiny smile as her aunt goggled at her.

Thinking about it in the carriage, Emily had decided that Caroline was right. Given her own strong reaction to the man, and everything they'd learned in Chinatown, Mr. Carstairs was probably their strongest suspect.

That didn't mean she was going to forget about Mr. Gainer, however.

"Well. I am disappointed," Aunt Louisa said. "However did you know?"

"You looked so engaged by what you'd learned," Emily said. "I knew it had to be someone you knew. And whoever this is, they're fanatical about their collection. Of the three men we know who belong to the Society and collect mid-century earthenware, only Mr. Carstairs was even slightly interested when I wanted to discuss it. And he lost interest the minute he realized I wasn't a true collector."

She was also very relieved that her aunt didn't seem too upset that Mr. Carstairs might be responsible for the theft, and possibly even for Betsy's death. After seeing the interaction between the two of them at the last meeting of the Collector's Society, she still hadn't been sure if Aunt Louisa was simply enjoying flirting with a fellow collector, or if she was genuinely interested in him as a romantic prospect. Clearly it had been the former.

With that concern dealt with, she filled her aunt in on what she and Caroline had learned in Chinatown. "Have you ever heard of Mr. Gainer?"

Aunt Louisa nodded. "He attends meetings occasionally. And I'd heard that he is a pottery man, with an especial interest in chinoiserie. But I've never heard his name coupled with an interest in mid-Victorian pottery, so he's probably not the man we're looking for."

"Unless Mr. Gainer is an even more fanatical collector, one who hides his precious collection from everyone," Emily said. "Could that be possible?"

Her aunt looked thoughtful. "I suppose it could. I've heard rumors of a collector or two like that. Usually it means that much of their collection is illegally obtained."

"Which would fit here," Emily said.

"So you think either Mr. Carstairs or Mr. Gainer could be the collector who bought my stolen pottery?" Caroline asked.

"They seem the likeliest," Aunt Louisa said.

"I think so too." Emily said. "But did one of them kill Betsy?"

"I hate to think either of them could have done so," Aunt Louisa said. "And I can't really speak for Mr. Gainer. But Mr. Carstairs *is* passionate about his collecting."

"I don't trust him," Emily said. "But that doesn't mean he's a murderer. And we still have no more than rumors about opium smoking for either of them. And worse, no proof that there are no other collectors fond of the opium pipe that we haven't heard about."

"So how do we prove who it was? And more important, how do we tie either of them to the thieves, and the thieves to the murder?" Caroline asked. "They certainly aren't going to tell us."

Both women turned and looked at Emily.

"If it is one of them, we'll need help from the man himself to prove it," Emily said with a smile. "Which is the entire point behind this dinner party we're holding on Friday."

41

G ranville and Scott had returned to the office and continued the discussion of the case when the telephone on his desk rang. It was Emily. And things went from bad to worse.

Scott glanced up as he hung up the telephone. "Granville, what is it? Emily?"

His partner had probably guessed some of it from his end of the conversation, but he was too polite to let on.

"Yes. She's narrowed her list of suspects for the collector down to two," Granville said.

"You have names?"

"Carstairs and Gainer. Though at this point they are simply collectors of pottery or china who fit a certain set of criteria. Which doesn't help us much."

Scott looked at Granville. "And?"

"What do you mean?"

"If Emily can name the collector, she can send the police after him. But you look like someone just swiped your favorite suit."

"Emily is making plans to confront both of her suspects publicly," he said. "Her new friend is holding a dinner for the members of their society."

"She's what?"

He nodded. "And I can't talk her out of it."

"That's not good." Scott blew out a breath. "Wait a minute. She told you all that over a telephone line when the operator could be listening in?"

"No, she implied most of it. No one who didn't know most of the details already would have understood a word."

"And when is this dinner?"

"Tomorrow night."

"Not much time, then."

"No. It isn't. Good thing we're due to for an update," he said, glancing at his watch.

Walking into their meeting room with Scott at his side, Granville found the rest of the team, with the addition of Carver, waiting for them. Looking around the table, he felt the pressure of Emily's upcoming confrontation with the collectors—and perhaps a killer—bearing down on him.

Carver started to say something, and Granville held up a hand. "Miss Rizzo is bringing in the tea. Let's hold off on our discussion until then."

Once the biscuits were laid out and everyone had a cup of tea steaming in front of them, he looked around the table. "We need to start looking for any local links to Emily's collector, whoever he is," Granville said. "Are the names Carstairs and Gainer familiar to anyone?"

"Who're they?" Trent asked, just as Miss Kent spoke up.

"Yes, I think so," she said. "I've seen both names recently. They may be clients with one of the lawyers on your lists. Something like that. Would that help?"

Finally, they might be making some progress. "Yes. It might help a great deal," he said.

"But who are they?" Trent said.

"They are two collectors who may be connected to the case

Emily is working in Victoria. Anything we find might help her. It's unlikely, but if they also have some connection to our big fish…"

"We need to know about it," Miss Kent said, making a note. "I could check now, if you'd like?"

"If you could, that would be very helpful."

"I'll just be a moment," she said as she stood and shook out her skirts. "Mac, if you wouldn't mind?"

"Of course," he said, and followed her out.

In less than five minutes the two of them were back. Miss Kent was looking flustered, but pleased. He hoped that meant good news.

"Were you able to find anything on Emily's suspects?" he asked.

"Yes, we did," Miss Kent said eagerly. "Both are clients of Konrad's."

"Are they indeed?" he said, thinking rapidly. "And what area of the law does he handle for them?"

"They were separate cases, but both apparently broker chinoiserie—Chinese porcelain," she explained. "For select clients."

"So there is some overlap between these two cases," Granville said. "It's clear that our focus needs to be on Emily's case as well as on our pufferfish, since Carstairs and Gainer are both clients of one of the lawyers we suspect. I'll make sure Emily is aware of that in time for her meeting."

"And we'll keep digging into any further connections," Mac said.

"I appreciate it. Anyone else? No?" He turned to Carver. "Can you fill in the others on the poison theory you developed?"

Carver was happy to do so, and Granville took note of the intent look on Mac's face. And the thoughtful one on Miss Kent's.

Trent, as usual, looked impatient. He was more comfortable with action than theory.

When Carver was done, it was Mac who asked, "This poisoner? He's going to be hiding in the shadows, isn't he?"

Carver nodded. "That he is."

"So he may be somewhere in the files we already have…"

"Probably is," Carver said.

"But he won't stand out. In fact," and Mac exchanged glances with Miss Kent. "Our big fish is probably the one we have the least documentation for."

"That would make sense," Carver said.

"We can't keep calling him the big fish. Not someone this poisonous," Scott said, and shot a look at Granville. "So at the meeting this morning, Granville officially named our villain the pufferfish."

Granville rolled his eyes while the table erupted into laughter. If he'd been less worried about Emily, he would have traded quip for quip. But Scott's little joke was welcome.

They all needed a release from the tension of pursuing a case that seemed to be going nowhere.

"I have a little more information to share," Granville said. And he filled them in on what Emily had told him about her upcoming dinner for the Collector's Society. There was a little silence as the others digested what he'd told them.

Trent broke it. "But Emily—that could be dangerous. She could be in danger."

He hoped not. "She's handling her case beautifully."

To his surprise, Miss Kent spoke up. "Emily is smart. She knows how to take care of herself."

She was right, dammit. He needed to trust his fiancée. Which he did.

It was the separation from her that made this situation tough.

BACK IN HIS OWN OFFICE, Granville kept replaying Emily's call in his mind. Finally he grabbed his hat, bid everyone good night and headed towards the water. He'd had enough for one day.

Scott caught up with him at the bar in the Carlton, and slid onto the stool beside him.

"Why are you here?" He looked past Scott. "And how did you manage to escape without our shadow?"

"Trent?" Scott said with a grin. "Told him he couldn't come. Mood you're in, he'd only make things worse."

"Probably," he said. And drained the shot in front of him.

Scott gave him a sideways glance, signaled the bartender for two more whiskeys. "What's up?"

"We're chasing shadows."

"The six lawyers?"

"All of it. Whispers, and half-truths. And I suspect Emily and I were both lied to."

Scott immediately knew what—and who—he meant. "Wong Sun? But what did he have to gain?"

"You might as well ask what Benton had to gain."

"Okay, I'll bite. What did Benton have to gain?"

Granville ignored his partner's attempt at humor. "Look, we've been chasing this fellow for more than a week now. And we're still nowhere near catching him. Which should tell us something."

"We need new careers?"

"Maybe we do. But first I want to know why we're being misdirected at every turn. And who is behind this. Whoever the pufferfish is, he can't be so powerful he can operate invisibly from behind the scenes."

"Benton already explained that," Scott said as the bartender slid their drinks in front of them.

"Did he? I must have missed it. Cheers," Granville said, raised his whiskey in a mock toast, and drained it.

Scott rolled his eyes and drained his own whiskey. "So what's your plan? You going to challenge Benton? Again?"

The whiskey hit the spot. Granville signaled for another round. "I would. Except I don't have time to play his games."

Because Emily's dinner party, where she intended to unmask the Collector—and possibly confront a killer—was tomorrow.

All traces of humor fell away from Scott's face. "This is about Emily, isn't it?"

"She's hunting a killer. And I'm not there. I need to take our pufferfish down, and quickly. That way I can be on the next ferry if I'm needed."

"We do need to deal with this pufferfish, once and for all," Scott said cautiously.

"We do." He drained this glass, signaled for another. Said, with an attempt at humor that had no laughter in it, "As soon as I figure out who he is."

Scott considered him. "What you need is a steak," he said.

Granville had to laugh. A good thick steak was Scott's answer to everything. And he was probably right. Steak would go nicely with the whiskey.

Maybe it would even help.

42

Thursday, September 6, 1900

On Thursday morning Granville woke abruptly from an uneasy half sleep. He had no hangover, which surprised him. And he was still worried about Emily.

But he had a working telephone. And he knew Emily would be awake early today.

A brief conversation with her, and hearing about some of the preparations she'd made, helped to diminish his concerns about her dinner that evening. She wouldn't be confronting a killer. She was subtler than that.

He wished her well. And asked her to be careful anyway. She promised she would.

Somewhat easier in mind, he met Scott at the hospital. Randall's floor was quiet, the narrow corridors deserted. There was no sign of the doctor, so Granville gave a quick nod to the nurse on duty, who recognized him by now, and led Scott directly to Randall's private room.

The narrow iron bedstead was empty, the thick linen sheets thrown back.

Granville drew in a harsh breath. Had they lost Randall?

The nurse he'd seen earlier swept in after him, her nun's robes immaculate. "I tried to catch you," she said. "He's been taken down to be x-rayed."

It had been ten days since the attack. Why were they x-raying him now? "Thank you, Sister," he said. "Did something go wrong?"

"Not at all," she said. "They are simply checking that his leg is healing properly. He should be back here shortly."

He checked his pocket watch and turned to Scott. "We have a little time."

"We might as well wait, then," Scott said as he sat in one of the wooden visitor's chair along the wall. "We don't need to get back to the office until our meeting, anyway."

It was nearly half an hour before they heard the unmistakable creak of a gurney being wheeled down the hall. Granville braced himself—this was the first time he'd seen Randall when he was conscious, and he wasn't sure what to expect. Despite the doctor's assurance that their lawyer was healing well, he knew how unpredictable recovery from a really bad beating could be.

The gurney squeaked closer. "I don't know why they can't oil those things better," Scott said, after a sideways look at him.

Granville's focus was on the occupant of the gurney as the door swung inwards. Randall's swelling had decreased enough that he looked like himself again, and his bruises had faded to a greenish yellow. Neither of which affected the intelligent eyes or the broad smile.

"Granville. Scott. Am I glad to see you two," Randall said. "I feel like I've been trapped in this hospital forever. No offense, sister," he added to the nun that accompanied him.

"None taken," she said. "We are always glad to have patients impatient to return to their normal life. It's the best sign of healing there is."

Between them, the orderly and the nun helped Randall back into bed, while he and Scott chatted quietly, pretending not to notice. As the orderly wheeled the gurney back out, the nun turned to them.

"You may visit for a few minutes, but don't tire him. He's had a busy morning," she cautioned them, then swooshed out.

Leaving Granville staring at Randall. Even lying down, he looked more alive than he had since the attack.

"I believe I have you to thank," Randall said in a raspy voice. "For getting me here, and for making sure I was cared for."

"You'd have done the same for me."

"Regardless."

"Just tell us what you can of the attack. Who did this to you?"

"There were three men," Randall said. "All in black. Someone set up a fake appointment, and these thugs showed up."

"What did they say?" Granville asked.

"None of them said a word. Just went after me."

"And then what?"

"I fought back, but I couldn't get to my gun in time, so the odds were against me. And these three knew their business. They had me incapacitated in no time," Randall said, as calmly as if he were laying out facts in court.

"Did you recognize any of them?"

"Not exactly. But one of them looked familiar. I think he's used to be one of Dagan's henchmen."

"Gurak?"

"No, him I'd be sure of. This was one of the big, burly guys in black."

Granville and Scott exchanged glances. That fit most of Dagan's —now Gurak's—men.

"Any other details?"

"I'm afraid not. It's mostly a blur," Randall said, and his lips tightened.

Granville nodded. He knew exactly what the lawyer meant.

"Did they say anything to you?" Scott asked. "Even a word or two?"

"Not from the time they burst in until I lost consciousness," Randall said. "Sorry I can't be more help."

"It doesn't matter," Granville said. "We'll get them. Carver's working with us."

"Good. He knows that world," Randall said. "Is this all part of the campaign against me?"

"We think so," Granville said. "We're working to narrow down who's really behind all of this."

"When you find out, I want to know," Randall said. "Lying here, I've had nothing to do but think. And it still makes no sense to me."

"To us either," Scott said.

"That's why it's taking so long," Granville said. "The motive is hidden, as is whoever ordered the hit on you."

"So you do think they were trying to kill me?" Randall asked.

Dammit. He hadn't meant to let that out. Their lawyer clearly hadn't lost any of his quickness of mind, which was a relief. But it was inconvenient, just now.

"Yes, I do. As you say, they knew what they were doing. And you nearly died."

"I'd suspected as much," was all Randall said.

"Which is why we've put it about that you're dying," Granville said, watching his friend closely.

That could be a hard thing to hear, even for someone who appreciated strategy as much as their lawyer did.

"So I'm dead, am I?" Randall said with a grin that looked like it hurt. "Well played. Is it helping?"

"You're still alive, aren't you?" Granville said with an answering grin.

Anything to keep from telling Randall they were still getting nowhere on exposing the poisonous villain who'd tried to have him killed.

LEAVING THE HOSPITAL, Granville and Scott walked briskly back to the office. Mac and Miss Kent were already waiting in the meeting room, and they'd again invited Robert Carver to join them. Trent wasn't in yet.

Granville could hear the outer office door slamming open, a murmur from Miss Rizzo and hasty footsteps heading their way.

Breathing hard, Trent rushed into the room and slid into a seat beside Scott with a red face and muttered apologies.

He acknowledged him with a nod, then looked around the table, aware of each tired face. "Good morning, everyone. Carver, thank you for joining us. Before I start, does anyone have anything to add to our discussion from last night?"

"I do," Miss Kent said. "Mac—Mr. McAndrews and I looked a little deeper into Lessing and his interactions with Randall. And there wasn't much to find. Other than the upcoming case we already knew about."

"So Lessing hasn't lost a case to Randall in court?"

"No," she said. "Not that we could find. Not even as a junior lawyer on someone else's case."

"Leaving him with no obvious motive against Randall," Granville said thoughtfully.

"I don't know all the elements of these cases," Carver said then. "So forgive me if I'm out of line. But I gave this a lot of thought last night. And everything you have on both cases—yours and that of your fiancée—is still based on speculation and rumor.

From what you've said, she is closing in on her killer. But you're no closer to finding this pufferfish than you were when Randall was attacked. And you still haven't got a single fact in either case that would stand up in a court of law."

Granville considered the lawyer's determined expression. Carver did have a point. It was the same thing Scott had pointed out earlier. They had too few facts on both these cases.

What both of them missed was that it was the slow work of finding the right theory that had enabled them to solve their previous cases.

But theories weren't going to convict the pufferfish.

Or help Emily get the killer arrested before she staged a confrontation at this dinner of hers.

They needed to move faster now. Which meant a different approach.

"You're partially right," he said. "We do have too many theories, none of which fit the few facts we have. But perhaps we need to look at those facts in a new light."

"Go on," Carver said.

"When Scott and I spoke with Konrad, he pointed at Gurak for the beating," Granville said. "And also suggested that Lessing was behind the attack on Randall."

"We know all this," Carver said impatiently.

"Bear with me," he said. "Gurak told us he didn't know the name of the fellow that hired him, but he described a man very similar to Oliver Lessing."

Carver was beginning to frown.

"The facts we have so far point to Oliver Lessing as our puffer-fish, and Lew Gurak as the man paid to attack Randall."

Carver's frown deepened. "Fine. But we still have no proof."

"And the deeper we dig for truth, the more we seem to be uncovering lies and misdirection rather than truth," he said.

"How do you mean?" Trent asked.

Granville smiled wryly. "For instance, if Konrad and Lessing are indeed engaged in a long-standing feud, then Konrad's motives for accusing Lessing are suspect. And Gurak's description of the man who hired him either damns Lessing, or suggests Gurak himself is deflecting our investigation for an unknown reason."

"Even the legal and financial records seem to contradict each other," Mac said.

"Indeed," he said. "The few facts we've managed to gather so far are suspect. I believe we're being lied to and deliberately misdirected by everyone we've spoken to so far. So today we are going to hunt down every one of those facts, and find out what's hiding behind the lies."

"Good," said Trent. "How are we going to do that?"

So much for an inspirational speech.

"Scott and I will pay a visit to some of those lawyers, and see if we can shake anything loose," Granville said. "The three of you have more digging to do in the records. You're looking for connections between Randall, Carstairs or Gainer, and any of the six lawyers. Or their clients, though we don't seem to have turned up anything on the clients to date. We'll meet back here at five."

Carver grinned. "And I'll join you in visiting those lawyers, if I may. You might find me useful. I speak their language, after all."

He considered for a moment, and decided Carver was likely right. And with Emily's dinner only hours away—if there was any connection between her case and his, he wanted the pufferfish behind bars before then. He'd take all the help he could get.

"Thank you," he said.

He hoped it would be enough.

4 3

"So how do you want to do this?" Carver asked as the three of them took the stairs down to the street.

"We need to either find this poisoner, or prove he doesn't exist," Granville said. "What do you suggest?"

Carver shrugged. "If he exists, he's not going to be who we expect. That much is clear."

"What about gettin' them all together," Scott said, lowering his voice as they reached street level and stopped at the far end of the white and grey marble lobby. "Put 'em in a room, and bait them. Like trout."

Granville had to laugh. "Trout? Seriously?"

"It's not a bad idea," Carver said. "Lawyers like to argue. You could say it's a strength. Get them arguing with each other, and see what happens."

"Yesterday you called the poisoner subtle. Do you really think he'd get so caught up in a debate that he gives himself away?"

"Frankly, I'm out of ideas," Carver said. "Do you have a better one?"

"What if we invite them all to lunch at some tavern, get the whiskey flowing?" Scott said.

"Get them all drunk?" Carver said. "I like it."

"Think that would get the pufferfish to give himself away?" Scott asked.

"It just might," Carver said. "The trick will be to get all of them to agree to lunch."

It wasn't the best idea Granville had ever heard, but it wasn't the worst, either. And he was out of time. "We can tell them it's in memory of Randall," he said.

"Randall died? When? Why didn't you say something?" Carver said, looking shocked.

Granville and Scott exchanged glances. Caught.

"Frankly, because I'd forgotten you didn't know the truth," he said.

Carver looked from him to Scott and back. "He's not dead, is he? And probably not even dying."

"It was touch and go for a few days," he said. "He developed a nasty fever. But he's recovering fast now."

"Why didn't you tell me?"

"We needed the other lawyers to believe he was nearly dead. The best way for you to convince them was to believe it yourself," Granville said.

"Thanks a lot."

"I'm sorry for that. But you know as well as I do that if the pufferfish had the least inkling Randall was recovering…"

"He'd go after him again. I still don't appreciate the lie. But I'd have done the same," Carver said.

He nodded acknowledgment. "Randall was finally well enough to talk to us this morning. And he remembers being attacked by three thugs, but not much more."

"Did he recognize anyone?"

"Only one man, as being one of Dagan's thugs."

"Now one of Gurak's?" Carver asked.

"Presumably."

"At least that tells us that none of our six lawyers were involved in the attack itself. Randall would have recognized any one of them immediately," Carver said.

"That was my assumption as well."

"Then we're right about someone, probably the pufferfish, hiring an attack on Randall. So we know that much for certain," Carver said.

"Yes. We do," Granville said.

Then it occurred to him that Gurak himself could have ordered the hit, in revenge for Dagan. But the idea seemed unlikely, given the six lawyers spreading hate about Randall. So he kept the thought to himself.

Though Randall had been instrumental in putting Dagan behind bars. And most of Dagan's men—especially Gurak—were still very loyal to him.

"Wait a minute," Carver said, staring from him to Scott. "Randall is recovered enough to talk about his attackers. And you're proposing to make the lie even bigger? A memorial lunch?"

"I think it's a great idea," Scott said. "Or how about a 'we've just been told he won't live out the day and we want to drown our sorrows and remember him' lunch."

"That's even better," Granville said.

"But then why ask the six to join us?" Carver asked.

"Because they're really good at remembering him," he answered as if it was obvious.

The lawyer started to laugh. "Yes, because they hate him. You two truly are crazy, you know that?"

"Perhaps. But we get results."

"Can't argue with that," Carver said. "They're lawyers, though. They'll know you're looking to blame someone for Randall's death. And they'll be on the defensive, every one of them."

"I'm counting on it," Granville said. "And on the arrogance of the pufferfish. He'll think he's succeeded, that his enemy is dead, or nearly so, and that we don't have a clue. In his mind, it will be his own private celebration."

Carver nodded slowly. "That fits. You've been giving this a lot of thought."

When he wasn't thinking about Emily and the dangers she was up against. "Yes."

"Both of us have," Scott said. "And I still don't get why this guy has it in for Randall so bad."

"For what it's worth, I can't figure it out either," Carver said. "And I'm a lawyer, too. But you're both right, that kind of thinking fits with his actions so far."

"And for now, his actions are all we've got," he said. "I don't think we'll have a hope of figuring out his motive until we've identified him."

"So you're hoping arrogance and liquor together will equal a loose tongue?" Carver said. "It might work, too.

Fine, we'll invite the pufferfish and friends to a slightly premature wake for their enemy. But it can't be at the Terminal City Club. It'll have to be the right atmosphere, if we're going to get them to talk."

"There's a small back room at the King's Arms pub we can use," Granville said. "It's private enough, but the atmosphere in the main room tends to be, shall we say, anything but discreet."

"It's the opposite of Terminal City, which is all business, then," Carver said. "That should do. So what time?"

"All of the six are in town this week?"

"Yes."

"And are any of them in court today?"

"Cheever is," Carver said. "But this judge insists on a lunch break from eleven-thirty until two."

"Then our lunch is at eleven-thirty. Is that enough notice for these lawyers to join us? Or should we do this tomorrow?"

Carver consulted his pocket watch. "There's enough time. And I like the immediacy of your calling them together the same day Randall is expected to die. They'll be too curious to stay away."

"Good," Granville said. "Then if you can get the word, out, Scott and I will see you at the King's Arms at eleven-thirty."

Granville sat in the back room at the King's Arms with Scott on his right, and watched the six lawyers—plus Carver—file in. Their faces were all equally bland, they all wore trained expression of a professional lawyer. But there were tiny differences, if you looked for them.

And he did.

A very slight frown creased Cheever's wrinkled brow, a hint of tension he couldn't quite erase, while Peabody's thin lips were pursed, as if he tasted something bitter.

Griggs' eyelids were drooping, as if to hide secrets, and Bragg's thick lips curled, giving him a disdainful look.

Konrad's hands shook slightly. He looked worried. And Lessing's jaw was tightly clenched, in anger or in some other emotion Granville couldn't name.

If one of these six was the pufferfish, he was doing an impressive job of hiding the triumph he must be feeling.

When they were all seated, with Carver on his left and the others ranged around the table in front of him, steaks, chips and bottles of whiskey were brought around. Granville waited until the servers had left the room, then stood and lifted a brimming glass. "To Randall," he said, and downed half of it.

"Randall," Carver said, raising his glass high. "He was always a better lawyer than any of us."

"May he soon rest in peace," said Briggs ironically as he copied the gesture.

"To Randall," Peabody said, downing the remainder of his own glass. "He won't be missed," he muttered, as the others rushed to refill their glasses.

Starting off the next round of toasts. Which got nastier and nastier as the toasts continued.

By the time they'd finished the first rounds of toasting and taken a break to demolish their steaks, it was a very merry group gathered in the backroom of The King's Arms. As the levels of whiskey in the bottles on the table diminished, the toasts became less veiled and increasingly insulting.

Granville watched and listened, drinking far less than he

appeared to be. He found himself wishing he could take notes of exactly who said what, but he had to content himself with listening for anything the pufferfish might let slip.

Two hours later, they'd gone through another round of steaks and another three bottles of whiskey, and the tone had become maudlin. The only thing Granville was sure of was that Bragg was going to lose his case, if he made it back to the courtroom at all.

And that he detested each and every member of this group of six. Even maudlin, they expressed nothing but hate and contempt for Randall. Each toast built on the rantings of the last. They seemed unable to think of anything else.

It was as if they were determined to rub his and Scott's noses in it.

If he could prove that all of them had conspired to kill Randall, he'd be a happy man. But there had to be one man behind this. The pufferfish.

Unless…

For a moment, he contemplated the bizarre notion that this was indeed a conspiracy of six, looking from face to face as he did so. If this was a conspiracy, it was a remarkably stupid one. And far too obvious.

Except it had escaped him so far, hadn't it?

And while he was too busy looking for whoever was really behind all the rumors, Randall had been attacked and nearly killed, his good name and his business both almost destroyed.

Or was that the whiskey talking?

Cheever, Griggs, Peabody, Bragg, Konrad and Lessing.

They had all either lost to Randall, or knew that they'd lose the next case they argued against him. And most likely the one after that, too. And Randall was too honest to be bought, too good to be outmaneuvered—and he knew the law better than any of them.

These lawyers were capable at best, yet they were some of the most successful ones in town. Which told him something about their ethics.

Randall, on the other hand, was brilliant. And articulate. And incorruptible.

No wonder they hated him.

Could it really be that simple? And that ugly?

He was still thinking about it when the lunch drew to an end, and the celebrants poured themselves into several hackneys that jangled and creaked as they rolled away.

44

As soon as the six lawyers had left the back room, Granville had made some excuse and left as quickly as he could. He hadn't managed to shake Scott, though. He'd no sooner turned down along Water Street, than he could hear his partner's steady tread behind him.

"Where's Carver?" he asked as Scott increased his stride to walk alongside him.

"Dunno."

Granville had to smile at the thought of Carver left alone in the mess their "memorial" had left behind. The poor fellow probably thought he'd been left with a huge bill.

He hadn't, of course. They'd made arrangements ahead of time with the manager of The King's Arms to bill the office for the meal. And the whiskey. It would be expensive, but it might have been worth it.

Now he had some thinking to do. He needed to walk. And he knew just the place. Hopping on a streetcar, with Scott right behind him, he headed for Stanley Park.

Walking in the dense greenness of a grove of ancient cedar trees, Granville drew in a deep breath. The very smell of the air, a heady mix of cedar, pine and ocean breeze, was enough to clear his head. And it was quiet here—the slow, solemn quiet of long years undisturbed.

Standing here, it was impossible to believe the downtown was one streetcar ride away. If he turned left, he'd break through the trees, and find himself walking towards the bathing huts along English Bay. He turned right, and made his way deeper into the forests.

With Scott walking silently at his side, his feet sought the paths leading into the trees, thickly covered in pine needles. His breathing deepened, and he began to mentally review everything that he knew about Randall's case.

The harder he tried to disprove the idea of a conspiracy amongst the six lawyers, the more the facts shifted. He cursed under his breath, and Scott gave him a worried look.

There still had to be a ringleader, didn't there? The big fish had to exist, even if he wasn't a pufferfish, and played a different role than the one they'd thought he played.

But if it was a plot between the six of them, it explained why they couldn't pin that leader down. Each of the six had played a role.

And unfortunately for his investigation, they'd played it rather well.

Granville cursed under his breath when he realized that if he'd put this together sooner, the case would have been wrapped up by now. And he'd have been free to go to Victoria to assist Emily. If she needed assistance, off course.

She hadn't asked for any.

But still. She might have appreciated an escort for her dinner party, at least.

He couldn't even plan to head for Victoria tomorrow. There was no way he could wrap this mess up tonight. And he couldn't leave town with it unsolved, leaving Randall still in danger.

He still couldn't quite see clearly what was going on with the six lawyers, though. Without that, his next move could prove disastrous.

They'd had too little to go on from the start.

"You still thinking through our lawyer's lunch?" Scott's voice, out of place in this silence, startled him out of his train of thought.

"I am. You?"

"Just enjoyin' the walk."

Granville chuckled. "Of course you are."

"Unless you want to talk about it?"

"Not yet. I'm trying to sort a few things out."

"Well, sort faster. We'll need to leave soon if we're going to make it to the office before the meeting. And didn't you want to talk to Emily before she left for her dinner?"

He checked his pocket watch. Scott was right. "In fact, we need to leave now," he said.

"You might. Your legs are shorter'n mine."

"Very funny." He turned back the way they'd come, Scott walking beside him, matching his stride.

He caught his partner giving him a sideways glance. "What?"

"You sure you don't want to talk about what went on at lunch?" Scott asked. "Left to yourself, you come up with some odd conclusions, sometimes."

He grinned. "So do you. And these are some odd circumstances we're dealing with."

"At least Randall's doing better."

"And we need to keep him that way." He paused to sweep a low hanging cedar bough out of their path. "I'd rather wait until the meeting. I'm still sorting things out in my head, and I'm hoping hearing everyone's opinions will help."

"You sure about that?"

He just grinned.

"Well, it's your party," Scott said. "Don't blame me if Carver gets on your case again."

"It isn't Carver I'm worried about."

"Or Trent does," Scott added, earning himself another grin.

"I'll risk it," Granville said, and increased his pace.

He wasn't about to rush to the wrong conclusion now and risk endangering the case and everyone involved.

His call to Emily was a brief one, and unsatisfactory since there was so little they could actually say. And she would need time to dress for her dinner party. Still, it was good to hear her voice.

"Call me tonight, as soon as you're home?" he said just before he rang off.

"Of course," she'd promised.

"And stay safe."

"Granville, it's a dinner," she said with a laugh. "But I have to run if I'm to be on time. Good night."

"Until later," he'd said, but all he heard was the dial tone.

Hanging up, he found Scott staring at him. "Did I hear you hinting to her about Carver's poisoner theory?"

"You did."

"You think she understood? Just from that?"

"I know she did."

Scott gave him a funny look. "Well, good then," he said, then muttered something about it being past time they got married.

Which didn't help, since he agreed. Strongly. "Come on, they'll be waiting for us," he said.

At five everyone met again in the meeting room. Granville thought they all looked even more tired than they had that morning. Miss Rizzo brought in tea and biscuits, then left the room.

Once the tea had been poured, Granville again turned to Mac and Miss Kent. "One thing occurred to me today. You established this morning that both Carstairs and Gainer, Emily's suspects, are clients of Konrad's. And both broker Chinese porcelain. Does Konrad have a specialty in that area as well?"

"Yes, he does," Miss Kent said. "Mr. McAndrews and I dug into it further, and in fact, Mr. Konrad advertises that specialty," she said. "As does Mr. Lessing."

"It's one of the main areas where the two compete for clients," Carter said.

"Let us not forget about Lessing," Granville said thoughtfully. "Or Randall. Whose recent cases, then, must be costing these four quite a bit."

"The successful ones would be taking money directly out of all four pockets," Carver broke in.

"Lessing's, Konrad's, Carstairs's and Gainer's," Granville clarified.

"Yes," Carver said, and Miss Kent nodded her agreement.

"Which would seem to give all of them equal incentive to remove that threat to their income," he said.

"Carstairs and Gainer weren't in town when Randall was attacked," Trent said. "I checked the newspaper reports of arrivals and departures."

Granville was sure those reports could be evaded, but he gave Trent an approving nod for his initiative anyway. "Lessing and Konrad are the more likely suspects in any case."

And he was rather more interested in whether either lawyer was the man who had hired the pottery thief in Emily's case. "Do you know if either Lessing or Konrad spend much time in Victoria, or have reason to know it well?"

"I can find out," Trent said. "I know a few people."

"Do so," Granville said. "That would be helpful."

And Trent beamed.

Carver looked distinctly unhappy, though. Now what? "Problems, Carver?" he asked.

"I'm not sure Lessing and Konrad are the most likely suspects," the lawyer said. "From their behavior at lunch today, anyway. Even drunk, they weren't sounding guilty."

Seeing the confused looks around the table, Granville quickly explained the luncheon they'd held for the six lawyers.

"So how did it go?" Trent asked.

"We told them Randall had died and fed them whiskey," Carver said dryly.

Trent punched the air. "Good one."

"And it went downhill from there," Granville said. "I've never heard the like. The gloating at Randall's death, and the hatred we heard expressed towards him today?" He shook his head, and wished it was whiskey in front of him, rather than tea.

"Even when they heard he was dead?" Miss Kent asked, her face pale.

"Especially once they heard he was dead," Carver said.

"Which still suggests someone subtle but lethal who is orchestrating that reaction from behind the scenes. Our pufferfish, if you will," Granville said. "And I'd agree that Lessing with his bluster and threats seems an unlikely candidate for that."

He turned to Carver. "You don't think either Lessing or Konrad are the pufferfish?"

"No, I don't."

"Of the six, which seemed the most likely to you, then?"

Carver scowled. "None of them, unfortunately. But if I had to pick one, I'd pick Bragg."

"Why?"

"Because he so clearly hates Randall," Carver said. "He didn't have a single good thing to say about someone who he believed wouldn't live out the day."

"Yes, that was obvious," Granville agreed, and turned to Scott. "Who do you suspect is the pufferfish?"

Scott grimaced. "My first opinion hasn't changed. I still think it's Konrad."

"Even after today's lunch?" Carver asked.

"Especially after today's lunch."

"Why?" Granville asked, genuinely curious.

"As far as I could tell, they all hate Randall about equally," Scott said. "Or think they do. But I caught Konrad looking smug a few times, just for a second. And he seemed to be energized by the news of Randall's death—way more than when we saw him the other morning. Remember?"

"Yes, I do. And I'd agree that he was happy about something, and trying to hide it."

"But you don't think Konrad is our pufferfish either, do you?" Scott asked.

"No, I don't. I think he was being a little too obvious to be the pufferfish."

"Then who do you think it is?" Carver asked, leaning forward.

"I think there's another reason we've been finding it so hard to crack this case and find our pufferfish," Granville said deliberately. "I think they all did it. Together."

And pandemonium reigned as all five of them began talking at once.

Surprisingly, it was Miss Kent's voice that rose above the din. "That makes no sense," she said. "Excuse my forthrightness, but this goes against every fact we've been talking about. I get that they all hate Randall, but… are you saying there *is* no leader? No big fish —I mean pufferfish—at all?"

"And what is their motive?" Carver added. "Surely you don't think they'd go this far just to get even with the man? Aside from the fact that I can't imagine those six effectively working together, what do they stand to gain by this?"

Granville held up a hand. "Bear with me for a moment. I gather we all agree that these six at best dislike Randall, and at worst hate him, correct?"

He looked around the table.

They all nodded.

"What if they don't?"

Blank stares met him this time. He grinned. "I had trouble with this too, believe me. I'm still not certain I'm right. Let's see if I can convince all of you."

"Go on," Mac said, leaning forward.

"All six of them hate Randall," Granville said. "But except for Peabody, we couldn't figure out why they felt so strongly about him. So we began looking for someone behind it all. Someone who's deliberately making trouble for Randall."

"Poisoning the water," Scott put in.

"Exactly. And the three of us," he indicated himself, Scott and

Carver. "Spent a frustrating few hours earlier today trying to get that poisoner—the pufferfish—to betray himself.

Which was a failure, and told us nothing.

There was no hint of the pufferfish. Or his motive. Despite the quantity of whiskey they all downed. So I started asking myself what we were missing. And I realized we'd known the motive all along."

"Those cases," Mac said, on a note of dawning discovery.

Now Miss Kent was leaning forward too. "Randall kept winning them. And they all—the six—had businesses that were being affected by those wins."

"And Randall couldn't be bought off," Scott said slowly.

"We kept missing it because we were looking for an emotional reason for the attack on Randall. Not a business one," Granville said.

"Because they made it all about hating Randall, so we focused on that," Scott said.

"They were feeding off each other," Carver said in disgust. "Building the story taller and taller. And we fell for it."

"Not entirely," he said. "We knew someone was feeding us lies, trying to distract us."

"We just didn't realize they all were," Scott said.

"Because that made no sense," Carver said.

"It does if it serves as a distraction from what's really going on," he said.

"So who attacked Randall?" Mac asked at the same time. "Still Gurak and his thugs?"

"Randall says at least one of Gurak's thugs was part of the gang that attacked him," Scott said. "And Gurak's men are the ones trying to stop us, too. It's got to be them."

"The real question is, who hired Gurak? It's unlikely to have been all six of them," Granville said.

"In a court of law, there are two things that matter most," Carver said. "Who inflicted the blows? And who paid for the attack?"

Scott looked across the table at Granville. "I'll lay you odds that they all paid."

"That's a wager I won't be taking," he said with a grin. "I think you're right."

"So we know who did it," Trent said with an air of finality that amused Granville. "How do we prove it?"

And that was the real question.

"It would be easier if Randall really was dead," Carver muttered, then looked up to find himself the target of five hostile stares. "I'm sorry, but legally, the penalty for 'conspiracy to commit murder' is harsher if he dies than if he recovers. If their defense lawyer is good, they could walk away with a fine."

"What about the fraud they've been perpetrating and the way they've twisted the import laws?" Mac said. "Can't we do something with that, and tie it to the conspiracy?"

"Now you're talking. We might just have enough evidence," Carver said. Then his face fell. "Though it's the kind of case where you'd need a mind like Randall's to convince a judge of what was really going on."

Granville's eyes narrowed as he watched the two of them. There was something in what Carver had said…

"What if Randall was your main witness in this trial?" he asked the lawyer.

"But Randall's still in hospital."

"Mostly for his own protection, now. Nothing wrong with his mind. And he's getting stronger by the day."

"You're thinking of setting these six lawyers up?" the lawyer asked. "Like you did in the Sinclair trial, where everyone thought I was dead until Randall called me as a witness?"

"Exactly like that," he said. "Would it work?"

"We'd need more proof to make arrest charges stick," Carver said. "But if we can find that, and with Randall explaining things? Then yes. I think it might work."

Granville smiled. "Especially if we play our defendants off against each other."

"We'd have to get them arrested first," Mac said.

"Not if I'm representing Randall in court," Carver said thoughtfully. "What's the status of Peabody's lawsuit against Randall?"

"It's on the docket, but pending Randall's recovery," Miss Kent said, after flicking through a few pages in her green-lined stenographer's notebook.

"And since it's a civil suit, which means no jury, I'm sure I could persuade the judge to move it forward," Carver said. "Randall's final request, or some such nonsense. We'd likely want to countersue, naming all six of them, as well."

"Then they'll know he's not dead," Trent said.

"Not necessarily. Given how they operate, I'm certain they'll think we're playing the same game of lies and misdirection as they are," Granville said. "They'll probably be quite smug about it, thinking they have us on the run."

"I like it," Scott said.

"Then we have work to do," he said.

And putting their heads together, they began to plot.

Later that evening, a special meeting of the Victoria Collector's Society was held at the Herron mansion. After a sumptuous, multi-course meal featuring oyster soup, fresh-caught salmon, Beef Wellington and two kinds of pudding, Caroline Herron thanked them all for coming.

"I also owe a 'thank you' to my great friend Louisa here, for suggesting your society members as the answer to my dilemma," Caroline said smoothly. Sitting halfway down the table, Aunt Louisa nodded and beamed.

There was a great deal of excitement at her words, and several of the ladies exclaimed quite loudly, "Whatever can she mean?" and words to that effect.

Emily sat opposite her aunt, sipping a glass of wine and watching carefully. This was going to be interesting. Or at least she hoped it was.

"You will all have heard of the unfortunate event that took place here a few weeks ago," Caroline said.

There was a murmur of agreement and expressions of condolence among the guests. Their hostess nodded regally. "Thank you. It has been a difficult time."

She took a sip of her wine as her guests murmured amongst themselves.

"I can only blame the confusion of that awful day for how long it took me to notice that the pottery we inherited from my husband's beloved great-aunt had gone missing. It was a particularly fine set of what I believe is known as naturalist earthenware, decorated with thistles and dating from the opening exhibit at the Crystal Palace. But it has a sentimental value as well," and here Caroline and her husband exchanged glances, "For those who treasure such pottery, as we do."

"You are not saying it was stolen?" A gruff looking man with a military bearing said.

"I fear so," Caroline Herron said. "And worse, I fear that pottery may have been the reason for the murder of that poor girl."

"But I thought Ying…?" an overdressed woman in pink blurted out.

Only to be shushed by her neighbor.

"I fear the police think so as well," Mrs. Herron said. "But I haven't yet told them about the missing pottery," and she broke off, dabbing at her eyes with a lacy handkerchief.

Emily was impressed at how well Caroline was handling this. Especially since none of the guests seemed to recognize it for the performance it was.

"Well, why ever not?" The military type said. "We—I mean you must inform them immediately."

"I plan to do so tomorrow," Mrs. Herron said. "But I hoped to consult with you first."

There was a silence at her words, as the members of the society exchanged glances.

"I don't understand," Emily heard one of the ladies at the far end of the table say.

"I fear the police will not see the missing pieces as sufficient cause for the murder," Mrs. Herron said. "If I can place a value on the pieces when I report the theft, it might be easier to persuade them to take the matter of the theft seriously."

She glanced around the room. "I'm afraid I have no idea of the current value of the pieces and I was hoping that the society could help me with that assessment. You are the experts. I need your help."

"Of course we will help," the military gentleman said gruffly. "More than happy to assist you and your husband in this matter. Justice must be done. However, I myself am unfortunately not an expert on pottery, much less naturalist pottery. Anyone?"

It was clear to Emily from the quick discussion that followed that the society members were well aware of which items each member collected. All eyes, including Mr. Gainer's, were soon fixed on Mr. Andrews, Mr. Martin, and Mr. Carstairs.

There was some little discussion between Mr. Andrews and Mr. Martin about the true value of the collection. Once Caroline Herron had confirmed that it included a full dinner set as well as the tea set —which widened a few eyes—the two men agreed.

"With both sets complete, it could be worth as much as five thousand dollars," Mr. Andrews said, as Mr. Martin nodded. "And perhaps more to the right buyer. Don't you agree, Mr. Carstairs?"

"Oh, hardly that much, I think," he said quickly. "Perhaps a thousand dollars to the right collector, but hardly more."

As Mr. Andrews and Mr. Martin argued vociferously with him, Emily noted that Mr. Carstairs held strongly to the value he'd proclaimed for the collection, but he seemed to be looking to his left a bit too frequently. And his usual oily charm was missing. Why?

Each time Mr. Carstairs's eyes swiveled to the left, Emily tried to follow his gaze and see what—or who?—he was looking at. It was hard to tell. At first she thought he was checking the reaction of the military type who had been so quick to assure Mrs. Herron that they'd value her missing pottery.

Then she realized that Mr. Carstairs's gaze was looking too high for his target to be any of the guests. And the spot where he was looking changed slightly each time, too.

Finally she realized he was watching Mr. Lau—borrowed for the occasion—as he brought out several trays of fruit, nuts and cheese, then went around the table topping up sherry glasses.

Was Mr. Carstairs worried about what Mr. Lau might overhear? That seemed beyond odd.

Emily mulled it over as she continued to watch the drama in front of her. Mr. Carstairs dabbed several times at the sweat that beaded on his brow. His full lips tightened as the figure that Mr. Andrews and Mr. Martin discussed grew higher.

They seemed to be trying to outdo each other, Emily thought with amusement. But judging by the deepening lines in his forehead, Mr. Carstairs didn't find it amusing in the slightest.

And he kept glancing at her aunt's cook.

Was Mr. Lau involved in the theft somehow? Or perhaps Mr. Carstairs knew that Mr. Lau must have connections in Chinatown and was worried that he would talk about this dinner?

But why should it matter?

Unless Mr. Carstairs had paid for the stolen pottery based on a value he himself had given? And likely one that was substantially lower than the current market value, given the current discussion.

In fact, Mr. Andrews and Mr. Martin had started with a valuation that was close to the one the fine china dealer had given. And all three sets of figures were more than five times higher than the figure Mr. Carstairs was suggesting

As she watched and listened, Emily thought about the conversation they'd had with Mr. Lau. She had believed him when he said he wasn't involved in the theft. But how had the thieves found out about the valuable pottery in the first place?

Mr. Ying had taken the blame, saying he had talked too much about his employer's lovely home and things. But talked to whom?

Most of the stolen pottery collection had still been packed in boxes that were stored in the depths of the cellar. Which was hardly a place where someone could easily spot it. And no one touring the house would ever be shown pottery that wasn't even displayed.

So either Mr. Ying had bragged about that pottery collection in particular—one that his employers didn't even value. Or someone else who'd spent time in the Herron's cellar had seen the pottery, and passed on that information, likely for money. Or maybe for favors, if a *tong* was involved, and worked anything like Mr. Benton's gang did.

Emily had no idea where this thought was taking her—except that she was nearly certain Mr. Carstairs was the one who had ended up purchasing Mrs. Herron's stolen pottery. Which was bad enough, though it didn't necessarily make him the killer.

And much as she disliked him, she had difficulty picturing him as a killer. But at the very least, it meant he probably knew who had killed young Betsy. And he hadn't come forward with that information to the police.

Which was despicable.

A girl had been killed. Just so he could own a few pieces of pottery. He deserved whatever was coming to him.

Emily caught Caroline's eye, glanced at Mr. Carstairs, and then gave her a little nod. Caroline Herron returned the nod, then cleared her throat, catching the attention of most of her guests.

"This discussion has been most useful, giving me some idea of the value of the pottery," she said. "Even at the lower end of the range, it is more than high enough for the police to pay attention. I thank you."

"I know I speak for all of us when I say you are most welcome, dear lady," the military fellow said.

Caroline smiled at all of them, held up a hand.

"But you should know there is one other fact that affects this matter," she said. "You see, the earthenware that was stolen…well, it was a copy. We keep the real set safely in the vault."

The members of the collector's society broke into excited talk. Emily was keeping a close eye on Mr. Carstairs and Mr. Gainer, as well as the other two collectors of naturalist earthenware. Mr. Andrews, Mr. Martin and Mr. Gainer looked shocked, but Mr. Carstairs had gone alarmingly purple and was tugging at his collar.

Caroline waved for silence. As the talk died away, Emily noticed that Mr. Carstairs had drained his wine and poured himself a refill. His color was better, but he was frowning heavily.

"But if it was only the copies that were stolen, then what can it matter what the real items were worth?" the lady in pink asked.

"Well, the thieves presumably didn't know they were copies," Mr. Audley, a lawyer, said. "Since the real collection is worth so much, the police will have to recognize that the thieves could have seen it as worth killing for. The value of what they actually stole is not really relevant."

"You really think so?" Caroline asked.

"Definitely," he said firmly.

"That is very good to hear," Caroline said with a smile, and he flushed a little and fussed with his dessert fork.

Emily was impressed by Caroline's acting ability, though most of her attention was on Mr. Carstairs. Everything rested on what he would do next.

A disturbance at the other end of the table drew her attention to Mrs. Smith, who was angrily brushing at her skirts with a table napkin. It seemed Mr. Lau had spilled the sherry as he refilled her glass.

Emily took in Mr. Lau's fixed expression and wide eyes. He was staring at Mrs. Herron. Then his gaze switched to Mr. Carstairs.

As if he'd felt her looking at him, Mr. Lau gave a muttered apology to Mrs. Smith, bowed and hastily departed through the baize door leading to the kitchen.

Emily blinked and looked back at the dinner guests. Aunt Louisa looked horrified, and was apologizing to Mrs. Smith for Mr. Lau's behavior. Caroline was looking surprised. Was she was asking herself the same question Emily was?

And Mr. Carstairs had pushed back his chair with a grating sound and was making his apologies to his hostess. Who immediately said all the right things, and encouraged him to stay for another glass of sherry. "Or we have a lovely port, if you'd rather?"

When he pleaded an urgent engagement, she turned to her husband. "Dear, would you see our guest out, please?"

Mr. Herron nodded, and the two men disappeared down the hallway. Emily and Caroline Herron exchanged glances. This was unfolding more quickly than they'd expected.

"Shall I see if everything is all right in the kitchen?" Emily offered

"I'd be very grateful," Caroline said. "Let me know if you need me."

They exchanged a knowing look, then Emily quietly vanished through the green baize door and into the kitchen.

4 6

The kitchen was empty. Mr. Lau was nowhere to be seen. And he'd apparently left in quite a hurry.

The tray holding the half-full decanter of wine had been shoved haphazardly onto one end of the counter amongst the used dessert plates and forks. The dinner plates on the side of the sink had not yet been scraped or rinsed. And it smelled like the coffee percolator on the stove was starting to burn.

Emily turned down the heat under the coffee, then moved to stand on one side of the door. From here she could peer out into the darkened yard without being seen.

Nothing moved in the darkness. Perhaps Mr. Lau hadn't left this way.

She moved to the door at the top of the stairs, which was slightly ajar. Carefully opening the door wider, she looked down the stairs. There was no sign of Mr. Lau—or anyone else. She stood motionless, listening hard.

It was an eerie feeling, being alone in the deserted kitchen, and knowing Betsy had been murdered just a few feet from where she stood now.

There was no sound from the cellar below. And all she could hear from the dining room was a low murmur of voices.

Emily peered down into the darkened cellar again. Had Mr. Lau gone this way?

She thought about turning on the light, but didn't want to let him know he'd been followed, in case he had gone this way. She took a few steps down the stairs, telling herself she would only go far enough to hear more clearly if anyone was moving in the cellar.

Emily was nearly halfway down the cellar stairs, peering ahead of her into the shadows cast by the dim light from the kitchen, when a hand landing on her shoulder from behind nearly had her heart stopping.

Only lack of breath saved her from screaming long and loud.

"Shhh, it's me," Aunt Louisa stage whispered from behind her.

"Aunt! What are you doing? He'll hear us," Emily whispered back once she found her voice. It took an effort of will to keep her words low.

"Oh, and he wouldn't have heard you?" Aunt Louisa said. "Your mother told me you were too fond of risks. Which is a trait I quite admire, usually."

Emily rolled her eyes but held her tongue.

"But you're taking it too far, now. I suppose that fiancé of yours encourages it," Aunt Louisa continued. "Which I suspect he'll come to regret. Though he seems a lovely young man otherwise."

"We need to find Mr. Lau," Emily said quietly. "From his reaction, he was very surprised at the actual value of the stolen pottery."

She needed to get her aunt back on track, before she got too distracted. Aunt Louisa did love to talk.

"Which means he lied to us," her aunt said. "He said he knew nothing about the pottery."

"Yes. It also means he's involved with the theft somehow. But his abrupt departure suggests he's planning to tell someone about the true value of the stolen pottery. And what matters now is to find out who he plans to tell."

"Someone needs to follow him," Aunt Louisa said.

"Yes. We need to know where he goes. And the police are only expecting to follow one person."

"Mr. Carstairs."

"Yes."

"Mr. Herron has already confirmed that the police are following Carstairs," Aunt Louisa said. "We'll have to follow Mr. Lau ourselves until we find one of the officers and get him to take over. It will be safer if there are two of us."

Emily wasn't sure that was true, but she saw no other option. At least for now. She'd rather have done this alone, but there wasn't time to talk her aunt out of coming along.

With a little luck, they could pick up Mr. Lau's trail without his ever suspecting he was being followed. And find one of the policemen Mr. Herron had managed to convince to watch the house tonight, and get him to take over.

NAVIGATING THE DIM, crowded cellar with only the light reflecting down from the kitchen was hard. Emily was aware of Aunt Louisa behind her with every step, and the possibility that they could run into Mr. Lau.

She wondered if the cook was armed. And just how good he was with a knife.

The image of poor Betsy with the handle of a knife protruding from her chest replayed itself in her mind, and she couldn't seem to get it out.

What if Mr. Lau was the killer?

The thought hadn't occurred to her before, but there was something about the shadowy cellar with shelving towering over her in the dark that made her imagination run wild. And Mr. Lau could have been the man Carstairs hired. Wong Sun could have got it wrong. Or maybe he'd bent the truth for reasons of his own.

Emily's steps slowed, and she felt her aunt's breath warm on the back of her neck in the chill of the cellar.

She shook off the thought and sped up again.

Mr. Lau was hardly likely to be the killer.

And she couldn't lose him. Not if there was any hope he might lead them to the killer.

He had to be desperate, though. To have spilled the wine on Mrs. Smith and then just left, as he'd just done? And that desperation might make him dangerous.

If he'd been the one to pass information about this valuable pottery to Mr. Carstairs, or even to one of the *tongs*, what would their vengeance be if that pottery was—as almost everyone present at dinner now believed—a worthless copy? Was Mr. Lau running to tell someone what he'd learned? And hoping do so before Mr. Carstairs did?

Or was he just running?

All the while, part of her mind was navigating the rows of shelves, hoping she'd remembered the path correctly, since she couldn't see the map of lights along the ceiling when they were turned off. It was getting harder to remember the way with each turn she made.

Finally she had to stop. She had no idea which way to turn—was it left, and then right? Or the reverse?

"What is it, dear?" Aunt Louisa whispered in her ear, nearly making her jump, it seemed so loud in the stillness.

Which made Emily realize just how lucky they'd been so far, that neither of them had blundered into one of the crowded shelves. It would have made an almighty racket. And given them away completely.

"I'm not sure which way to turn," Emily said very softly, half turning her head so her aunt could hear her better.

It was then she saw the pale reflection of light off the ceiling ahead of them. It had to be Mr. Lau. And he was nearly to the door!

But even that little bit of light was enough to show her the path she needed. Reaching back, she touched her aunt's shoulder, and gestured. Emily could just make out the outline of Aunt Louisa's head as she nodded.

Emily moved forward quickly. He would be outside soon, and their chance of following him gone too.

But for once on this case, her luck was in. The light reached the door and held there for a moment. Then it went out, but now she was close enough to see moonlight coming through the window in the door. The moon would guide her way. She quickened her pace, determined not to lose him. And listened hard for the sound of the door opening.

She didn't hear it. Which meant he was still in the cellar.

Why was he hesitating?

He'd have looked through the window before going out. Maybe there was someone outside the door? One of the policemen? Emily's hopes rose. Perhaps this was truly going to work out, after all.

Likely he was just being cautious, and taking the time to check that his way was clear.

Or maybe he'd heard the two of them behind him.

Emily's heart beating so loudly in her ears she was sure he'd hear it, though she knew that was nonsense. It didn't stop her. But it did make her cautious.

Holding up a hand to tell her Aunt to move slowly, she carefully made her way to the edge of the shelf and peered around it.

And she could see him.

He was crouched against the door, raising his head a little every few seconds to peer out the window. There must be someone outside. If she made enough noise, they'd come to investigate, and it would all be over.

But what if there wasn't anyone there?

And what if Mr. Lau was the killer? Was he desperate enough to kill both her and his employer?

Emily reined in her fearful thoughts, but this time she paid attention to them. Was her intuition trying to tell her something? What did she know of her aunt's cook, after all?

What *was* his involvement in this case?

Recalling the look Mr. Carstairs had given Mr. Lau right before he fled had made Emily question everything her aunt's cook had told them. And it was becoming even clearer that he was involved in all of this. Somehow.

Could it have been just the two of them behind the theft and the murder? Mr. Carstairs and Mr. Lau?

But that would make everything Wong Sun had told her a lie. And surely that didn't explain Mr. Ying's silence. Or his fear. Mr. Lau was hardly a threat.

Was he?

No, it had to be the *tong* that Mr. Ying was afraid to take on.

Unless Mr. Lau's concern for Mr. Ying been faked? What if he had lied to hide his own involvement? That possibility raced through Emily's mind as she stood frozen, watching the outline of his head against the moonlit glass, and trying not to breathe too loudly.

Mr. Carstairs and Mr. Lau? One of them had money and the desire to own that collection, the other had the knowledge that the collection existed and access to the cellar. They wouldn't have needed more.

Except it meant that one of them must have killed Betsy.

Emily shuddered, her muscles aching from leaning forward, and wished she wasn't here at all. But it was too late to back out.

And she couldn't let Mr. Ying hang for a murder he didn't commit. Or let Betsy's murder go unsolved. Just because she was feeling overwhelmed.

Emily moved back a little to rest her legs, and felt her aunt's hand on her shoulder. She patted it absently while her mind raced through possibilities.

There were policemen right outside. All she had to do was set one of them after Mr. Lau.

Except—if one of the policemen arrested him, they still had nothing to tie him to the theft or the murder. Though her aunt's cook clearly knew the Herron's cellar, having made his way unerringly to the door even in the dim light.

But that wasn't proof. They'd be no further ahead if Mr. Lau was arrested.

No, there had to be a way to follow Mr. Lau—and hope his actions incriminated him. Perhaps he might run to whoever had hired him. Or perhaps he'd attempt to flee.

If indeed he'd done something wrong. Which still wasn't certain.

BEFORE EMILY COULD THINK herself to a standstill—or her aunt's increasingly restless movements could give them away—the sound of the door creaking slowly outwards froze both the them where they stood.

After a long moment of silence, Emily carefully lifted her head and peered around the corner of the shelf again. Mr. Lau's silhouette had vanished. The door still hung slightly open—he wouldn't have risked it creaking again as he closed it. But there was no sign of him.

Gesturing to her aunt to stay put, Emily made her way forward as quickly and as carefully as she could. She had to be sure he was gone.

She kept to the shadows of the shelf, just in case, and hoped she wouldn't brush against some garden implement or other and knock it off. The noise would give her away immediately.

Reaching the door, she stood on tiptoes to look out the window. Seeing nothing, she edged her way out the door, standing sideways to make a smaller, less visible target for anyone who might be watching.

Emily stopped just on the other side of the doorsill, pressing herself back against the wall. A slight breeze teased her nostrils with the scent of freshly cut grass and sent clouds chasing across the sky. Peering into the moonlit shadows, Emily couldn't see Mr. Lau. Or any of the policemen.

Unfortunately, she knew exactly where her aunt was. Aunt Louisa had emerged from the cellar on her heels, and opened her mouth to say something. Before she could give their presence away, Emily put her fingers against her lips. Aunt Louisa nodded, and stopped where she was.

Together they surveyed the edge of the garden in front of them.

"Is he gone?" Aunt Louisa whispered.

"I can't see him," Emily said. "But he can't have gone far—there hasn't been time. The breeze is stirring the bushes, so he could be crawling through those and we wouldn't know. There are too many of them to be sure."

"So what do we do now?" Aunt Louisa asked.

"If Mr. Lau were headed for Chinatown, which direction would he go?" Emily asked.

"He would have to find his way out to the main road, then head south," Aunt Louisa said. "With the cliffs below us here, the road is his only choice."

"Then we find one of the police officers, and send them after him," Emily said. "If he's on foot, and headed for Chinatown, he shouldn't be too hard to spot. The moon is quite bright."

They both scanned the yard in silence for a moment.

"Your house is north of here, isn't it?" Emily asked suddenly.

"Yes. But why do you ask?"

Emily didn't want to tell her aunt what she was thinking, because if her cook had sold information about the Herron's pottery collection to the *tong*, he might indeed head for Chinatown.

But if he was the one behind this, and not the *tong* as he'd implied, then he'd want to leave town with Carstairs's money as quickly as possible—before Carstairs could catch up with him and demand his money back.

Mr. Lau would have to gather up his things, first. And a careful planner, one who had nearly pulled off a robbery and a murder with no one suspecting him, might have hidden anything important at his place of work, not in his rooms in Chinatown.

"I think we should see if there is an officer available to see us home, as well," she said.

Aunt Louisa gave her a funny look. "I think you worry too much, Emily," she said. "Mr. Lau's ethics may be questionable, but he's harmless. He can't even slice roast very well."

It didn't seem the best time to point out the holes in her aunt's logic. "Let's see if we can find two officers, anyway. Including one willing to see us home," Emily said.

Unfortunately, even Mr. Herron's persuasive powers hadn't convinced the local constabulary to send out more than three policemen. Two of them had followed Mr. Carstairs when he left the dinner party in such a hurry, leaving only one free to try to intercept Mr. Lau on his route to Chinatown.

As she explained the situation to Constable Fryer—who seemed rather uncertain of himself for a police officer—Emily began to have second thoughts.

"Perhaps you could see us home first," she said. "And then pursue Mr. Lau to Chinatown."

Both Constable Fryer and her aunt gave her dubious looks.

"But Emily," Aunt Louisa said. "You just explained how important Mr. Lau's visit to Chinatown could be for this case. It makes no sense for the constable to delay pursuing him. We will be quite fine."

Constable Fryer didn't say anything, but his expression made it clear he was in full agreement with her aunt.

Emily thought about explaining what she'd been thinking, but it would take too long. And she had a feeling they wouldn't believe her anyway.

She wished Granville was here. He'd understand what she meant, and together they'd have worked out a plan. But he wasn't here, so she was going to have to do the best she could.

"Never mind, Aunt," she said. "I'm sure one of the guests will see us home. Or perhaps Mr. Herron will do so."

Though really, if her fears about Mr. Lau's involvement were accurate, they needed someone with a gun. Emily had never owned one, never even thought of it. But for the first time, she could see the benefit of owning a gun.

If she didn't shoot someone by mistake.

"REALLY, Emily. I can't understand why you're making all this fuss about nothing," Aunt Louisa said as Constable Fryer departed and they went indoors.

"I'd just feel safer if we had an escort," Emily said lightly. "Unless you own a gun, of course."

"Of course I do," Aunt Louisa said. "Your late uncle was always over-concerned for my safety. A little like you are right now," she added with a slight smile. "He gave it to me."

Aunt Louisa had a gun? Emily hadn't expected that. "It won't help us tonight unless you have it with you, though."

"Oh, is that all?" Aunt Louisa said, opening her evening purse and drew out a small, silver plated revolver. "Your uncle always insisted I carry it if I went out without him. And that I knew how to use it, too."

Emily just stared for a moment. She couldn't imagine Papa's reaction if Mama had wanted to carry a gun. And Aunt Louisa was Papa's sister. But clearly the two of them were different in more ways than Emily had realized.

And perhaps carrying a small gun was something she should consider. Granville carried a gun, after all, and it often came in useful on a detective case.

"Then we just need to thank Mrs. Herron and we can be on our way home," Emily said.

"Thank goodness," said Aunt Louisa. "My feet hurt. I never would have worn these evening slippers if I'd realized we'd be trekking through the cellar. They are made to be seen, not to walk in."

As the carriage Aunt Louisa had hired for the evening drew up to her front door, both of them could see that the house was in darkness.

"That's odd," Aunt Louisa said. "I could have sworn I left a light on in the hall."

"Perhaps the bulb burned out," Emily said. "Or maybe Mr. Lau really did come here."

"But Lau would be turning lights on if he was here. Not turning them off. "

"Unless he doesn't want anyone to know he's here. And even a shadow crossing a lighted window can raise suspicions, you know."

"Especially in this neighborhood," Aunt Louisa said thoughtfully. "And several of my neighbors knew we would be out this evening. So, what do we do now?"

"I don't know how to shoot a gun," Emily said. "How comfortable are you with doing so?"

"Well, I've never shot an actual person. But I used to enjoy going shooting with your uncle, which we did quite regularly. And I'm considered an expert shot. "

Another surprise. Emily suddenly regretted her earlier harsh judgements of her aunt. There was much more to her than she'd realized.

"I hope it won't come to shooting anyone," she said. "But if your feet are up to it, I think we should sneak around the side, and see if the lights are on in the kitchen. If Mr. Lau is there, I'd like to take him by surprise. "

"And going in the front way would give everything away," her aunt said with a brisk nod. "It's a good plan. And don't worry, I won't shoot the man unless I have to. And if I do have shoot him, I won't kill him. I'm quite capable of hitting an arm or a leg."

Emily swallowed hard. Even with training, she wasn't sure she'd be so calm about having to shoot someone. But she was very glad Aunt Louisa was so confident.

"I think we should send the driver to fetch the police," Emily said. "As a precaution, in case Mr. Lau is more dangerous that we think."

Aunt Louisa considered that, then nodded. "Your uncle would have approved," she said.

The driver protested about leaving them to go into a darkened house alone, but he wasn't up to arguing with her aunt.

They watched the carriage leave, then Emily turned back towards the house. "Follow me, then," she said, slipping from the gravel of the drive that crunched underfoot to the soft, silent grass that ran around the side of the house.

As they rounded the corner of the house, Emily could see a dim light burning in the kitchen. But she couldn't see any sign of Mr. Lau.

"Where could he be?" she said softly.

"Pantry," was her aunt's terse reply. "It's where I'd hide things if I needed a quick getaway. "

Emily pictured the layout of the kitchen. The pantry was a narrow windowless room that opened off the far side of the kitchen, beside the stove. "We'll have to go in. And quietly, or he'll hear us. "

The moon was high now, the moonlight creating bright spots and deeps shadows everywhere, though the breeze had died down.

It felt easier when the shadows weren't moving. Keeping their heads low, and staying in the shelter of the bushes, they ghosted across the lawn to the back door.

Opening the screen door slowly and gently, Emily handed it off to her aunt to hold open while she opened the door itself just as slowly. Then they were in.

Holding a finger her lips, then beckoning her aunt to follow her, Emily tiptoed across the shadowy kitchen.

Mr. Lau was still out of sight, so she was more worried about being heard than being seen. The silence in the kitchen was so thick, it felt like she could touch it. The ticking of the clock on the far wall seemed to boom around them.

As she grew closer, Emily could see a thin line of light under the pantry door. She'd been right, Mr. Lau had come here. Was she right about everything else, too?

Even now she couldn't fully believe it. Aunt Louisa's cook, of all people. It seemed too outlandish to be real.

The door creaked. "He's coming out," Emily said over her shoulder, keeping her voice low enough that only Aunt Louisa would hear her. "Is your gun ready?"

She glanced back and saw the pretty little sliver pistol. Which looked suddenly lethal in Aunt Louisa's determined grip.

There was no time for more, as Mr. Lau came into view. He was carrying a small leather bag, heavy with coins that clicked as he moved.

"I'd stop right there if I were you. We have a few more questions for you about the robbery at the Herron's," Aunt Louisa said as he caught sight of them and froze. "And this time we need honest answers. Lies won't suffice."

Mr. Lau looked even more shocked than she felt. For a moment Emily thought he'd obey her aunt, but then his face twisted into a snarl, and his dark eyes bored into hers.

Suddenly he looked lethal, and more than capable of killing anyone who got in his way. Emily's hand flew to her throat, and she took an involuntary step back.

With a lithe swiftness, he moved to the counter and reached

for the knife block. His hands closed around two of the bone-handled knives. Emily watching in horrified fascination as the muscles in his arms and shoulders tensed through the thin tunic he wore.

Her mind raced frantically, looking for some way out of this.

"I suggest you don't move," Aunt Louisa said firmly, her gun held steady in her white gloved hand.

The cook glanced over at her, then froze.

"Good. Now let go of the knives and lace your hands together on top of your head. Slowly," Aunt Louisa said. "Then turn and face us. Even more slowly."

Mr. Lau did as she instructed.

The relief Emily felt as he did so was so strong, and the contrast with her aunt's usual manner was so astonishing that she was nearly surprised into a laugh. Or perhaps it was the shock of it all.

She kept her gaze focused on Mr. Lau and tamped down her unwieldy emotions. "We know everything," Emily told him. "So you might as well confess."

And that quickly he must have weighed the situation and made a different decision. He turned and darted for the door.

Now what was she to do? If the threat of a gun didn't stop him…?

The bark of the revolver from beside her answered her question as it set her ears ringing. Aunt Louisa had shot him!

Before the sound had died away, Emily was in motion. Pulling her long skirts up and out of her way, she ran to where Mr. Lau lay bleeding on the tile floor. Dropping to her knees beside him, she could see he was alive.

And probably not badly injured, though he seemed too stunned to realize it yet. He hadn't expected his employer to fire, any more than she had.

The bullet had gone through his calf, and he was bleeding steadily, but not in the spurts that would have meant death. Emily grabbed a linen napkin from the counter, folded it, and pressed it against his leg.

"We need something to bind his wound," she said, glancing over her shoulder and hoping her aunt would hear the words she left unspoken.

"I know just the thing." With a decisive nod, Aunt Louisa handed the gun to Emily, then circled around them and disappeared into the pantry.

Pressing down on the injured man's wound with one hand, Emily aimed the gun at him with the other. She was very conscious that she needed to keep it out of his reach.

Mr. Lau seemed harmless enough now, but he's seemed so earlier, as well. She wasn't making the mistake of underestimating him again.

Emily heard the sound of fabric ripping, then her aunt emerged from the pantry holding long strips of white fabric. "This should work," she said briskly, sweeping her skirts out of the way, then kneeling down beside Emily.

Who noted with amusement that her aunt had still managed to keep her skirts out of the blood.

"These sheets were ready for the rag bag anyway, but they're absorbent and sturdy enough. How is he doing?" Aunt Louisa asked.

As she spoke she put a hand on the injured man's wrist as if feeling for a pulse, then quickly grabbed his other wrist and tied them efficiently together with several strips of sheet. The minute he'd felt his wrists being tied, the cook's eyes sprang open and he begun to struggle.

But the two of them were too fast for him.

Emily had been watching him carefully, and the minute his eyes opened she stopped putting pressure on the hole in his calf and sat down heavily on his legs so he couldn't move them.

Aunt Louisa grabbed the gun from Emily and leveled it on him. "I wouldn't," she said.

While the two engaged in a silent glaring match, Emily used more strips of the sheet and tied his ankles tightly together. Then she quickly used another strip to tie the linen napkin tightly around the wound in his calf. That done, she glanced around, and retrieved the small bag he'd been carrying.

"I wonder how much is in here?" she said, hefting the bag so that the coins inside jingled. "It feels quite heavy. "

Mr. Lau didn't answer, just watched the two of them as if waiting for his moment. Being tied hand and foot didn't seem to bother him. In fact, he looked like a rattlesnake ready to strike. Emily had seen one at the zoo, once, and never forgotten that sense of coiled power.

"How much did you say you were paying him?" she said lightly to her aunt, though her eyes never left their captive.

"Not enough to explain that much money," her aunt said tartly.

"I wonder where he got it," Emily said, as if thinking out loud. "And how long it will take the officers to get here and arrest him."

"It probably means that you were right, and that he was involved in the theft, at the very least," Aunt Louisa said. "Mr. Carstairs probably paid him for his part in stealing the pottery. Though from the look of that bag, and the discussion at dinner, he probably didn't pay him as much as he should have."

"Care to tell us?" Emily said, deliberately needling their prisoner.

She didn't really expect him to tell them anything, but he clearly wasn't afraid of them. Maybe he thought he could get loose, and that Aunt Louisa wouldn't shoot him again. In the meantime, he might let something slip.

His face expressionless, Mr. Lau didn't say a word.

"You do realize Mr. Carstairs has been arrested," Emily said, inventing as she went. She shot a quick glance at her aunt, who luckily hadn't reacted to the lie. "He's probably telling the police right now that it was all you—that you're responsible for the theft and the murder."

Some strong expression crossed Mr. Lau's face, but it was gone so quickly Emily wasn't sure what it was. "You'll hang for it," she said, watching him closely. "While Mr. Carstairs goes free."

Aunt Louisa was standing a few feet back from them, her gun pointed unwaveringly at the middle of the cook's forehead. "And Ying will go free, as well," she said.

Mr. Lau grimaced. "No. Moving dishes took two men. Ying hang for his part in this."

It was hatred she'd seen, Emily realized with a sense of shock. "Mr. Ying wasn't involved," she said.

"Ying plan all," he said.

Emily wanted desperately to look at her aunt, but she didn't dare take her eyes off their prisoner. If Mr. Lau was telling the truth, both men would hang.

But even if the fellow was lying, he was likely to be believed anyway—and Mr. Ying would still hang.

Sentiment ran strong against the Chinese community in general —except when it came to household chores, growing vegetables, and providing laundry or tailoring services. And guilt was more believable than innocence. Especially if it meant that Mr. Carstairs, one of their own, went free.

Because Mr. Lau was probably telling the truth when he said it had taken two men to move the pottery.

Desperately searching for a question that would wring the truth out of their captive, Emily was distracted by the sound of pounding feet and loud voices from the floor above. The police had arrived.

Too soon. Now Emily was wishing she and her aunt had longer to question Mr. Lau. The police would believe his story without digging any further.

But they didn't have the whole story yet. Emily knew it in her bones. There was something that didn't quite fit—but in the darkened kitchen with the smell of blood and cordite in her nostrils, her nerves jumping with the after effects of adrenaline, she couldn't quite put it all together.

And they'd run out of time, she thought in despair as heavy boots clattered down the stairs.

Emily felt like screaming in frustration. But that wouldn't be professional. And would probably upset her aunt. Gun or not, she had no wish to insult her aunt's generous hospitality and willingness to help by worrying Aunt Louisa even more than she already had.

There were answers here. Somewhere. She just had to find them.

"WE HAVE to talk to Mr. Carstairs," Emily said to Aunt Louisa as they both collapsed on the sofa in the parlor. The policemen had at last taken their departure, after far too many unnerving questions, taking Mr. Lau with them. "You didn't believe Mr. Lau, did you? When he said that Mr. Ying is guilty I mean?"

"I don't know," Aunt Louisa said. "It's been quite an evening. I just wish the police hadn't taken my gun with them."

"I know," Emily said. "Do you think they believed what we were saying?"

"We've done what we can," Aunt Louisa said. "You need to rely on them to sort all this out. It's out of our hands now."

"But that's just it," Emily said. "How can I rely on them? They've always thought that Mr. Ying was guilty, and refused to look any further."

"Well, we've done the looking for them," Aunt Louisa said. "And now they have the culprit in custody."

"They have *a* culprit in custody," Emily said. "I am not convinced that Mr. Lau is *the* culprit. And he is far too ready to say that Mr. Ying was in on it."

"*In on it*? Where do you come up with these sayings?" her aunt said. "I am beginning to believe your Mr. Granville is a bad influence."

Emily knew he was, or at least in the eyes of those of her parent's generation. It was one of the things that made him so perfect.

"He's not a bad influence," she said. "It's just this case. I still think we're missing something. I only wish I knew what it was."

"Whatever do you mean?" Aunt Louisa said. "Mr. Lau ran when he heard what the stolen pottery was worth. And he had the money. Which likely ties him to the robbery, since he never could have earned that amount honestly. They've just arrested him. What more do you want?"

"Well, we still have no idea how the theft happened. Or why

poor Betsy was killed. Or who killed her. Or even what happened to the pottery."

"I thought it all quite clear," Aunt Louisa said. "Lau and Ying conspired to sell the pottery to Mr. Carstairs. In the process of stealing it, Betsy saw them, and they killed her to silence her."

"Exactly," Emily said. "And where was Mr. Carstairs in all of this?"

"That's easy," Aunt Louisa said. "He's the collector, the one with a passion for pottery, and the money to pay for it. He was likely sitting in his study, waiting for his new toy to be delivered to him."

"And that is his only role? Paying for the collection?" Emily asked.

"Now that I know Lau is in on this," Aunt Louisa said. "Yes. Trust me, I spend a lot of time around collectors. When they have a passion for a thing, they are determined to have it. And they will do anything, spend any amount of money to get it, no matter how ridiculous."

Emily waited for her aunt's own words to hit her. Aunt Louisa was no lightweight, no matter what she sometimes pretended.

"Oh," Aunt Louisa said.

"Yes." Emily said. It amused her as much as it pleased her to see the light in her eyes as Aunt Louisa too started to put the pieces together.

"So you think Mr. Carstairs…?"

"From the little I know of him, I don't see him as a man who would be content to sit in the background while there was a possibility of making a rare addition to his collection."

Aunt Louisa sighed. "You might be right. But it's too late now to do anything about it. The police already have their suspects in custody. And all the evidence they need."

"Which we gave them. And it's never too late."

"But what can we do?"

"That's why I want to talk to Mr. Carstairs."

"You don't seriously think he will just tell you what he did. Whatever that might have been."

"No, of course not. We still have no proof that Mr. Carstairs was involved at all, even in buying the stolen pottery. That's where you come in."

"Where I come in?" Aunt Louisa said. "You want me to talk to him? How do you expect me to get answers out of him?"

And then she redeemed herself for all time in Emily's eyes when she added, "I don't even have my gun."

4 8

Friday, September 7, 1900

Friday morning Granville woke early. He hadn't slept well. Emily hadn't called after her dinner party, as she'd promised.

He'd waited until ten last night, when a normal dinner party would have ended, then called her aunt's home repeatedly for over an hour. There had been no answer.

Grateful that the telephones had been installed in his new house, he telephoned again as soon as the clock struck seven this morning. The telephone at her aunt's home rang several times unanswered, and he'd begun to think he'd have to ask the operator to intervene. Or possibly call the police.

When suddenly he heard the click as the mouthpiece was raised. "Good morning, Atkin residence."

It was Emily.

"Emily? Are you all right? I didn't hear back last night. And I haven't been able to reach you."

"You were worried. Oh, Granville, I'm so sorry," she said. "I'm fine. I really am."

"You don't sound like yourself."

"I'm just fine," she assured him. "All in one piece and every-thing. I'll fill you in on every detail as soon as I'm back home."

He wondered how much she was avoiding telling him. "Which means you'll be coming home soon?"

"Yes, I hope—and believe—that I will be," she said, to his relief. "If everything goes well today."

So the evening must have been a productive one. "And your evening?" he asked formally. "Your dinner party also went well?"

"There were a few unexpected surprises," she said, clearly picking her words carefully. "But yes. Very well."

Oh, yes. There was a lot she wasn't saying. But as long as she was out of danger, it could wait until she was home. "But every-thing worked out well?"

"It did," she said, then quickly deflected the question. "And you? How are things proceeding there?"

"You're not injured, are you?" he persisted.

"No, not a bit."

He could hear the truth in her voice, and let out a relieved breath. "Then to answer your question, Carver will be countersuing Peabody on Randall's behalf. And he was able to get a quick trial date, given the tragic circumstances."

He heard Emily draw in a quick breath at his mention of tragedy. Then her even quicker brain worked out what he couldn't say. "Randall?" she said, with a note in her voice told him she under-stood the ruse.

"Yes, sadly. So Carver will be calling a lot of witnesses. Six lawyers will be served this morning. Which will keep the focus on what's happening here, not whatever might be going on in Victoria."

"I'm glad to hear it," she said. "That sounds quite helpful. So when is the trial?"

Quite helpful meant she was up to something, and glad not to have to worry about a big fish. Not even a smallish big fish. So perhaps he'd solved his own case in time to help hers, after all. "Tuesday," he said.

"If all goes well, I hope to be back in town for the trial," she said.

She must be very close to finishing her case. Which was excellent news. "I'd be very pleased to have your company on Tuesday," was all he said, still mindful of listening ears. "You'll be careful?"

"Of course. And you too."

"Also of course. And I'm looking forward to Tuesday."

"Me too," she said ungrammatically. And this time her tone wasn't careful at all.

Granville hung up the mouthpiece with a grin, and whistling, hied himself off in search of breakfast.

HALF AN HOUR LATER, the team had gathered in the meeting room again. It was fast becoming a favored place to work. Granville looked up from jotting down cryptic notes and glanced around the table.

Carver, Mac and Miss Kent were busily arguing over some legal document or other. They'd sent Trent off to the newspaper archives to dig further into where each of the parties had been prior to the attack on Randall.

Scott was scowling over a long, densely worded document.

And Miss Rizzo was again in the outer office on reception and handling the telephones. That arrangement seemed to be working out far too well. He wondered how long it would be before someone tried to persuade him to add her to the team.

He went back to his own notes with an inward smile, and considered another team. The six lawyers. Even with all of them working together, there was probably still a leader. Of sorts. Someone who came up with the plan, stirred up the others.

Not quite a pufferfish, because most of the poison they'd been slinging around was for show. But a big fish in their little legal pond, anyway.

Or better yet, a small fish with delusions of grandeur, he thought with a grin. Mostly it was relief. Both cases were nearly done. And Emily was coming home.

But small fish or not, the fellow had managed to stay invisible. So far, anyway. Most likely he was simply sneakier than the others.

A deluded small fish. Who still thought nothing would stick to him.

Well, he'd be called to the stand and made to look an incompetent idiot, then arrested and charged along with the rest of them, so maybe it didn't matter what he thought.

But it irked Granville that they hadn't found him. And that the fellow would get off with no larger penalty than any of his cohorts. To his mind, the small fish bore more of the responsibility, and should pay a bigger price. No matter what the law said.

He felt the same way about Gurak and his thugs.

Carver's earlier comment that the legal fight would be simpler and the penalties higher if Randall had died applied to Gurak's gang, too. They hadn't been part of the importing schemes, which seemed to be where Carver was busy building proof against the six to use in court. Did that mean that after nearly killing Randall, Gurak and his thugs might get away with nothing but fines?

As he considered that, he remembered a snippet of conversation he'd overheard at Clara's sister's wedding. Something about the downtown not being safe anymore, and too many killings.

That day, he'd been worried about Emily's safety from whatever he and Scott had stirred up, and he hadn't really paid attention. But it had stuck at the back of his mind, and thinking about the attack on Randall had triggered the memory.

He looked up as Carver and Mac's voices rose. They seemed to be debating some complex issue of what did or did not constitute financial fraud. Fascinating though it might be, it wasn't helping his thinking processes any.

Miss Kent was intent on the argument, but Scott had a broad grin on his face. That was enough to decide him.

"Scott, do you have a moment?" he asked.

At his partner's nod, he raised his voice. "Scott and I are going out to stretch our legs for a bit," he said. The others didn't even look up.

He and Scott ended up in Mary's Diner, at their usual table in the back, cups of coffee steaming in front of them.

"You hear anything about a killing or killings in town sometime in the last few months?" Granville asked his partner in low tones.

"A killing?" Scott said, his heavy brows drawing together.

Granville repeated what he remembered of that half-overheard conversation.

"Oh, those killings," Scott said. "If they were killings."

"You've heard about them?"

"I'm surprised you hadn't," Scott said. "But we were pretty focused on the Steveston case at the time."

"One murder?"

"Two. Or maybe three. There have been some pretty wild rumors, but I don't know that they were murders."

"Three deaths, then. What happened?"

"One looked like an accidental fall, only he wasn't found 'til the next morning, and he was dead of his injuries by then. And there were some questions about how he'd managed to fall and injure himself so badly, though it was just gossip, far's I know.

The second was the same deal. He'd been out celebrating some real estate deal or other, and got roaring drunk. His buddies wanted to call a hack, but he insisted on walking home. Never made it."

"Any signs of a fight?"

"Nothing. It looked like he'd tripped over an uneven walkway, one where the street had been built up. Fell a couple of feet, and hit his head or something. Or was it a broken neck? Something of the sort."

"That's two," Granville said. "What about the third?"

"The third was a fight broke out at one of the pubs, and both guys got chucked out. One guy didn't make it home."

"He was beaten to death?"

"No," Scott said. "Or not in the way you mean. Nothing like poor Randall. He'd taken a blow to the head during the fight, but he seemed okay when he left the pub and started to walk home.

He was found hours later, unconscious, about halfway to his

house. They talked about a brain bleed or some such. Anyhow, they couldn't revive him, and he died."

"Any connection between the three dead men?"

Scott shook his head. "Not that I heard. I think they were just random guys, out for an evening, who drank a little too much."

"That's a lot of coincidences," Granville said. "And hearing about it now, I have a few questions. Especially given what happened to Randall. I think we need to talk to Daniels."

"I don't think they were his cases," Scott said.

"That doesn't surprise me. If it had been, there would be more answers and fewer rumors."

"You really think these deaths might be related to Randall? Whoever beat him up didn't even try to make it look accidental."

"I think Gurak is even more violent than Dagan was. And with less honor. When he was hired to attack Randall, I wouldn't be surprised if he saw a chance to get even for Dagan. And send a message at the same time."

He paused, considered what he knew. "I do think the fact that Randall is still alive was an accident, though. Maybe if I hadn't arrived so quickly, he would have died of his injuries."

"Like the others," Scott said heavily.

"Indeed. And I think that we need to know more about these other deaths."

"Then let's go see Daniels," Scott said as he stood, drained his coffee and threw a few coins on the table.

GRANVILLE TRACKED Daniels down at the police station, where he'd just written up his latest arrest.

"You heading out again?" Granville asked.

"Yes, why?"

"We'll walk with you," he said. The police station was no place to discuss this crime. Not where so many ears might be listening.

Several blocks away, he detoured the three of them into a temporarily deserted alley. Where he raised the three earlier cases, and the possibility of them being murders, with Gurak and his gang behind them.

Daniels was skeptical, to put it kindly. But when Granville laid out his speculations about the three deaths, pointing out their similarity to the attack on Randall—with Scott adding pertinent details—the policeman's eyes took on that glint.

They'd caught his interest. Good.

"How do you want to proceed?" Daniels asked.

"I want to see Gurak and his thugs arrested and brought up on trial for murder. They need to be stopped. And they need to pay for what they've done," he said.

"How do you plan to achieve that?"

"Using any means necessary."

"Any legal means, I'm sure you mean," Daniels said.

"Of course," Granville said, exchanging a grin with Scott. "Didn't I say that?"

Daniels smiled back, and shook his head.

Not sure if that was an answer or a comment, Granville ignored it. "The thing is, we need the arrests to happen soon, because in Randall's case, at least, we're pretty sure someone hired Gurak's boys to kill him. And we have a court case coming up that should prove it."

"I see," Daniels said. "And what do you hope I can accomplish for this plan of yours?"

"Tie Gurak to the deaths, and find enough evidence to prove they were murder. Or, in Randall's case, attempted murder," he said.

"Is that all? And by when?"

"Tuesday morning at the latest," Scott said, deadpan. "We have a court date."

Daniels rolled his eyes. "I don't know why I bother with you two. You know that's impossible."

"You've earned some nice arrests because of us," he said. "How's that promotion to detective looking?"

The corner of Daniels mouth ticked up in a reluctant smile. "Better all the time, thanks."

"Glad to hear it. Now imagine how pulling together these cases and proving them murders will look."

Daniels held up his hands, half-laughing. "Whoa. There simply isn't enough time between now and Tuesday. Even if I had help. Which I won't, because it would take at least a week to convince the Chief to consider those deaths were murder."

"You'll have help. Ours." And Granville pointed to himself and Scott.

Daniels muttered something, but he stopped arguing. For now.

"Can you get your hands on the files for the first three cases?" Scott asked.

"Probably," Daniels said. "But not until after my shift."

"Then Scott and I will start looking for connections between the three victims. And we'll buy you dinner."

"You should have started with that. On my pay, I'd never turn down a free meal." Daniels grinned. "I'll meet you at Mary's. Seven?"

"Done." And Granville headed for the door, with Scott matching him, stride for stride.

Emily's conversation with Mr. Carstairs, not surprisingly, had to wait until the next morning. Unfortunately, in the meantime she and Aunt Louisa received a hastily written note from Caroline Herron.

The police had followed Mr. Carstairs, as promised, but he hadn't gone to Chinatown the previous evening at all. Instead, he had gone straight to his residence in tony James Bay. They'd watched his house for the next hour, but all he'd done was sit in his study, drinking brandy and writing letters.

"Unfortunately, Lau continues to implicate Ying," Caroline had written. "And won't be swayed from the story. Not that the police are trying very hard."

"However, it's a good thing you caught Lau with that money," she'd added. "Or the police would be seriously upset with all of us."

Emily took little comfort from that. It didn't get them any closer to finding out who had really murdered poor Betsy.

And could it mean that she'd been wrong? That Mr. Carstairs wasn't involved at all?

Then why had he been so angry at dinner last night?

"Well, it's a good thing we hadn't yet arranged to meet with the man," Aunt Louisa said as she came back into the breakfast room with a fresh pot of tea. "I need to advertise for a new cook as soon as possible. Unless you're a better cook than I am, we're not going to be eating very well until I can find someone."

"Mmm," said Emily, not really paying attention. She could make tea, and boil an egg, if you weren't too picky about how the yolk was cooked. And there were good restaurants and bakeries in town. They wouldn't starve.

Aunt Louisa gave her a sharp look. "Emily are you listening to me?"

"If Mr. Carstairs isn't the collector who bought the stolen pottery, who else might it be?" Emily asked. Knowing that the appeal to her aunt's collector's heart would be the best distraction.

"We've already been through this," Aunt Louisa said. "And my opinion hasn't changed. Mr. Carstairs is the most likely one. Especially after his behavior last night."

"Which is what I've been thinking, too. But we have no way of proving that he's the one who bought those ugly thistle plates. And if he didn't go to Chinatown last night, then how was he communicating with the thieves?"

"According to Caroline, the police only watched him for an hour. How do we know he didn't go out again after that?" Aunt Louisa said calmly, pouring them each another cup of tea.

She sat forward, staring at her aunt. "You're right. He could easily have done so. Or perhaps he was writing someone to set up a meeting for today."

Aunt Louisa smiled and sipped her tea.

Emily nibbled at one of the currant-filled scones her aunt had made earlier, after they'd realized there was no bread left. The scones were rather good. Perhaps she should learn how to bake such things. She'd never realized what a useful skill it could be.

Nor, she suddenly realized, had she given sufficient thought to how she and Granville were to live once they married. He'd already moved into the house he'd bought for the two of them—a house that she had chosen. Small enough to maintain easily, it was still big enough to house a small staff if they needed them.

She had decided to manage without live-in staff, though, having seen the difficulties her mother sometimes had. Mama had trained her in the basics of running a household, after all. Though she was much better at cleaning than she was at cooking. And she'd never had to do everything herself. It was all about training others to perform the various tasks to your standards.

She hadn't really thought about who would do the cooking and cleaning, if she was working with Granville in his detective agency. Nor considered that it might be difficult to find such people, especially if she wasn't there during the day to train them and supervise their work.

And she seriously doubted Granville had ever cooked a meal in his life. Except perhaps over an open fire on the goldfields. Which wouldn't translate well—though it meant he might be marginally better at making a meal than she was. How was this ever going to work?

"Emily?" Aunt Louisa said.

Emily blinked, realized she'd been staring into space as she tried to imagine her life as a married woman. This was going to be more complicated than she'd thought.

"What do you know about Mr. Carstairs?" she asked her aunt.

"He's an American. From somewhere back east, Boston, I think. He doesn't have that Brahmin accent, though, so I'm not sure that's accurate."

"He must have money, to collect the way he does?"

"He seems well enough off, though no one knows where the money comes from," Aunt Louisa said.

"Has he been a collector long?"

"He's been a member of our society for nearly two years. He joined when he first moved to town."

Which didn't really help at all. "Well, if Mr. Carstairs was writing to someone about the stolen pottery…Is there any way we can read the letters? Or at least who they're addressed to?"

"Interfering with the mail is illegal," Aunt Louisa said. "And I don't know how we'd manage it anyway." She paused, and poured more tea.

Emily was about to say something, but she was beginning to recognize that look on her aunt's face. She waited.

"Of course, Marion Parker down at the post office is an absolute busybody," Aunt Louisa said. "I swear she must memorize where half the letters are going, given how much she seems to know about what's happening in town."

"Is there any chance she'll talk to us?"

Aunt Louisa nodded. "If we ask her the right way. Leave this to me."

MARION PARKER at the post office had proven surprisingly helpful. By the time Emily and Aunt Louisa met Mr. Carstairs for lunch in the dining room at the Empress Hotel, they had several extra questions to ask him. For once, Emily ignored the elaborately beautiful surroundings, and focused on her opponent. For so she considered him.

She and Aunt Louisa had spoken at length as they walked over from the post office, working out their strategy. Emily was to take the lead, which she did as soon as the pleasantries were over and their orders placed.

"Mr. Carstairs," she said. "I hope you will forgive an impertinent question, but I find myself so confused by the discussion at dinner last night. How much is the collection of naturalist earthenware belonging to the Herrons actually worth?"

He gave her a tight smile. It looked as if hurt. "Any collection is worth exactly what a collector will pay for it. No less, and certainly no more."

"But I don't understand," she said. "Why do Mr. Andrews and Mr. Martin think the collection is worth so much more than you do? It doesn't make sense."

"Their opinions are different than mine," he said with a frown.

"But why?"

Judging by Mr. Carstairs's expression, the waiter's interruption as he served their oyster soup was welcome distraction. No doubt he was hoping she'd forget that line of questioning, Emily thought with glee. It wasn't going to happen.

"But how could you value the collection so much less than Mr. Andrews and Mr. Martin do, when all three of you collect the same kind of pottery?" she persisted just as he took a mouthful of soup. "How is that possible?"

For a moment she thought he was going to choke on his soup. Or spit it back at her. There was a charged silence.

He glared at her. "Are you accusing me of something?"

Emily was enjoying herself as she gave him a wide-eyed look. "What...? Accusing you? I don't understand. How could you think such a thing?"

She wished she could squeeze out tears on demand, but that skill was beyond her, so she looked plaintively at Aunt Louisa instead.

"My apologies. I misunderstood you," he said curtly.

"The apologies should be on our side," Aunt Louisa said in soothing tones. "I am afraid my niece sometimes leaps in without considering her words, where she should treat her elders with more consideration."

She and Mr. Carstairs exchanged a look. He smirked a little as Aunt Louisa said, "Ah, youth."

Emily held back her grin. This was exactly what she had hoped would happen. Aunt Louisa had stepped in, and now she had brought Mr. Carstairs onside. Hopefully he would be more open with her.

If she asked the right questions.

"It was certainly an eventful evening last night," Aunt Louisa said. "You've heard that the police later arrested my cook in connection with the theft of the pottery?"

"No, I hadn't heard," he said. "And I'm sorry to hear it. Has the fellow confessed?"

"No, he continues to blame Ying," Aunt Louisa said. "I'm just so confused and upset by the whole thing. It seems a shame that collecting always seems to have this dark side to it. You know what I mean, don't you, Mr. Carstairs?"

"Well," he said slowly, "Yes, I suppose I do. We collectors do tend to get carried away at times. And there are always unscrupulous folk willing to take advantage of us. But as they say, anything worth having is worth fighting for."

"I know. It makes me sad," Aunt Louisa said. "That these beautiful things don't always exist in beauty."

He nodded as though she had said something profound, instead of something that Emily found almost incomprehensible. However, she suspected that was the point. Aunt Louisa was firmly in character, and it wasn't so much what she said, it was how Mr. Carstairs responded.

"And if you'll forgive my curiosity—with all this fuss, I've been dying to know. It appears whoever stole the collection found a buyer," Aunt Louisa said. "And I haven't heard a single rumor about who that could be, which is most unusual. Usually the Society members are the first people to know. Have you heard anything?"

"No, nothing," he said. "Which, as you say, is odd. I always keep my ears open for rumors of anything relating to any of my collections. You'll be surprised how often that has paid off."

"Not at all," Aunt Louisa said. "It's the nature of being a collector, is it not? Finding the hidden gems before another collector does, I mean. But please, go on."

"Well, in this case it has not."

"I suppose it doesn't matter now," Aunt Louisa said. "Aside from the inconvenience of finding a new cook. Because as we learned last night, what was stolen was only a copy. The Herrons still have the real items."

"True," Mr. Carstairs said.

"But I wonder, what is going to happen to the real collection?" Aunt Louisa said. "If they were to sell it, I mean. Would you buy it?"

"Normally I would be very interested," he said with a smile that almost looked genuine to Emily. "Unfortunately, thanks to those idiots Andrews and Martin..." He looked at Aunt Louisa. "My apologies, ma'am."

Aunt Louisa shook her head. "Not at all. Most understandable."

"Their babble last night has driven up the Herron's expectation of the collection's value, based on little or no knowledge. So even if they were willing to sell, I doubt I could meet their terms."

"Wouldn't that only matter if Mr. Andrews or Mr. Martin were also trying to purchase the collection?" Emily asked.

Mr. Carstairs gave her an irritated look. "They are collectors too. Of course they'll try to purchase it."

Aunt Louisa gave him a knowing look. "Yes, but will they be willing to buy at their own inflated prices?"

He nodded, looking thoughtful. "It's all about negotiation. But I'd give a lot to own that collection," he added, half to himself.

"Oh?" Emily said. "How much is a lot?"

She tried to look young and naïve and surprised all at the same time. She was afraid it was a dismal failure, but carried on anyway.

"I'm afraid that's confidential for now," he said calmly. But the quick swallow of coffee he took gave him away.

Emily considered him carefully. Based on what he'd just said, coupled with his behavior last night, she was more convinced than ever that he had bought the Herron's collection. Which he now thought was fake.

And judging by his comments the previous evening, he'd likely paid a thousand dollars or more for it. It was a lot of money, money he couldn't recover, which might leave him unable to bid on what he now believed to be the real collection.

What Emily still didn't know—and desperately needed to know—was what part Mr. Carstairs had played in the robbery itself. And in the murder of young Betsy.

Was *he* the murderer?

Mr. Lau had said it took two people to clear the collection out of the cellar. He'd implied that Mr. Ying had been the second person. And he'd apparently reiterated that claim to the police.

But Wong Sun had identified the two people involved as a non-Chinese 'hasty man' as the killer. And a Chinese thief, hired with the help of someone who didn't live in Victoria—possibly one of the lawyers Granville was now investigating?

Mr. Carstairs and Mr. Lau? It was seeming more likely the more they found out about what had happened that day.

But why would Mr. Lau have been hired through a lawyer in Vancouver? He was her aunt's cook—Mr. Carstairs probably already knew him.

Unless whoever Wong Sun's informant was, he hadn't known about Mr. Lau? And the thief was yet another man—a third man—who had been hired from Chinatown?

Emily thought about that for a moment. All that pottery had to be heavy. It was also fragile, so those boxes had to be handled carefully. And if the thieves had timed the theft to coincide with Mrs. Herron's afternoon tea, then they had a limited amount of time available to pull it off.

Were two people even enough to handle the task?

The timing of the theft had always seemed an odd choice to Emily. Surely the risk of discovery would be lessened late at night, rather than in the middle of a tea party. Had the distraction provided by the commotion of such a large entertainment seemed worth the risk?

Staging the theft during the afternoon tea still didn't feel right to her. Not unless the thieves had always intended Mr. Ying to be the scapegoat.

Then an ugly thought occurred to her. Surely that didn't mean the young Betsy's death was planned? Emily sipped her tea to hide the horror that had probably crossed her face at the very idea.

Neither Mr. Lau nor Mr. Carstairs could be that ruthless. Could they?

But what role had the third man played? If indeed there had been a third man.

She glanced at Mr. Carstairs, whose attention was focused on Aunt Louisa. Luckily her aunt had recognized the moment and was busily apologizing for Emily's latest too blunt question. Mr. Carstairs was accepting her soft words as his due, even smiling a little.

She didn't like him at all, but he didn't look like a ruthless killer. Still, even her limited experience with detection told her that evil didn't always look ugly. Not on the outside, at least.

When they'd caught him trying to flee with the money, Mr. Lau had looked far more evil than Mr. Carstairs did now. Which didn't mean he was evil.

Nor that he wasn't.

Emily shook her head. This case was beyond frustrating. And it was time to bring this visit to an end and go home. To Granville.

If it weren't for poor Betsy, she'd probably have given up by now. Except that she never gave up on anything.

Someone was a murderer and a thief. And they were going to pay for it, if she had to stay at her aunt's until… and here Emily gave up on the thought. She'd been here quite long enough, thank you, and she didn't want to jinx herself.

Wrenching her mind back to the situation at hand, Emily debated bringing up the information they'd got from the post-mistress. After another glance at Mr. Carstairs self-important face, she decided now was not the time.

Emily exchanged glances with Aunt Louisa and shook her head slightly. Her aunt gave her the subtlest of nods. Good. She agreed.

So where did that leave them?

Pursuing an address or three, apparently.

"Mr. Carstairs seems very defensive, didn't you think?" Emily said as she and her aunt walked out through the heavy double doors of the Empress and strolled towards the Inner Harbor.

It was cloudy today, with a breeze that set the clouds scudding across the sky, but still warm enough to be pleasant. The threat of rain appeared to have kept most people indoors, though. There were so few people strolling along the seawall, Emily felt quite safe discussing the case as they walked.

"Defensive is exactly the word for it," Aunt Louisa said.

"But what was he defensive about?" Emily said. "We didn't get much out of him. And I keep thinking about the letters he wrote last night. Thanks to Marion at the post office, we know who he wrote to. If not what he wrote about."

"Today's luncheon was not the time to ask."

Aunt Louisa was right, but it was so frustrating.

"No. But those letters must be in response to him thinking the pottery is fake. And we still don't have enough facts. And every time we guess, we risk wasting time on information that doesn't lead anywhere."

"I thought you wanted to be a detective," Aunt Louisa said with a sideways look and a small smile. "At least, I've heard your Papa complain about it often enough. Isn't this what detectives do?"

"You're right," Emily said, laughing a little at herself. "Please ignore my rants, Aunt. I'm just frustrated. It seems with this case I keep running into dead ends. And I want to see Betsy's killer in jail."

"So you don't think either of the men now in jail killed her?"

"Mr. Lau or Mr. Ying? No. I don't."

"Why ever not? I don't see that we've gathered enough information to even point at Mr. Sinclair as a killer, much less to be sure it's him."

It was a good question. Indeed, it was a very good question.

"I may not have facts," Emily said slowly, thinking it through as she spoke. "But the further we dig into this case, the stronger my feeling is that Mr. Carstairs is the one behind all this. And not just because he agreed to buy the stolen pottery, setting everything in motion."

She brushed an errant strand away from her eyes, frowning a little. "I didn't fully realize it until right this moment. I'm increasingly sure he's the killer. But even now I can't seem to find the facts that would prove it."

Aunt Louisa nodded. "So far I'm not convinced," she said. "But I find it interesting that you are. From everything I've seen so far, your detective instincts are good. And I'm very proud of you for persisting in following that career."

She smiled. "Even in the face of my brother's resistance."

Emily blushed a little. Aunt Louisa was the first member of her family to say anything positive about her determination to be a detective, and so much a part of Granville's world. It had been hard, hearing their doubts and criticisms.

She was so lucky that Granville, at least, was supportive.

"We'll need a confession from Mr. Carstairs," she said. "Nothing else will be strong enough for him to be arrested, much less brought to trial. Especially for such a senseless murder."

"I agree," Aunt Louisa said. "But how are you going to get him to confess?"

"We have a few people to talk to first," Emily said. "I'd start with the letter to his bank, but unless you know the manager at the Bank of British Columbia?"

"No, I'm afraid not."

"Then he is unlikely to tell us anything. So I suggest we start with this milliner Mr. Carstairs wrote to. I can't think why, in the midst of his fury with Mr. Lau, Mr. Carstairs would take the time to write to someone who owns a hat shop. Can you?"

Aunt Louisa gave her a wry look. "Oh, I can think of one or two," she said.

Emily blushed. "Well, apart from the obvious, I mean. I meant a reason connected with this investigation. For him to write her now... She must know something."

Emily contemplated that thought for a moment, watching the breeze pushing small waves across the harbor. "I wonder what it is? Mr. Carstairs doesn't seem the type to confide in anyone."

"He has a very high opinion of himself. Which I'm sure the information at last night's dinner bruised considerably."

"Oh. You think his ego needs stroking, so he's turning to his, ah, friend?" Emily watched a gray and white seagull dip and swoop over the harbor, looking for its dinner. "I've never heard of Mrs. Adamson. Have you?"

"Yes, she has a certain clientele for her hats. They are very modish, but too young for me."

Emily nodded. "The address isn't too far to walk, but I think we'll make a better impression if we arrive in the carriage. Is that all right?"

"Good idea. My feet are getting tired," Aunt Louisa said.

THEY SWEPT up to "Lucille's Hat Boutique" in a polished carriage from Aunt Louisa's preferred stable. The shop was tiny, but the front window sparkled, the goods were well laid out, and the hats were intriguing. Emily's eye was caught by a stylish straw braid turban, the brim covered with folds of pale green taffeta that ended in a twist around a cluster of tiny pink and white flowers. Granville would love it on her, she just knew it.

"This is lovely," she said impulsively, looking around for the milliner. "May I try it on?"

A young blonde woman looked up from the counter where she was assisting another customer, and smiled. "Please do," she said in a pleasant voice.

She looked to be only five or so years older than Emily herself, and was dressed in an understated pale blue shirtwaist and a darker blue skirt that fell unadorned to the floor. She wore a dashing bonnet of straw braid with a matching twist of blue velvet and tulle.

Aunt Louisa hid a smile as Emily pretended she was her friend Clara, who never saw a hat shop she didn't like, or a hat that she didn't need. Emily wasn't usually that fond of hats, but she liked this one. And it really did suit her.

She turned this way and that, admiring the tilt of it on her head, while she waited for the other customer to leave. When that lady left carrying a distinctive striped hat box, and the blonde stepped across to assist her, Emily was ready for her. "You are Lucille Adamson?"

The blonde's eyes widened. "Yes, I am. And it's Lucy. How may I help you?"

"We know Mr. Carstairs sent you a check yesterday," Emily said, keeping her voice low. Aunt Louisa moved to stand beside her.

As the woman's eyes widened, Aunt Louisa said, "He's your protector, isn't he?"

Lucy looked from Emily to her aunt. "Oh please, you can't tell anyone. I'd be ruined."

"Don't worry," Emily said. "We don't want to do anything that might ruin you, or your business. We'd like your help."

"My help? What do you mean?"

"Tell us about Mr. Carstairs. How long have you been together?"

"A year and a half," Lucy said. "He's good to me. I'd never be able to set up shop like this, otherwise."

Aunt Louisa looked surprised. "But you do beautiful work."

"I couldn't even find employment when I arrived. No one would take a chance on me. He did. I owe him loyalty, at least."

"You know Mr. Carstairs is a collector of china and pottery?" Emily said.

"Yes," Lucy said. "He's quite open about it. And he really does love his collections. He always shows off his newest pieces to me, and swears me to secrecy to so that his fellow collectors can't get the jump on him."

She gave Emily a tiny smile. "Though not even loyalty can make me like some of his pieces."

Emily rolled her eyes. "Those thistles."

The unsuspecting girl nodded. "Aren't they hideous? Every detail so carefully sculpted—as if that could ever be a good thing on a vase, let alone a dinner plate."

Emily looked at that sensitive face and decided to take a risk. "I'm sorry to tell you that collection was stolen."

Lucy's hand flew to her mouth. "Stolen? But... No, I'm sure it's fine."

She knew where the collection was?

"No, I mean that Mr. Carstairs doesn't own it," Emily said. "The set was stolen from its original owner. And Mr. Carstairs knew it."

Lucy looked shocked. "But he'd never."

"I'm afraid so. And what is worse, a young woman, a girl, really —who'd been hired to assist in the kitchen that day? She was stabbed to death during the theft."

"No!" It was a heartfelt cry.

Aunt Louisa moved across the room to the woman and wrapped her in her arms. "I'm afraid it's true," she said softly.

"He couldn't have," Lucy said, her head buried in Aunt Louisa's soft shoulder.

"You know he's capable of it, for his collections. Don't you?" Emily said.

"I never thought it possible. I hoped it wasn't," she sobbed. "Oh, I can't believe it."

"I'm sorry, but it really is true," Aunt Louisa said, still sheltering the girl.

"He'd do anything for one of his collections," Emily said. "Wouldn't he?"

"Yes," the girl sobbed. "Yes, I believe he would."

"What do you know?" Emily asked.

It didn't take much for the girl to tell them everything. She still swore he was kind to her, and gentle.

"But when it comes to his collecting," she sobbed. "He gets that look in his eyes. Fanatical like. I know that look. My brother had it —only it was politics for him. And got him killed, too."

The girl raised her head from Aunt Louisa's shoulder and straightened her back. "I tried not to see it. But I recognized it."

Aunt Louisa nodded. "I know what you mean. Not all collectors have the bug that strongly, but the ones who do..."

She shook her head. "It's always worried me about my fellow collectors, but I've never known one who took it this far. Or at least, I've never known about it if they did."

She exchanged a knowing look with the girl in her arms. "Sometimes it's easier not to believe it."

Lucy nodded. "Yes, exactly. You tell yourself you're over-reacting, that they're not like that. But deep in your heart, that little fear? It never goes away."

Emily sensed Lucy was talking as much about her brother as she was about Mr. Carstairs. "But this time, you weren't sure, were you?"

Lucy gave her a grateful look. "No. Or at least, not all the way sure. It was easier to tell myself that he wouldn't really do anything wrong. Or violent like. It's just things—not people's lives. Not like it was with Bran. My brother."

She sniffed, and Aunt Louisa passed her a handkerchief. Lucy took it with thanks, then pulled away and sat up straight.

"But if he's done this thing, killed this girl, I mean," she paused, and met Emily's gaze. "Are you sure? Sure that it's him, I mean?"

Emily met Aunt Louisa's eyes, then nodded.

"Then it is that bad," Lucy said. "And he needs to pay for it. I have something to show you."

And she locked the front door, flipped the sign to closed, and led the way towards the back of the store. Following close on Lucy's heels, Emily glanced around in curiosity. She'd never seen the back room of a store before, and half expected to see a cluttered maelstrom of opened boxes and half-made hats.

She should have known better. Like the well-ordered showroom, the back room was neat and organized. Boxes were stacked everywhere, it was true, but they were orderly stacks, the boxes labelled, and well out of the way.

There was a wooden folding table set up with scissors and pins, measuring tapes, bolts of fabric and bins of trimming material in all colors. An exuberant jar of peacock feathers caught Emily's eye, and her fingers itched to stroke the beautiful things.

Looking back towards the shop door, Emily saw a low window cut into the wall of the back room that gave someone sitting at the trimming table a clear view of the door. The window was covered by a wrought iron decoration whose flowing lines depicted a peacock. The piece was backed with a piece of sheer white tulle that kept shoppers from noticing the window, while letting the person sitting trimming hats see everything.

"Did you design that window?" Emily asked the milliner. "It truly is a brilliant concept. I'd never have thought of it."

But she could think of several places such an element could be useful. Especially in the new offices of Granville and Scott Investigations. She'd have to talk with Laura about what might work best. And with Granville, of course.

"Yes, I did," Lucy said, but her attention was on a set of low cupboards behind the trimming table. She'd crouched down in the far corner, and was pulling out boxes of various feathers and setting them on the table. Then she stepped back, and waved Emily towards the cupboard.

"There," she said.

Emily stepped forward to look, and was stunned to recognize several packing boxes that looked suspiciously similar, right down to the markings, to the ones she'd seen in the Herron's basement.

"Are those…?" she began. Then found herself speechless.

As Aunt Louisa crowded forward and bent forward to peer into the cupboard, Lucy nodded.

"But I don't understand," Aunt Louisa said. "What are we looking at?"

"The Herron's pottery," Emily said, realizing it had been too dark in the cellar the other night for her aunt to recognize that the boxes were the same. "And it looks as if the entire collection is here."

"Really? Here?" Aunt Louisa said. She looked over her shoulder at Lucy. "Mr. Carstairs must have a great deal of confidence in you."

"He has a great deal of confidence in the power of his money," Lucy said.

"May I?" and she reached past Aunt Louisa's shoulder and lifted out a medium sized basket. Unwrapping the top item, she drew out an undamaged naturalist earthenware candlestick holder, with a large, realistic and remarkably ugly purple thistle decoration, complete with sharp clay thorns.

"Oh my," Aunt Louisa said.

Emily laughed at her aunt's expression. She sobered quickly as she took in Lucy's. "I'm sorry. I suppose he asked you to keep these hidden for him?"

Lucy nodded.

"And last night's letter? Another caution against mentioning these to anyone?"

"Yes. Along with a check," Lucy said bitterly. "Both of which would make me guilty of theft, seeing as he stole them. What can I do to help you put him behind bars?"

"Are you willing to testify against him?" Emily asked.

"You are certain he was involved in that girl's death?"

"Yes," Emily said. And she'd have proof of it before she asked Lucy to appear in court.

"Then yes," Lucy said. "Yes, I am."

"I suspect that a visit to Lau is next on your list," Aunt Louisa said as their carriage pulled away from the hat shop. "Since his is the most damning name of those Mr. Carstairs wrote to."

"And you'd be right," Emily said. "We might not be certain why Mr. Carstairs wrote to him, but I'd venture that Mr. Lau is."

She shifted the elegant hat box she'd been carrying onto the bench seat opposite her. "And thank you so much for my new hat. You really shouldn't have."

"Nonsense," Aunt Louisa said. "I've never seen you fall in love with a hat before. It was too good to miss."

"Well, thank you. I really do love it," Emily said. She grinned at her aunt. "And with regard to seeing Mr. Lau, I'm sure you have a connection at the courthouse. One who could get us a meeting with him?"

Emily had spent time with her father's sister often over the years, but it was only this week that she'd truly begun to appreciate her for the force that she was. She'd been learning that Aunt Louisa had connections in the most unlikely places, connections that opened doors that would otherwise have been firmly closed to them.

In response to Emily's statement, Aunt Louisa rapped on the carriage roof, and re-directed the driver to the courthouse.

"Of course I have," she said.

Finding herself in the same windowless room she'd been in when she and Mrs. Herron talked to Mr. Ying, Emily glanced at her aunt. Who looked remarkably calm about the whole experience. "Have you been here before?" she asked.

"No, never. This is a side of Victoria I've never had the need to explore."

Aunt Louisa considered the drab walls, the slightly too-bright lighting. "I can't say I'd like to spend much time here, but investigating has proven much more entertaining than I'd imagined," she said with a sparkle in her eye. "You'll have to visit me more often."

Emily was smiling as Mr. Lau was ushered into the room, wearing the same kind of chains the Mr. Ying had worn. Which sobered her immediately.

When the guards had left the room, Mr. Lau looked sullenly from his employer to Emily and back. His mouth was set in a thin line and his eyes looked sunken. There was no trace of yesterday's arrogance.

Aunt Louisa was looking at the bandage wound around the man's calf. It looked ragged, and the edges were dirty. "Has that wound been treated by a doctor?" she asked.

He just looked at her and didn't answer.

"I'm sorry for shooting you, but you left me no choice," Aunt Louisa said. "And I do want to be sure you're receiving the care you need for it. Otherwise it could get infected."

"So? They hang me anyway," he said.

He was probably right.

Emily thought about Granville's Lost Mine case, where ten years before, the fellow who first discovered the mine, a native named Slumach, had been accused of murder and jailed, then nursed back to health from a fever before being tried and hung. It still made her shudder.

But that had been more than ten years ago. Surely such things couldn't still happen—they couldn't still be so cruel? Though now she thought of it, the way the law treated the Chinese people was similar to the treatment they gave the native Indians. Both were just wrong.

And she couldn't blame Mr. Lau for looking at her with such resentment. Though he was probably a thief, and possibly a blackmailer—since something had to explain Mr. Ying's silence—she didn't think he was a murderer.

No, that was Mr. Carstairs. Who would get away with it if they couldn't figure out how to catch him.

Freeing Mr. Lau in exchange for catching Mr. Carstairs seemed like a good bargain. She glanced at Aunt Louisa.

Who nodded. "I think you need to hear what my niece has to propose," she told Mr. Lau.

"We know Mr. Carstairs now has the pottery that was stolen from the Herrons. I don't know exactly what happened during the theft," Emily said, her voice soft. "And I'm not asking you to tell me."

Though Mr. Lau's expression didn't change, and he leaned a little away from her, Emily thought from a slight change in the angle of his head that he was at least listening to her.

She kept her voice low, partly so the guards couldn't hear, but mostly to keep the prisoner's attention focused on her. "My only interest is to see that whoever stabbed and killed that young woman in the Herron's kitchen pays for what he did."

No reaction from the prisoner.

"In fact, the Herrons don't intend to prosecute the thief or thieves for the theft of the pottery. *If,*" she added, "and only if, the thieves help in identifying the killer. I have their word on it."

Mr. Lau turned his head away.

That was fine. Emily didn't expect him to believe her. "What you may not know, is that Mr. Carstairs left immediately after you did last night. I would have expected him to go after you, and maybe you did as well, since you'd obviously made plans to leave town immediately."

Still no reaction.

"Instead, Mr. Carstairs went home and wrote and mailed several letters, including one to you, in care of your Benevolent Association. Had you not been in jail, you would likely have received it by now. Would you care to guess what might be in that letter?"

Mr. Lau's jaw tightened, but he didn't answer.

Emily let the silence stretch for a moment, then continued. "We both know that Mr. Carstairs has the stolen pottery. And that he knows now that the pottery he bought is a fake. I suspect that knowledge has seriously upset him. Don't you agree, Aunt?"

"More than that. From what I know of the man, he'd be furious. And looking to take that fury out on someone else," Aunt Louisa said.

"Like the man who told him about the pottery in the first place?" Emily said. "I think so too. I wonder how he'd express that fury? Was that what happened to poor Betsy, Mr. Lau? She made Mr. Carstairs angry?"

More silence.

"I don't think even getting back the money he paid you would be enough to satisfy him, Mr. Lau," Emily said.

"Nor do I," Aunt Louisa said. "Not from everything I now know of Mr. Carstairs."

"You'll never run fast enough or far enough to hide from a man like that," Emily said.

"Even China might not be far enough," Aunt Louisa said.

"No choice," the prisoner said.

"But you do have a choice," Emily said. "Help us prove the Mr. Carstairs killed that girl, and he will be arrested. Probably he will hang. You will go free. With no prison sentence. No record."

He just pressed his lips tightly together.

"Lau," Aunt Louisa said. "It doesn't have to end like this for you. You've worked with me long enough to know that when I give my word on something, I stand by it. And I give you my word that if you help us, you will walk out of here a free man."

Mr. Lau stared at her for a long moment. Emily held her breath. Would it be enough?

Finally he gave a sharp nod. "Mr. Carstairs killed her. You set me free, I help you."

"No, Lau," Aunt Louisa said firmly. "The only way you will be released from here is if the police arrest the real killer."

At her words, Mr. Lau's jaw set.

"Mr. Carstairs will not forget that he's been cheated," Emily said. "Not ever."

"Not my fault," he said. "Ying told me it was real."

"Do you think Mr. Carstairs will care? He paid you," Emily said, hoping she was right about this fact, at least. "Unless you help us get him arrested, your life is in danger. And we need to know everything."

Mr. Lau glared at her, but she refused to look away.

"Fine," he said. "I help you."

"Thank you," Emily said. "Now, we need to know everything."

ONCE MR. LAU agreed to talk, he didn't hold anything back. The story was a simple one, for all its ugliness. And the connection between the three men was something Emily would never have imagined.

All three were fond of the opium pipe. As Mr. Lau put it, "A pipe or two help us relax, think deep thoughts."

Opium wasn't illegal, and Emily knew from Granville that there were several opium dens in Vancouver's Chinatown. So it hadn't surprised her to learn that the same was true in Victoria. In fact, there were even more opium dens here.

But opium use was frowned on in society, and discussed only in hushed tones. You wouldn't expect to know anyone who used opium. And none of the ladies who relied on their Chinese house-boys believed that their valued employee would ever use opium.

Of course not. They'd be horrified to find out the truth. And likely fire the poor man on the spot.

And yet these same ladies thought nothing of taking a dose of laudanum to calm their nerves. In fact, laudanum was often prescribed by their doctors to soothe overwrought nerves. Emily had never realized that harmless little bottle of laudanum was derived from opium, until Granville had told her so last year.

She suspected very few of the ladies who depended on the stuff were aware of the connection. And if they were, they'd likely still argue that taking a few drops of labeled and packaged laudanum in the privacy of your own home was very different than going to a horrid opium den hidden somewhere in Chinatown to smoke a lump of smelly, sticky black sap. Which for them, was probably true. But it was the same drug.

And it was thanks to opium that Mr. Lau had heard about the naturalist pottery from Mr. Ying. Though not in the way either had previously described.

It seemed that both men were in the habit of frequenting the same opium den several times a month. Though they were not friends, they knew each other, and would occasionally help one another out in navigating the strange expectations of their employers. Which was how Mr. Lau had first heard of the Herron's disregarded pottery collection.

Mr. Ying's own disregard for the set had apparently exceeded even that of his employers. But the description of the ugly but very detailed thistles adorning the pottery had caught Mr. Lau's interest. He'd heard Mr. Carstairs and another collector talking about such pottery, and how valuable it could be when he was serving at a dinner Aunt Louisa had given for the Collector's Society.

And he'd seen Mr. Carstairs a number of times at an opium den he also frequented, but which Mr. Ying did not. It wasn't difficult for Mr. Lau to approach Mr. Carstairs and offer to sell him the pottery. But he hadn't appreciated the extent of Mr. Carstairs's passion for the pottery.

"It not enough I bring him the pottery," Mr. Lau said. "He want to know exactly where, and how, and when. Then he want to hire someone to help me steal the boxes. Then he insist he is there too. He find it exciting. I think he a fool, but a fool with much money."

Mr. Lau stared at his hands, which sat loosely on the table in front of him, the handcuffs heavy on his thin wrists.

Emily and Aunt Louisa sat in silence opposite him. Once Mr.

Lau had begun to talk, it had become clear that he wanted to tell this story, but it would be at his own pace. Sometimes halting, sometimes with long pauses.

It seemed to pain him to speak of what had happened, and several times Emily thought he would stop altogether. But each time he began again, speaking as if the words were dragged from somewhere inside him.

"He hire another Chinaman, but a very dangerous one. I see him, I know I not make mistake, or my life is finish."

So there *had* been a third man, Emily thought, pleased she'd been right about that much.

Mr. Lau swallowed hard and stared at the hands clenched in his lap. Then resumed. "I take both of them down to cellar. We wait until drive is clear. Then find boxes, start to carry them out. All, easy."

"Until girl come into cellar. See us take boxes. She give little scream. And Mr. Carstairs, he chase after her. Face all red. I try and stop him, but…"

He hung his head. "Too late. I go after him, climb stairs. Other Chinaman behind me. I see kitchen almost empty. But Mr. Carstairs standing over girl, holding knife. I say no. He stab. She die."

This time Emily broke the silence. "And what of Mr. Ying? Where was he?"

"He come in other door then, with silver platters. See Mr. Carstairs, see girl. Run at them. Mr. Carstairs go red again, hit Ying. Many times.

I tell him no, Ying will not talk. I make sure. Mr. Carstairs curse, but can hear voices near. He run past me to cellar.

I say to Ying, you talk? I tell them about opium. He still wants to tell. I say, Mr. Carstairs would hurt family, children. He still argue, then he see other Chinaman on stairs below. He know the man, know what I say is true. His eyes open up, and he stop argue. He has fear."

"You were on the cellar stairs?" Emily asked.

"Yes. Voices outside, come near."

Emily nodded, feeling sick. It all fit with what Jane and the other three serving girls had said.

What if Betsy hadn't been alone in the kitchen when Mr. Carstairs followed her upstairs? There had been so much activity for Mrs. Herron's tea—it was probably the only time Betsy had been alone all day.

What if the kitchen had still been full of activity? Would the poor girl still be alive? It hurt even to think about.

"So you managed to keep Mr. Ying quiet?" Emily said. "Even to lie about what he'd seen?"

"He see other Chinaman," Mr. Lau said, as if it answered every-thing. "Then he believe me about Mr. Carstairs, and threat to little boys. Ying love the boys. He know men like third man. Carstairs, too. Violent men, angry."

Emily thought about the elegantly dressed man she'd first met at the Collector's Society meeting. There had been no sign of that side of Mr. Carstairs then. But she'd seen it last night, at Mrs. Herron's dinner, when he thought his prized new collection was a fake.

She glanced at her aunt, whose face had gone white, though there was resignation in her eyes. She knew as well. There were too many such men in polite society, and they hid what they were too well. As long as their manners were polished, no one looked too closely.

"Did Mr. Ying see Mr. Carstairs stab Betsy?"

"No. He come in, see Mr. Carstairs stand over her. She dead on floor."

Emily cringed a little at the blunt words and the image they brought with them. "If Mr. Carstairs is arrested, would Mr. Ying testify in court about what he saw?"

"Yes. Mr. Carstairs in jail, boys safe. I testify, too."

"Thank you," Emily said. "Thank you so much."

"And we will see you released from jail soon," Aunt Louisa said. "You have my promise."

———

THE REST of the afternoon was a flurry of activity. The first thing Emily and her aunt did was to call on Mrs. Herron and share everything they had learned with her. Then Emily watched in amazement as Aunt Louisa and Caroline Herron swung into action.

Between the two of them, they knew everyone that mattered in town—and exactly how to prod each of them into action.

Once they knew what they were looking for, and inspired by some curt words from their Chief, the detectives and officers assigned to the case quickly assembled the evidence they needed. By the end of the day, Mr. Carstairs was in jail and charged with murder, the pottery had been collected as evidence, and both Mr. Ying and Mr. Lau had been freed.

The trial was scheduled to begin in three weeks. And Betsy would finally see justice.

That evening, Emily and Aunt Louisa joined the Herrons for a quiet dinner, which had been prepared by Mr. Ying.

Emily complimented Caroline on the food, which was quite amazingly tasty, with complementing flavors and textures that she'd never have considered using together. But Caroline lifted her wine glass in toast to Emily.

"You are the one who deserves the compliments," she said. "It is such a joy to have Ying back. And a relief, too. I was beginning to think the situation hopeless. I still don't know how you managed to solve it."

"With a great deal of help. Mostly from the two of you," Emily said, looking at the faces of the two women she'd come to know so much better through the work they'd done together. "I'd have been lost without both of you. Between you, you know everyone and everything there is to know about this town."

"And we would have been lost without you," Aunt Louisa said. "Without you to put the pieces together for us, and to ask the right questions, our knowledge was useless."

"Let me make the toast, then," Mr. Herron said. "To the three of you. For solving the case, and doing a better job of it than the entire police force managed. There is no doubt in my mind that with the evidence we now have, Carstairs will be hanged. And deservedly so. So, my very sincere compliments to all three of you for a job well done. And my thanks."

Emily could feel herself blushing a little, and took a quick swallow of wine to hide it. It hadn't been easy, but she'd enjoyed working with the other two women. She'd learned a lot.

But she was glad Betsy's murder was avenged. And the case finished.

It was time to go home. She'd missed her family, but she'd missed Granville more. It would be good to see all of them again.

It was nearing ten by the time they returned from the impromptu dinner party and Emily had a chance to call Granville. When he picked up the telephone, she found herself unexpectedly at a loss for words. And more emotional than she'd anticipated.

"Granville, I…we've wrapped up this case," she said. And had to fight back the tears that wanted to choke her. "I'm coming home. I'll be back in time for your trial."

"That is very good news," Granville said. "And congratulations on solving a major case, and a very complicated one. It's an impressive accomplishment. Especially for your first case."

She could hear the sincerity in his voice, and a wave of longing for him swept over her. Just to be held in his arms for a moment, in a world that suddenly felt unsteady beneath her feet. And she couldn't tell him any of that—not here.

"Thank you," she managed to say.

"Which ferry were you thinking of taking?" he asked prosaically.

Why was she suddenly sure he knew exactly how she was feeling, and that this was his version of anchoring her? And a reminder that it wouldn't be long now. Not even two more days.

"The morning ferry on Monday," she said, pleased to hear that she sounded nearly as matter of fact as he had done. "Now that the case is done, I've promised Aunt Louisa that we'll have a quiet day, then go to church on Sunday."

There was much to be thankful for.

"Then I'll meet you at the ferry terminal on Monday afternoon," he said, his voice calm, but just a little deeper.

Suddenly Monday couldn't come soon enough.

"I'd love that," she said. "I'm so looking forward to seeing you. And telling you everything. And hearing everything that's been going on."

5 2

Monday, September 10, 1900

W hen the *Princess Louise* neared the docks, Emily could barely contain her excitement. She was home. And very shortly, she'd be with Granville again. It wasn't until the case was done that she'd allowed herself to realize how much she'd missed him.

Phone calls were very unsatisfying.

She peered across the stretch of water that was rapidly closing between where she stood at the railing and the crowd awaiting the ferry, and spotted Granville's tall figure. There was no sign of Scott beside him. Which meant it would just be the two of them in the carriage. Her heartbeat picked up at the thought.

Despite some prodding from Aunt Louisa, she hadn't actually committed to moving forward the date of her wedding to Granville. But now, seeing his much-loved features coming ever clearer, ever closer? The idea of waiting the two years Mama expected seemed impossible.

She'd have to talk to her mother. Perhaps a spring wedding might be possible. April was often lovely…

Once the bustle of disembarking and sorting out her luggage was done, Emily sat side by side with Granville in the same carriage he'd hired a week ago. And found herself feeling unexpectedly shy with him. With the decision to move up their wedding now firm in her mind, she wasn't quite ready to discuss it with him.

Instead she turned to him with a smile she hoped didn't look as forced as it felt. "So tell me about your case," she said. "You have a court date. Does that mean you've found the big fish?"

He gave her an odd look, which she suspected meant her smile had looked exactly as odd as it felt. But to her relief he didn't comment on it, just began to tell her how the search for his big fish had unfolded since they'd last been able to talk freely. When he got to the legal six, and his realization that it was a conspiracy with all six working together, she put a hand on his arm.

"You mean there is no big fish?"

"Well, I suspect one of them is a ringleader of sorts. But really, he's only a deluded small fish," he said.

Emily burst out laughing. "A deluded small fish? Oh, I love that," she said. "And just imagine how he'd feel if you were to call him that to his face."

He grinned at that. "One of these days I plan to do exactly that. And you can bet I'm looking forward to it."

She could just picture it. "But I'm a little lost, here. Which one of your six *is* the deluded small fish?"

"That's the best part. Or perhaps the worst. We still don't know."

She gaped at him. "You're going to court, and you don't know whom you're after?"

"That's it."

"But... but..." She paused, and gave him the stink eye, as only a small girl with two tormenting older sisters could have learned to do. "You must have *some* idea who it is."

"Oh, I do. The evidence we have so far, including a description from Gurak, suggests that it's one Oliver Lessing, one of the six lawyers who hate Randall for winning too many cases."

Emily looked at him askance. "But you don't think it's him, do you?"

"No, I don't. The evidence is too neat. It's like someone tied him into a neat package for us."

"So who do you think it is?"

"Another of the six, a lawyer named Jasper Konrad. Even if he is a spineless weasel."

Emily recognized one of Granville's worst insults. He really didn't like the lawyer. "And why do you suspect him?"

"He's clever enough to have pulled it off. Then there's the fact that he gave us quite a few facts that helped tie Lessing up tightly. And he hates Randall."

"That's it? I can't believe you're going to trial with so little." Emily shook her head. Then she sat back, and considered him in silence for a moment. "You have a plan, don't you? And it's going to unfold in court, just like the last times you've done this."

"Guilty," he said, and this time it wasn't a grin, but a heart melting smile he gave her. "I knew you'd figure it out."

She was trying not to gape again, and for totally different reasons. But there was no way she was admitting it. "You're going to get your proof in court, get the silly little fish to expose himself in front of everyone."

"That's the plan."

"But… the last few times you pulled this off, you had Randall arguing for you. Now you don't. Is Carver a good enough lawyer to pull this off?"

"Who says I don't have Randall?"

Emily started to laugh. "You're going to use Randall as your ace in the hole?"

"One of 'em."

"Does that mean he's out of hospital? If he can appear in court, I mean?"

"No, he's still in hospital. He's ready to be released, but he can use the extra rest. And since he's still rumored to be on death's doorstep…"

"They're hiding him for you until tomorrow," she concluded. "So he'll go straight to court, and arrive just in time for his appearance. Carver will set it up, and… Oh, I'm so glad I'm home in time to see this. It's going to be so exciting."

"It should be entertaining, anyway. If it all comes together."

And that was still a worry, she could see it in his eyes. "You can't tell me you felt any more certain your plan would work before the Sinclair trial. Or before Scott's trial, either, come to that. And look how well those turned out," she said.

He gave her a sideways glance, and another smile. "Enough about my case. Tell me about yours?"

"I'm happy to," she began, and told him every detail of her case, everything she'd been forced to keep back since she last saw him.

"So Carstairs was the 'hasty man' after all."

"He was. And now I know a little more about him, that description fits very well."

"And the police are satisfied with what you've uncovered?"

"They said the evidence proves Mr. Carstairs was guilty of young Betsy's murder, as well as the theft of the Herron's pottery. Even the prosecutor said there were no questions left," she said, feeling a little shaky with relief all over again, just saying that.

"So your case is finished, you've found the killer, and made sure the police have ample evidence to ensure he hangs," Granville said. "Congratulations. You've done an amazing job of putting this one together."

"It wasn't easy," she admitted.

"If it had been, you probably had the wrong man," he said.

"Really?"

"I'm afraid so. Especially in a case as complicated as this one proved to be. Now, when is the trial?"

"In three weeks. And I intend to go back to Victoria for it," she said. "And I was wondering if you'd have time to accompany me?"

"I'll be there," he said, and it was a promise.

"Thank you," she said, and reaching for his hand, squeezed it. "That means a lot. But there's one question I still have, and I've been wanting to discuss it with you…"

"Go on."

"They—the police, I mean—discounted the idea of a third man on the robbery. The one Mr. Ying and Mr. Lau were both afraid of."

"By the third man, you mean the thief that Wong Sun told you about. The one hired by a non-Chinese man?"

"Yes, that's the one," she said. "Well, the police still don't believe Mr. Ying and Mr. Lau that this third man exists."

"Or they don't expect to be able to find him," Granville said.

"Yes, that too. And I still don't have a name for him. Or any way to find him. So he's getting away with theft. And that isn't right."

"You took this case on to solve young Betsy's murder. And you've done that. So unless you think this thief had a hand in murdering young Betsy, does it really matter if he's arrested?"

"I don't know," she said, thinking about it. "Maybe not. There's no indication the third man—the thief—was directly involved in Betsy's death. It's just… a loose end, I guess. And I find I don't like loose ends."

"Sometimes you don't get all the answers on a case."

"Yes, I've seen that on some of your previous cases. And since the thief wasn't part of killing Betsy, I suppose I can be…resigned to not knowing who he is. Or seeing him brought to justice."

"But you're struggling with it," he said.

"Yes, I am," she said. "But I don't see what I can do about it." Her hands tightened on her reticule as she spoke. She was feeling more unsettled by this than she'd admitted to herself, she realized. And forced her fingers to release their grip.

"Especially since my only real source for information about the thief was Wong Sun," she added. "I can't even imagine going back now and asking Bertie's uncle for more information."

He grinned at that. "I doubt that would go well," he said, then sobered, frowning a little. "Wong Sun told you that the fellow who hired this third man wasn't Chinese. That fellow would know the thief's name. You've found no sign of him, either?"

"No, nothing more than the connection you mentioned between Mr. Carstairs and two of your conspiring lawyers," she said.

He nodded. "From what we've dug out, both Konrad and

Lessing were in cahoots with Carstairs, as Scott would say, and could have hired this thief for him. But we've found nothing to corroborate that. And they're not likely to be cooperative."

"So we're unlikely to learn the thief's name from them," she said. "Or even know for sure which of them hired the thief. Maybe that's part of what's bothering me."

"The deluded small fish is bothering you?"

She had to laugh. "It sounds silly, but that small fish makes yet another unnamed player in this case. One who has ties to Mr. Carstairs and hired the thief for him. And I don't know who he is, or even what role he plays."

"I can see why that's bothering you. It's all part of that loose end."

"It is," she said. "But, as you asked me earlier, does the loose end connect to Betsy's death? And I really can't see that it does."

"And you stopped a killer," he reminded her. "Which may have been the point Wong Sun was making in telling you what he did. That young woman's death is on the "hasty man". And no one else."

"That's what Mr. Ying said, too." She frowned a little. "Do you think that's why Wong Sun chose to talk to us?"

"I think it's possible. Especially since the police were focused on Ying, and the real killer isn't even Chinese."

She nodded. "Maybe this thief also works sometimes for Bertie's uncle. And either the thief or Wong Sun himself wanted Mr. Carstairs punished for killing Betsy."

"It's a possibility," Granville said. "Do *you* want to ask him?"

She shivered at the thought. "I think I'll be satisfied that Betsy's killer is in jail, and let this loose end stay the way it is."

"That's probably a good idea." He glanced out the carriage window. "Because you're home. And I know they waited dinner for you. Knowing your mother, we won't get another chance to talk privately until I collect you tomorrow for the trial."

She laughed. "You're right about my mother. What time should I be ready?"

"Just after eight. It's beautiful weather. I thought we'd walk."

"Perfect," she said, as he held out his arm to assist her down from the carriage, and her mother and sisters appeared on the porch. "Now we face the onslaught. Onwards."

53

Tuesday, September 10, 1900

On Tuesday morning, the court was more than half empty as Granville strolled into the courthouse with Emily on his arm. One lawyer suing another apparently didn't attract spectators in the way a murder trial did. Not even when one of those lawyers was rumored to be dead after a violent attack.

As they joined Scott, Trent, Mac and Miss Kent in the third row, all the empty seats struck him as an insult to Randall. But he knew they'd all appreciate the thin turnout later today. The courtroom was pleasantly cool now, but as the heat of the day built up, the heat and humidity would build in the courtroom as well—despite anything the four large overhead fans could do. If the place was crowded, the air in here would be unbearable.

Judge Alexander Graham was presiding today, and he sat ramrod straight in the heavy chair. His narrow, intelligent face dominated by the curled white wig and heavy robes he wore. From behind the elevated judge's bench, he looked down on the witness stand to his left, and the prosecutor's table to his right.

Peabody sat alone at the prosecutor's table, since for this

trial he was both the accuser and the accuser's lawyer. The defendant's table was located more towards the middle of the room, where Carver also sat alone. His client, Randall, could hardly appear, being presumed dead. Or very nearly dead, at the least.

There were rows of the low-backed benches for the onlookers—two on each side of the aisle—running from behind the defendant's and prosecutor's tables, all the way to the double exit doors at the back.

Granville guided Emily towards the first row of benches, choosing to sit right behind Carver. It gave them a good view of the witness stand, which would be key in this trial. And even more important, it allowed him to confer with Carver—and Carver with him—as the need arose.

The empty benches behind them filled a little more in the next few minutes, but it was still markedly quiet. Emily leaned a little closer to him, placing a neatly gloved hand on his arm. It felt right to have her there, next to him.

"Where are your six lawyers?" she said in a whisper that wouldn't carry beyond his ears. "From everything you've told me since I came home, I almost feel as if I know them. But I could pass any one of them on the street and never know it. Well, except for Mr. Peabody, of course."

"None of them are in court," he said, equally softly. "Because when he filed a counter suit on Randall's behalf, Carver called all six of them as defense witnesses."

"Really? Why?"

"They can testify to the animosity that Peabody bore for Randall."

"Because of their little club," she said with a quiet laugh. "That undoubtedly made all of them quite nervous."

"I suspect it did. It also keeps them out of the courtroom for all of the other testimony, so they'll have no idea what is said here. Which could prove very useful later."

She nodded, her attention on the other spectators. "I see Officer Daniels," she said. "Is he here on official business?"

"Officially he doesn't have a role to play here today," he said blandly.

"But he does have a part to play in the drama that's about to unfold here, doesn't he?"

"He does indeed," he said, wondering how Emily managed to convey a sense of foreboding in a whisper.

"And that's Mr. Draper from the *News Advertiser* beside him, isn't it? Do they know each other?"

"I hadn't thought so. But even a business reporter must need information from the police, now and again."

"Especially when it comes to fraud. He'd have to keep up on criminal activities in town, wouldn't he? At least the business-related ones."

"He would indeed." And he suddenly wondered who Draper's source was among the officers. Not that it mattered now—but still, it was interesting. And it might be a useful thing to know for the future.

A rustle among the spectators distracted him, and he and Emily both turned to look as the judge banged his gavel twice to quiet the gallery—quite unnecessary today—and begin the trial. Everyone was in place.

Since this was a civil trial, rather than a criminal one, there was no jury. The judge was the final authority here today.

Emily was now sitting very straight-backed, with her gaze fixed firmly on the judge, and her white-gloved hands tucked neatly together in the lap of her favorite green summer suit. As if feeling his gaze, she looked sideways at him and the corners of her mouth quirked up.

She was clearly intending to enjoy the coming spectacle.

As was he.

JUDGE GRAHAM INVITED the two lawyers to make their opening statements. Since he'd filed the original suit against Randall, Peabody had the first shot.

"Thank you, m'lord," he said to the judge. "I intend to prove that Mr. Randall has maliciously and without provocation or cause defamed my character and attempted to destroy my reputation. And I will also prove that he is a dangerously incompetent lawyer, who deserves to be disbarred."

Judge Graham held up a hand to stop him there, which was most unusual. "You do understand that this court does not have the authority to disbar any lawyer?"

"Of course, m'lord," Peabody said smoothly. "But it is germane to the defamation charge. And you do have to ability to make recommendations on the matter of disbarment to the appropriate body."

The judge's expression didn't change, but he signaled for him to continue.

Whereupon Peabody launched into a very carefully framed attack on Randall that went on at some length.

"It sounds like he's describing himself and his own cases, not Randall," Emily whispered in his ear. "Doesn't he realize how bad he's making himself look?"

"I doubt it," Granville said. "No one would ever accuse Peabody of being aware of his own weaknesses."

She smiled. "Good."

When it was Carver's turn, the fellow stood up behind the defense table and brushed back the dark hair that had flopped over onto his forehead. His opening was short, to the point, and promised to demolish every claim Peabody had made.

"In fact," he said. "I will prove that all of the accusations Mr. Peabody has aimed at my client, including the charge of defamation, should more properly be directed against Mr. Peabody himself. Thank you," he finished, and sat down.

"Mr. Peabody? Will you call your first witness?" Judge Graham said.

"Thank you, your honor," Peabody said. Then with a spiteful look directed at Carver he called Lester Bragg to the stand.

"But he's one of the six, isn't he?" Emily whispered. "I thought he was testifying for the defense?"

"So did I," Granville said. "This should be interesting."

"What can he possibly say against Randall? Especially since he's testifying under oath. He can't lie, can he?"

"It seems we're going to find out."

Emily grinned, and focused her attention on the witness stand, where Bragg had settled his considerable bulk. He was quickly sworn in.

"Now, sir," Peabody began, walking towards the witness stand. "Can you describe for the judge and the court your last interaction with Mr. Randall in this court?"

"I object," Carver said immediately, standing up to speak. "How is this relevant to your suit against Mr. Randall?"

Peabody shot him an irritated look, and turned to the judge. "If you will grant me a few minutes here, your honor, I'm sure it will all become evident, even to my learned colleague."

"Very well," Judge Graham said. "I'll give you some leeway. But mind you keep it civil."

"Of course, of course," Peabody said, and turned back to his witness. "Mr. Bragg? Shall I repeat the question?"

"Of course not," Bragg said, sounding a little testy to Granville's ears. "The last occasion was several months ago. Randall's client had accused my client, a small importer, of fraud. The case was quite without merit, but neither Randall nor his client would see reason."

"I thought Randall won that case?" Emily whispered.

"He did."

"Then... how could it be without merit?"

"Because Peabody is trying to get something on the record, probably. Let's see if the Judge heard about that case."

Apparently he had not, because he didn't stop the line of questioning.

Nor did Carver object again, leaving Granville wondering what Peabody's unexpected approach was doing to Carver's strategy.

"And what was your experience of opposing Mr. Randall in court?" was Peabody's next question.

"I hate to speak ill of him in these circumstances," Bragg said, with a smug look that belied his words. "But I found him most unreasonable. He was dismissive to the point of rudeness, and quite lacking in the courtesy normally extended from one lawyer to another."

Granville had a quick mental picture of Bragg's open glee at the news of Randall's imminent demise, his maligning of the other lawyer's character and ethics, and he had to fight to keep his disgust from showing on his face.

"And in your opinion, did he fairly represent his client?" Peabody asked.

"No, he did not," Bragg said hotly. "He refused to allow his client to even consider a settlement. Which was hardly in the client's best interest."

"I see. Thank you, Mr. Bragg," Peabody said. "No further questions, your honor."

5 4

s Judge Graham turned to the defense bench, Granville glanced over at Peabody. Who was pale and starting to sweat heavily. Was he even going to make it through the trial? Those wigs and heavy robes had to be insufferable in this weather, but it was the mess that Peabody had put himself into that was the real problem.

"Mr. Carver? Do you have questions for this witness?" the judge asked.

"Just one or two, m'lord," Carver said, looking cool and collected as he stood to approach the witness. "Now, Mr. Bragg, I believe you had another lawyer assisting you with your defense that day, did you not?"

"I did."

"And who was this?"

"Mr. Jasper Konrad, who was a junior lawyer in my office at that time, assisted me with the case."

"Isn't Mr. Konrad's another one of the six?" Emily whispered. "Why is Mr. Carver linking them like this? Is he up to something?"

"Always," he said. "I have no idea what his strategy is. But

Bragg doesn't look too happy about being cross-examined. I don't think he expected Peabody to raise that case in court."

"He should have done a better job of preparing his witness, then, shouldn't he?" she said.

"I see," Carver was saying. "And can you refresh my memory on the outcome of that specific case? You won, I assume?"

"Well… not exactly." Bragg said.

Carver looked surprised. "It was a split decision, then?"

"Not exactly."

"Come now. It's a matter of record, after all. How did the judge find?"

"He found for the defendant," Bragg said, spitting out the words. Then he glanced at the judge and grimaced.

"I believe there was a substantial settlement, as well, wasn't there?" Carver said. "Or am I misremembering the case?"

"You are not. There was."

"And yet you believe Randall did not serve his client well?"

"Yes. I mean no, he didn't."

"I see," Carver said. He glanced at the judge, then walked a little closer to Bragg where he sat on the witness stand. "You are remembering you're under oath. Sworn to tell the truth?"

"Yes."

"And you still stand by your statement?"

"Yes. I do."

"I see." Carver looked from the witness to the judge and back again. "Can you explain this to us? Was Randall's client not sufficiently compensated by the judge's ruling? Would your client have settled the suit for more?"

Bragg was silent.

Carver looked towards the judge.

Who spoke immediately and firmly. "The witness will answer the question."

"Yes, there is a possibility that my client would have settled out of court for a larger sum."

"I find it surprising that the judge ruled that your client should receive the smaller amount, given his harsh words to the defendant at the time," Carver said. "But perhaps he did not have all of the facts at the time."

"I object," Peabody said, bobbing up from his seat like a cork. "Counsel is testifying."

"The objection is sustained. Ask a question, counsellor," Judge Graham said. Then he turned to the witness. "And remember you are under oath."

"The judge doesn't seem to trust this witness to answer honestly," Emily said softly into Granville's ear. "That's good for us, isn't it?"

She didn't miss a thing. "It is indeed. But it's too early in the trial to mean much."

"Did Judge Hardy have all the facts when he ruled on the case you're describing?" Carver was asking.

Briggs was looking flushed and uncomfortable now. "No. Not exactly. You see…"

"Thank you, Counsellor," Carver said. "That will do. Now, you mentioned Mr. Konrad assisted you on that case. And does he still work for you?"

"He does not."

"Do the two of you ever discuss cases? Or other lawyers? And I would remind you again that you are under oath."

"I object," Peabody was saying. "How is this relevant?"

"Overruled," the judge said, without taking his eyes off the witness. "Answer the question."

"At times we do," Bragg said.

"I see. And have you and Mr. Konrad ever discussed Mr. Randall, and his cases?" Carver asked. "Beyond this particular case, I mean."

"We have," Bragg said.

"And you and Mr. Konrad are indeed part of a select group, are you not? A group, in fact, that frequently discusses Mr. Randall."

"I object," Peabody began.

"Overruled," the judge said without letting him finish. "Mr. Bragg?"

"I am part of a group of other lawyers who meet occasionally. To discuss various legal matters."

"Including all the cases in which each of you have faced, or will face, Mr. Randall?"

"Yes, those cases certainly came up."

"And is Mr. Peabody here a member of that group of lawyers?"

"I object," Peabody said strongly.

Carver looked over his shoulder at him. "On what grounds?"

"It's... it's irrelevant."

"Overruled," Judge Graham said. "The witness may answer."

Bragg sat silent for a moment. Then at a look from the judge, he said, "Yes, Peabody is one of the members."

"And there are how many members of this group?"

"Since it is informal, it varies. There is no official membership."

"I see. The last time you were all together, how many of you were there?"

Bragg looked trapped. "Six."

"Including yourself, Mr. Konrad and Mr. Peabody."

"Yes."

"And the time before that?"

"Six."

"And the time before that?"

"Six."

"I see." Carver looked to the judge. "I have no further questions for this witness. Though I may need to recall him later."

"So noted," the judge said. "Next witness?"

Peabody, predictably, called each of the four other lawyer who made up what Bragg had called their informal group and what Granville had come to think of as their little conspiracy. With each witness, Peabody tried to destroy Randall's reputation. And with his cross examination, Carver undermined each lawyer's testimony, and verified that they were indeed members of the legal six.

He didn't accuse any of them of fraud. Not quite. But their answers to the questions he did ask set them up nicely for that charge. And then Carver let them go.

But in each case, he also stipulated that he might need to recall them.

"He must have been taking notes when Mr. Randall tried the Sinclair case," Emily leaned over to say softly into his ear. "This is very similar to the strategy Mr. Randall used then."

"Indeed it is," he said. "And you aren't the only one to think so. Look at Peabody."

"He looks rattled. And so did the other lawyers, when they left the stand. They hid it better, though. Did you notice?"

It had been subtle, but after that lunch he'd got a sense of each of the six. And despised them for what he'd seen. So he'd taken appreciative note of how uneasy Carver had made them. But he was impressed that she had seen it so easily.

"I did indeed. I'm wondering if Peabody is done, and if not, whom he'll call next."

Peabody was done, it seemed, because he rested his case.

When the judge called for a lunch recess, Emily gripped Granville's arm. "It's like the judge did that on purpose."

"What, called a recess?" he asked, amused.

"Gave us time to let the tension build up," she said.

"Since he did, would you like something to eat?"

"I couldn't enjoy it. Why don't we have a late lunch once this is all over."

"It could be hours yet."

"I don't care. Not when all I can think about is what Mr. Carver is going to do now," she said. "Everyone has to be wondering the same thing."

He grinned. "You'll all have to wait and see."

55

W hen court resumed after the break, Emily's gaze was pinned to Mr. Carver as he stood to call his first witness. She was feeling very pleased to be sitting in this courtroom, at this moment, with Granville at her side. And her own case firmly behind her.

She couldn't wait to see what happened next.

Mr. Carver was fascinating to watch, and Peabody…Well, he certainly wasn't the deluded small fish they'd been looking for. She hid a smile at the thought.

He might be considered deluded, though. And he was playing straight into Mr. Carver's hands.

"I call Mr. Josiah Randall to the stand," Mr. Carver said.

There was a rustle of excited whispering in the room as the bailiff escorted Mr. Randall into the room. He didn't exactly look healthy, Emily noted. He was too pale and thin for that, and he walked slowly, leaning on a black-topped cane. But for a man who was reported to be hovering near death, he looked very well indeed.

She glanced from his pale face to the judge's intent one. Judge Graham didn't look surprised. Mr. Carver must have briefed him on what to expect.

Would the judge have to agree to this breach of normal procedure? Probably. But given the recent attack on Mr. Randall's life—and the possibility that threat was ongoing—the judge had clearly been persuaded.

She looked over at Mr. Peabody, curious what his reaction would be to his opponent's return to health. He'd flushed, then turned nearly as pale as Mr. Randall was. Now he was gulping down water from the glass on his table.

"Mr. Randall. Thank you for leaving your hospital bed to join us today," Mr. Carver said smoothly, drawing the attention of everyone in the court. "Now, before we begin, are you familiar with the particulars of this suit Mr. Peabody has brought against you?"

"I am."

"And, remembering you are under oath, have you ever maligned or defamed Mr. Peabody there?"

Mr. Randall looked over at Mr. Peabody, then back at his own lawyer. "I have not."

"Not even in jest?" Mr. Carver persisted.

"No. Not under any circumstances. I don't consider such behavior professional."

"He has no need of it," Granville said quietly in her ear. "He can demolish any of them in court without effort. And all of them know it."

Emily nodded, but her attention was on Mr. Peabody, who was puffing and blowing like a landed fish. This trial was proving even more entertaining than she'd expected. It probably helped that it wasn't a murder trial.

Not yet, at least.

"I see," Mr. Carver said, seemingly unaware of the antics of his opponent. "And what of Mr. Peabody's accusations that you have attempted to destroy his career? Have you ever said or done anything that might have had that impact on his career?"

"Never," Mr. Randall said firmly.

"I object," Mr. Peabody said loudly, standing up with his chest puffed out. Since his face had turned bright red, Emily thought he looked like an undersized turkey, all puffed up for a fight.

"On what charge?" the judge asked.

"He's lying," Peabody yelled. "He can't lie under oath."

"Overruled. Sit down, Mr. Peabody."

"But…"

"Sit down, I say," the judge said. "Continue, Mr. Carver."

Mr. Carver was staring at Mr. Peabody with no expression at all on his face. At the judge's words he nodded, and turned back to his own client. "You say you have never done anything to undermine Mr. Peabody's career. And yet, it was following a case where he was prosecuting one of your clients that he was fired from that position. How do you explain that?"

"I can't," Mr. Randall said.

"You can't explain it?"

"No."

"And why not? I will remind you that you are under oath."

"I can't explain it because I had nothing to do with whether Mr. Peabody lost his position. Or retained it, for that matter."

At those words, Mr. Peabody again leapt to his feet. "I…" The judge gave him a hard look, and he closed his mouth and sat down again.

"So you never said a word about Mr. Peabody's role in that case? To anyone?"

"I did not."

"You didn't drop a word in someone's ear, for instance, that he lost the case because he handled it so badly? Or pointed out that if he'd done his job ahead of time, he would have known that I was alive, for instance."

"Objection," Peabody said loudly. "He's testifying."

"Overruled. You may answer the question, Mr. Randall."

"Thank you, m'lord. And no, I did none of the things that Mr. Carver has suggested."

"Then what did you do, in that case, Mr. Randall?" Mr. Carver asked.

"I did my job. I defended my client, to the full extent of my ability, while staying within the law."

Emily had to turn and see Mr. Peabody's response to that. And she noted that nearly everyone else in the courtroom had done the same. Including the judge.

Peabody was still seated, but he was breathing hard, and gripping the edge of the table with both hands. She couldn't imagine anything further from Mr. Randall's calm, reasoned statement.

"I see," Mr. Carver said, somehow managing not to look smug.

Which was an impressive feat, to Emily's mind. It was clear to her, and probably the rest of the spectators, that he'd struck a major blow for his client.

"And did Mr. Peabody afford you the same respect? Did he refrain from belittling you and maligning your character?" Mr. Carver continued.

"I am sorry to say that he did not."

"I see. And do you have proof of this?"

"I suspect that Mr. Peabody's witnesses from earlier today could provide the proof you're looking for. If they haven't done so already," Mr. Randall said calmly.

There was quite a bit of excited whispering in the courtroom after this statement. The judge had to bang his gavel twice to restore order.

"I see," Mr. Carver said when order was restored. "And Mr. Peabody, in his opening statement, said that he"—and here he consulted his notes—"would also prove that you are a dangerously incompetent lawyer, who deserves to be disbarred. In your opinion, does he have reason to make such a statement?"

"He does indeed," Mr. Randall said calmly.

This statement prompted much discussion and some very audible comments from the spectators. It took significantly longer to quiet the courtroom this time, and Judge Graham looked decidedly irritated when the questioning recommenced.

"And what reason might Mr. Peabody have had to say you were —and I quote—'dangerously incompetent'?" Mr. Carver asked.

It was impressive the way he was hammering his points home with a little judicious repetition, Emily thought. But why had Mr. Randall agreed with the statement? She waited breathlessly for the answer.

"Mr. Peabody's attempts to discredit me are rooted partly in his need to have someone to blame for his own failures," Mr. Randall said. "That is not a matter that can easily be proven in this court, however."

Peabody leapt to his feet. "I object. The witness is slandering me."

"Sustained," the Judge said. "Strike that testimony from the record," he directed the court reporter.

"My apologies, m'lord," Mr. Carver said. "If I may redirect that question?"

"Go ahead."

The defense lawyer turned back to his client. "Is there a reason—one that can be proven in this court—why Mr. Peabody might want to somehow prove that you are, and again I quote his own words, 'dangerously incompetent'?"

"Indeed there is," Mr. Randall said. "Mr. Peabody, along with some of his clients—as well as the other five lawyers whom he conspired with and their clients—have been committing fraud. All of them have been profiting through a coordinated, consistent flaunting of our import laws. And Mr. Peabody, along with every one of the other five lawyers in this conspiracy, has either lost fraud-related court cases to me, or has a similar case scheduled."

Mr. Peabody lurched to his feet. "Objection. This is slander."

"And is this statement provable, Mr. Carver?" Judge Graham asked.

Mr. Carver turned back to his client. "Can this fraud on the part of Mr. Peabody and his five conspirators be proven in this court?"

"It can," Mr. Randall said. "In addition to my own testimony, that proof rests with my accountant. And with the six co-conspirators."

"Your objection is overruled," the judge said to Mr. Peabody, who sat down hard.

"Thank you," Mr. Carver said. "I have no further questions, though I may need to recall this witness at a later date."

"Do you wish to cross-examine?" Judge Graham asked Mr. Peabody.

Who made as if to rise, then shook his head. "Not at this time."

"Peabody is beginning to see the trap he's set for himself," Granville said quietly to her.

"I can't believe it took him this long," Emily whispered back.

"This witness is dismissed. Call your next witness, Mr. Carver," Judge Graham said.

"I call Mr. McAndrews, who is Mr. Randall's accountant. And I intend to recall all of the five lawyers who have already testified. But I would like to call Mr. Peabody as a witness, as well."

The judge looked startled. "I have no problem with your other witnesses. But your request to call Mr. Peabody is unprecedented. And I'm afraid I can't allow it, since he is representing himself. And he can hardly cross-examine himself while he is sitting on the witness stand, can he?"

Emily noted that Carver didn't look surprised. But Mr. Peabody looked…was that relief?

"In that case, I have another request," Mr. Carver said. "Since my recent witness is also the defendant, I'd like to request that Mr. Randall join me here at the defense table for the rest of the trial."

"And if you need to recall him as a witness?" the judge asked.

"I would still like to do so."

Judge Graham pondered that for a moment. "Again, this is unprecedented. But in my opinion, the two situations cancel each other out. Since I denied your previous request, I'll allow this one. Mr. Randall may take his place at the defense table. And that decided, we'll take a brief recess."

"Thank you, m'lord," Carver said.

Emily turned to Granville. "I knew this trial was going to be interesting, but it just keeps getting more suspenseful. Is it going the way you had hoped it would?"

"Indeed it is. But what comes next should be even better," he said with a grin.

WHEN COURT RESUMED, Mac McAndrews was called to the stand,

and he and Mr. Carver went through what seemed to Emily like volumes worth of files on the various fraud trials. Though there were only perhaps seven or eight documents that Mr. Carver introduced into evidence.

Usually she found some of the business details fascinating, but today they didn't invoke the same tension that the interaction with Mr. Peabody had just done.

She knew that Mr. McAndrew's testimony was essential. And that Mr. Carver's questions were laying the groundwork for recalling the other lawyers. But she just couldn't bring herself to pay attention.

Instead, her eyes kept wandering to Mr. Peabody's frustrated expression. It must be awful to sit there like that, unable to stop them as they tore his career apart. What was he thinking?

And she couldn't stop worrying that without Mr. Peabody's testimony, Mr. Carver wouldn't be able to get the other five lawyers to implicate each other in the fraud they were so painstakingly detailing.

Finally, finally the examination of the ledgers was done. After Mr. Peabody again declined to cross-examine, the judge dismissed the witness. She leaned over to Granville and whispered, "Will they have enough to prove fraud, do you think?"

"I think so. The team worked hard to fill in all the missing pieces. Having access to Randall yesterday helped quite a bit. And Carver is doing a stellar job of asking the right questions, in the right way. Look at Randall's face. Even he's impressed."

Emily glanced at the defense bench. It was true. Mr. Randall didn't let much show on his face, but his expression was engaged. And he was leaning forward a bit, holding himself as if he was standing right behind Mr. Carver while he recalled Mr. Bragg.

56

Unfortunately, Carver's interrogation of the other conspirators didn't yield any of the fireworks Emily had been hoping for.

There might have been tension in Mr. Bragg's face, Mr. Griggs might have gritted his jaw over a question or two, but these were experienced lawyers. They weren't about to expose themselves so easily.

With practically every other question they cited client confidentiality and refused to answer, or so it seemed to her. It was just too bad that Mr. Peabody wasn't going to testify. Of them all, he had the least control over himself. And his anger.

Which would hopefully help their case anyway, since she noted that the judge checked Mr. Peabody's very obvious reaction with every question that Mr. Carver asked.

When Mr. Cheever proved even more deadly dull than Mr. Griggs had been—even spouting off a mind-numbing list of figures at one point—Emily really started to worry. As he presented them, the numbers involved weren't small, but they weren't exactly huge, either. Was the information they had ever going to be enough to implicate all six of them in major fraud, as Granville hoped?

And what if it wasn't?

Where did that leave their case?

She slid a glance over at Granville's intent face. He at least seemed to be following everything. And he didn't look discouraged in the least.

What did he know that she didn't?

Perhaps when Mr. Lessing or Mr. Konrad were recalled as witnesses, all this detail might seem more relevant. Those were the two he suspected the most of being the ringleader, after all.

Granville had said Mr. Lessing seemed the obvious choice, and that Mr. Konrad seemed too smooth. Which one would Mr. Carver choose to call next?

To everyone's surprise, including Judge Graham's, Emily thought, going by the murmuring in the court and the hand the judge traced over his jaw—Mr. Carver called his client back to the stand. Once Mr. Randall had been reminded he was still under oath, Mr. Carver strode forward until he was standing a little to one side of the witness box.

"He just made sure all of us, and especially the judge, can clearly see Randall's expression," Granville said quietly, his eyes alert.

"I see it. And Mr. Peabody's expression at the same time. That's a smart move, and it means this is important. But the last three witnesses didn't say anything too dreadful. Why recall Mr. Randall now?"

"Don't worry. Carver's sticking to his plan. And the strategy is sound."

So they had planned to keep the other two lawyers in reserve. Why? What were they expecting Mr. Randall to say that they'd do that?

At least the excitement was back in the trial, she thought, sitting forward on the hard wooden bench.

Mr. Carver put his hands behind his back, and contemplated his client.

"Earlier in the day, Mr. Peabody accused you of trying to destroy his career, which you have denied," he said in a clear, carrying tone. "Did Mr. Peabody attempt to end your career, in the same way he accuses you of trying to end his?"

"He did," Mr. Randall said. "Though not in quite the same way."

"In what way would that be?"

"I was attacked, and left for dead."

A hush fell over the courtroom, as if every person there had been waiting for this moment.

"You were. Are you saying that Mr. Peabody had something to do with the attack on you?" Mr. Carver asked.

"I am. Mr. Peabody and his fellow conspirators were behind the attack."

"Several of them attacked you?"

"No. They hired the thugs who attacked me."

"And do you have proof of this?"

"Yes. If you call Mr. Lew Gurak, he can tell you who hired him and his thugs."

"Are you saying that it was Mr. Gurak's thugs who attacked you?"

"Yes. I clearly recognized one of the three thugs who attacked and nearly killed me as being one of Mr. Gurak's gang."

This caused such an out-roar in the courtroom that the judge gave up pounding his gavel and called for another recess. "And if this courtroom isn't absolutely silent when I return in ten minutes, I'm tossing the lot of you out," Judge Graham thundered, then left the courtroom.

Emily turned to Granville. "Did Mr. Randall just accuse Mr. Peabody of trying to murder him?"

"That isn't quite what he said," Granville replied, sounding every bit as calm as his lawyer had.

"Oooh. You're all up to something," Emily said, knotting her hands together. "I can't stand the waiting to find out what the plan really is. And you're not going to tell me anything, are you?"

"Of course not. Where's the fun in that?" he said. And winked at her.

WHEN THE JUDGE returned to an unnaturally silent courtroom, Emily put a gloved hand over her mouth to hide her smile. Then the trial resumed with a literal bang of the judge's gavel.

Mr. Carver had no further questions for Mr. Randall. And Mr. Peabody passed on cross-examining him, again simply retaining the right to recall him later.

Emily thought that was a surprisingly wise move on the latter's part. Given Judge Graham's current mood, accusing the defendant of lying at the top of his lungs would likely have earned Mr. Peabody an enormous fine.

Besides, Mr. Peabody seemed too angry to frame a rational question, let alone to cross examine someone like Mr. Randall. Which was too bad.

It would have been an education to watch Mr. Randall tear Mr. Peabody's arguments to shreds. Which the other lawyer seemed to have realized. Unfortunately.

Still, if Mr. Carver had hoped that his opponent would sabotage his own case in an attempt to cross examine Mr. Randall, he was handling the loss well. And perhaps his next witness would make up for it.

Which he did.

"I call Mr. Lew Gurak to the stand," Carver said to the still silent courtroom.

There was a subdued murmur from the onlookers, quickly hushed. And a few nervous glances at the judge.

"I thought Officer Daniels arrested Mr. Gurak," Emily whispered to Granville.

"He did. I believe he's out on bail."

"And did someone make a deal with him in exchange for his testimony here today?"

"Excellent question. Wait and see if Peabody thinks to ask it," was all he'd tell her.

As Mr. Gurak was brought into the courtroom by the bailiff, there was a ripple amongst the spectators as people craned to see the notorious thug. Emily noticed that the judge was watching the witness carefully. Once he was sworn in, Mr. Carver strode towards the witness stand.

"Mr. Gurak, good afternoon."

The witness stared past him into the courtroom.

Mr. Carver hadn't yet asked the witness a question. He seemed to be silently contemplating him instead. And the judge, for some reason, was allowing it.

It was like they were all following a script that she couldn't see. Which was just annoying. But it did build the tension.

And the judge's interest, she thought, watching Judge Graham's eyes narrowing.

Was he about to reprimand Mr. Carver? Or was he as curious as everyone else as to what the defense lawyer was up to? Curious enough to let this play out?

But the judge's eyes narrowed still farther. That couldn't be good.

And at that very moment, Mr. Carver spoke. "I understand that at least one of your men was involved in an attack on my client, Mr. Randall. Is this true?"

His timing was impeccable. Everyone's eyes were riveted on Mr. Gurak, now. Including the judge's.

"I am sad to say it is."

"And why did he do so?"

"They are hired to kill Mr. Randall. To look like accident."

"So they were hired to kill Mr. Randall, but make his death look like an accidental one?"

"Yes, as you say."

"You also said 'they'. So more than one man was hired to kill Mr. Randall?"

"Three men are being hired."

"I see. And these three men were hired to kill Mr. Randall but to make it look like an accident."

Emily was intrigued by how often Mr. Carver repeated that someone had hired the thugs to kill his client. And how much the tension in the courtroom increased every time he did so.

"Yes. They are," Mr. Gurak said.

"And how were they to do that?"

"Is their choice. Broken neck, a fall. A thing that look like accident."

"And yet, Mr. Randall was beaten nearly to death. Which hardly appears accidental. Can you tell us how that occurred if they were hired to make his death look accidental?"

"Mr. Randall betrays our boss. The men are loyal. And angry."

"So they were angry, and beat Mr. Randall instead of what they'd been hired to do?"

"No. They are being hired to kill him. So they beat him, it look like burglary. The accident?" Mr. Gurak made a dismissive gesture. "Not so important."

"And yet my client is still alive. How is that?"

"He is?" Gurak's shoulder tensed.

"He is, despite the severity of the beating."

"Well, if he is alive, that is good, no?" the fellow said with an easy smile that Emily thought looked even more sinister than his normal expression.

"Yes, it is," Mr. Carver said. "But why is Mr. Randall alive? Did your men decide not to kill him?"

"No, no. They are paid. They know the job. If he is alive, this is… is accident. Help maybe come too soon."

"I see. So your men acted as they were hired to."

"Yes," Gurak said.

Was that pride on his face? Emily wondered. Or defiance?

"And who hired them for this? To kill Mr. Randall, I mean?" Carver asked.

"I never hear name. And he pay cash."

"Can you describe him?"

"Yes. He is not tall." And Gurak stood up, measuring a height of about five foot six with his hand against his own chest. Then sat down slowly when reprimanded by the judge.

As Mr. Gurak described him, Emily was picturing Mr. Lessing, just as he'd sat on the witness stand for Mr. Peabody not two hours ago. It fit.

"Go on," Mr. Carver said.

"He is a little man. And scrawny. Brown hair, pale blue eyes. Easy to forget. He wear a brown suit."

Everything he'd described fit, right down to the brown suit Mr. Lessing had been wearing, she thought. Granville had been right, despite his doubts.

"And how old a man would he be?" Mr. Carver asked.

"More than thirty."

"How much more?"

"Thirty to forty, maybe."

"That is a good description. But you don't know his name?"

"No."

"Do you see this man anywhere in court?"

The courtroom fell completely silent, as Gurak's eyes scanned the room. Emily waited for the no. Then they'd have to recall Mr. Lessing, and…

Then Mr. Gurak's eyes fell on Mr. Peabody, and he pointed. "Him."

Emily's eyes widened, and she stared at the accused lawyer in disbelief. And wondered if he the suit he was wearing under his flowing black robes was a brown one.

"This is the man who paid you to have Mr. Randall killed?" Mr. Carver said, with the tone of a man who wanted to be absolutely certain. "The one sitting behind the prosecutor's desk?"

"Yes. Him," the witness said.

Apparently she wasn't the only one who hadn't been expecting quite this outcome.

The courtroom erupted. Mr. Peabody was on his feet, howling about false accusations and insisting he'd been framed. The voices of the spectators rose louder and louder, drowning out the determined hammering of the judge's gavel.

Emily just sat there, stunned. Mr. Peabody was the one responsible for the attack on Mr. Randall?

Which would make him the deluded small fish. Well, that part fit. Even if she hadn't expected him to be capable of organizing anything. Maybe he just wasn't good under pressure?

And Mr. Gurak seemed not to notice he'd just admitted to a

crime, she thought in amazement. But accepting payment for a killing? She wasn't sure what the charges would be—or the penalties—but they had to be steep.

She slid a glance over at Granville. He looked pleased. As well he should.

She couldn't wait to discuss it with him.

5 7

Stepping out of the courthouse several hours later, Emily was almost surprised to find herself walking into the warm, golden air of an autumn afternoon. The courtroom had been poorly lit, and stuffy, and it felt like they had been inside forever.

She took an appreciative sniff of air that smelt like the sea and… was that chrysanthemums? She was fond of their bright, shaggy heads and the sharp, spicy smell of them. They seemed to fit so perfectly with this time of year, when all the greens were fading and the trees were taking on their scarlets and yellows and golds.

Hand tucked safely into the crook of Granville's arm, she dared to close her eyes as they strolled, savoring the mingled scents.

"Are you hungry?" came Granville's voice from beside her. "Emily? Why are your eyes closed?"

"I'm resting them," she said. And opening them, she grinned up at him. "I spent too much time today staring at lawyers, and I think I'm feeling the strain."

"Well, I can understand that," he said with an answering grin. "They were a particularly noxious lot today. Our own two lawyers excepted, of course."

"Of course," she said.

"It feels good to be free of it all, doesn't it?"

"Particularly good when it's all done with," she agreed. "Both of our cases are complete. Mr. Carstairs will pay for what he did to Betsy. Mr. Gurak and his thugs will pay for the harm they did to Mr. Randall, as well as those three unfortunate men they killed."

He nodded. "And Peabody and the rest of the group of six will be charged with fraud, and possibly attempted murder for their part in all of this. And probably disbarred."

"Attempted murder? Really?"

"Really."

"And will all six of them be charged? I thought it was all Mr. Peabody? Mr. Gurak only mentioned him."

"It will all come out in Peabody's trial," he said. "But I strongly suspect that they'll find out that they money Gurak received can be traced back to all six."

"Oh, I can see that," she said, picturing the six faces she'd watched so carefully in court. "It's what you've suspected all along, isn't it? But won't that be hard to prove?"

"If that is the case, Peabody will be the first to accuse the others. And if he does so under oath, it gives them reason to dig into their financials to trace the money."

"What if only Mr. Peabody is convicted? Is Mr. Randall still in danger?"

"No. None of them will be able to go after Randall again. And I doubt that, after today, they'd even have the stomach to try."

"Good," she said. "Then that takes care of your case. Just like mine is taken care of."

"It's satisfying when a case is finished, and neatly wrapped up, isn't it?"

She gave a satisfied sigh. "It really is."

"Which will give us time to turn our attention to a few other important things."

Emily gave him a wary look. She knew that note in his voice. "Oh? Such as?"

"I notice you haven't mentioned our wedding since you got back. Have you changed your mind?"

"Of course not. As you know very well."

"Not even about the date of our marriage?"

She knew that note in his voice. He was teasing her, but serious behind it. "Well…," she said, letting the word stretch and teasing him right back.

"So you did talk to your aunt about it."

"I'm not sure you could say we talked," she said in a considering kind of tone. "More that I listened to her talk. She has a great many opinions on the subject of my marrying you, you see."

"Ah. Having met your aunt, that doesn't surprise me. Should I be worried?"

Emily squelched the laughter she was feeling at the look he gave her.

"Hardly. Aunt Louisa thinks you are perfect for me. And that I'm an idiot for not marrying you as quickly as possible."

"Your aunt is a much wiser woman than I gave her credit for," he said.

"I've come to agree with that observation. But not because of her opinion of you," she added quellingly. "Though I am glad she has noted your good qualities."

"Alas, they are so few," he said.

"Now you're just trying to annoy me," she said with a sideways look and a grin.

"No, I'm hoping you'll take pity on me," he said. "I've been living all alone in an empty house with almost no furniture. And it's no way to live."

"If it's furniture you need, I'm sure Clara would be most happy to help the two of us chose some," she said. "But that's hardly a reason for moving up our wedding date."

"It was worth a try," he said.

At his grin she let out the laughter she'd been suppressing. It was a good thing they'd reached a residential neighborhood and were walking along a quiet, treelined street. There was no one within earshot to hear their conversation, or her inappropriate burst of laughter.

"But I am going to tell Mama that we've decided on a spring

wedding. Perhaps in April. No matter how difficult that might be to plan," she said when she'd caught her breath.

"And if your mother doesn't agree?" he asked.

"Then I think we should elope," she said decidedly. "I missed you."

"I'm glad. Because I missed you, too," he said, and her heart skipped a beat at the look in his eyes. "And now I wish I'd hired a carriage for today."

The abrupt shift in topic left her floundering. "Oh?" she managed to say. "Why? It's a beautiful time of day for a walk."

"But I can't kiss you on the street," he said reasonably. "And I'd very much like to kiss you right now."

"Oh," she said, suddenly breathless. "Yes. I… My parent's home isn't far. And the entrance hall should be empty. And it's quite private."

He smiled. "Then I suggest we walk a little faster. Don't you think?"

"Yes, indeed," Emily said, and quickened her pace to match his.

AUTHOR'S NOTE

Thank you for joining me on this journey. I hope you enjoyed reading *The Hidden City Murders* as much as I enjoyed writing it.

The title is a reference Victoria, B.C.'s Chinatown. Established in 1841, Victoria played key roles in the fur trade, three Gold Rushes, as a major naval base, and—until it was banned in 1908—as one of North America's largest importers of opium. I've always loved the city—the setting, the people, the history—and thought it would be a great place to set a historical novel. Or as it turned out, part of one.

In researching the book, I was fascinated to learn that the X-ray machine was invented in 1895, and in widespread use in hospitals worldwide by 1897. St. Paul's Hospital was one of the first hospitals in Vancouver to purchase their own X-ray machine, that didn't happen until 1906. Until then, shared facilities were used.

I'd like to thank the staff at St. Paul's Hospital, the Vancouver Public Library Special Collections, the Vancouver Archives, the Royal British Columbia Museum and the Museum of Vancouver.

A number of historical works and on-line sites have also been invaluable to me; you can find them listed on my website at: www.sharonrowse.com